Praise for the Kate Daniels novels

MAGIC SLAYS

"Delivers nonstop action and a few surprises while adding considerable background and depth to Kate's character as she begins stretching her magic usage . . . Top-notch urban fantasy."

—*Monsters and Critics*

"Simply amazing. The Kate Daniels series honestly gets better with each new release. I had high hopes for this book, and the authors simply blew me away with the quality and depth of this story."

—*Night Owl Reviews*

"It takes both talent and hard work to keep a series consistently high quality . . . Andrews's intricate, detailed world-building provides such a rich backdrop for the story that it nearly becomes a character itself. Add in clearly defined and layered characters, not to mention amazing, kick-butt action, and you've got one unbeatable series. No one does it better!" —*RT Book Reviews* (4½ stars, top pick)

"The conclusion is heart-stopping as Kate fights to secure Atlanta's survival in a dramatic finale that left me satisfied but ready for book six. Ilona Andrews once again hits a game-winning home run with *Magic Slays.*" —*Smexy Books*

MAGIC BLEEDS

"Ilona Andrews is one of the few authors whose books just keep getting better . . . It's books like *Magic Bleeds* that make television and movies seem like an inferior form of entertainment."

—*Romance Reviews Today*

"I have read and reread this book and it's perfect. The action, the romance, the plot and suspense . . . I cannot wait for the fifth in the series." —*Smexy Books*

continued . . .

"Balancing petrifying danger with biting humor is an Andrews specialty, leaving readers both grinning and gasping. Put this on your auto-buy list immediately!" —*RT Book Reviews* (4½ stars, top pick)

"Delivers on the promise of 'One hell of a good read.' You will not be disappointed!" —ParaNormal Romance.org

MAGIC STRIKES

"Andrews blends action-packed fantasy with myth and legend, keeping readers enthralled. *Magic Strikes* introduces fascinating characters, provides a plethora of paranormal skirmishes, and teases fans with romantic chemistry." —*Darque Reviews*

"Ilona Andrews's best novel to date, cranking up the action, danger, and magic . . . Gritty sword-clashing action and flawless characterizations will bewitch fans, old and new alike."

—*Sacramento Book Review*

"Doses of humor serve to lighten the suspense and taut action of this vividly drawn, kick-butt series." —*Monsters and Critics*

"From the first page to the last, *Magic Strikes* was a riveting, heart-pounding ride. Story lines advance, truths are admitted, intriguing characters are introduced, and the romance between Kate and Curran develops a sweetness that is simply delightful." —*Dear Author*

"Write faster . . . I absolutely love the relationship between Curran and Kate—I laugh out loud with the witty sarcasm and one-liners, and the sexual tension building between the couples drives me to my knees, knowing I'll have to wait for another book." —*SFRevu*

MAGIC BURNS

"Fans of Carrie Vaughn and Patricia Briggs will appreciate this fast-paced, action-packed urban fantasy full of magic, vampires, were-beasties, and things that go bump in the night."

—*Monsters and Critics*

"With all her problems, secrets, and prowess both martial and magical, Kate is a great kick-ass heroine, a tough girl with a heart, and her adventures . . . are definitely worth checking out." —*Locus*

"[*Magic Burns*] hooked me completely. With a fascinating, compelling plot, a witty, intelligent heroine, a demonic villain, and clever, wry humor throughout, this story has it all." —*Fresh Fiction*

"A new take on the urban fantasy genre, the world Kate inhabits is a blend of gritty magic and dangerous mystery."

—*The Parkersburg News and Sentinel*

"If you enjoy Laurell K. Hamilton's early Anita Blake or the works of Patricia Briggs and Kim Harrison, you need to add Ilona Andrews to your reading list." —*LoveVampires*

MAGIC BITES

"Treat yourself to a splendid new urban fantasy . . . I am looking forward to the next book in the series or anything else Ilona Andrews writes."

—Patricia Briggs, #1 *New York Times* bestselling author of *Fair Game*

"Andrews shows a great deal of promise. Readers fond of Laurell K. Hamilton and Patricia Briggs may find her work a new source of reading pleasure." —*SFRevu*

"Andrews's edgy series stands apart from similar fantasies . . . owing to its complex world-building and skilled characterizations."

—*Library Journal*

"Fans of urban fantasy will delight in Ilona Andrews's alternate-universe Atlanta." —*Fresh Fiction*

"The strong story line coupled with a complex alternative history . . . will have readers hoping for more." —*Monsters and Critics*

Ace Books by Ilona Andrews

The Kate Daniels Novels

MAGIC BITES

MAGIC BURNS

MAGIC STRIKES

MAGIC BLEEDS

MAGIC SLAYS

MAGIC RISES

MAGIC BREAKS

MAGIC SHIFTS

The World of Kate Daniels

GUNMETAL MAGIC

The Edge Novels

ON THE EDGE

BAYOU MOON

FATE'S EDGE

STEEL'S EDGE

Specials

MAGIC MOURNS

MAGIC DREAMS

MAGIC BITES

ILONA ANDREWS

ACE BOOKS, NEW YORK

THE BERKLEY PUBLISHING GROUP
Published by the Penguin Group
Penguin Group (USA) Inc.
375 Hudson Street, New York, New York 10014, USA
Penguin Group (Canada), 90 Eglinton Avenue East, Suite 700, Toronto, Ontario M4P 2Y3, Canada (a division of Pearson Penguin Canada Inc.) • Penguin Books Ltd., 80 Strand, London WC2R 0RL, England • Penguin Ireland, 25 St. Stephen's Green, Dublin 2, Ireland (a division of Penguin Books Ltd.) • Penguin Group (Australia), 707 Collins Street, Melbourne, Victoria 3008, Australia (a division of Pearson Australia Group Pty. Ltd.) • Penguin Books India Pvt. Ltd., 11 Community Centre, Panchsheel Park, New Delhi—110 017, India • Penguin Group (NZ), 67 Apollo Drive, Rosedale, Auckland 0632, New Zealand (a division of Pearson New Zealand Ltd.) • Penguin Books Rosebank Office Park, 181 Jan Smuts Avenue, Parktown North 2193, South Africa • Penguin China, B7 Jaiming Center, 27 East Third Ring Road North, Chaoyang District, Beijing 100020, China

Penguin Books Ltd., Registered Offices: 80 Strand, London WC2R 0RL, England

MAGIC BITES

"A Questionable Client" was previously published in the anthology *Dark and Stormy Knights*.
Cover art by Juliana Kolesova.
Cover design by Jason Gill.

PUBLISHING HISTORY
Ace mass-market edition / April 2007
Ace trade paperback edition / January 2013

Ace trade paperback ISBN: 978-0-425-26420-1

PRINTED IN THE UNITED STATES OF AMERICA

10 9 8 7 6 5 4 3

For my daughters,
Anastasia and Helen

CONTENTS

ACKNOWLEDGMENTS
xi

MAGIC BITES
1

BONUS MATERIAL
277

KATE DANIELS SERIES
FREQUENTLY ASKED QUESTIONS
279

CHARACTERS
285

FACTIONS
293

FACTION QUIZ
305

CURRAN POINTS OF VIEW
313

"A QUESTIONABLE CLIENT"
325

ACKNOWLEDGMENTS

I'm greatly indebted to my editor at Ace Books, Anne Sowards, for her excellent editorial guidance and her great kindness and patience during all those times I needed reassurance, which was far too often. I would also like to thank my agent, Nancy Yost, for her wonderful advice and unfaltering support. I'm grateful to Jason Gill and Laura K. Corless, the designers, and Juliana Kolesova, the artist, for the fantastic cover and design; to Michelle Kasper, the production editor, and her staff for making this book possible; and to Rosanne Romanello, Ace's publicist, for all of her hard work.

I'm most grateful to Charles Coleman Finlay, Ellen Key Harris-Braun, and Jenni Smith-Gaynor of Online Writing Workshop for Science Fiction, Fantasy, and Horror for believing in my work before anybody else did. I thank Deanna Hoak for answering my endless questions. And a big thank-you to everyone who has read and commented on the draft of this work: Hannah Wolf Bowen, Jeff Stanley, Nora Fleischer, Lawrence Payne, Mark Jones, Del Whetter, Steve Orr, A. Wheat, Betty Foreman, Catherine Emery, Elizabeth Hull, Susan Curnow, Richard C. Rogers, Aaron Brown, David Emanuel, Jodi

Meadows, Christiana Ellis, Kyri Freeman, Elizabeth Bear, Mary Davis, and especially Charlene L. Amsden.

Finally I would like to apologize to the city of Atlanta, whose beautiful architecture I've treated so badly in the name of artistic license.

CHAPTER 1

I SAT AT A TABLE IN MY SHADOWY KITCHEN, STARING down a bottle of Boone's Farm Hard Lemonade, when a magic fluctuation hit. My wards shivered and died, leaving my home stripped of its defenses. The TV flared into life, unnaturally loud in the empty house.

I raised my eyebrow at the bottle and bet it that another urgent bulletin was on.

The bottle lost.

"Urgent bulletin!" Margaret Chang announced. "The Attorney General advises all citizens that any attempt at summoning or other activities resulting in the appearance of a supernaturally powerful being can be hazardous to yourself and to other citizens."

"No shit," I told the bottle.

"Local police have been authorized to subdue any such activities with all due force."

Margaret droned on, while I bit into my sandwich. Who were they kidding? No police force could hope to squash every summoning. It took a qualified wizard to detect a summoning in progress. It required only a half-literate idiot with a twitch of power and a dim idea of how to use it to attempt one. Before you knew it, a three-headed Slavonic god was wreaking havoc in downtown Atlanta, the skies were raining winged snakes, and SWAT was screaming for more ammo. These were unsafe times. But then in safer times, I'd be a woman without a job. The safe tech-world had little use for a magic-touting mercenary like me.

When people had trouble of a magic kind, the kind that cops couldn't or wouldn't handle, they called the Mercenary Guild. If the job happened to fall into my territory, the Guild then called me. I grimaced and rubbed my hip. It still ached after the last job, but the wound had healed better than I expected. That was the first and last time I would agree to go against the Impala Worm without full body armor. The next time they better furnish me with a level-four containment suit.

An icy wave of fear and revulsion hit me. My stomach lurched, sending acid to coat the root of my tongue with a bitter aftertaste. Shivers ran along my spine, and the tiny hairs on my neck stood on end.

Something bad was in my house.

I put down my sandwich and hit the mute button on the remote control. On the screen Margaret Chang was joined by a brick-faced man with a high-and-tight haircut and eyes like slate. A cop. Probably Paranormal Activity Division. I put my hand on the dagger that rested on my lap and sat very still.

Listening. Waiting.

No sound troubled the silence. A drop of water formed on the sweaty surface of the Boone's Farm bottle and slid down its glistening side.

Something large crawled along the hallway ceiling into the

kitchen. I pretended not to see it. It stopped to the left of me and slightly behind, so I didn't have to pretend very hard.

The intruder hesitated, turned, and anchored itself in the corner, where the ceiling met the wall. It sat there, fastened to the paneling by enormous yellow talons, still and silent like a gargoyle in full sunlight. I took a swig from the bottle and set it so I could see the creature's reflection. Nude and hairless, it didn't carry a single ounce of fat on its lean frame. Its skin stretched so tight over the hard cords of muscle, it threatened to snap. Like a thin layer of wax melted over an anatomy model.

Your friendly neighborhood Spiderman.

The vampire raised its left hand. The dagger talons sliced the empty air, back and forth, like curved knitting needles. The vamp turned its head doglike and studied me with eyes luminescent with a particular kind of madness, born of bestial blood thirst and free of any thought or restraint.

In a single motion I whipped around and hurled the dagger. The black blade sliced cleanly into the creature's throat.

The vampire froze. Its yellow claws stopped moving.

Thick, purplish blood swelled around the blade and slowly slid down the naked flesh of the vampire's neck, staining its chest and dripping on the floor. The vampire's features twisted, trying to morph into a different face. It opened its maw, displaying twin fangs, curved like miniature ivory sickles.

"That was extremely inconsiderate, Kate," Ghastek's voice said from the vampire's throat. "Now I have to feed him."

"It's a reflex. Hear a bell, get food. See an undead, throw a knife. Same thing, really."

The vampire's face jerked as if the Master of the Dead controlling it tried to squint.

"What are you drinking?" Ghastek asked.

"Boone's Farm."

"You can afford better."

"I don't want better. I like Boone's Farm. And I prefer to do business by phone, and with you, not at all."

"I don't wish to hire you, Kate. This is merely a social call."

I stared at the vampire, wishing I could put my knife into Ghastek's throat. It would feel very good cutting into his flesh. Unfortunately he sat in an armored room many miles away.

"You enjoy screwing with me, don't you, Ghastek?"

"Immensely."

The million-dollar question was why. "What is it you want? Make it quick, my Boone's Farm's getting warm."

"I was just wondering," Ghastek said with dry neutrality particular only to him, "when was the last time you saw your guardian?"

The nonchalance in his voice sent tiny shivers down my spine. "Why?"

"No reason. As always, a pleasure."

In a single powerful leap the vampire detached itself from the wall and flew through the open window, taking my knife with it.

I reached for the phone, swearing under my breath, and dialed the Order of Knights of Merciful Aid. No vampire could breach my wards when the magic was in full swing. Ghastek had no way of knowing when the magic would ebb, so he must have been watching my house for some time, waiting for my defensive spells to fail. I took a swig from the bottle. That meant a vamp had been hiding someplace close when I came home last night, and I didn't see or feel it. How reassuring. Might just as well write "Alert R Us" on my merc ID.

One ring. Two. Three. Why would he ask me about Greg?

The phone clicked and a stern female voice delivered a practiced blurb, "Atlanta Chapter of the Order, how may I help you?"

"I would like to speak to Greg Feldman."

"Your name?"

A faint note of anxiety pulsed through her voice.

"I don't have to give you my name," I said into the receiver. "I wish to speak to the knight-diviner."

A pause issued and a male voice said, "Please, identify yourself."

They were stalling, probably trying to trace the call. What the hell was going on?

"No," I said firmly. "Page seven of your Charter, third paragraph down: 'Any citizen has a right to seek counsel of a knight-diviner without fear of retribution or need for identification.' As a citizen, I insist that you put me in contact with the knight-diviner now or specify the time he can be reached."

"The knight-diviner is dead," the voice said.

The world halted. I skidded through its stillness, frightened and off balance. My throat ached. I heard my heart beating in my chest.

"How?" My voice was calm.

"He was killed in the line of duty."

"Who did it?"

"The matter is still under investigation. Look, if I could just get your name . . ."

I pushed the disconnect button and lowered the receiver in its place. I looked at the empty chair across from me. Two weeks ago Greg had sat in this chair, stirring his coffee. His spoon had made small precise circles, never touching the sides of the mug. For a moment I could actually see him right there, while the memory played in my mind.

Greg was looking at me with dark brown eyes, mournful, like the eyes of an icon. "Please, Kate. Suspend your dislike of me for a few moments and listen to what I have to say. It makes sense."

"I don't dislike you. It's an oversimplification."

He nodded, wearing that very patient expression that drove women mad. "Of course. I didn't intend to slight or simplify your feelings. I merely wish us to concentrate on the substance of what I have to say. Could you please listen?"

I leaned back and crossed my arms. "I'm listening."

He reached inside his leather jacket and produced a rolled-up scroll. He placed the scroll on the table and unrolled it slowly, holding it taut with the tips of his fingers.

"This is the invitation from the Order."

I threw my hands in the air. "That's it, I'm done."

"Allow me to finish," he said. He didn't look angry. He didn't tell me that I was acting like a child, although I knew that I was. It made me madder.

"Very well," I said.

"In a few weeks you'll turn twenty-five. While in itself that means very little, in terms of readmission into the Order it carries a certain weight. It's much harder to gain entrance once you turn twenty-five. Not impossible. Just harder."

"I know," I said. "They've sent me brochures."

He let go of the scroll and leaned back, lacing his long fingers. The scroll remained open even though every law of physics dictated that it should snap back into a roll. Greg forgot about physics sometimes.

"In that case, you're aware of the age penalties."

It wasn't a question, but I answered it anyway. "Yes."

He sighed. It was a small movement, only noticeable to those who knew him well. I could tell by the way he sat, very still, craning his neck slightly, that he had guessed at my decision.

"I wish you would reconsider," he said.

"I don't think so." For a moment I could see the frustration in his eyes. We both knew what was left unsaid: the Order promised protection, and protection to someone of my lineage was paramount.

"Can I ask why?" he said.

"It's not for me, Greg. I can't deal with hierarchy."

For him the Order was a place of refuge and security, a place of power. Its members committed themselves to the values of the Order completely, serving with such dedication that the organization itself no longer seemed a gathering of individuals, but an entity in itself, thinking, rationalizing, and incredibly powerful. Greg embraced it and it nurtured him. I fought it and almost lost.

"Every moment I spent there, I felt as if there was less of me," I said. "As if I was shrinking. Dwindling away. I had to get out and I won't go back."

Greg looked at me, his dark eyes terribly sad. In this dim light, in my small kitchen, his beauty was startling. In some perverse way I was happy that my stubbornness forced him to visit and now he sat in a chair less than a foot away, like an ageless elven prince, elegant and sorrowful. God, how much I hated myself for this little girl fantasy.

"If you'll excuse me," I said.

He blinked, startled by my formality and then rose smoothly. "Of course. Thank you for the coffee."

I saw him to the door. The outside had turned dark, and the bright light of the moon enameled the grass on my lawn with silver. By the porch, white Rose of Sharon flowers glowed against the shrubs like a scattering of stars.

I watched Greg descend down the three concrete steps into the yard.

"Greg?"

"Yes?" He turned. His magic flared about him like a mantle.

"Nothing." I closed the door.

My last memory of him, poised against the moonlight-drenched lawn and clothed in his magic.

Oh, God.

I cradled myself with my arms, wanting to cry. The tears would not come. My mouth had gone dry. My last link to my family severed. Nobody was left. I had no mother, no father, and now no Greg. I clenched my teeth and went to pack.

CHAPTER 2

THE MAGIC HAD HIT WHILE I WAS PACKING THE ESSENtials into my bag, and I had to take Karmelion instead of my regular car. A beat-up rusted truck, bile green in color and missing the left headlight assembly, Karmelion had only one advantage—it ran on water infused with magic and could be driven during a magic wave. Unlike normal cars, the truck did not rumble or murmur or produce any sound one would expect an engine to make. Instead it growled, whined, snarled, and emitted deafening peals of thunder with depressing regularity. Who named it Karmelion, and why, I had no idea. I bought it at a junkyard with the name scrawled on the windshield.

Lucky for me, on a regular day Karmelion had to travel only thirty miles to Savannah. Today I forced it into the ley line, which in itself wasn't bad for it, since the ley line dragged it almost all the way to Atlanta, but the trek across the city didn't do it much good. Now the truck was cooling off in the parking lot behind me, dripping water and sweating magic. It would take me a good fifteen minutes to warm the generator back up, but that was alright. I planned to be here for a while.

I hated Atlanta. I hated cities, period.

I stood on the sidewalk and surveyed the small shabby office building that supposedly contained the Atlanta Chapter of the Order of Knights of Merciful Aid. The Order made efforts to conceal its true size and power, but in this case they had gone overboard. The building, a concrete box three stories high, stuck out like a sore thumb among the stately brick houses flanking it on both sides. The walls sported orange rust stains made by rainwater dripping from the metal roof through the holes in the gutters. Thick metal grates secured small windows, blocked by pale venetian blinds behind dusty glass.

There had to be another facility in the city. A place where the support staff worked while the field agents put on a nice modest front for the public. It would have a large, state-of-the-art armory, and a computer network, and a database of files on anyone of power—magic or mundane. Somewhere in that database my name sat in its own little niche, the name of a reject, undisciplined and worthless. Just the way I liked it.

I touched the wall. About a quarter of an inch away from the concrete, my finger encountered elastic resistance, as if I was trying to squeeze a tennis ball. A faint shimmer of silver pulsed from my skin and I withdrew my hand. The building was heavily warded against hostile magic. If someone with a lot of juice was to hurl a fireball at it, it would probably bounce off without so much as scorching the gray walls.

I opened one half of the metal double doors and walked inside. A narrow passage stretched to the right of me, terminating at a door boasting a large red-on-white sign: Authorized Personnel Only. My other option was a flight of stairs leading upward.

I took the stairs, noting they were surprisingly clean. Nobody tried to stop me. Nobody asked why I was there. *Look at us, we are helpful and nonthreatening, we live to serve the community, and we even let anyone walk into our office.*

The need for an unassuming building I could understand, but public records claimed that the entire Chapter consisted of nine knights: a protector, a diviner, a questor, three defenders, and three guardians. Nine people, overseeing a city the size of Atlanta. Yeah.

The stairs ended on a landing with a single metal door painted dull green. A small dagger gleamed weakly on its surface at about my eye level. Knocking didn't seem like a good idea, so I swung the door open and let myself in.

A long hallway stretched before me, offering a variety of color to my tired eyes: gray and gray, and yet more gray. The ultra-short carpet boasted plain gray pile; the walls were painted in two shades of gray: lighter on top and a darker gray runner at the bottom. The small warts of electric lights on the ceiling looked gray, too. No doubt the decorator chose a particularly dull smoky glass out of esthetic considerations.

The place looked spotless. Several doors branched from the hallway, probably leading into the individual offices. At the very end a large wooden door supported a kite shield enameled black. In the middle of the shield reared a steel lion, polished to a bright gleam. The knight-protector. Just the fellow I needed to see.

I marched through the hallway, aiming for the shield and glancing into the doorways as I passed them. On my left I saw a small armory. A short, well-muscled man sat on a wooden bench polishing a dha. The wide blade of the short Vietnamese sword shimmered slightly as he drew an oiled cloth against its bluish metal. On the right lay a small but immaculate office. A large black man dressed in an expensive suit sat behind the desk, talking on the phone. He saw me, smiled with automatic courtesy, and kept talking.

In his place I wouldn't have given myself a second glance either. I wore my work clothes: jeans loose enough to let me kick a man taller than me in the throat, a green shirt, and comfortable running shoes. Slayer rested in its sheath on my back, partially hidden by my jacket. The saber's hilt protruded above my right shoulder, obscured by my hair gathered into a thick plait. The braid was cumbersome—it slapped my back when I ran and made for an excellent hold in a fight. If I were a little less vain, I would've cut it off, but I'd already sacrificed feminine clothes, makeup, and pretty underwear in the name of functionality. I would be damned if I gave up my hair, too.

I reached the protector's door and raised my hand to knock.

"Just a moment, dear," said the stern female voice I had heard through the phone yesterday.

I glanced in its direction and saw a small office cluttered with file cabinets. A large desk sat in the middle of the floor and on top of the desk stood a middle-aged woman. The woman was tall, prim, and very thin, with a halo of curly hair dyed platinum gray. She wore a stylish blue pantsuit. A matching pair of shoes rested near the leg of the chair she must have used to get on the table.

"He's with someone, dear," the woman said. She raised her hands and proceeded to change the twisted bulb in a feylantern affixed to the ceiling next to an electric light. "You don't have an appointment, do you?"

"No, ma'am."

"Well, you're in luck. He's free for the morning. Why don't you give me your name and the reason for your visit, and we'll see what we can do."

I waited until she finished with the feybulb, told her that I was here in connection with Greg Feldman, and gave her my card. She took it down, showing no reaction at all, and pointed behind me. "There's a waiting area over there, dear."

I turned and walked into the waiting area, which turned out to be just another office, equipped with a black leather sofa and two chairs. A table stood against the wall by the door with a coffeepot, guarded by two stacks of small clay cups. A large jar of sugar cubes stood next to the cups and next to the jar sat two boxes from Duncan's Doughnuts. My hand twitched to the doughnuts, but I restrained myself. Anyone who had the pleasure of trying one of the old Scot's doughnuts quickly learned you couldn't eat just one, and waltzing into the protector's office covered in hand-whipped chocolate cream wasn't a good way to make the right impression.

I found a safe spot by the window, away from the doughnuts, and glanced past the bars to the outside, at the small stretch of the overcast sky, framed by roofs. The Order of Knights of Merciful Aid offered just what its name suggested: merciful aid to anyone who asked. If you could pay, they would charge you; and if you couldn't, they would kill shit on your behalf pro bono. Officially their mission statement was to protect humanity against all harm, by magic or by weapon. Trouble was, their definition of harm seemed rather flexible and sometimes merciful aid meant they lopped your head off.

The Order got away with a lot. Its membership was too powerful to be ignored, and the temptation to rely on it was too great. It'd been endorsed by the government as the third part of the Law and Order triumvirate. The Paranormal Activity Police Division, the Military Supernatural Defense Units, and the Order of Knights of Merciful Aid were all supposed to play nice together and keep the general public safe. In reality, it didn't exactly happen that way. The knights of the Order were helpful, competent, and lethal. Unlike the mercenaries of the Guild, they were not motivated by money and they stood by their promises. But unlike the mercs, they also made judgments and they believed that they always knew best.

A tall man stepped into the waiting room. The stench hit me almost before I saw him, a sickeningly sweet, lingering odor of rotting garbage. The man wore a sweeping brown trench coat stained with ink and grease spots, and smeared with so many varieties of foodstuff and plain trash that he looked like young Joseph in his coat of many colors. The coat hung open in the front to allow a glimpse of an abomination of a shirt: blue and red with green tartan stripes. His filthy khaki pants were held up by orange suspenders. He wore old steel-toed paratrooper boots and leather gloves with their fingers cut off at the first knuckle. On his head sat a felt hat, an old-fashioned fedora, soiled and stained beyond belief. Thick mousy hair dripped in limp strands from under the hat.

He saw me and tipped his hat, holding its rim between his index and middle finger the way some people hold cigarettes, and I got a glimpse of his face: hard lines, three-day stubble, and pale eyes, quick and cold. There was nothing especially threatening in the way he looked at me, but something behind those eyes made me want to raise my hands in the air and back away slowly until it was safe to run for my life.

"Maaaa'am," he drawled.

He scared the shit out of me. I smiled at him. "Good morning." My greeting sounded a lot like "niiice doggy." I'd have to squeeze past him to get to the door.

The receptionist came to my rescue. "You can go in now, dear," she called.

The man stepped aside, bowing slightly, and I walked by him. The side of my jacket brushed against his trench coat, probably picking up enough bacteria to knock out a small army, but I did not pull away.

"Nice to meet you," he murmured as I passed him.

"Nice to meet you, too," I said and escaped into the protector's office.

I found myself in a large room, at least twice the size of the offices I'd seen so far. Heavy burgundy draperies covered the windows, letting in just enough light to create a comfortable gloom. A massive desk of polished cherrywood dominated the room, supporting a cardboard box, a heavy mesquite wood paperweight with a Texas Ranger badge on top, and a pair of brown cowboy boots. The legs in the boots belonged to a thick-shouldered man, who leaned back in an oversized black leather chair listening to the phone at his ear. The knight-protector.

At some point he must have been very strong but now his muscle was sheathed in what my father had called "hard fat." He was still a large, strong man and he could probably move fast if he needed to, despite the unsightly bulge around his middle. He wore jeans and a navy blue shirt with a fringe. I did not know they even made those anymore. The clothes in which the West was won—or sung into submission—were meant for whiplash-lean men. They made the protector look like Gene Autry gone on a long Twinkie binge.

The knight looked at me. He had a wide face with a massive square jaw and probing blue eyes under heavy eyebrows. His nose was misshapen from being broken too many times. The hat hid the hair or, more likely, the absence of it, but I was willing to bet that what was left of the growth on his head had to be gray and short.

The protector motioned me to one of the smaller red chairs set before the desk. I sat, getting a look into the cardboard box on his desk. It contained a half-eaten jelly doughnut.

The knight resumed listening to the phone conversation, so I looked around his office. A large bookcase, also of dark cherrywood, stood at the opposite wall. Above it I saw a large wooden map of Texas decorated with strips of barbed wire. Golden script etched under each piece announced the name of the manufacturer and the year.

The protector finished his conversation by hanging up the phone without saying a word. "You've got some paper to show me, now's the time."

I handed him my merc ID and half-a-dozen recommendations. He flipped through them.

"Water and Sewer, huh?"

"Yes."

"Gotta be tough or dumb to go down into the sewers these days. So, which one are you?"

"I'm not dumb, but if I tell you I'm tough, you'll peg me for a bravo, so I'm going to smile cryptically." I gave him my best cryptic smile. He did not fall down to his feet, kiss my shoes, and promise me the world. *I must be getting rusty.*

The protector squinted at the signature. "Mike Tellez. I've worked with him before. You do regular work for him?"

"More or less."

"What was it this time?"

"He had a problem with large pieces of equipment being dragged away. Someone told him he had a baby marakihan."

"They're marine," he said. "They die in fresh water."

An overweight slob who eats powdered jelly doughnuts, wears shirts with fringe, and identifies an obscure magical creature without a momentary pause. Knight-protector. Camouflage expert extraordinaire.

"You got to the bottom of Mike's problem?" he asked.

"Yes. He had the Impala Worm," I said.

If he was impressed, he did not show it. "You kill it?"

Very funny. "No, just made it feel unwelcome."

The memory stabbed me, and for a moment I stumbled again through a dim tunnel flooded with liquid excrement and filth that rose to my hips. My left leg burned with icy pain and I struggled on, half-dragging it, while behind me the enormous pallid body of the Worm spilled its lifeblood into the sludge. The slick green blood swirled on the surface, each of its cells a tiny living organism consumed by a single purpose: to reunite. No matter how many times or how many miles apart this creature appeared, it was always the same Impala Worm. There was only one and it regenerated endlessly.

The protector put my papers on his desk. "So, what do you want?"

"I'm investigating the murder of Greg Feldman."

"On whose authority?"

"My own."

"I see." He leaned back. "Why?"

"For personal reasons."

"Did you know him personally?" He delivered the question in a perfectly neutral tone, but the underlying meaning was all too clear. I felt happy to disappoint him.

"Yes. He was a friend of my father."

"I see," he said again. "Your father wouldn't be available for a statement?"

"He's dead."

"I'm sorry," he said.

"Don't be," I said. "You didn't know him."

"Do you have anything that might support your relationship with Greg Feldman?"

I could easily provide him with corroboration. If he was to look me up in his files, he would find that Greg had sponsored my application to the Order, but I did not want to go in that direction.

"Greg Feldman was thirty-nine years old. He was an intensely private man, and he disliked being photographed." I handed him a small rectangle of the photograph. "This is a picture of me and him on the day of my high school graduation. There is an identical picture in his apartment. It's located in his library on the third shelf of the central bookcase."

"I've seen it," the protector said.

How bloody nice. "Can I have that back, please?"

He returned the photo. "Are you aware that you're named as a beneficiary in Greg Feldman's will?"

"No." I would've welcomed a moment to deal with my guilt and gratitude, but the knight-protector plowed on.

"He bequeathed his financial assets to the Order and the Academy." He was watching me for a reaction. Did he think I cared about Greg's money? "Everything else, the library, the weapons, the objects of power, is yours."

I said nothing.

"I've checked on you with the Guild," he said. The blue eyes fixed me in place. "I've heard you're able but hurting for money. The Order's prepared to make you a generous offer for the items in question. You'll find the sum to be more than adequate."

It was an insult and we both knew it. I thought of telling him that if it wasn't for Oklahoman cowboys and Mexican whores having a bit of fun, there would've been no Texans, but that would be counterproductive. One didn't call a knight-protector a whoreson in his own office.

"No, thank you," I said with a pleasant smile.

"Are you sure?" His eyes took my measure. "You look like you could use some money. The Order will give you more than you'd get auctioning it off. My advice, take the money. Buy yourself a decent pair of shoes."

I glanced at my beat-up sneakers. I liked my shoes. I could bleach them. It took the blood right out.

"Do you think I should get some like yours?" I asked, looking at his boots. "Who knows, they might throw a cowboy shirt with fringe in with them. Maybe even a girdle."

Something stirred in his eyes. "You got a mouth on you."

"Who, me?"

"Talk's cheap. What can you really do?"

Thin ice. Proceed with caution.

I leaned back. "What can I really do, Sir? I won't do anything to threaten or antagonize the knight-protector in his own office no matter how much he insults me. That would be stupid and highly hazardous to my health. I came here in search of information. I just want to know what Greg Feldman was working on when he died."

For a moment we sat there looking at each other.

The knight-protector sucked the air into his nose with an audible whoosh and said, "You know anything about investigative work?"

"Sure. Annoy the people involved until the guilty party tries to make you go away."

He grimaced. "You know that the Order's investigating this matter?"

In other words, run along, little lady, and let people who are more competent handle it. "Greg Feldman was my only family," I said. "I'll find who or what killed him."

"And then what?"

"I'll burn that bridge when I cross it."

He laced the fingers of his hands into a single fist. "Anything able to take out the knight-diviner is packing some power."

"Not for long."

He thought about that for a while. "So happens I could use you," he said.

That was unexpected. "Why the hell would you want me?"

He gave me what he must have considered his cryptic smile. It reminded me of a grizzly awakened in midwinter. "I have my reasons. Here's what I'll do for you. You get a Mutual Aid sticker on your ID, which should open you some doors. You get to use Greg's office. You get to look at the open file and police report."

Open file meant I would get the case as it came to Greg: bare facts and no or little findings. I would have to retrace Greg's steps. It was bloody more than I expected.

"Thank you," I said.

"The file doesn't leave the building," he said. "No copies, no quotes. You'll make a complete report to me and only to me."

"I'm bound by the Guild's disclosure of information act," I said.

He waved it aside. "It's taken care of."

Since when? This knight-protector was going far out of his way to help a worthless merc. Why? People who did me favors made me nervous. On the other hand, it was bad manners to look a gift horse in the mouth. Even if you're getting it from an overweight cracker in a fringe shirt.

"Officially you have no status with me," he said. "Screw up and you're persona non grata."

"Understood."

"We're done," he said.

Outside the receptionist waved me over and asked for my ID. I gave it to her and watched as she affixed a small metallic Mutual Aid sticker to it, an official "stamp" of the Order's interest in my humble work. Some doors would open to me and more would slam in my face. Oh, well.

"Don't mind Ted," the receptionist said, returning my ID. "He's harsh sometimes. My name's Maxine."

"My name's Kate. Would you point out the late knight-diviner's office to me?"

"I'd be glad to. The last one on the right."

"Thank you."

She smiled and went back to her work. Peachy keen.

I reached Greg's office and stood in the doorway. It didn't look right.

A square window spilled daylight onto the floor, a narrow desk, and two old chairs. To the left, a deep bookshelf ran the length of the wall, threatening to collapse under the weight of meticulously arranged volumes. Four metal file cabinets as tall as me towered at the opposite wall. Stacks of files and papers crowded in the corners, occupied the chairs, and choked the desk.

Someone had gone through Greg's papers. They'd done it carefully. The place wasn't ransacked, but someone had looked at each of Greg's files and didn't return them to their proper place, instead choosing to stack them on the first horizontal surface available. These were Greg's private papers. For some reason, the idea of someone touching Greg's things, going over them, reading his thoughts after his death bothered me.

I stepped through the doorway and felt a protective spell close behind me. Arcane symbols ignited with a pale orange glow, forming complex patterns on the gray carpet. Long twisted lines connected the symbols, crisscrossing and winding about the room, their intersections marked by radiant red dots. Greg had sealed the room with his own blood, and more, he had keyed it to me, otherwise I wouldn't be able to see the spell. Now any magic I did in this room would stay in it, leaving no echo beyond the door. A spell of this complexity would take weeks to set up. Judging by the intensity of the glowing lines, it would absorb one hell of an echo. Why would he do that?

I walked between the files to the bookshelf. It held an old edition of the Almanac of Mystic Creatures, an even older version of the Arcane Dictionary, a Bible, a beautiful edition of the Koran bound in leather and engraved with gold, several other religious volumes, and a thin copy of Spenser's *Faerie Queene*.

I made my way to the metal cabinets. As expected, they were empty. The shelves were marked in Greg's own unique code, which I couldn't read. It didn't matter really. I picked up the closest stack and carefully slid the first file onto the metal frame.

Two hours later, I finished with the papers on the floor and the chairs and was ready to start on the stacks covering the desk when a large manila envelope stopped me. It lay on top of the central stack, so my name, written with black marker in Greg's cursive, was plainly visible.

I lowered the stacks to the floor, pulled up a chair, and emptied the envelope onto the desk's surface. Two photographs and a letter. In the first photo two couples stood side by side. I recognized my father, a hulking, red-haired man, enormous shoulders spread wide, one arm around a woman who had to be my mother. Some children retain memories of their deceased parents, a shadow of a voice, a hint of a scent, an image. I recalled nothing of her, as if she had never existed. My father kept no photographs of her—it must have been too painful for him—and I knew only what he told me. She was pretty, he had said, and she had long blond hair. I stared at the woman in the photograph. She was short and petite. Her features matched her build, well-formed, delicate, but devoid of fragility. She stood assured, with easy, natural poise, clothed in a kind of magical allure and perfectly aware of her power. She was beautiful.

Both he and Greg told me I resembled her, but no matter how hard I studied her image, I could see no resemblance. My features were bolder. My mouth was larger and not pouting by any stretch of the imagination. I did manage to inherit her eye color, dark brown, but my eyes had an odd cut, almond shaped, slightly elongated. And my skin was a shade darker. If I overloaded on eyeliner and mascara, I could easily pass for a gypsy.

There was more to it than that—my mother's face had feminine gentleness. Mine didn't, at least not when compared to hers. If we were to stand side by side in a room full of people, I wouldn't get a single glance. And if someone had stopped to chat me up, she could've stolen him with a single smile.

Pretty . . . Yeah. Nice understatement, Dad.

On the other hand, if the same people had to pick one of us to kick a bad guy in the kneecap, I'd get the vote, no problem.

Next to my mother and father, Greg stood by a lovely Asian woman. Anna. His first wife. Unlike my parents, those two stood a little apart, each maintaining a barely perceptible distance as if their individualities would strike a spark if they reached for one another. Greg's eyes were mournful.

I put the photograph facedown on the desk.

The other photo was of me, about nine or ten years old, diving into a lake from the branches of a giant poplar. I didn't know he had it or even when it was taken.

I read the letter, a few sparse lines on the white piece of paper, a part of Spenser's poem.

One day I wrote her name upon the strand,
But came the waves and washed it away:
Again I wrote it with a second hand,
But came the tide, and made my pains his prey.

Below four words were written in Greg's blood.

Amehe
Tervan
Senehe
Ud

The words blazed with red fire. A powerful spasm gripped me. My lungs constricted, the room blurred, and through the dense fog the beating of my heart sounded loud like the toll of a church bell. A tangle of forces swirled around me, catching me in a twisted mess of slippery, elastic power currents. I reached out and gripped them, and they carried me forth, far into the amalgam of light and sound. The light permeated me and burst within my mind, sending a myriad of sparks through my skin. The blood in my veins luminesced like molten metal.

Lost. Lost in the whirlwind of light.

My mouth opened, struggling to release a word. It wouldn't come and I thought I would die, and then I said it, pouring my power into the weak sound.

"Hesaad." Mine.

The world stopped spinning and I found my place in it. The four words towered before me. I had to say them. I held my power and said the words, willing them, forcing them to become mine.

"Amehe. Tervan. Senehe. Ud."

The flow of power ebbed. I was staring at the white piece of paper. The words were gone and a small puddle of crimson spread across the sheet. I touched it and felt the prickling of magic. My blood. My nose was bleeding.

Pulling a dressing from my pocket, where I always carried some, I pressed it against my nose and leaned back. I'd burn the bandages later. The watch on my wrist said 12:17 p.m. Somehow within those few instants I had lost almost an hour and a half.

The four words of power. *Obey, Kill, Protect,* and *Die.* Words so primal, so dangerous, so powerful that they commanded the raw magic itself. Nobody knew how many of them there were, where they came from, or why they held such enormous hold over magic. Even people who had never used magic recognized their meaning and were subject to their power, as if the words were a part of some ancient racial memory we all carried.

It wasn't enough to merely know them; one had to own them. When it came to acquiring power words, there were no second chances. You either conquered them or you died trying, which explained why so few among the magic workers could wield them. Once you made them yours, they belonged to you forever. They had to be wielded with great precision and using them took a chunk of power that left the caster near exhaustion. Greg and my father both warned me that the power words could be resisted, but so far I hadn't had a chance to use them against an opponent that did. They were the last resort, when all else failed.

Now I had six words. Four given to me by Greg and two others: *Mine* and *Release.* My father taught them to me long ago. I was twelve and I almost died making them mine. This time it had been too easy.

Maybe the power of the blood grew with age. I wished Greg was alive so I could ask him.

I glanced to the floor. The orange lines of Greg's ward had grown so dim, I could barely see them. They had absorbed everything they could.

The words clamored in my head, shifting and tossing, trying to find their place. Greg's last gift. More precious than anything he could have given me.

Gradually I became aware of someone watching me. I looked up and saw a lean black man in the doorway. He had smiled at me when I passed by his office some three hours earlier.

"Are you alright?" he asked.

"Tripped a residual ward," I mumbled, the rag still covering my nose. "Happens. I'm okay."

He eyed me. "You sure?"

"Yeah." Okay, I'm an incompetent moron, go away now.

"I brought you Greg's file." He made no move to enter the room. Smart. If I had tripped a trap set up by Greg, it could hit him as well. "Sorry it's so late. One of our knights had it."

I walked to him and took the file from his hands. "Thanks."

"No problem." He regarded me for a moment and walked away.

I rummaged through Greg's desk for a mirror. Every self-respecting mage had a mirror close to hand. Too many spells required it. Greg's was a rectangle set in a plain wooden frame. I caught my image in it and almost dropped the rag. My hair glowed. It radiated a weak burgundy luminescence, which shifted when I ran my hands through it, as if each individual strand of hair was coated with fluorescent paint. I shook my head, but the radiance didn't dim. Growling at it didn't help either and I had not the faintest idea how I could get rid of it.

I hid in the farthest corner of the room, invisible from the door, and opened the file. If you can't make it go away, wait it out.

The last time I assimilated words of power, I was exhausted. Now I felt exhilarated, high on magic. The energy filled me, and I struggled to contain it. I wanted to jump, to run, to do something. Instead I had to hide in a corner and concentrate on the file before me.

The file contained a coroner's report, a summary of a police report, some hurried notes, and several photos of a crime scene.

A wide shot showed two bodies sprawled on the asphalt, one corpse stark, pale, and nude, and the other a bloody mess of mauled, shredded tissue. I found the close-up of the mauled corpse first. The cadaver lay spread-eagled upon a blood-soaked cloth. Something had ripped into its chest, snapped the breastbone, and torn it away with unbelievable force. The chest cavity lay exposed, the wet, glistening mass of the smashed heart dark against the spongy remains of lungs and the yellow white of broken ribs. The left arm, wrenched clear of its socket, hung by a thin, bloodied filament.

The next shot showed the close-up of the head. Sad eyes I knew so well looked up into the camera and straight at me. Oh God. I read the caption. This battered piece of human meat was all that remained of Greg.

A lump rose in my throat. I struggled with it for a few agonizing seconds and forced it down. This was not Greg. It was only his corpse.

The next photo provided me with a close look at the other body. This one appeared untouched, all except for the head, which was missing. A broken shard of the spine jutted from the neck stump framed by limp shreds of torn tissue. No other evidence of the head ever being there remained. There was hardly any blood. There should have been pints of it. The body lay at an angle and both carotid and jugular were cleanly severed, so where did all the blood go?

I found four more shots of the corpse and arranged them next to each other on the floor. The smooth marble-white skin of the cadaver stretched tightly over his musculature, as if the body had no fat at all, only lean muscle. Not a single hair marred the epidermis. The scrotum looked shriveled and unusually small in size. I needed a close-up of the hand but there was not one. Somebody had dropped the ball. It did not matter too much, since all of the other telltale signs were there. Even without the nails, the conclusion was plain. I was looking at a dead vampire.

Vampires are dead by definition, but this one had ceased its undead existence. Not even Ghastek, with all of his necromantic powers, could fix a vampire without a head. The sixty-four-thousand-dollar question was who did this vampire belong to? Most People branded their vampires. If this one was branded, it didn't show in any of the shots the moron photographer had taken.

What could wipe out a vampire and a knight-diviner? The vampire, super fast and able to take out a SWAT team unaided, would prove hard prey by itself. The vampire plus Greg made for a near impossible kill. Yet there they were, both dead.

I leaned back, thinking. The killer would have to possess great power. He would have to be faster than a vampire, strong enough to tear the head off a body, and able to shield himself from Greg's magic and his mace. Off the top of my head the list of possible murderers was rather short.

First, the People could have sought to kill Greg and used one of their vamps as bait. An aged vampire in the hands of an experienced and able Master of the Dead was a weapon like no other. If there was more than one, they could've taken out Greg and their own bloodsucker. It was expensive and improbable, since Greg was particularly effective against vampires, but it wasn't impossible.

Second, the condition of Greg's ravaged corpse pointed to the shapechangers. That kind of damage had to be done with claws and teeth, and by more than one set of them. Perhaps it was a loup, a deranged shapechanger. The bodies of those afflicted with Lycos Virus, or Lyc-V for short, yearned to slaughter without discrimination while their minds sought to restrain the bloodlust. If the mind won over the body, a shapechanger became a Free

Man of the Code, existing within a well-structured and highly disciplined Pack. If the body conquered the mind, a shapechanger became a loup, a cannibalistic murderer driven mad by hormones, hunting everything and hunted by everyone.

The loup theory was even less probable than the People theory. For one, the beheaded vamp was untouched except for its neck, and loups tore into everything with maniacal frenzy. Next, Greg would've killed more than one of them, and no other bodies littered the scene. Third, if the murderer was a loup, or more likely, several of them, they would've left a ton of evidence at the scene, everything from saliva and hair to their own blood. The medical examiner's office had genetic profiles on almost all known shapechanger types. As far as I could discern, the file contained no paper showing that any shapechanger DNA had been found at the scene.

Rubbing my face didn't give me any special insights into the situation. Most likely, the murders had been committed by none of the above, and for the time being I had to leave it at that.

The autopsy report confirmed the beheaded cadaver as *Homo sapiens immortuus*, a vampire. An ironic name since the mind of a human died the moment vampirism took hold. The vampires knew no pity and no fear; they couldn't be trained; they had no ego. On a developmental level they stood close to insects, possessing a nervous system and yet incapable of forming thoughts. An insatiable hunger for blood ruled them and they slaughtered everything in their path in their urge to quench it.

I frowned. The file contained no m-scan. All crime scenes involving death or assault were routinely scanned for magic. Technically both the police and MSDU could demand access to this file and be granted such access by a court order. The fact that an m-scan was missing meant that it showed something the Order didn't wish to reveal to the general public. Unless the same cretin that took the photographs somehow managed to drop the scan in the trash.

The only remaining page in the file listed several female names. Sandra Molot, Angelina Gomez, Jennifer Ying, Alisa Konova. None of them sounded familiar, and no explanation of the list was offered.

A fresh examination of my hair revealed that it was no longer glowing. I made a quick dash to the desk and dialed the number listed in the police report.

A gruff voice answered the phone. I introduced myself and asked for the lead detective. "I'm looking into the murder of the knight-diviner."

"We've spoken to you people," the man on the other end said. "Read the goddamned report."

"You haven't spoken to me, sir. I would very much appreciate any time you could find for me. Any time at all."

The phone clanged and I was greeted by a disconnect signal. So much for interagency cooperation.

The watch on my wrist showed 12:58 p.m. I'd have time to hit the morgue. The mandatory one-month waiting period for the dead vampire was nowhere close to running out, and the MA sticker would ensure that I'd have no problem taking a look at the bloodsucker's body.

I closed the file, placed it into the closest filing cabinet, and made my escape.

THE CITY MORGUE STOOD IN THE MIDDLE OF THE downtown district. Directly across from it, past the wide expanse of the Unnamed Square, rose the golden dome of the Capitol Building. The old morgue had been leveled twice, first by a rogue Master of the Dead, and second by a golem, the same one that created the Unnamed Square when it reduced the five city blocks to rubble in its failed attempt to break through the Capitol's wards.

Even now, six years later, the city council refused to rename the empty space surrounding the Capitol, reasoning that as long as it had no name, nobody could summon anything there.

The new morgue was constructed on the principle of "third time's the charm." A state-of-the-art facility, it looked like the bastard offspring of a prison and a fortress, with a bit of medieval castle thrown in for good measure. The locals joked that if the Capitol Building came under attack again, the State Legislature could just run across the square and hide in the morgue. Looking at it, I could believe it, too. A severe, forbidding building, the morgue loomed among the dolled-up facades of the corporation headquarters like the Grim Reaper at a tea party. Its mercantile neighbors had to be unhappy about its presence in their midst, but could do nothing about it. The morgue got more traffic than all of them. Another sign of the times.

I walked up the wide staircase, between granite columns, and moved through the revolving door into a wide hall. The high windows admitted plenty of light, but failed to banish the gloom completely. It pooled in the corners and along the walls, lying in wait to clutch at the ankles of an unwary passerby. Polished tiles of gray granite covered the floor. Two hallways radiated from the opposite wall, both flooded by blue feylantern light. The tiles ended there, replaced by yellowish linoleum.

The air smelled of death. It wasn't the actual nauseating odor of the rotting flesh, but a different kind of stench, one of chlorine and formaldehyde and bitter medicines, reminiscent of a hospital smell, but nobody would confuse the two. In the hospital, life left its sure signs. Here only its absence could be felt.

There was an information desk between the two hallways. I

made my way to it and introduced myself to a clerk in green scrubs. He glanced at my ID and nodded. "He's in seven C. You know where it is?"

"Yes. I've been here before."

"Good. Go ahead, I'll get someone to open it for you."

I took the right hallway to a flight of stairs and went down, into the basement level. I passed section B and came to a stop at its end, where a steel gate barred my progress.

After five minutes or so, hurried steps echoed through the hallway and a woman wearing green scrubs and a stained apron came rushing around the corner. She carried a thick three-ring binder in one hand and a jingling key chain in the other. A few thin wisps of blond hair had escaped her sterile hair net. Dark circles surrounded her eyes, and the skin on her face sagged a little.

"Sorry," I said.

"Nahh, don't worry about it," she said, fumbling with the keys. "It didn't hurt to take a walk."

She unlocked the gate and swept past me. I followed her to a reinforced steel door. She opened two locks, stepped back, and barked, "It is I, Julianne, who commands you, and you shall do my bidding. Open!" The magic shifted subtly as the spell released the door. Julianne swung it open. Inside, on a metal table riveted to the floor, lay a nude body. Stark against the stainless steel, it was a queer shade of pale, whitish pink, as if it had been bleached. A silver-steel harness enclosed the cadaver's chest. A chain as thick as my arm stretched from the harness to a ring in the floor.

"We usually just collar them, but with this one . . ." Julianne waved her hand.

"Yeah." I glanced at the stump of the neck.

"Not that he'll rise or anything. Not without a head. Still, if anything . . ." She nodded toward the blue circle of a panic button on the nearest wall. "You armed?"

I unsheathed Slayer. Julianne jerked back from the shimmering blade. "Whoa. Okay, that'll work."

I slid the saber back into its sheath. "There was a second body brought in with this one."

"Yeah. Kind of hard to forget that one."

"Any trace evidence?"

"Nice try." Julianne smirked. "That's classified."

"I see," I said. "What about an m-scan?"

"That's classified, too."

I sighed. Greg with his dark eyes and perfect face, mangled and broken, locked away in some cubicle in this lonely, sterile place. I fought the urge to double over and cradle the empty space in my chest.

Julianne touched my shoulder. "Who was he to you?" she asked.

"My guardian," I told her. Apparently my efforts to appear impartial had suffered a spectacular failure.

"You were close?"

"No. We used to be."

"What happened?"

I shrugged. "I grew up and he forgot to notice."

"Did he have any kids?"

"No. No wife, no children. Just me."

Julianne glanced at the vampire's corpse with obvious disgust. "You'd think the Order would have enough sensitivity to assign someone not related to this mess."

"I volunteered."

She gave me an odd look. "How about that. I hope you know what you're doing."

"So do I. There is no chance you'd let me glance at the m-scan?"

She pursued her lips, thinking. "Did you hear that?"

I shook my head.

"I think someone's at the gate. I'm going to go and check on it. I'm putting my binder right here. Now, these are confidential reports. I don't want you looking at them. In particular, I don't want you looking at the reports from the third of this month. Or taking any copies out of this file." She turned and marched out of the room.

I flipped through the notebook. There were eight autopsies on the third. Finding Greg's didn't prove to be a problem.

The trace evidence consisted of four hairs. In the origin column someone penciled Un. Psb Feline der. Unidentified, possibly a feline derivative. Not a feline shapeshifter. They would've pegged it as *Homo sapiens* with a specific *felidae* genus.

The long folded sheet of the m-scan came next. Obeying the shake of my hand, it unfolded to its full three feet, presenting a graph drawn by the delicate needles of the magic-scanner. The faint colored lines on the graph wavered, a sure sign of many magic influences colliding in one spot. It was inconclusive by the most lax of standards and no court would have permitted it into evidence. The small header in the top corner identified it as a copy. Oh, goodie.

I squinted, trying to make sense of it. Greg's body had continued to release its magic even after his death, and the scanner recorded it as a sloping gray line, sometimes an inch wide, sometimes almost invisible. The deep jagged purple cutting across it had to be the vampire's magic. I looked harder. There was a third line, actually a series of lines, faint and dashing at irregular intervals through the reading. The longest was about a quarter of an inch long and the color was undeterminable. I raised the graph so the light of the ceiling bulb shone through it. The ink stood out. Yellow. What the hell registered yellow?

I tugged at the graph, tearing it along the perforated lines and slid it into my folder. Julianne returned shortly. "Nobody there. Well, I'll leave you to it."

She took the binder and walked out, leaving me with the vampire's corpse. I slipped on a pair of medical gloves and approached the body. The placement of brands depended on the personality of the Master of the Dead. Phillian marked his with a big Eye of Horus smack in the middle of the forehead. Constance marked hers in the left armpit. Since the forehead on this one was conveniently missing, it could have belonged to Phillian. Theoretically. I set about finding the brand.

The armpits were clean, so was the chest, the spine, the back, the buttocks, the inside of the thighs and ankles. The only place remaining was the scrotum, so I spread the vampire's legs. The testicles diminished immediately after the human's death and continued to shrink during the vampire's life. There was a whole study on dating the bloodsuckers based on the size of the reproductive organs. I didn't care how old this one was, but judging by the signs he had to be pushing fifty. And he was clean. No brand. There was a scar, however, cleaving the scrotum at the base on the left side. It looked like it had been stitched together.

A quick glance about told me I would find no scalpel in this room. I took Slayer from its sheath. It smoked, sensing the undead. Thin tendrils of pale haze curved from the blade.

"Don't start dripping," I murmured and pressed the very tip of the edge against the scar.

The undead tissue hissed as the blade sank into the flesh. I let it cut about a quarter of an inch and withdrew the saber, leaving a neat incision. Taking the flap of the skin, I pulled on it lightly, and it came away from the groin, revealing a smooth burn scar about an inch wide and three quarters of an inch long. In the middle of the burned scar sat a neat scorch mark, an arrow tipped with a circle instead of an arrowhead. Ghastek's brand. Why wasn't I surprised?

"You do know there are penalties for mutilating corpses?" said a male voice.

I spun around, blade in my hand. A tall man stood leaning against the doorway. He wore scrubs, which meant he had more right to be here than I did.

"Watch out there," he said.

"Sorry," I lowered the saber. "I don't like being startled."

"Neither do I. Except by young attractive women." He looked to be in his mid-thirties. The colored stripe on his shoulder shone bright orange. Third-level clearance. The tag clipped to his suit confirmed it: I'd gotten a bloody unit supervisor.

A unit supervisor could make a person non grata in the morgue faster than I could blink.

The man waited until I finished staring at his tag and held out his left hand. "My name's Crest."

I peeled off my left glove without putting down Slayer and shook his hand. "Kate. Is there a first name that goes with Crest?"

"Yes, but I don't like it."

A funny guy. Perhaps I would get away without a black eye for dicing a corpse.

"It's a vampire," I said. "I was looking for the brand."

"Find it?"

"Yes."

He approached the table to examine my handiwork. I moved to stand across from him. Dr. Crest was actually on the appealing side. Auburn-haired, tall, and quite muscular, judging by the forearms. A pleasant face, open and honest, with large, well-defined features and nice eyes, honey brown and warm. The full mouth was downright sensuous. Attractive fellow, not strictly handsome in a classical sense, but still . . . He looked up from the body, smiled, and became handsome.

I smiled back, trying to radiate integrity and decency of character. That's right, I'll be very nice to you, sir, just please don't bar me from the morgue.

"Interesting," he said. "I've never seen one concealed in this way."

"Neither have I."

"You see a lot of vampires in your line of work?"

"Unfortunately."

I caught him glancing at me and he lowered his gaze back to the body.

"Dr. Crest?"

He blinked. "Yes?"

"Do I need to let Julianne know about the brand?" It was the least I could do.

"No. I can tell her myself if you have to run."

A little warning bell went off in my head. The good doctor was a little too accommodating. I would have to make sure that Julianne got my message.

Crest was frowning at the corpse. "A devious place to put a brand."

Ghastek was a devious fellow. "Indeed."

Another pause issued. "Let me walk you upstairs," he said.

How charming. He was trying to make sure that I didn't go on a mutilating rampage. I gave him my knockout smile. "Sure."

He didn't look dazzled. Damn it, that's the second time today my smile had misfired.

We left, walking side by side. I waited while he locked the grate behind us. "So what do you do here, Dr. Crest?"

He grimaced. "I suppose one can call it charity work."

I made the appropriate noise, "Charity?"

"Yes. I perform reconstructive surgery." He glanced at me as if afraid I would demand a nose job. "I make corpses presentable. Not everyone can afford it, so twice a week I do it here pro bono."

I nodded.

"It's kids mostly," he said. "Torn up and mauled. Not a pretty sight. Such a waste."

We reached the upper floor. He waited while I checked out with the clerk and wrote down Julianne's number, and then walked me to the door.

"So I'll see you again sometime?" he said.

"Hopefully not on the operating table," I said and left the building. As I walked away to where Karmelion waited for me, I could feel Crest watching my back.

A man was leaning against my truck. He wore a dark gray shirt, black jeans, tucked in soft boots, and a black cloak that wanted very much to be a cape. While I was in the morgue, the sun had broken through the clouds, flooding the streets with sunshine. He seemed to shrug off the sun's rays—not a man, but a rectangle of darkness cut in the shroud of sunlight.

The human current streaming up the street bent away from him. People didn't eye him; in fact, they concentrated so hard on ignoring his presence, one could have dropped a twenty dollar bill on the ground and it might have gone unnoticed.

The man's eyes tracked my movement. I stopped a few feet away and looked at him.

He reached into an inside pocket of his cloak and flicked what looked like a long yellow ribbon at me. I caught it in midflight. The smooth, cold body coiled about my wrist, and the serpentine head reared to strike at my face. I clamped its neck with fingers of my left hand and stopped it three inches from my cheek. The snake's tongue danced between the scaly lips. Blood-red membranes tinged with brilliant purple flared on both sides of the head, spreading like the wings of an enormous butterfly. The baby winged snake shuddered, trying to take flight, but I held it in check.

"I'm sorry, Jim."

He held up his arms, indicating something about three feet wide. The cloak parted enough to show muscle roll across his chest under the fabric of his shirt. "The nest was this big, Kate." His voice had the smooth, almost melodious tone of a less dangerous, much prettier man. It clashed badly with his bulldog-ugly mug. "You owe me and you stood me up. I had to do the gig single-handed."

The snake twisted in a feeble attempt to sink its fangs into my arm. The long triangular teeth contained no poison but the bite hurt like hell.

"Greg's dead," I said.

There was a tiny pause before he asked, "When?"

"Two days ago. He was murdered."

"You on it?"

"Yeah."

We stood for a while, caught in a painful silence. He peeled himself from my truck, moving with the liquid, animal grace that only a master shapechanger could achieve.

"You need anything, you know where to find me."

I nodded and watched him walk up the stairs to the morgue.

"Jim?"

He scowled at me over his shoulder. "Yeah?"

"What are you doing at the morgue?"

"Pack business," he said and moved on.

Everyone had business in the morgue these days. Even Jim. I still owed him for this winter when he pulled me out of a mud pit full of melted snow and hydra. He was the closest thing to a partner I had. Once in a while we shared merc jobs from the Guild. This time I had stood him up. I'd have to make it up to him. But first, I'd have to find out who killed Greg. To do that I would have to figure out what Ghastek's vampire was doing at the murder scene.

I eased the pressure on the snake's neck and gently tossed it into the air. The serpent plummeted and suddenly took flight. It soared higher and higher, far above the rooftops into the sunshine, until it finally disappeared from sight.

WHEN IN DOUBT AND IN NEED OF INFORMATION, FIND a snitch and squeeze him. That was one of the very few investigative techniques I was aware of. As a matter of fact, that and the "annoy principals involved until the guilty party decides to kill you" pretty much summed it up for me. Move over, Sherlock.

I was definitely in doubt and in need of information concerning Ghastek's dead vampire, and I knew just the person to squeeze. He had spiky hair, wore black leather, and called himself Bono after some long-forgotten singer. He was also Ghastek's journeyman.

If you had a talent for necromancy or necronavigation, the care and piloting of the dead, you qualified as an apprentice. Once you added a bit of knowledge to that, you became a journeyman. To move higher required a genuine power and a drive to succeed. Most People never graduated from journeymanship. Bono was on his second year. His knowledge of the dead was almost encyclopedic. The last time we met, he gave me a cut-out article to put into my Almanac—something about some Slavic corpse-eater creature called an upir. But I had a feeling his expertise ended with theory. My guess was he would not grow into a Master of the Dead any time soon.

Bono was easy to find. He frequented Andriano's, a peaceful joint as bars went, unlike the newly redesigned establishments of Atlanta Underground, where bars leaned toward the rowdy and most clubs had the word "pain" in their name. Andriano's occupied a nice little spot on Euclid Avenue in Little Five Points and catered to an almost middle-class crowd.

Bono's pretty face, his hair, and his jacket made sure he was noticed. Women enjoyed his company. He enjoyed them too, but his focus was on quantity. I'd never seen him with the same woman twice. Once in a while someone tried to kick his ass and left a few smears of their blood on the floor and furniture. Anyone who spent his formative years tending to a stable of vampires proved a hard person to fight.

I could've gone straight to the source and just asked Ghastek about his vampire. Trouble was, confronting Ghastek meant I'd have to physically walk into the Casino, where the People had their HQ. Walking into the Casino meant I'd have to meet Nataraja, the People's grand poo-bah in the city and Ghastek's boss and supervisor. Nataraja was the worst kind of worm, but he had an uncanny sensitivity to magic. My guess was, he wasn't quite sure what he felt when I was around, but he wanted very much to find out. Every time we met our conversation degenerated into him trying to force me into a show of power. That I couldn't afford, especially not now with the four new words of power rattling in my head. I'd have to go to the Casino eventually, but for now squeezing Ghastek's journeyman would suffice.

It was almost 11:00 p.m. when I made it to Andriano's. Bono rarely showed up before dark and I had used the time to hop the ley line back to my place and bring back Betsi, my beat-up old

Subaru. It looked like I would be stuck in the city for a while. Since the magic would fall, the way it always did, I'd eventually need a car that worked during tech.

It cost me fifty bucks to have Betsi towed to Greg's place. I was in the wrong business.

I entered Andriano's. The bar stretched the length of the room, guarded by a row of tall stools. A couple of patrons stared into their drinks on the far end. A blonde with her war paint on sipped something fruity from a margarita glass. Through the arched doorway I could see the second room, crowded with red privacy booths, which Andriano must have pilfered from some fast-food joint.

The barkeep, long of limb and dark-haired, nodded at me. Lean and phlegmatic, with a narrow, intelligent face, he looked more like a campus intellectual than a bartender. His name was Sergio and he knew how big of a lime slice to put into a Corona, which made him a worthwhile man to know. I passed him two twenties. Sergio bent an eyebrow at me.

"What for?"

"In case anything gets broken. Bono and I are going to chat a bit. Is he here?"

Sergio nodded toward the room with booths and shrugged, palming the twenties. "Stay away from the windows," he said. "Too expensive for you."

The back room was dimly lit with feylanterns. Bono preferred a corner booth, the farthest from the door. I stood for a moment, surveying the scene, and caught sight of his spiky black hair. I marched toward the booth with flags out and guns ready.

Bono had company. Judging by the mystical "hey-baby-I'm-a-student-of-magic" smile that stretched his lips, he had female company. No matter.

He paused his wooing to glance around the room and noticed

me. He must have seen something he did not like, because the smile slid off his face. He sat straighter.

I reached back. My fingers grasped Slayer's hilt and withdrew it in a smooth fluid motion. Bono's hand dropped under the table, groping for a gun. He carried a 9mm Colt in his jacket pocket.

I crashed to a halt before the booth. A thin redhead in a strapless short dress sat opposite Bono. I put my saber on the table. Bono "stank" of vampires and the saber fluoresced weakly, a sliver of moonlight against the dark wood. The redhead's eyes went wide. Bono's face relaxed a bit but his gaze never left mine.

"Hey, Bono," I said. "Nice to see you. Fuck any corpses lately?"

The last hope for a relaxing evening bled from his face. "Not any you'd care about."

The redhead scrambled out of the booth and fled, trying to salvage some shred of dignity. Bono threw a wistful look after her retreating backside and turned to me.

"You scared her. Not nice, Kate."

I raised an eyebrow at him and slid in the seat vacated by the redhead.

"Did you read the article I gave you?" he asked.

"No."

"You should read it, Kate. You should read about the upiri."

I traced Slayer's blade with my finger. It stung a little as the magic discharge touched my skin.

"I want to know about the diviner's death. I want to know why one of Ghastek's bloodsuckers was at the scene. I want to know who was piloting it and what they saw. I want to know what tore his head off. And whatever else you'll find necessary to add."

Bono showed me his teeth. "Feeling a bit on edge today, are you?"

My hand closed about the hilt. "You have no idea."

He leaned back. "Go ahead," he said. "Make a play. I'll ass-fuck you with that saber."

I grinned at him. "You can't take me, Bono. Go ahead and try. You telegraph your punches, you drop your left shoulder, and your gun isn't worth piss with magic up. So come on. Show me what you've got."

I saw his eyes and knew my grin had turned into a hungry grimace. "I really need to hurt something. It'll make me feel good." I was almost laughing, having a hard time containing myself. "Give me a reason. Come on, Bono. Just give me a fucking reason."

Magic built around me, drawn from the environment by the emanations from my blood. If magic had color, I would be sitting in a whirlpool of red. Slayer flared bright silver, feeding off my anger. It wanted to slice into warm flesh and I was about to let it.

Bono blinked. He sensed the magic influx and sucked the air into his lungs in a sharp breath. "You're crazy."

"Very."

His face went slack, and I knew we had stepped away from a cliff. The fight would not happen today.

Bono leaned forward. "What if I told you that we have no involvement with the diviner's death? And even if we did, we don't have to speak to you."

That proverbial "we." I chewed on it for a little while and said, "In that case, I'll get up and walk over to the bar, where I'll make two phone calls. First, I'll call the knight-protector, for whom I now work, and tell him that a vampire belonging to Ghastek was involved in his diviner's murder. I'll tell him that an effort was made to conceal its brand—which is illegal—and that Ghastek's journeyman declined to discuss the matter with me and threatened my life. Then I'll call Ghastek and inform him that I know the reason why the world just started crashing down around his ears. And I'll explain to him that the reason is you."

He stared at me. "I thought we were on good terms. We nod to each other across the room. We don't bother each other. I shared my research with you."

I shrugged.

"You won't do this to me," he said with great surety. "You know what Ghastek would do to me. You're a nice person."

"Just what exactly in my track record gives you the idea that I'm a nice person?"

He had no answer and shook his head. "Why me?"

"Why not? Give me what I want and I'll go away. Or I'll hurt you one way or another."

Bono was in the corner. No way to go but outside the ring. "They're called shadows," he said, his handsome face marked with resignation. "Vampires with concealed brands. Ghastek isn't the only one using them but he uses his a lot, if you catch my drift."

"What was that particular one doing?"

"Tailing the diviner. I don't know why."

"Who was piloting it?"

Bono hesitated. "Merkowitz."

"What did he see?"

Bono spread his hands. "Your guess's as good as mine. Do you know what happens to a navigator when the vamp he's piloting dies?"

I had a general idea but more info never hurt. "Enlighten me."

"Unless you guard yourself, you'll suffer death-shock. Meaning you think it's your head being torn off, which leaves your brain very confused. Add to it the explosion of shit the diviner threw around and whatever magic the attacker emitted, and you'll get Merkowitz. I never liked the asshole. I have to admit, he makes a fine vegetable."

My heart sank. "Nonresponsive?"

"About as responsive as a brick wall."

"How long will he be like this?"

"They're working on him now, but when he'll come out, nobody knows. It's hard work convincing someone that he isn't dead when his own mind has decided otherwise."

"Do the People have any idea who might have enough juice to beat a diviner and a vampire to a pulp?"

Bono looked past me at the wall.

"I need a name," I said.

"Corwin. You didn't hear it from me." He rose in a fluid motion and left.

I waited a few minutes, went to the bar, and drank a cold Corona with a wedge of lime in it. I had frightened Bono. A small part of me felt bad about it. The larger part reminded me that he piloted vampires for a living and kicked his opponents when they decided to stay down.

Greg's face came to my mind. I took a big swig of Corona. I felt defeated and tired. What a long day . . . I had hoped for more than Bono had given me. Still, I had a name. And I had Greg's database, against which I could reference it. The day was not a total waste.

DARKNESS CLOAKED THE STAIRWAY OF GREG'S APARTment building. Not a single lamp illuminated the concrete steps. When I came to the first landing, I saw why—the electric bulbs had exploded. It happened once in a while during a hard fluctuation in places where the magic hit the strongest. The fluorescent feylamps usually did the job just fine—they ran by converting environmental magic to weak, bluish light—but tonight they were dark, too. The fluctuation must have been too strong, and the lamp converters had overheated and burned out.

I felt odd going back to Greg's place. Not exactly ill at ease, but not happy to be there either. Unfortunately I had no choice. I would have to spend some time in this rotten city and I needed a base. Greg's apartment was perfect: its wards were keyed to me and Greg had maintained a fair collection of basic herbs, reference books, and other useful things. His arsenal was decent, but he leaned toward bludgeoning arms, while I preferred swords. Maces and hammers required too much strength. I was strong for a woman but I harbored no illusions. In a contest of strength a man of my size and my training would pummel me into the ground. Lucky for me very few men had my training.

I climbed the dark stairs, fantasizing about food and a shower. The ward guarding the apartment's door clutched at my hand and opened in a pulse of blue. I entered, kicked off my shoes, and went into the kitchen. The upside of having a magic sword was that its secretions liquefied the undead flesh. On the downside, the blade had to be fed at least once a month, or it would become too brittle and break.

I slid a four-foot-long fish tank from the bottom cabinet and found the bag of feed I've kept at Greg's apartment for emergency purposes. Grayish-brown, the feed resembled coarse wheat flour. Most of it actually was wheat flour, that and metal shavings, copper, iron, and silver, and seashells ground to fine dust, together with bonemeal and chalk.

I filled the tank with water, added a cup of feed, and stirred the mixture with a long wooden spoon until the solution became cloudy and none of the feed remained stuck to the bottom. That done, I dropped the saber into it and washed my hands.

The little ruby light on the answering machine was blinking. It shouldn't have, since the magic was in full swing. Magic was a funny thing. Sometimes phones worked and sometimes they failed.

I settled into my chair and pushed the button on the answering machine. Anna's anxiety-laced voice filled the room. "Kate, it's me." I sat up straighter. Anna didn't get anxious. Perhaps it was Greg's death. Their divorce was ten years old, but still she must've felt something for him.

"Listen very carefully, while I remember." Exhaustion crept into her voice and I realized she was fresh from a vision. The fact that she knew I would be in Greg's apartment was so mundane to her she didn't bother to comment on it. Sometimes being a clairvoyant had its uses.

"Woods," Anna's voice said. "Very green, very healthy, late spring or early summer. The air smells of moisture. There are tall wooden idols set under some of the trees. They are old. Time has smoothed the edges of the carvings. The idols shift and change shapes. One looks like an old man, but also a bear with horns, holding something . . . a saucer of water maybe. Another old man stands on a fish; I think he holds a wheel in his hand. A man with three faces, his eyes covered, sitting deep in the shadow. I can barely see him."

The first was Veles, the third was Triglav. Slavic pantheon. I'd have to look up the second one.

"A man stands before them, surrounded by a brood of his children. They are very *wrong*. They do not fit, neither human nor animal, neither living nor dead. Behind him stand his servants. They smell of undeath." Anna took a deep breath. "The man is masturbating. To the right something is shimmering in and out of existence, a child maybe? To the left you're sitting cross-legged on the grass and eating a corpse."

Lovely.

"I know Greg's dead," she said. "And I know you're looking for the murderer. You must drop it, Kate. I know you'll ignore me, but I have to warn you. This isn't good, Kate. It's not good at all."

CHAPTER 3

I AWOKE EIGHT HOURS LATER, TIRED AND PLAGUED BY a migraine. I had meant to call Anna, but instead I somehow had fallen into bed and my body turned off my brain for the entire night.

The phone no longer worked. I sat on the bed and stared at it. So far I had some data for a hair but not the actual specimen; I had some lines that may or may not be the result of an m-reader malfunction; and I had a name of some nocturnal character given to me under duress by a People journeyman who'd pretty much do anything to get me off his back. On top of it I had what was probably a feline hair on a dead vampire, which set the Pack and People on a collision course. I pictured two colossi running at each other across the city, like monstrosities from an antique horror movie, and myself, a gnat in the middle.

It would be a bloodbath, which most of the city wouldn't survive. So the trick wasn't to survive it, but to keep it from happening.

In my daydream the gnat kicked one colossus in the groin and hit the other with a vicious uppercut.

I tried the phone again. It still didn't work. I cursed and went to dress.

An hour later I slipped into Greg's office. Nobody challenged me. Nobody glared and asked me why the hell the case was not solved or why I was so late arriving. The lack of drama was very disappointing.

I sifted through Greg's data. The cabinets contained no files marked "Corwin," but in the last cabinet I found a stack of folders marked with a question mark, so I went through them on the faint hope that I'd find something. Anything. Otherwise I'd be reduced to grabbing people on the street and screaming, "Do you know Corwin? Where is he?"

The files secured Greg's notes, written in his particular code. I frowned as I scanned one indecipherable entry after another. "Glop. Ag. Bll.–7." "Bll" had to be bullets. "Ag" could be Argentium, silver. What the hell did "Glop" mean?

My hopes dimmed as I flipped through page after page, and when I came across it, my brain almost did not register it. On a single page there was a scratchy "Corwin" and next to it were two drawings. One was a very clumsy rendition of a glove with sharp blades protruding from its knuckles. The other was some sort of bizarre doodle against a dark semicircle. I stared at the doodle. It meant nothing to me.

The phone rang.

I looked at it. It rang again. I wondered if I should answer.

The intercom came to life and Maxine's voice said, "You should, dear. It's for you."

How did she know? I picked up the phone. "Yes?"

"Hello, sunshine," said Jim's voice.

"I'm kind of busy."

I turned the file on its side and examined the doodle. Still nothing.

"No shit," he said.

"Yeah. No gigs for me."

"That's not why I'm calling."

I frowned at the phone and turned the file upside down. "I'm all ears."

"Someone wants to meet you," he said.

"Tell him to get in line," I mumbled. The doodle almost looked like something.

"I'm not joking."

"You never joke because you're too damn busy proving that you're a badass. Come on, black leather cloak? In mid-spring Atlanta? Besides I don't have time to meet anybody."

Jim's voice dropped low and he spoke each word very distinctly. "Think very carefully. Do you really want me to tell *the man* no?"

Something about the way he said "the man" stopped me. I sat still and thought very hard about what kind of "man" would inspire Jim to use that voice.

"What did I do to warrant the Beast Lord's attention?" I asked dryly.

"You're sitting in the diviner's office, aren't you?"

Touché.

The Beast Lord was the Pack King, the lord of the shapechangers, and he ruled his brethren with an iron fist. Few ever saw him and the mention of his title was enough to make the loudest shapechanger shut up. In other words, he was precisely the kind of fellow my father and Greg had warned me to avoid. I ground my teeth, thinking of a way to weasel out of it. I would have to go and see the People sooner or later to find out about the vampire. But so far nothing necessitated my walking into the Pack's lair.

"Your safety's guaranteed," Jim said. "I'll be there."

"That's not the reason," I murmured. There had to be a way to dodge this invitation. I glared at the stubborn doodle . . .

"Look," Jim said, making an obvious attempt to sound reasonable, "consider the . . ."

"Tell him I'll meet him tonight someplace private," I said. "I'll answer his questions if he answers mine."

"Agreed. Eleven o'clock, corner of Unicorn and Thirteenth."

He hung up. I tapped the desk with my fingers. I finally made sense of the doodle. The head of a howling wolf silhouetted against the semicircle of the moon. The sign of the Pack. Corwin belonged to the Pack.

There was the small matter of Maxine to attend to. I concentrated and whispered so quietly I couldn't hear myself. True communicators could focus enough to broadcast their thoughts without vocalization, but I still had to move my lips like a dufus.

"Maxine?"

"Yes, dear?" Maxine's voice said in my head.

"Were there any other calls for me?"

"No."

"Thank you."

"You're welcome."

I put the file back into its place and walked out of the office. Maxine was a telepath. A strong one. From now on, there would be no thinking done in the office.

I left quickly, almost breaking into a run on the stairs. The idea of someone digging in my head took some getting used to.

I went back to the apartment. I sat on the floor, leaned against the door, and took a deep breath. All my life I was taught to stay out of the way of the powerful. Don't draw attention to yourself. Don't show off. Guard your blood, because it will betray you. If you bleed, wipe it clean and burn the rag. Burn the bandages. If someone manages to obtain some of your blood, kill him and destroy the sample. At first it was a matter of survival. Later it became a matter of vengeance.

Meeting the Beast Lord meant plunging headfirst into the supernatural politics of Atlanta. He was one of the heavyweights. I could choose not to meet the Beast Lord. All I had to do was walk away. It would be so easy. A vision of me squatting over a human corpse, stuffing shreds of limp meat into my mouth flashed before my eyes.

The apartment was silent. It felt like Greg. It was suffused with his lifeforce, with everything that made him what he was. He was like my father, direct, unbending, doing his own thing and never worrying about how the world would look upon him.

I couldn't let it go. I would find whoever killed him and punish them, if not for Greg, then for me, otherwise I wouldn't be able to look myself in the eye.

WHEN LIFE BACKS YOU INTO A CORNER AND OFFERS you no escape, when your friends, your lover, and your family abandon you, when you're at the end of your rope, panicked, alone, and losing your mind, you know you'd give anything to make your problems go away. Then, desperate and eager, you will come to Unicorn Lane, seeking salvation in its magics and secrets. You'll do anything, pay any price. Unicorn Lane will take you in, shroud you in its power, fix your problems, and exact its price. And then you will learn what "anything" really means.

Every city has one of those neighborhoods—dangerous, sinister places—so treacherous that even the criminals who prey on other criminals shun them. Unicorn Lane was such a place. Thirty city blocks long and eight blocks deep, it cut through what used to be Midtown like a dagger. Half-crumbled skyscrapers stood there, mute witness to the past's technology, the husks of GLG

Grand, Promenade II, and One Atlantic Center, gnawed down to the bones by magic. Rubble choked the streets and sewage overflowed from the busted pipes in foul-smelling streams. Magic pooled there, lingering even in the strongest of tech waves, and hideous things that shun the light found refuge there, among the dark carcasses of gutted high rises. Lunatic mages, vicious, perverted loups who feared death at the hand of an unforgiving Pack, Satanists, and rogue necromancers all ran to the Unicorn, for if they could make it there and survive, no lawman on this earth would force them out. Unicorn Lane held on to its own.

Hell of a place for a rendezvous.

I drove up Fourteenth Street, parked Karmelion in a secluded alley, and walked the two remaining city blocks. Ahead a stone wall had crumbled, a pitiful attempt of some fool on the city council to contain Unicorn Lane. I climbed over the wreckage. A large block of concrete barred my way. It looked slick, almost slimy, and I leaped over it.

Here, even the moonlight snapped and growled like a rabid dog, and magic bit without warning.

Five minutes into the Unicorn a sign on the side of an abandoned house announced that I had reached my destination, corner of Thirteenth and Unicorn. In front of me, an old apartment complex stared at the street with empty windows. To the right, a tangled mess of concrete and steel framework marked a collapsed office building. The debris blocked the street, burying the pavement beneath the rubble. The street was open on the left, but shrouded in darkness. I stood very still, waiting, listening.

The moonlight spilled onto the ruins. Thick, inky darkness pooled in the alcoves and burrows and stretched forth, mingling with light, spawning half-shadows, and blurring the lines between real and illusory. The eerie landscape appeared false, as if the ruined buildings had vanished, leaving behind treacherous shadows of their former selves. Ahead in the depths of Unicorn Lane something howled, giving voice to a tortured soul. My heart skipped a beat.

Someone or something watched me from the darkness. I felt their stare press upon me like a physical burden. Moments dragged by, with minutes in tow. After a while I glanced at my watch. It had stopped.

Somewhere in the darkness the Beast Lord prowled. I didn't know what he looked like. I didn't know the species of his beast. Few people outside of the Pack claimed to have met him and nobody seemed willing to discuss the experience. The only thing certain about him was power. By the latest count, he commanded a force of three hundred and thirty-seven shapechangers in Atlanta alone. He wasn't in charge because he was the smartest or the most popular; he ruled because of those three hundred and thirty-seven he was unquestionably the strongest. He was in charge by the right of might; that is, he had yet to meet anyone who could kick his ass.

Among the shapechangers, wolves were the most numerous, then came the foxes, the jackals, the rats, and then the hyenas and the smaller felines: lynxes, bobcats, and cheetahs. There were the exotic forms too, the werebuffalos and wereserpents, but the buffalos formed their own herd in the Midwest and the serpents were solitary. All of the beast-forms were larger than their natural counterparts; an average shapechanger in a wolf form came close to two hundred and twenty pounds while the natural gray wolf weighed a hundred pounds less. From a biological point of view, the transformation of a hundred-and-seventy-pound human into a two-hundred-and-twenty-pound animal made no sense, but then when it came to shapeshifting, the fluctuating mass was the least of the anomalies. Magic could not be measured and explained in scientific terms, for magic grew through destroying the very natural principles that made science as people knew it possible.

Another howl ruptured the quiet, still too far away to be a threat. The Beast Lord, the leader, the alpha male, had to enforce his position as much by will as by physical force. He would have to answer any challenges to his rule, so it was unlikely that he turned into a wolf. A wolf would have little chance against a cat. Wolves hunted in a pack, bleeding their victim and running them into exhaustion, while cats were solitary killing machines, designed to murder swiftly and with deadly precision. No, the Beast Lord would have to be a cat, a jaguar or a leopard. Perhaps a tiger, although all known cases of weretigers occurred in Asia and could be counted without involving toes.

I had heard a rumor of the Kodiak of Atlanta, a legend of an enormous, battle-scarred bear roaming the streets in search of Pack criminals. The Pack, like any social organization, had its lawbreakers. The Kodiak was their Executioner. Perhaps his Majesty turned into a bear. Damn. I should have brought some honey.

My left leg was tiring. I shifted from foot to foot . . .

A low, warning growl froze me in midmove. It came from the dark gaping hole in the building across the street and rolled through the ruins, awakening ancient memories of a time when humans were pathetic, hairless creatures cowering by the weak flame of the first fire and scanning the night with frightened eyes, for it held monstrous hungry killers. My subconscious screamed in panic. I held it in check and cracked my neck, slowly, to one side then another.

A lean shadow flickered in the corner of my eye. On the left and above me a graceful jaguar stretched on the jutting block of concrete, an elegant statue encased in the liquid metal of moonlight.

Homo Panthera onca. The killer who takes its prey in a single bound.

Hello, Jim.

The jaguar looked at me with amber eyes. Feline lips stretched in a startlingly human smirk.

He could laugh if he wanted. He didn't know what was at stake.

Jim turned his head and began washing his paw.

My saber firmly in hand, I marched across the street and stepped through the opening. The darkness swallowed me whole.

The lingering musky scent of a cat hit me. So, not a bear after all.

Where was he? I scanned the building, peering into the gloom. Moonlight filtered through the gaps in the walls, creating a mirage of twilight and complete darkness. I knew he was watching me. Enjoying himself.

Diplomacy was never my strong suit and my patience had run dry. I crouched and called out, "Here, kitty, kitty, kitty."

Two golden eyes ignited at the opposite wall. A shape stirred within the darkness and rose, carrying the eyes up and up and up until they towered above me. A single enormous paw moved into the moonlight, disturbing the dust on the filthy floor. Wicked claws shot forth and withdrew. A massive shoulder followed, its gray fur marked by faint smoky stripes. The huge body shifted forward, coming at me, and I lost my balance and fell on my ass into the dirt. Dear God, this wasn't just a lion. This thing had to be at least five feet at the shoulder. And why was it striped?

The colossal cat circled me, half in the light, half in the shadow, the dark mane trembling as he moved. I scrambled to my feet and almost bumped into the gray muzzle. We looked at each other, the lion and I, our gazes level. Then I twisted around and began dusting off my jeans in a most undignified manner.

The lion vanished into a dark corner. A whisper of power pulsed through the room, tugging at my senses. If I did not know better, I would say that he had just changed.

"Kitty, kitty?" asked a level male voice.

I jumped. No shapechanger went from a beast into a human without a nap. Into a midform, yes, but beast-men had trouble talking.

"Yeah," I said. "You've caught me unprepared. Next time I'll bring cream and catnip toys."

"If there is a next time."

I turned and there he stood, wearing a loose T-shirt and sweatpants. A modest shapechanger, how refreshing. You wouldn't even know that he had changed, save for the glistening sheen of dampness on his skin.

He looked me over slowly, judging, taking my measure. I could blush demurely or I could do the same to him. I chose not to blush.

A couple of inches taller than me, the Beast Lord gave an impression of coiled power. Easy, balanced stance. Blond hair, cut too short to grab. At first glance he looked to be in his early to mid-twenties, but his build betrayed him. His shoulders strained his T-shirt. His back was broad and corded with muscle, showing the power and strength a man developed in his early thirties.

"What kind of a woman greets the Beast Lord with 'here, kitty, kitty'?" he asked.

"One of a kind." I murmured the obvious reply. Eventually I had to look him in the eye. Better sooner than later.

The Beast Lord had a strong square jaw. His nose was narrow with a misshapen bridge, as though it had been broken more than once and hadn't healed right. Considering the regenerative powers of the shapechangers, someone must've pounded his face with a sledgehammer.

Our stares met. Little golden sparks danced in his gray eyes. His gaze made me want to bow my head and look away.

He regarded me as if I was an interesting new snack. "I'm the Lord of the Free Beasts," he said.

"I figured." Perhaps he expected me to curtsy.

He leaned forward a little, puzzling over me as if I were an odd-looking insect. "Why would a knight-protector hire a no-name merc to investigate the death of his diviner?"

I gave him my best cryptic smile.

He grimaced. "What have you found out?" he asked.

"I'm not at liberty to tell you that." Not with the Pack suspect.

He leaned forward more, letting the moonlight fall on his face. His gaze was direct and difficult to hold. Our stares locked and I gritted my teeth. Five seconds into the conversation and he was already giving me the alpha-stare. If he started clicking his teeth, I'd have to make a run for it. Or introduce him to my sword.

"You will tell me what you know now," he said.

"Or?"

He said nothing, so I elaborated. "See, this kind of threat usually has an 'or' attached to it. Or an 'and.' 'Tell me and I'll allow you to live' or something like that."

His eyes ignited with gold. His gaze was unbearable now.

"I can make you beg to tell me everything you know," he said and his voice was a low growl. It sent icy fingers of terror down my spine.

I gripped Slayer's hilt until it hurt. The golden eyes were burning into my soul. "I don't know," I heard my own voice say, "you look kinda out of shape to me. How long has it been since you took care of your own dirty work?"

His right hand twitched. Muscles boiled under the taut skin and fur burst, sheathing the arm. Claws slid from thickened fingers. The hand snapped inhumanly fast. I weaved back and it fanned my face, leaving no scars. A strand of hair fell onto my left cheek, severed from my braid. The claws retracted.

"I think I still remember how," he said.

A spark of magic ran from my fingers into Slayer's hilt and burst into the blade, coating the smooth metal in a milky-white glow. Not that the glow actually did anything useful, but it looked bloody impressive. "Any time you want to dance," I said.

He smiled, slow and lazy. "Not laughing anymore, little girl?"

He was impressive, I'd give him that. I turned the blade, warming up my wrist. The saber drew a tight glowing ellipse in the air, flinging tiny drops of luminescence on the dirty floor. One of them fell close to the Beast Lord's foot and he moved away. "I wonder if all this changing has made you sluggish."

"Bring your pig-sticker and we'll find out."

We circled each other, our feet raising light clouds of dust from the dirty floor. I wanted to fight him, if only to see if I could hold my own.

His lips parted, releasing a snarl. I swung my blade, judging the distance between us.

If we fought, and if I survived, I'd never find out who killed Greg. The Pack would tear me to shreds. This was getting me nowhere. I had no choice but to lose face. I stopped and lowered my blade. The words didn't want to leave my mouth, but I forced them out anyway. "I'm sorry. I'd love to play but I'm not my own person at the moment."

He smiled.

I did my best to ignore the condescension I saw in his face. "My name is Kate Daniels. Greg Feldman was my legal guardian and the closest thing to a family I've had for many years. I want to find the scum who killed him. I can't afford to fight you and I won't show off my magic. I just want to know if the Pack had something to do with Greg's death. Once I find the killer, I would be more than happy to indulge you."

I offered him my hand. He halted, studying me, and then the fur melted away, absorbed through the follicles that produced it. The Beast Lord took my hand in his human palm and shook.

"Fair enough. Right now I'm not my own person either," he said. Being a Beast Lord, he probably never was.

The gold in his irises shrank to mere flecks. His control was unbelievable. The most adept of shapechangers could choose between three forms: human, animal, and beast-man. To change a part of your body into one form while keeping the rest of it in another, as he had, was incredible. Before this night, I would have said it couldn't be done.

The Beast Lord sat down on the dirty floor. I had no choice but to follow, feeling like an idiot for dusting my jeans off earlier.

"If I prove to you that the Pack had no interest in removing the diviner, will you share?"

"Yes."

He reached into his sweatshirt, produced a black leather folder zipped shut, and offered it to me. I held my hand out, but he retracted it before my fingers touched the supple leather. I wondered if he was quicker than me. It would be interesting to find out.

"Between us," he said.

"Understood."

I took the folder and unzipped it. Inside were photos. Shots of corpses, some human, some partially animal, mangled and bloody. The bright, awful crimson dominated the images, making it difficult to analyze them. I looked over the photographs anyway. Corpse after corpse after corpse, torn, disemboweled, drenched in their blood. It made me ill.

"Seven," I murmured, holding the pictures by their edges as if the blood on them would stain my fingers. "Yours?"

"Every one." He reached over to tap one of the shots. "This one. Zachary Stone. The alpha-rat. Tough, vicious sonovabitch."

I tried to see beyond the blood, focusing on the injuries. "Something chewed on him."

"Something chewed on five of them. And would have chewed on the other two as well if it wasn't scared away."

A little light went off in my head. "Greg was working on this."

"Yes. And keeping it quiet. The People want power. They lust after it the same way their vampires lust after blood. They see us as rivals and they'll attack any weakness. To admit that we can't take care of our own is a weakness. Nataraja would cream his jeans if he knew."

"You think they are responsible?"

"I don't know," he said, his face grim. "But I'm going to find out."

It made sense. The Order had little love for the Pack, which was too organized and dangerous for their liking, but faced with a choice between the People and the shapeshifters, the Order would side with the Pack. Greg could have been tailing a vampire when something killed him, preventing him from revealing what he saw or was about to see. The vampire could have been caught in a struggle. Or the vamp could have been following Greg when something killed him because he was getting too close. Or . . .

"I would like to speak to Corwin," I said.

His face showed no reaction. "Is he a suspect?"

There was no point in lying. "Yes."

"Done," he said. "You'll have your talk. On our premises."

"That's fine."

"I did my part," he said.

I took the m-scan I stole from the morgue and spread it in the dirt.

"What am I looking for?" he asked.

"These." I pointed to the yellow lines.

"Looks like a scanner malfunction."

"I don't think so."

He frowned. "What would register yellow?"

"I don't know. But I know an expert who might."

"You have something more to go on, besides that?"

There was the hair, and I considered not telling him about it. Forewarned is forearmed. And he didn't give me anything that I couldn't have gotten from the knight-protector. Theoretically. Still, the Beast Lord saved me a lot of work and I doubted the texture of Corwin's hair could be altered so severely that DNA mapping would not match it to the sample.

The Beast Lord looked at the photographs, shifting through them with marked slowness. He looked almost human. I realized that I was biased. Biased against Nataraja and his college of death-devotees, with their clinical indifference to tragedy and murder. For them, a dispatched vampire and a comatose journeyman equaled a loss of an investment, costly and inconvenient, but ultimately not emotionally painful. The man in front of me, on the other hand, had lost friends. They were people he knew well and they had placed themselves in his charge. The Pack leader's ultimate duty was to protect his Pack—and he had failed them. As he looked at the snapshots of their deaths, his face reflected determination and anger, cold crystallized anger, born of guilt and grief. There was an old word for that kind of anger. Wrath.

This I understood. I felt it every time I thought of Greg. I'd have to be very careful from now on, because I was no longer neutral. If the Beast Lord did kill Greg, I would have to work harder to convince myself of his guilt.

To think that I had found a kindred spirit in the Beast Lord. How touching. Greg's death was making me lose my mind. Perhaps I could hack off the murderer's head while the Beast Lord held him down.

"Several hairs were found at the scene," I said. "The medical examiner's office doesn't know what to make of them. They contain fragments of both human and feline genetic sequences. It's not any kind of shapechanger that the ME's analysts have seen. It's weird as hell, and no, I don't have the exact printout of the base pairs."

"Does Nataraja know?"

"I think he does," I said. "One of his journeymen gave me Corwin's name. He didn't say they thought he did it, but it's obvious they do."

A small muscle twitched in the Beast Lord's cheek, as if his face wanted to twist into a feral snarl. "Figures."

"Are you satisfied?" I asked.

He nodded. "For now. I'll call on you."

"I won't come here again," I said. "Unicorn Lane makes my skin crawl."

His eyes shone again. "Really? I find it relaxing. A scenic location. Moonlight."

"I never was much for scenic locations. Next time I'd like an official invitation."

He put away the snapshots.

"Can I keep those?" I asked.

He shook his head. "No. It's enough that they exist."

I turned to leave and paused before the gap in the ruined wall. "One last thing, Your Majesty. I'd like a name I can put into my report, something shorter than typing out 'The Leader of the Southern Shapechanger Faction.' What should I call you?"

"Lord."

I rolled my eyes.

He shrugged. "It's short."

This was turning out to be a difficult night, and it showed no signs of being over. I climbed out, over the heap of rubble. Jim was gone.

Something touched my shoulder. I whirled and saw the Lord of Beasts looking at me from the gap ten feet away.

"Curran," he said, as if granting me a boon. "You can call me Curran."

He melted into the darkness. I waited for a moment to make sure he was gone. Nobody jumped me from the shadows.

Beyond the Unicorn, I could see the blue feylanterns of the city. Time to take the m-scan to my expert. He rarely minded late-night visits.

CHAMPION HEIGHTS WAS AN EASY PLACE TO FIND. IT was about the only high-rise still standing. Once it was called Lenox Pointe, but it had undergone so many renovations and changed hands so many times that its old name was all but forgotten. Nestled among the artfully pruned evergreens, the seventeen-story building of red brick and concrete loomed above the shops and bars of Buckhead like a mystic tower. Pale haze clung to its walls and balconies, blurring the crisp man-made edges, as a web of wards worked tirelessly to convince the very magic which fed it that the high-rise was nothing but a large rock. A distortion, the side effect of the spells' labor, spread unevenly across the structure, and sections of the high-rise looked like portions of a steep granite cliff.

The enchantment must have cost a small fortune, and although it had kept the high-rise standing so far, there was no guarantee it would continue to do so. I thought it would. The entire setup had that bizarre illogic peculiar to complex magic. Understanding it required a mind with a specific twist—just like quantum physics. Whatever the future held for Champion Heights, the owners had already recouped their investment several times over. Many couples would be happy to retire on what they charged for a year's rent.

I parked Karmelion in a lot among the Cadillacs, distinguished Lincolns, and bizarre mechanisms designed to transport their drivers during the magic waves. There was no convenient way to carry an m-scan, so I folded it and slid it between the pages of my Almanac. The night wind came, bringing smells from far away: a touch of wood smoke, the aroma of seared meat. I crossed the lot and made my way up the concrete stairs, flanked by some picturesque shrubbery, to the revolving glass doors. Enchanted glass lost a little of its transparency, but I had no trouble making out the heavy metal grate barring the lobby and the small cage with the guard who leveled a shock crossbow at me.

I reached to my left and pressed the button of the intercom. It hissed.

"Fifteenth floor, one fifty-eight, please."

His voice came back, distorted by the static. "Code, please."

"Forth he fared at the fated moment, sturdy Scyld to the shelter of God." Without the code he would keep me outside while he queried one fifty-eight, and even then I wouldn't get in without being frisked and surrendering Slayer. Parting with my saber was not an option.

The metal grate slid aside. "Proceed."

A revolving door admitted me to the lobby, flooded with the light of feylanterns. My steps, loud on the tiled floor of polished red granite, sent little echoes scurrying into the corners. I approached the elevator. The magic was still up, but I'd visited Champion Heights in the middle of a magic fluctuation before. Their elevator worked no matter the circumstances.

A luxurious green carpet lined the fifteenth floor. The pile was thicker than some mattresses I've seen. Sinking into it, I made my way to the metal door marked 158, pressed the button of the bell, and knocked in case the magic had short-circuited it. Nobody home.

The metal box of an electronic key card reader, about six by three inches, secured the door. Like all things in Champion Heights, the lock was not what it seemed, magic masquerading as tech. Slayer whispered as it left its sheath, and I slid its blade into the narrow slit of the key card reader. Concentrating on the saber, I put my hand onto the blade. A jolt of magic pulsed from my fingers.

Open!

The lock clicked and the heavy door gave under the pressure of my palm. Retrieving Slayer, I stepped inside and locked the door behind me.

Reaching for the feylantern, I turned the round handle and a wide tongue of blue flame flared into existence, illuminating the apartment. I would never make a living as an interior decorator. My home was a comfortable chaos, my furniture mismatched but highly functional. The esthetic properties of any given piece were secondary to its convenience, and luxury for me meant having a small table by my couch to support a reading lamp and a mug of coffee.

Not so here. The moment I stepped into this apartment, it was clear that its owner had crafted his environment with a deliberate goal in mind. I was looking at years of selective purchases made by a person for whom the word "sale" held no meaning. The furnishings, the carpet, the spare decorations—all blended to present a distinctive whole, and looking at it produced the same feeling as viewing the reconstruction of an African savannah in a zoo. It was a harmonious but alien habitat of glass, steel, and white plush, all ellipses and curves. Three doors led from the room, one to the bedroom, another to a bathroom with a double sink and a walk-in shower, and the third to the lab.

The spell-haze did not affect the view from the inside and huge windows offered a vision of midnight Atlanta under the endless black sky. The weak light of the single feylantern caressed the window glass, rendering it invisible, and permeated the darkness outside as if the apartment itself was but a piece of midnight sky, defined by glass and stone but not separated from the world outside. If I stood very close to the window, I could imagine that I was flying high above the city . . .

As I watched, the tech hit. Thousands of tiny lights sparked into existence, like jewels among the folds of black velvet, and the street lamps flooded the avenue below me in man-made sunshine. The feylantern flickered and died, and bright electric lights came on inside the apartment, murdering the illusion and separating me from the infinite blackness. The glass became impenetrable, and I stood confined by it as if locked in the middle of a transparent cage. Suddenly I felt vulnerable so I turned off the lights, all but a single reading lamp of steel and opaque glass.

I washed my face and arms up to my elbow, dried them with a fluffy white towel I found hanging on a hook near the sink, and took up residence on the ultramodern couch. Curran's question nagged me: why would the knight-protector give Greg's investigation to a no-name merc? On the surface, it made no sense. I finally managed to look past my own ego. One of the Order's own was dead, a well-known man of substantial power. They wouldn't handle it themselves. They would bring in a crusader.

The crusaders served as the Order's equivalent of a lancet. Got a nasty boil ready to rupture—throw a crusader at it. Loners, highly skilled and deadly, they were great at what they did, and after they did it, they returned to where they came from. Ted expected me to "investigate the crime," meaning he expected me to make lots of noise and draw attention to myself, while the crusader quietly worked under my smoke screen. It chaffed at me for about two seconds, but in the end both parties got what they wanted: Ted got his lightning rod and I got to search for Greg's killer. Everybody won.

I flipped open the Almanac and pulled the m-scan and the folded cutout of the article Bono had given me from between the book's pages. Glancing at the m-scan one last time, I slid it onto the glass table, unfolded the article, and began to read. The owner of the apartment would arrive shortly. He rarely stayed out past two in the morning—he thought 3:00 a.m. to be an unlucky hour.

IT WAS CLOSE TO TWO O'CLOCK WHEN A SINGLE CAB made its way up the avenue below me. I raised binoculars to my eyes.

The door of the cab opened and a blonde stepped onto the pavement. She was tall and very slender. The short black dress clung to her narrow hips and long waist, flaring to artfully enclose breasts that looked too large for her body. Her hair, so pale it shimmered white, fell to her shoulders without a trace of a curl.

Her face was perfectly formed, with high prominent cheekbones, aquiline nose, huge eyes, and a full mouth. As she strode to the high-rise, her face wore an expression that on someone less attractive would be called a sneer. Elegant, graceful, and arrogant in her beauty, she was like a young Arabian horse, haughty and cruel and an irresistible challenge to any male.

A lone passerby stopped, struck by the sight of her. I thought he whistled but could not tell for sure. The blonde ignored his presence without even trying; for her, he simply did not exist. I put away the binoculars and returned to my Almanac.

Five minutes later the lock clicked and the blonde walked through the door. She saw me and stopped. The sneer vanished. "Oh, good. I have something for you."

Not again.

She went to the kitchen, retrieved several protein cans from a cabinet, and put them onto the bar. A bag of dried apricots joined the cans, together with a bag of sugar, a block of chocolate, and an oversized blender. She took a carton of eggs from the fridge and cracked three into the blender. Two handfuls of apricots followed, with several cups of sugar, the chocolate, and the contents of at least six cans. "Ice water," the blonde murmured, nodding to the drink I had gotten myself. "You could've gotten something from the bar."

"I wanted water," I said.

The blonde smiled, a strange expression on her face, and turned on the blender. The blades spun, converting the contents into a thick uniform paste. She unplugged the blender, detached the top with a practiced twist, and drank straight from it.

"What is it, about two-thirds of a gallon?" I asked.

She stopped drinking for a moment. "Closer to three-quarters, actually."

She finished and unceremoniously pulled her dress over her head. I looked at my book again.

"Are you uncomfortable?" the blonde laughed, stripping her stockings.

"No, just giving you a bit of privacy." And hoping to miss the glorious moment when my stomach would clench and squirt its burning contents into my throat.

"You could just admit that I make you ill."

"There is that."

"How do you like her?" the blonde asked.

I glanced up and saw her standing nude on the floor. "Not bad for an ice queen. The breasts are too large."

The blonde grimaced. "Yes, I know."

"Why a woman?" I wondered.

"Because I deal in information, Kate, and men tend to blab their secrets to beautiful women." She smiled. "As you well know."

"I usually have to threaten men with bodily harm before they tell me secrets."

"Then I feel sorry for those men. They obviously have poor taste. Do you know who makes the converters that go into our feylamps?"

"I have no idea."

"There are four companies, actually. By the end of the week the city council will decide which one of them gets a municipal contract for the next three years. Right now there are three people in this city who know how they will vote."

"Let me guess, you're one of them?"

The blonde didn't answer, but her smile widened just a little, permitting a brief glimpse of white teeth. Even a financial moron like me knew the price of that kind of information had to be astronomic.

Her muscles moved, stretching, twisting, as if a tangle of worms suddenly came to life under her skin. My stomach lurched. I clenched my teeth and tried to keep my dinner where it belonged. The blonde's pelvis shifted, her shoulders grew broad, her legs thickened, while her breasts dissolved, forming a massive male chest. Ropes of muscles coiled, shaping powerful legs and huge arms. The bones of her face crawled, the nose thickening, the jaw becoming strong and square. The eye color darkened to piercing intense blue. The hair dissolved and grew again, this time turning dark brown. I blinked and a man stood before me. Muscular with the crisp exactness of a professional body builder, he was towering and quite well endowed. Blue eyes glared at me from the flat face of a born fighter—no sharp edges, no jutting bone to shatter under a punch. A bit of armor and he would earn the loyalty of any barbarian horde.

"What do you think?" he asked, his voice deep and commanding.

I eyed him. "Impressive, but too much."

He leaned toward me, the blue eyes smoky with a promise I was sure he could fulfill. I tried not to think of the bedroom.

"Too much?"

"Yes. I like the menace. It's very masculine, but he looks like he would screw everything in sight and call me 'wench.'"

The barbarian king before me rubbed the bridge of his nose. "What exactly leads you to that conclusion?"

"I'm not sure. Something in the eyes, I think."

"So it's a no?"

"It's a no."

"I'll have to work on him."

The barbarian deflated, his awesome musculature slimming into a leaner build. The hair vanished, leaving the head bald, and the face grew longer, with intelligent dark eyes and a large nose. The man I knew as Saiman strode to the bar and drew a glass of water from the sink faucet.

"Business?" he said, glancing at the m-scan.

"Yes."

He nodded, drained his glass, and refilled it.

"I can't feel a trace of magic," I said. "Yet you seem to have no problem metamorphosing. Why is that?"

He arched an eyebrow at me—a gesture so much like my own

that I could've sworn he copied it from me. It was likely. Saiman often mimicked the mannerisms of his clients. He did it consciously, knowing it unnerved them.

"The key word is 'seem.' Metamorphosis now requires concentration, while during the magic tide it flows naturally. But to answer the essence of your question, I believe my body stores magic. Like a battery. Perhaps it even produces its own."

He downed the second glass and approached the couch. "How long have I kept you waiting?"

"Not too long."

For a moment I thought he would make a comment about the view, and then I wouldn't be able to help myself and have to ask him to shield his own "view" with some clothes. Fortunately he withdrew to the bedroom.

Saiman was driven by the desire to create his own Uberman, a super-male that would be irresistible to women. The sexual aspect of his quest interested him much less than the scientific motivation to craft an image of a perfect human being. He engaged in this pursuit of an ultimate shape for purposes unknown, for I truly had no idea what he would do with his Uberman if he ever succeeded. He approached the challenge with the same methodical logic he applied to everything, attempting to gather feedback from a wide pool of subjects, most of whom had no idea what he truly looked like.

Long ago I argued that his Uberman simply could not exist. Even if he did succeed in creating an image of the essential male, it would fail his expectations. Too much depended on the interaction between two human beings, and ultimately it was that interaction that led to intimacy. He debated me with great passion and I had learned not to argue anymore.

We met during a merc gig a year ago, bodyguard detail. All mercs did one sooner or later, and it was just my luck I drew

Saiman. He was injured at the time, confined to his bed by a post-operative complication from a stomach surgery. His body kept changing while it fought the infection, and he proved very difficult to guard. I managed to kill two of the assassins sent to dispatch him. He killed the third with a pencil through the eye. I thought I had botched the job but he had seemed grateful ever since. I didn't complain. His services didn't come cheap.

Saiman returned wearing loose clothes of dark blue that were cut like common sweats but looked too expensive to be soiled by that moniker. He looked at the Almanac still opened in my lap, the article Bono had given me a few days back lying on the page.

"Cut from the *Volshebstva e Kolduni.* What a pretentious title. As if writing 'Spells and Warlocks' in Russian would somehow lend them more credibility. I didn't know you read that trash."

"I don't. The article was given to me by an acquaintance."

"The problem with those rags is that the people who publish them don't realize that magic is fluid. They print erroneous information."

It was an old argument and a valid one. People affected magic just as magic affected them. If enough people believed something to be true, sometimes the magic obliged and *made* it true.

Saiman scanned the article. "It's incomplete and full of garbage as always. They classify the upir as a corpse-eating undead. Look, they correctly state the upir has an enormous sexual appetite, but are unaware of the contradiction: an undead has no urge to mate, therefore an upir cannot be undead. They also mention that it will try to mate with anything mammal it can secure long enough to achieve a climax but fail to note that the product of such union usually survives to serve the upir." He dropped the article in disgust. "If you ever need to know more about this creature, let me know."

"I will."

"So what brings you to my humble abode?"

"I need an m-scan evaluated."

He arched his eyebrow again. I could learn to hate him. "Very well. I'll charge you by the hour. Our usual discount starting . . ." He glanced at his watch. "Now. Do you want a complete workup?" he asked.

"No, just the basics. I can't afford the fancy stuff."

"Cheap client?"

"I'm working pro bono."

He grimaced. "Kate, that's a horrible habit."

"I know."

He took the chart, holding it gently with his long fingers. "What interests you?"

"A series of small yellow lines toward the bottom."

"Ah."

"What would register yellow? And how much is the answer going to cost me?"

"A great question. Let me run a test to make sure this isn't a mechanical failure."

I followed him to the lab. A forest of equipment that would make the personnel of an average college lab giddy with joy rested on black surfaces of flame-resistant tables and counters. Saiman donned a green waterproof apron and a pair of slick opaque gloves, reached under the table, and produced a ceramic tray. With a practiced, economic movement, he took the tray to a glass cube in the corner.

"What are you doing?" I asked.

"I'm going to scan the m-scan to pick up any residual traces of magic. Full enclosure. I don't want any contamination."

"I can't afford it."

"It's free. Your altruism infected me. You still have to pay for my time, of course."

He touched a lever and the cube rose upward on a metal chain. Saiman slid the tray onto the ceramic platform and lowered the cube, so the glass enclosed the tray. His fingers danced across the keyboard and an explosion of green color flooded the cubicle. It died, flashed again, died, and a printer chattered on a different table, belching a piece of paper.

He ripped it free and handed it to me. It was blank—a control to make sure no magic traces contaminated the tray.

Saiman attached the m-scan to the tray, slid it into the cube, and repeated his elaborate high-tech dance. This time the printer produced an exact copy of my m-scan.

Saiman pondered it for a moment and leaned against the table, m-scan in hand. "The problem is, the m-scanner is imperfect."

My heart sank. "So, it's a malfunction?"

"In a manner of speaking. As of now, the scanner is an imperfect instrument. It registers humans in various shades of light blue to silver, but it frequently fails to document the subtle tint of their magic. Almost anything except the most radical variations, such as purple for a vampire or green for a shapechanger, escapes it. A clairvoyant and a diviner of roughly equal power would register in the same color, even though their magic inclinations differ. And," Saiman allowed himself a thin-lipped smile. "It registers all *fera* magic as white."

"Fera as in feral? Animal magic?"

"Each animal species exudes its own specific magic. The common m-reader documents it as white so we don't even see it. Recently some bright minds in Kyoto examined a wide variety of animals using a hypersensitive scanner. They conclusively proved that each species of animal produces its own color. Faint, pastel, but distinct, and always a derivative of yellow."

"So the yellow lines mean animals?"

"On a superb scanner, yes. But on our piece of junk the animals would most likely register white. The only way we would notice them is through mixing with some other magical influence."

"You lost me."

"Look at your lines. They have a light peach tint. It's very faint but that peach is the only reason we can see the lines in the first place. It means that you are facing something that is mostly animal but has been tainted with something else."

My head swam. "Okay. Let me reiterate this. All animal magic registers as white but is truly pale yellow. A very weak yellow that is easily dominated by all other colors. There is no way to see that pale yellow, except when it's mixed with some other color. The yellow of the wolf mixing with the blue of a human makes the hunter green of a lycanthrope. By this reasoning, the wolf-were, an animal shapeshifting into human, would register as swampy green. Am I right so far?"

He nodded.

"The fact that I can see the yellow lines means that the scanner showed the presence of something with strong animal magic and a touch of something else. Since the lines are peach, then the likely suspect would be . . . orange."

I bit off the last word. Orange came from red, and red was the color of necromantic magic.

Saiman confirmed my deduction. "It's an animal that has some connection with necromantic magic. I don't know of what kind. It certainly isn't an animal zombie. That registers as a dark red. Have fun."

I groaned.

"Time is money," he said, "so I suggest you save your ruminations for later. Do you have anything else for me?"

"No."

He looked at his watch. "Thirty seven minutes."

I wrote a check for nine hundred and sixty-two dollars, which left exactly four hundred dollars and nine cents in my checking account. I had five hundred in savings to use in case of emergency. If more money didn't come my way soon, I'd have to consider a change of venue.

I handed him the check. He didn't bother looking at it.

"Let me know how it turns out," he said with his customary smile.

"You'll be the first to hear."

"And Kate? If you change your mind about my latest prototype, the offer still stands."

The piercing blue eyes and enormous muscles flashed before my mind's eye. That way lay dragons. "Thanks, but it isn't likely."

As I strode out of the apartment, I decided that I didn't like the tint of smile playing on Saiman's lips.

CHAPTER 4

I AWOKE IN GREG'S APARTMENT CLOSE TO SEVEN AND reached for the phone. Dialing Jim's number resulted in three rings, a click, and a beep of the answering machine without any forewarning message. I left a laconic "call me" and hung up. He would be none too pleased. The morning after a night of hunting was the time for serene contemplation, as sacred to the shapeshifters as meditation to a Shaolin monk. Caught between Man and Beast, the shapechangers sought complete control over each, and so they met the sunrise looking inward. Their moment of self-reflection completed, they succumbed to peaceful sleep. I had little doubt that Jim had hunted last night in the Unicorn. He was likely to be asleep already, and the machine would beep announcing the message until it drove him crazy. I smiled at the thought.

I stretched, working the kinks out of my shoulders and back. I kicked at the shadow on the wall, putting all I had into it but never touching my imaginary opponent. I cycled through some basic kicks, front snap, roundhouse, thrust, finishing with more elaborate forms. After ten minutes I broke a sweat and pushed on for another twenty, working mostly on strength in my arms, shoulders, and chest. Greg did not own weights so I used a heavy lead-filled mace instead of a dumbbell. It was poorly balanced but it was better than nothing.

I had not lifted for a few days and I felt weaker than usual. Still, the controlled, determined exertion felt good and my mood improved gradually, so by the time the shower started calling to me, I was almost upbeat.

The phone rang just as my hand touched the bathroom door. I did a 180, expecting Jim on the line.

"Jim?"

"Hello," said a male voice. It was a pleasant voice, well modulated and clear. I'd heard it before, but it took me a minute to remember where.

"Dr. . . . Crane?"

"Crest."

Yes, the toothpaste-named charity worker. How the hell did he get my number? "Can I help you?"

"I was hoping you would have lunch with me."

Persistent bugger. "How did you get my number?"

"I called to the Order and lied to them. I said that I had information concerning the dead vampire and gave them my credentials. They gave me this number."

"I see."

"So will you join me?"

"I'm very busy."

"But you have to eat once in a while. I would really like to see you again, someplace less formal. Give me a chance, and if the lunch doesn't work out, I'll vanish from your horizon."

I thought about it and realized that I wanted to say yes. It was a completely ludicrous thing to do. I was sitting on top of a bomb and both the Pack and the People stood ready to light the fuse, and here I was, considering a date. How long had it been since I'd been on a real date? Two years?

"It's a deal," I said. "I'll meet you between twelve and twelve thirty at Las Colimas. Do you know where it is?"

He knew.

"And Dr. Crest?"

"Just Crest, please."

"Crest, please don't call the Order again."

I expected him to be taken aback, but he said cheerfully "Yes, ma'am!" and hung up.

Stepping into the shower, I tried to figure out why I had agreed to meet him. There had to be a reason, something besides feeling lonely and tired, and wanting normal human contact, *male* human contact, the kind of male that didn't warp into a monster or shift muscles around its frame with the ease of changing clothes. Perhaps, I would use this opportunity to pump him for information about the morgue's treatment of the dead vamp. Yeah, that was it.

Halfway through the shower the phone rang. I turned off the water and went to pick it up, dripping wet soap lather onto the linoleum.

"Yes?"

"This is Maxine, dear."

"Hello, Maxine."

"The protector wishes to see you in his office today at eight thirty."

"Thank you."

"No problem, dear."

I hung up and went back into the shower. The hot water hit me with a satisfying rush, soothing my muscles.

The phone rang.

I growled and stomped back to the phone, without bothering to shut off the water.

"What?"

"You've got some fucking nerve calling me in the morning," Jim growled.

"Forgive me for disturbing your beauty sleep!" I snarled.

"What the hell did you call me for?"

"I want you to claw your eyes open and give me a list of Pack murders: locations, times, and so on."

"You know that's classified information. Who the fuck do you think you are?"

"I'm the only person that gives a shit. Look out the window. You see a line of people waiting to help your furry asses?"

I slammed the phone and returned to the shower. The absence of steam should have alerted me, but I foolishly stepped right into the ice-cold cascade. While I was talking, the shower had run out of hot water. Choking the shower pipe would not bring the hot water back, as satisfying as it might feel, so I turned the shower off and toweled dry. It was going to be one of those days.

I SAT IN ONE OF THE VISITOR'S CHAIRS DEEP IN THE bowels of the knight-protector's office. This time Ted was not talking on the phone. Instead he regarded me from behind his desk like a medieval knight watching the besieging Saracens from the ramparts of his stronghold.

Moments stretched into minutes.

Finally he said, "I pulled your file from the Academy."

Oh, shit.

"You had an e-rating," he said.

E for electrum. Not that big of a deal, really.

"Do you know how many squires with e-ratings came to the Academy in its thirty eight years?" he asked.

I knew. Greg told me so many times that the number made holes in my ear membranes, but provoking the protector would do me no good, so I kept my peace.

"Eight," he said, letting the words sink in. "Including you."

I tried to look solemn.

Ted moved his pen two inches to the left, gave it a careful look, and leveled his gaze back at me. "Why did you leave?"

"I had a problem with authority."

"A bad case of honor student ego?"

"It went beyond that. I realized that the Order was the wrong place for me and I withdrew before I had a chance to do something really stupid."

In my mind Greg's voice said with a touch of reproach, *And so you became a mercenary, a sword for hire, without a purpose or cause.*

Ted said, "You're working for the Order now."

"Yes."

"How does it feel?"

"Well, Doctor, it feels rather sore and tingly."

He waved my quip aside. "I'm not fucking around. How does it feel?"

"Having a base in the city is nice. The MA sticker opens doors. There's a lot of responsibility."

"It bothers you?"

"Yes. When I'm on my own, I screw up and my paycheck goes down the drain, so I eat what I grow until the next thing comes along. Now I screw up and a lot of people might die."

He nodded. "Feel choked by authority?"

"No. You gave me a long leash. But I know it's there."

"Just as long as you remember."

"That's not something I would forget."

"I've got a complaint from Nataraja," he said.

I relaxed. The tide was changing. "Oh?"

"He claims that you're avoiding discussing the case with them. He had a lot to say."

"He frequently has a lot to say." I shrugged.

"You know why he's making noise?"

"Yes. Both the People and the Pack are suspects. He wants to put on a show of cooperation."

Ted nodded, approving of my assessment.

"I had no cause to go to the Casino," I said.

"You've got one now."

"Yes."

"Good. Then after we're done, go and shut him up."

I nodded.

"Tell me what you've got so far."

I unloaded. I told him about the dead vampire and the hidden brand; I told him about the meeting with the Beast Lord who wanted to be called Curran, and I told him about the yellow lines on the m-scan and Anna's dream.

He sat through it all, nodding with no expression on his stone face. When I was done, he said, "Good."

I realized that the audience was over and left the office. This time the Saracens escaped without burning oil scalding their backs.

I proceeded into Greg's office. Something had been bothering me since last night, tugging at my mind, and this morning, my wits sharpened by fury over the icy shower, I finally figured out what it was: the names of the women in Greg's file. I had forgotten about the four names, just let them slip from my memory, which was both irresponsible and stupid. I should have known better than that.

Finding the file and extracting the page listing the names took about five seconds. Sandra Molot, Angelina Gomez, Jennifer Ying, Alisa Konova. I checked Greg's files looking for the names, but none of the women had individual folders. Besides coming from different ethnic groups, they had nothing in common. I rummaged around for a phone book, found it in the lowest drawer, and looked through it. Gomez and Ying were common surnames, and Molot was not infrequent, so I looked for Konova. I found two men with the surname Konov, Anatoli and Denis. Russians denoted female gender by adding a vowel to the end of their surname, so a female form of Konov would be Konova. Given that, I thought the names were worth a try.

I dialed the first one and was informed by an indifferent female voice that the number had been disconnected. I tried the second number. The phone rang and an older female voice said with a slight accent, "Yes?"

"Hello, can I speak with Alisa, please?"

There was a long pause.

"Ma'am?"

"Alisa's missing," the woman said quietly. "We don't know where she is."

She hung up the phone before I had a chance to ask anything else. Since Molot was my second best bet, I looked for it and found six Molots. I hit pay dirt on the fourth one—a young male told me that Sandra was his sister and reluctantly informed me that she was also missing since the fourteenth of last month, but refused to say anything else, adding "the cops are still looking for her." I thanked him and hung up.

I called nineteen people with the last name Ying and twenty-seven with the surname Gomez. I could not find Jennifer Ying, but there were two Angelinas among the Gomezes. The first one was two years old. The second was twenty and missing.

It was a safe bet that Jennifer Ying had suffered the same fate as the other three women. I considered a visit to the precinct, but the rational part of my brain informed me that not only would they throw me out without any information, I'd also call enough attention to myself to make my job even more difficult. Cops had respect for full-fledged knights, but they did not cooperate with them unless the circumstances left them no choice. I was not even a knight.

It was possible that all four ladies grew claws and fur and called Curran "Lord," in which case it would be logical to suppose that they were missing, because they were among the seven dead shapechangers. I called Jim to verify, but either he was not home or he decided not to take my calls. I didn't leave a message.

With nothing left to do, I put away the file. It was nearly lunchtime and I had a plastic surgeon to meet.

THE DECORATOR OF LAS COLIMAS MUST HAVE BEEN A great admirer of both early Aztec and late Taco Bell architectural styles. The restaurant was a gaudy mess of bright booths, garish piñatas, and fake greenery. A resin skull rack modeled after the actual racks, which the ancient Aztecs filled with countless skulls of human victims, crowned the roof of the long buffet table. Small terra-cotta replicas of arcane relics sat on the windowsills among the plastic fruit spilling from wicker cornucopias.

The setting did not matter. The moment I walked in, the delicious smell enveloped me, and I hurried past the five-foot-high terra-cotta atrocity meant to personify the famous Xochopilli, the Prince of Flowers, which separated the entrance from the cash register. A redheaded waitress thrust herself in my way.

"Excuse me," she said with a smile that showed off her entire set of teeth. "Are you Kate?"

"Yes."

"Your party is waiting. This way, please."

As she led me past the buffet table, I heard a male voice asking the waitress, "Do you serve gravy with that?"

Only in the South.

The waitress delivered me to a corner booth, where Crest sat, immersed in the menu.

"I found her, Doctor!" she announced. The patrons at the neighboring tables glanced at me. If the restaurant was not so crowded, I would have strangled her on the spot.

Crest glanced from the menu and shot her a smile. "You remembered," he said, his voice filled with surprise. "Thank you, Grace."

She giggled. "Let me know if you need anything!"

She swept away, putting an extra kink into her walk. I would not have thought that a woman with an ass that bony could make it wiggle so much, but she proved me wrong.

I landed.

"A storm walking in," he said.

"Five minutes here and the waitresses already bat their eyelashes at you," I said. "It must be a talent."

He unrolled his napkin, took a round-tipped serrated knife from it, and mimicked being stabbed in the heart. "Actually, it's not a talent," he explained, waving the knife around. The knife's blade looked sharp. "Most people treat waitresses like dogs. They bring you food and wait on you, therefore they must be a lower breed of human being and don't mind being harassed."

I took the knife away from him before he hurt himself and put it on the table.

The redheaded Grace returned, dazzled us with another smile, and asked if we were ready to order. I ordered without looking at the menu. Crest asked for churassco and chimichurri in unaccented Spanish. Grace gave him a blank look.

"I think he would like the filet mignon in garlic and parsley sauce," I said. "The Chef's special."

Her face brightened. "Anything to drink with that?"

We both ordered ice water and she departed, wiggling furiously.

Crest grimaced.

"A sudden change of attitude?" I asked.

"I detest incompetence. She works in a restaurant that serves Latino cuisine. She should at least know how the names are pronounced. But then she probably does the best she can." He looked around. "I must say, this isn't a place to promote quiet conversations."

"You have a problem with my taste?"

"Yes, I do," he said.

I shrugged.

"You are quite . . . hostile." He did not say it in a confrontational way. Instead, his voice held quiet amusement.

"Was I supposed to pick a quiet place, tastefully decorated and private, that would promote intimate conversation?"

"Well, I thought you might."

"Why? You blackmailed me into lunch, so I thought I might at least enjoy the food."

He tried a different line of attack. "I've never come across anyone like you."

"Good thing, too. People like me don't like it when you try walking over them. They might break your legs."

"Could you actually do it?" He was grinning. Was he flirting with me?

"Do what?"

"Break my legs."

"Yes, under the right circumstances."

"I have a brown belt in karate," he said. I decided that he

found my tough woman persona amusing. "I might put up a fight."

This was actually fun. I gave him a full blast of my psychotic smile and said, "Brown belt? That's impressive. But you have to remember, I break legs for a living while you . . ."

"Fix noses?" he put in.

"No, I was going to say stitch up corpses, but you're right, 'fix noses' would've made a much better retort."

We grinned at each other across the table.

Grace arrived right on cue, holding two platters. She set them in front of us and was called away before she could blind Crest with another toothy smile.

"The food's wonderful," he said after the first two bites.

And cheap, too. I raised my eyebrow at him, meaning I told you so.

"I'll stop trying to impress you if you promise not to break my legs," he suggested.

"Alright, where did you learn to speak Spanish?"

"From my father," he said. "He spoke six languages fluently and understood who knows how many. He was an anthropologist of the old kind. We spent two years at Temple Mayor in Mexico."

I arched an eyebrow, took a bottle of hot sauce shaped like a stylized figurine, and put it in front of him.

"Tlaloc," he said. "God of rain."

I smiled at him. "So tell me about the temple."

"It was hot and dusty." He told me about his father, who tried to understand people long gone, about climbing the countless steps to the top of the temple, where twin shrines stared at the world, about falling asleep under the bottomless sky by the carved temple walls and dreaming of nightmarish priests. Somehow his voice overcame the noise of the restaurant, muting the conversations of other patrons to subdued white noise. It was so remarkable that I would have sworn there was magic in it, except that I felt no power coming from him. Perhaps it was magic, but of that special human kind—magic born of human charm and conversation, which I too often discounted.

He talked while I listened to his pleasant voice and watched him. There was something very comforting about him, and I was not sure if it was his easy manner or his complete immunity to my scowling. He was funny without trying to joke, intelligent without trying to sound erudite, and he made it plain he expected nothing.

The lunch stretched on and then suddenly it was close to one thirty and time for me to go.

"I had a great time," he said. "But then I talked the whole time, so I suppose that's obvious. You should've shut me up."

"I enjoyed listening to you."

He scowled at me, disbelieving, and warned, "Next time it will be your turn to talk."

"Next time?"

"Would you go to dinner with me?"

"I would," I found myself saying.

"Tonight?" he asked, his eyes hopeful.

"I'll try," I promised and actually intended to do so. "Call me around six." I gave him my address in case the magic knocked the phone out.

I insisted on paying my half of the lunch and declined an offer to be walked to my car. The day I needed an escort was the day I'd turn my saber over to someone who knew what to do with it.

"MR. NATARAJA WOULD BE DELIGHTED TO SPEAK WITH you," a cultured male voice informed me through the phone. "However, his schedule is extremely busy for the next month."

I sighed, tapping my nails on Greg's kitchen table. "I'm sorry I didn't catch your name . . ."

"Charles Cole."

"I tell you what, Charles, get Rowena on the line for me now, and I won't tell Nataraja that you've tried to stonewall the Order-appointed investigator he's been waiting for."

There was silence and then Charles said in a slightly strained voice, "One moment, please."

I waited by the phone, very pleased with myself. There was a click, and Rowena's flawless voice said, "Kate, my deepest apologies. What an unfortunate misunderstanding."

Score one for me. "No offense taken," I told her. I could afford to be gracious. "I was notified that Nataraja would like to speak to me."

"Indeed. Unfortunately, he's in the field. If he knew of your intention to visit, he would have postponed. He will be back this evening and I would be indebted to you if you could meet with us later, let's say at two tonight?"

Score one for Rowena. "No problem."

"Thank you, Kate," she said.

We said good-byes and hung up. She had a way of subtly turning every conversation personal, as if the matter discussed was vital to her and any refusal of her request would injure her. It worked both ways—when you agreed to something, she acted as if you did her a great personal favor. It was an art I would have loved to learn. Unfortunately I had neither time nor patience to spare.

Unsure what to do next, I tapped my fingernails on the table. Until I got my interview with Corwin, I could not eliminate him as a suspect, and I had no other suspects so far. Maybe if I annoyed Nataraja enough, he would supply me with other leads, but it wouldn't happen until tonight, which left twelve empty hours.

I looked around the apartment. It had lost its immaculate air. There was dust on the windowsill, and several dishes sat in the sink. I pushed myself free of the chair and started looking for the broom, rags, and bleach. Come to think of it, a nap wouldn't hurt either. I had a long night to look forward to.

When I woke up later in the now clean apartment, the light outside had turned the deep purple of late evening.

Crest hadn't called. Too bad.

An interesting thought occurred to me while I lay for a few extra precious seconds in my bed, staring out the barred window at the encroaching twilight. I held on to it, padded to the kitchen, and called the Order, hoping Maxine was still there. The phone was turning into my weapon of choice.

Maxine answered.

"Good evening, Kate."

"Do you always work late?"

"Sometimes."

"If I asked you to check on something for me, would you do it?"

"That's what I'm here for, dear."

I told her about the missing women. "The cops are involved so there has to be a file on at least one of those women, Sandra Molot. I need to know if they did a general homing spell using one of her personal effects. And same for the other three."

"Hold on, dear, I'll try to find out."

She put me on hold. I waited, listening to the small noises coming over the empty phone line. The night had fallen, and the apartment was dark, save for the kitchen, and eerily quiet.

Tap. Tap.

Something scratched at my kitchen window. It was a small sound, like a dry twig striking the glass.

I was on the third floor. No trees stood close to the building.

Tap.

Silently I backed into the hallway and picked up Slayer, cradling the phone between my cheek and my shoulder.

The line came alive and I almost jumped. "Jennifer Ying has no file," Maxine said.

"Aha." I turned the light off, drowning the kitchen in darkness.

Tap. Tap.

I moved to the window.

"They do have files on the other three women."

I reached for the curtain and jerked it aside. Two amber eyes glared at me, full of longing and hunger. A face that was a meld of wolf and human leaned on the glass. Its misshapen, horrid jaws did not fit together right and long strands of drool hung from its crooked yellowed teeth.

The skin around the lupine nose wrinkled. The nightmarish thing sniffed the glass, blowing air through its black nostrils and making a small opaque circle of condensation. It raised one deformed hand and tapped the glass with an inch-long claw.

Tap. Tap. Tap.

"Both standard and high-end locating spells were made in all three cases. They were blocked and produced no results. Kate?"

"Thank you very much, Maxine," I said, unable to take my gaze off the monster at my window. "I have to go now."

"Any time, dear. Play nice with the wolf."

Carefully I put the phone aside. Slayer in hand, I murmured the spell dissolving the ward around the glass and unlocked the window.

The claws hooked the window's edge and effortlessly slid it upward. The wolf-man stepped inside with marked slowness, one furry sinewy leg at a time, and stood seven feet tall in my kitchen. Dense gray fur sheathed its head, shoulders, back, and limbs, leaving the sickening face and the muscular chest bare. I could see round dark spots dotting the skin tightly stretched over his pectorals.

"Alright, pretty boy. What do you have for me?"

He reached toward me, holding a large envelope in his claws. A red wax seal with some sort of imprint secured the envelope.

"Open it," I directed.

The wolf-man clumsily snapped the seal, pulled out a single piece of paper, holding it with his claws, and offered it to me. I took it. His claws left small tears in the paper.

Four lines written in beautiful calligraphy said:

His Majesty Curran,
the chosen Lord of the Free Beasts,
requests your presence at the meeting of his Pack
at 22:00 of this night.

The paper was signed with a scribble.

"My own fault, huh," I said to the wolf-man. "I did tell him I wanted a formal invitation."

The wolf stared at me. His drool made small sticky puddles on the kitchen linoleum. I thought of being alone with two hundred monsters just like him, each faster and stronger than me, ready to tear me apart at the whim of their leader, and a sinking feeling sucked at my stomach. I didn't want to go.

"Are you supposed to escort me?"

The nightmare opened his mouth and produced a low guttural growl, the frustrated snarl of a mind gifted with the power of speech but locked in a body unable to produce the words. Only the most adept of the shapechangers could speak in a midform.

"Nod, if yes," I said.

The wolf nodded slowly.

"Very well. I need to change. Stay here. Don't move. This is a dangerous place for a wolf. Nod if you understand."

He nodded.

I stepped into the hallway and touched the wall, activating the ward. A translucent red partition materialized in the doorway, separating the kitchen and the monster within from the rest of the apartment. I went to get dressed.

I CHOSE LOOSE DARK GRAY PANTS, CUT TO FLARE AT the bottom. They masked my foot when I kicked. The prospect of many claws at my back made me think of light armor, but my suit waited for me at my real house along with the rest of my supplies, long overdue. Not that it would help anyway, not in the middle of the Pack. I dug in the closet, where I kept a couple changes of clothes. When Greg was alive, I only came to his apartment as a last resort, which usually meant I was bleeding and my clothes were ruined.

I thumbed through the outfits and my hands grazed leather. A black leather jacket. I could dimly recall wearing it at some point. Must've been during my "Oh look, I'm tough!" days. I slipped it on and looked in the bedroom mirror. I looked like a bravo. And it was hot. Oh well. It was better than nothing. I took the jacket off, changed my T-shirt for a dark gray tank top, slipped on the tangle of the back sheath, and put the jacket on again. Thugs are us. Great. Just add a super-tight ponytail and loads of mascara, and I'd be ripe to play a supervillain's evil mistress. Ve haf vays of making you gif us your DNA sample.

I settled for my usual braid.

Having rebraided my hair, I paused, considered the arsenal available to me, put on thin wristbands loaded with silver needles, and took nothing else except Slayer. To get clear of two hundred enraged shapechangers I'd need a case of grenades and air support. There was no reason to weigh myself down with extra weapons. Then again, maybe I should take a knife. One knife, as a backup. Okay, two. And that's it.

Armed and dressed to kill—or rather to die quickly but in style—I went to get the wolf-man, and together we took the gloomy staircase down to the street. I held Betsi's back door open for my guide and he slid into the backseat. As we started out of the parking lot, his claw tapped me on the back and pointed to the left. I took the hint and turned in that direction.

The traffic was light, almost nonexistent. Deserted streets, flooded with a yellow electric radiance, stretched before us. Few people owned cars that ran during tech. There was no need to invest in them, since it was plain that magic was gaining the upper hand.

An ancient blue Honda came to a stoplight in the left turn lane next to us. A man and a woman in the front seat were talking. I couldn't see the man except for his darkened profile, but the woman's face wore a blissful, slightly dreamy look as if she was remembering some happy moment. A small brown-haired boy sat in the backseat.

In a moment he would see the monster in my car. I braced myself for a scream.

The boy squinted and grinned. I glanced in the rearview window. The wolf-man was pretending to pant, black lips stretched in a happy canine smile. The gloom of the car hid most of his face and only the muzzle, illuminated by the outside light, and the glowing eyes were visible.

The boy mouthed something that might have been "Good dog." The light changed and the Honda drove on, vanishing into the night and carrying away the child and his parents, their reminiscing undisturbed.

We drove on, winding our way northeast toward Suwanee. It took us nearly an hour to reach the shapechanger compound and we had to leave the city behind to get there. All but invisible from the highway, the fortress sat in the middle of a clearing, defined by a dense wall of brush and oaks that looked decades older than they had any right to be. The only sign of its existence was a single-lane dirt road that veered so abruptly from the highway that I missed it despite my guide and had to double back.

The trail brought us to a small parking lot. I parked next to an old Chevy truck and held the door open for the wolf-man. He stepped out and paused in a kind of silent salute to the building. The compound loomed before us, a forbidding square building of gray stone nearly sixty feet high. Darkness pooled in the narrow arched windows, guarded by metal grates. The place looked like the keep of a castle rather than a modern fort.

The wolf-man raised his narrow muzzle and let out a long, wailing howl. Icy fingers of fear clawed their way up my spine and clutched my throat. The howl lingered, bouncing off the walls and filling the night with the promise of a long, bloody hunt. Another voice joined it from atop the keep, a third came from the side, then a fourth . . . All around us the sentries howled and I stood still in the whirlpool of their war cries. A bit dramatic, and yet it had the likely desired effect of turning a badass like me into just another frightened ape shivering in the darkness.

Satisfied, my guide strode toward the keep and I walked after him listening to the last echoes of the blood hymn flee into the night. The wolf-man stopped before a large metal door and knocked. The door swung open and we stepped inside, into a small chamber lighted with electric lamps.

A short woman with very curly blond hair waited for us. Some unspoken communication must have passed between her and my guide, and she looked at me. "This way, please."

I followed her through another door to a round room. A spiral staircase pierced the floor, stretching both up and down. I looked up and saw coils of stairs merging with darkness.

"This way, please," the woman repeated and led me down the stairs. We descended, making several loops, until my escort stepped into a dark side hallway. The hallway terminated in another heavy wooden door, and the woman pushed it open, motioning me inside. I stepped through.

A huge oval room lay before me, bathed in a comfortable glow of electric lights softened by opaque glass. The room sloped down gently, like a college auditorium, to culminate in a flat stage. On the left side of the stage, next to a door, fire burned brightly in a foot-wide metal brazier, its smoke sucked away into a vertical shoot. A smooth slanting path led from the doorway to the stage.

The rest of the sloping floor was terraced, segregated into five-foot-wide "steps," and on the steps, on uniform blue blankets, rested the shapechangers. Most were in a human form; some reclined by themselves; some sat together with their families, one family to a blanket, as if they had gathered for some sort of underground picnic. With a shock I realized there were more than three hundred of them. *Many* more.

And Curran was nowhere in sight.

The door closed behind me with a click. As one, the shapechangers turned and looked at me.

I wondered what they'd do if I asked to borrow a cup of sugar.

Behind me the door opened and two large males stepped inside, breathing down my neck. I got the message and started down the path to the stage. Ahead several males stood up from their blankets and barred the path midway down.

The welcoming committee. How nice.

I crashed to a halt before the men. "You're in my way," I said.

"Really?" The kid couldn't have been more than eighteen

years old, with an open face and longish brown hair. His brown eyes laughed at me, and I knew this was a setup. And I knew who orchestrated it. They wouldn't blow their noses without Curran's say-so.

"Really," I said, knowing what was coming.

"From where I'm standing, you're in our way," an older, stocky male said. A corner of his mouth curved, trying to hide a smile. He enjoyed the game.

A tall male, shaggy with red hair, called out from his blanket, "Hey, Mik, don't you know to step aside for a lady?"

"I don't see a lady here." The stocky male leered at me.

A wave of catcalls and growling rolled through the room, so sudden it might have been choreographed. Mik kept sizing me up. Even his leer seemed rehearsed. There was no threat here, only a test of what I would do. I had to resolve it quickly and without direct violence or the Pack would never work with me. The sheer stupidity of the situation was staggering.

The males grew bolder. The kid grinned. "What do you say, baby, let's you and me go to the side and I'll show you a good time."

The group exploded with laughter—this one must have been an improvisation. The kid, pleased with himself, reached out and his fingers brushed my cheek. The moment his skin touched mine, I whispered a single word so quietly that even I couldn't hear my voice.

"Amehe." Obey.

The word of power pulsed through my skin to his. The rush of so much magic leaving my body nearly brought me to my knees. The kid stiffened. The others did not notice, absorbed in making noise.

"That's a good one, Derek," Mik said. "I think she could take all of us on, unless you mind sharing."

I looked at the kid and said, "Protect me."

His body exploded into motion, the mist of body fluids drenching the floor. A sleek lupine shape hit the older male, knocking him off balance. Mik fell on his back, and the huge gray wolf was on top of him, fangs bared in a vicious feral snarl a hair away from his throat.

"Hold him," I said.

The wolf growled low, black lips quivering.

The room was suddenly quiet as a tomb. I hoped it wouldn't be mine.

"Derek," Mik said in a hoarse voice, the weight of the wolf on his chest making it difficult for him to speak. "Derek, it's *me*."

The wolf snarled.

"Don't move," I advised, reaching back and pulling Slayer from its sheath. It made a soft metallic whisper as it left the scabbard, and the gazes of the shapechangers fastened on the enchanted blade.

A woman rose from her seat to my left. Her lips quivered in a telltale precursor to a snarl. "What the hell did you do to him?"

I glanced around the room. The mood had changed. The game had ended, and their eyes burned like fire. The hair on their heads bristled, and the smell of murder was in the air.

"This is Slayer," I said, holding the saber so they could see it clearly. The saber seethed, and luminescent tendrils of smoke clung to its blade. "It has had many names. One of them was Wolfripper. Push me and I will show you how it got that one."

"You can't take all of us," a male snarled to the right.

"I don't have to." I lowered the blade onto the neck of the wolf. "Move and I'll kill him."

They became utterly still. Pack loyalty overrode their anger, but I didn't dare to push them any further.

"That's enough," Curran's voice said.

The shapechangers melted from my path and I saw Curran standing down by the fire. I looked at the wolf. "Come."

Hesitantly the beast took his paws off Mik's chest. I stepped over the stocky man and walked toward Curran, the wolf trotting at my side like an oversized guard dog.

I stepped onto the stage. Curran's irises were streaked with gold—he was pissed off. Ignoring him, I stepped toward the brazier, pulled up the right sleeve of my sweatshirt, and passed my forearm through the flame. Pain licked my arm. The stench of scorched skin and burned hair permeated the air. The room murmured. I proved my humanity and my control to the Pack as any shapechanger would. No shapechanger who abandoned the strict discipline and allowed his Beast to take charge could touch the fire. It was a vital and very private ritual, one they did not expect me to know.

Curran's face was stone. "Come," he said and the wolf and I followed him off the stage, through a door, into another, much smaller room, where eight people sat in padded chairs. They rose at Curran's approach and remained standing, three women and five men. Jim was one of them. So my old buddy was a member of the Pack Council. Fancy that.

The eight looked at the wolf, at me, at my arm, and then at Curran. Jim opened his mouth to say something and clamped it shut.

"Derek," Curran called.

The wolf glanced at him. The blaze of Curran's eyes seared him and he sat still, mesmerized. Curran made a strange sound, half growl, half word, but an unmistakable command. The wolf shuddered. Curran repeated the order. The wolf shook harder, his lean body convulsing, and whined weakly.

The lord of the shapechangers glared at me. "Release him."

"Is that a request or an order?"

A twitch ran through Curran's face as if the lion in him wanted to claw its way out. "It's a request," he said.

I kneeled by the wolf and touched his thick fur, making contact with the skin underneath. The beast trembled.

"Is the room warded with containment?"

Curran nodded. I looked at the wolf and whispered, *"Dair." Release.*

The strength of the power word rocked me. Red circles swam before me and I shook my head trying to clear my vision. The wolf sagged to the floor as if all strength suddenly left his sinewy legs. Curran growled, and the animal vanished in the dense mist, leaving the kid naked and wet on the floor.

"I couldn't," he groaned.

"I know," Curran said. "It's okay."

The kid sighed and passed out. One of the women, a long-legged lean brunette in her thirties, covered him with a blanket.

Curran turned to me. "Take one of mine again and I'll kill you." He said it in a conversational manner, matter-of-fact and flat, but in his eyes I could see a simple certainty. If he had to, he would kill me. He would not lose any sleep over it. He would not give it a second thought. He would do it and move on, untroubled by ending my existence.

It scared the shit out of me, so I laughed in his face. "You think you can do it by yourself next time, big guy? On second thought, you better bring some of your flunkies to box me in again—you *are* getting soft."

Behind him someone made a strangled sound. *That's it, I'm dead,* flashed through my head. Curran's face jerked. Bloodlust flooded him, and then, with a single massive exertion of will, he regained control. The effort was almost physical. I could see the muscles of his face relax one by one as his anger imploded. The rage in his eyes died to smoldering amber and he stood before me, relaxed, loose, and calm. It was the most frightening thing I'd ever seen.

"I need you for now," he said. Glancing at his Council, he asked, "Is Corwin ready?"

"Yes, my liege," boomed an older man. Barrel-chested and thick, with enormous shoulders and arms that would make any blacksmith proud, he looked to be in his fifties, his curly black beard and thick mane of black hair sparkling with isolated strands of gray.

"Good. Take her to the room. I'll join you shortly."

The black-bearded man approached the door on the left side of the room and held it open for me. "Please."

I made my exit.

We walked side by side through a winding corridor, the man with the black beard and I. "My name is Mahon," the man said. His deep voice held the slight burr of a Scottish accent.

"Nice to meet you," I murmured mechanically.

"It would have been much nicer under different circumstances," he chuckled.

"Knowing the extent of the Pack's welcome, I would've preferred Unicorn Lane."

"You must understand that Curran can't permit anyone to take something that's his. If he allows it to happen, his authority would come into question and some'd ask if you couldn't do the same thing to him as you did to Derek."

"I'm aware of the Pack's mechanics," I said.

"And you are an outsider. The Pack is distrustful of outsiders."

"I'm a human outsider. The Pack treated me as if I were a loner. With Curran's permission." Very rarely, a shapechanger chose to follow the Code in his own way, refusing the Pack. Such individuals were called loners. They were the ultimate outsiders, treated by the Pack with suspicion and dislike.

Mahon inclined his head, supporting my assessment of the situation. "Curran never does anything without a reason," he said. "I was told you'd met him. Perhaps you indirectly challenged him at that meeting."

Indirectly? I had challenged him *deliberately*.

"Your knowledge of our customs is unusual," he continued. "For a human outsider. How did you come by this information?" His voice promised no confrontation.

"My father," I said.

"A man of the Code?"

"In his own way. Not your Code but his own."

"You've learned well."

"No," I said. "He taught me well. I was difficult."

"Children can be sometimes," he said.

We stopped before a door.

"Do you need some ointment for your arm?"

I looked at the angry red welt marring my skin. "No. Unless you catch it right away, the ointment won't do any good. But I appreciate the offer." I shook my head. "Tell me, do you always pacify irate guests of the Pack?"

He opened the door. "Sometimes. I suppose I have a calming influence on misbehaving children. Please."

I stepped through the door and he closed it behind me. The room was small. A single lamp threw a sharp cone of light onto a table in its center. Two chairs stood by the table, the farther one occupied by a man. He had purposefully positioned himself so the light was turned away from him.

The setup reminded me of the spy movies from my childhood.

"Finessed you, didn't he?" the man said. His voice had a scratchy quality to it. "I bet another ten minutes and you ready to apologize."

"I don't think so." I pulled up a chair to the table. The man leaned back, remaining in the shadows.

"Don't beat yourself over it. He do it to everybody. Why I don't talk to him."

"You're Corwin?"

"No, I'm Snow White." He rocked back, balancing on the back legs of his chair.

"And who's the man that walked me here?"

"Mahon," he said. "The Kodiak of Atlanta."

"The Pack Executioner?"

"The very same."

I digested the news.

"He raise Curran, you know," the man said.

"Oh? And he calls him lord like the rest of you?"

The man shrugged. "That what Curran is."

"She has trouble with that concept," Curran's voice said from behind me.

I was learning. This time I didn't jump. "You may be their lord. You sure as hell aren't mine."

Curran was leaning against the wall.

"Where are the rest?" I asked. There had to be more people watching, probably the eight that greeted me in the room where I almost talked myself into death. The alpha male of the wolf pack, the head of the rats, the person that spoke for the "scouts," the smaller shapechangers, and someone who stood for the larger beasts.

"They are watching," Curran said, nodding toward the wall.

For the first time I noticed a one-way mirror.

I looked at Corwin. "Why don't you move into the light."

"You sure?" he asked.

"Yeah."

He leaned forward, letting the light play on his features. His face was horrible. Large, flint-hard eyes sat deep in his skull, overshadowed by heavy eyebrows. His nose was massive, his jaw too heavy and prominent to be human; he looked like he could bite through a steel wire with little effort. His reddish hair, thick and textured like fur, was combed back into a ponytail. Long sideburns hung from his cheekbones almost to his chest, framing tall, pointed ears with small tufts of fur on their ends. The same hair, only shorter and thicker, sheathed his neck and his throat, leaving his chin bare at such a precise line that he must have shaved.

His hands, resting on the table, were misshapen and out of proportion to his body. Despite short, thick fingers, each hand could enclose my entire head. Clumps of reddish fur grew between his knuckles.

Corwin grinned. His teeth were huge and pointed. Sickle claws shot from the tips of his stubby fingers. He spread his fingers in a catlike kneading motion, scraping the wooden surface of the table.

"Oh, boy," I said. "How do you fluff your pillows at night?"

Corwin licked his canines at me and glanced at Curran. "I like this one."

"Let's start," I said.

"You haven't asked me what I am." Corwin tapped the table with his claws.

"I'll figure it out." The familiar words from the long sessions at the Academy resurfaced. "I'm Kate Daniels. I'm a lawful and documented representative of the Order. I'm investigating a murder and you are one of the suspects. With me so far?"

"Yes," Corwin said.

"I'm here to question you with the purpose of establishing or eliminating you as a primary suspect. If you've committed this murder, you may incriminate yourself by answering my questions. I can't compel you to answer."

"He can," Corwin said in his scratchy voice, nodding toward Curran.

"That's between you and him. Just as long as we are clear that I can't force you to cooperate."

"We clear, sweetheart."

I flashed him a smile. "The information you provide today is confidential but not privileged."

"What do that means?"

"It means," Curran said, "that she'll keep it to herself but she'll have to give it up if subpoenaed by court."

"He's right." I looked at Corwin. "I must also warn you that if you murdered Greg Feldman, I'll try my best to kill you."

Corwin leaned back and a strange gurgling rumble emanated from his throat. A moment later I realized he was laughing.

"I understand," he said, his irises shining with green.

"Let's begin then. Have you taken any part, directly or indirectly, in the murder of Greg Feldman?"

"No."

I hit all of the major points. He knew what was in the papers and nothing more. He had never met Greg or the vamp in question. He had no idea why anyone would try to kill them. He did not know who Ghastek was.

"Would you be willing to donate some tissue for an m-scan?" I asked finally.

"Tissue?"

"Blood, spit, urine, hair. Something I can scan."

He leaned forward with a low murmur in his throat. "I could donate something to you. Something other than blood and spit."

I leaned to him until our gazes crossed. "Thanks," I said. "But I'm not available."

"Mated?"

"No. Busy."

"You won't stay busy forever."

On impulse I reached and scratched him under the chin. He closed his eyes and purred. "There are werecats," I said.

"Yeeeees." He turned to offer my fingers better access to his chin.

"And then there are cat-weres."

His eyes opened just a tiny bit, and green shone through the slits.

"Born an animal . . ." I said.

"And now I am man," he continued, turning again so my fingers would scratch a farther point on his jaw. "A man-lynx. I like to read. And human females are often in heat."

"Do you still hunt among the trees when the moon is out, lynx?" I asked softly.

"Come to the Wood at night," he said. "And you'll find out."

I sat back. "Do you have an m-scanner?"

"We have a portable," Curran said.

"That will be fine."

I waited until they brought the portable out. Even the portable scanner weighed over eighty pounds. A single woman carried it in and sat it in the corner, a large construction of metal and wood that resembled a sewing machine that had undergone a Celtic-warrior battle-warp. The woman examined it critically, picked it up with one hand and moved it a few inches farther from the wall. Strength was something the shapechangers had in abundance.

"You know how to work it?" the woman asked me. I nodded,

took the glass tray from the scanner's storage compartment, and smiled at Corwin. "About that hair sample?"

He held his sideburn taut and flashed his claws. A clump of reddish hair fell into the tray. I put it onto the examining platform. Green beams flashed and the printer whirred. Finally it stopped and the slip of paper slid from the slot. I pulled it. The lines were there, a series of short, faint slashes of color. But in the wrong place. I twisted the paper, trying to get the right angle of light. Light yellow-green. No match. There goes my only suspect.

"Are you satisfied?" Curran asked.

"Yes. He's clear."

Obeying Curran's nod, Corwin rose and left.

"We agreed to a trade," Curran said.

"I remember. What can I do for you?"

Curran looked to the open door and Derek staggered in, unsteady on his feet. He slumped against the doorframe, his face haggard. He looked like he needed a few more hours of sleep and a good dinner. I felt a pang of guilt. Just a tired kid, caught in a pissing contest between me and his boss.

"You can take him with you," Curran said.

I blinked. "As what?"

"As a bodyguard. As a connection to the Pack. Take your pick."

"No."

Curran just looked at me.

"We agreed to an exchange of information," I said. "At no point did I say that I'd take someone with me. Besides, why the hell would I want a wolf who'll report my every breath back to you?"

"I'll bind him with a blood oath. He'll do nothing to harm you, physically or otherwise. He won't spy on you."

Derek tensed against the wall and I tried to be reasonable. "Even assuming that I believe you, I can't take him with me. Look at him. He's a kid. If I get in a fight, I won't know whose neck to save, mine or his."

"I can hold my own," the kid said hoarsely.

"You can't force me to take him," I said. "I don't want his blood on my hands."

"If you won't take him, his blood will be on your hands." Curran crossed his arms over his chest. "You caused this. You took possession of my wolf in front of the entire Pack."

"You left me no choice. Was I supposed to squeal for your help? I came here in good faith and walked into an ambush. The responsibility is yours."

Curran ignored me and plowed on. "You've brought my authority into doubt. I can't just let it go. As of now I have three options. I can teach you a public lesson in humility, and oh, I would very much like to do that." His face left me no doubt as to exactly how much. "But I have to suffer you because you're the Order's point of contact. I can punish him, which I don't want to do. Or I can give him to you and let it be known that he was yours since our last meeting. You looked distressed and the blood oath had driven him berserk. It will let him save face."

I shook my head. "I won't take him."

"Then I'll kill him," Curran said.

All blood drained from the kid's face. He pushed himself from the wall and stood straight.

"He disobeyed me," Curran said. "He touched you, so I'm well within my rights." Fur sheathed Curran's arm. Claws shot from his huge paw and pricked the skin under Derek's chin. The kid winced.

"I like him," Curran's voice was almost a purr. "It won't be an easy kill."

"Bleed him and I'll skewer you like a stuck pig," I said through clenched teeth.

"No, you will try. You'll wave your sword around and talk a lot of shit and then back off at the last minute. And then I'll snap your neck and his."

Sickle claws danced dangerously close to the faint flicker of pulse on Derek's neck. Time to learn how to write checks I can cover.

"You win, Your Majesty. Please bind him now. I have an appointment in three hours."

THREE RED DROPS FELL ON THE COALS BURNING IN A metal brazier and hissed, bubbling. The smell of burning human blood permeated the chamber, fueling the tangled cords of magic. I grimaced.

A binding was taking place, a ritual of attaching Derek's oath to the magic of his blood. The trouble was that blood oaths guaranteed very little. Derek would have a strong aversion to breaking promises made under these circumstances, but that's where it ended. When given a choice between breaking a blood oath and a stronger obligation, such as loyalty to the Pack, he would most likely break the oath.

The tall, lean alpha-wolf intoned the words of the pledge. Derek repeated them, and the currents of power licked the round room, spiraling up the impossibly tall walls, to the ceiling lost in darkness. The Council, who had formed a circle around the brazier, uttered a single word in unison. Derek held his hand over the flame. The alpha-wolf slit Derek's forearm, letting his blood run into the fire of the brazier to seal the pledge. There were a lot of pledges. The shapechanger blood clotted quickly and the alpha had to reopen the wound every thirty seconds or so. The binding took nearly fifteen minutes. Halfway through it, Derek started clenching his teeth when the knife touched his skin. That arm had to be sore as hell.

I listened to the vows. Derek pledged to protect me with his life if need be. He pledged to be at my side in danger and in peace, for as long as the Pack required it. He pledged to uphold the honor of the Pack as a whole and of his Wolf Clan in particular. I was not getting a bodyguard. I was getting a second shadow, and if someone frowned at me, he was honor-bound to rip them to pieces.

He stood there, wincing over and over, looking lost and pitiful and somehow infinitely younger than me. I turned and quietly walked away, out of the room, into the shadowy hallway outside. The air was cool and smelled faintly of lemon of all things. I leaned against the wall and covered my face with my hands, shutting the world out for a moment. The blood oath took a while to set in and Derek would have to be at my side for the duration, otherwise his pledge would be worthless. He would have to sleep in my apartment, he would have to eat dinner with me and come with me to the Casino . . . Casino. Ugh.

"Weak stomach," Curran said at my side.

I didn't jump. It was more of a small hop, really. "You do this on purpose, don't you?"

"What?"

"Never mind."

I rubbed my face, but the fatigue wouldn't go away. Just an adrenaline cooldown. It would be over in a few minutes and then I would be as good as new.

"You're out of your league," Curran said.

No shit. "I really didn't handle this whole thing too well, did I?"

"No," he said. His voice held no sympathy.

I wanted to ask for a do-over. I would be more restrained the second time around. Less mouthy. Unfortunately in real life you rarely got a do-over.

"I'm heading to the Casino from here. I need to know if I can take Derek with me. Nataraja likes to fuck with me. If Derek goes wolf, it would really screw things up." An understatement of the year.

"You know anything of the Code?"

"'The Code is the Way,'" I quoted the Code of Thought. "'It is Order among Chaos; it is sanity amidst the oblivion.'" He glanced in my direction. Surprised, Your Majesty? Yes, I did read it. Many times over. "Without the Code, the shapechangers lose their balance. The Beast overwhelms them, compelling them to murder and cannibalize their victims. Consumption of human flesh triggers a cataclysmic hormonal response. Violent tendencies, paranoia, and sexual urges shoot into overdrive, and a shapechanger degenerates into a loup—a psychopath that engages in every perversion involving blood and sex that a human mind can imagine. A human mind can imagine quite a bit."

I was definitely tired now. Slowly I slid down and sat on the floor. Screw him, if he wanted to stand over me, so be it. "I was at Moses Creek when the Guild busted Sam Buchanan's compound of horrors," I said.

Like a servant overly eager to please, my mind thrust a memory before me. The front yard of Buchanan's holdout, past the trenches and the mud wall from which his deranged pack had sprayed shotgun blasts at us. Fall grass strewn with bodies of dead loups, a kiddy inflatable pool—blue with yellow ducks—full of blood and clumpy pale strings of entrails, and a woman, naked and bloody, black holes gaping where her eyes once were. Her hands spread before her, she stumbles on the corpses, searching blindly, grabbing the trunk of a pine for support, and calling, her voice barely above a whisper, "Megan! Megan!" And us, two dozen mercs in battle gear, unable to tell her of the tiny dark-haired body hanging from a noose in the branches of the tree to which she clings.

I clenched my teeth.

"Bad memories?" Curran asked.

"You have no idea," I said hoarsely and remembered whom I was talking to. "But then you probably do."

I shook my head, flinging the memories from me like a wet dog shakes off water. That was my third job with the Guild. I was nineteen and the nightmares were still vivid. And Buchanan had gotten away, ran into the woods while we pounded his berserk loups into wet mush. We never caught him. Knowing that was worse than any nightmare.

Curran was watching me. I opened my mouth to ask him why hadn't he done something about that rabid loup and then remembered that Jackson County had barred the Pack from interfering. That was six years ago. Today they would not dare.

My mouth was open so I said, "What does any of it have to do with Derek?"

"Derek's parents were Southern Baptist separatists. He was the oldest son and allowed to attend school. For a while at least, until his father had gone deeper into religion. He remembers burning books in the front yard, Dr. Seuss and Sendak."

I nodded. The shift to "deep religion" wasn't unusual. Half of the mountain towns had gone "deep" before the "Live-Life-with-God" movement gave them a new dogma.

Curran rubbed his neck, biceps rolling under the sleeve of his shirt. "When the kid was fourteen, they went to an end-of-the-world tent revival and daddy brought home the Lyc-V."

He sat next to me. "He didn't know what the fuck it was or how to deal with it. He didn't even know enough to get help. Went loup within days. Loups are contagious as hell. Derek's mother killed herself after she got infected and left her rabid husband alone with seven kids. Five of them were girls."

I swallowed the hard clump in my throat. "How long?"

"Two years." Curran's face was grim. "They killed a passing lycanthrope midway through the first year and Derek found the Code on his body. That and starvation kept him sane."

"So how did it end?"

"The way it always does. The kid became competition for the females and the father tried to kill him. The kid has a good beast-form and he can keep it steady."

The beast-form is the warrior form, superior to both animal and man. Most first-generation shapechangers have trouble with beast-form, unable to maintain it longer than a few seconds. They get better with practice, but it takes years of trial and error.

"Derek killed his dad?"

"And set the house on fire."

"What of the other children?"

"Dead. Two from starvation, three from daddy's affections, and the last one burned to death. We went through the rubble and buried the bones."

"And now you're giving him to me? Why, Curran? I can't be responsible for him, I'm doing a piss-poor job of being responsible for myself."

His gaze held enough contempt to drown me. "Derek can handle himself. I don't tolerate loss of control. He's been tested and he won't lose his way when he smells the blood. In your place, I'd worry more about your own ass."

"Well, you're not in my place." I rose to my feet. Time to go.

We walked back to the room, where Curran said a few words to Mahon and left. Mahon approached me. "I'll show you out. Derek'll meet us at the entrance."

"Please make sure he takes a shower," I said. "Lots and lots of Irish Spring. I don't want the People smelling blood or wolf on him."

Mahon led me a different way, through the maze of dim passages and branching tunnels that brought us to a wooden door. Mahon leaned his palm against it and it swung open.

"Curran wanted you to see this before you left," he said.

In the room, on a simple metal table under a glass hood laced with preserving spells, lay the head of Sam Buchanan.

CHAPTER 5

BETSI WOULD NOT START. A WERERAT MECHANIC TOOK one look under the hood, mumbled something about the alternator, and pointed me toward the stables.

Before we left, I popped Betsi's trunk, untied the strings holding the long oiled-leather roll and pulled it open, displaying swords and daggers secured in leather loops. The moonlight silvered the blades.

"Wow," Derek said.

Men and swords. My father said that if you put any able-bodied man, no matter how peaceful, into a room with a sword and a practice dummy and left him alone, eventually the man would pick up the sword and try to stab the dummy. It is human nature. This young wolf was no different.

"Choose a weapon."

"Whatever I want?"

"Whatever you want."

He examined the row of cutlery, his face thoughtful. I thought he'd go for a leaf blade, but he ignored it and his fingers strayed toward Bor instead. It was a good sword, especially for a beginner, with a thirty-two-inch blade and an ash-sheathed hilt just under eight inches long. It had a straight steel guard with sharp tips pointing downward and a no-nonsense steel pommel. Like all weapons I owned, it had a superb balance.

Derek held it upright.

"It's light!" he said. "I went to a sword fair once, and the swords there were way heavier."

"There is a difference between a sword and a swordlike object," I said. "What you saw at the sword fair were mostly reasonable imitations. They are pretty and heavy and they make you slower than a slug on vacation. This one only weighs two pounds."

Derek swung the sword in a practice slash.

"It's a working sword," I said. "It won't break and it doesn't send a lot of vibration back to your hand when you strike a target."

"I like it," he said.

"It's yours."

"Thanks."

I grabbed my utility bag and we were ready to go. Derek made some sniffing noises at the bag. "I smell gasoline."

"You smell right," I told him and left it at that. Explaining that I carried a large canteen filled with gasoline in my bag in case I spilled some of my blood and had to clean it up in a hurry would've been too complicated.

THE PACK LENT ME A MARE. HER NAME WAS FRAU. THE stable master swore that while she wasn't the swiftest beast in the stables, she was obedient, strong, and steady as the rock of Gibraltar. So far, I had no reason to doubt him.

Derek's dun gelding was perfectly content to let Frau take the lead. The kid rode with the stiffness of a moderately trained rider who had never gotten quite comfortable with horses. Some shapechangers rode like they were centaurs. Derek wasn't one of them.

Neither of us had spoken since we left the shapechanger keep fifty minutes ago.

If I was to work with him, we had to at least be able to talk. I dropped back, drawing side by side with him. The sounds of hoofbeats echoed on the deserted street.

"Why the arm?" Derek asked.

He was looking at my burn. The custom called for a hand to be thrust into the flame.

"Because I don't heal as quickly as you do. I need my hand to hold my sword."

"Oh. That was a dumb question." He looked away toward the city. Atlanta sprawled, looking relieved to be free of magic and yet also apprehensive, knowing its reprieve would be short-lived.

The moon shone on the sable of the night sky, a pale sliver of a face behind a veil of shadows. Its delicate radiance, a tangle of light and darkness, was all but lost, held at bay by bright street lamps. Electric lights, like the sun, offer no compromises. There are no shadows mixed with their glow, no duality, no promise of hidden depth and mystery, nothing but light, pure and simple.

"Have you ever noticed how some things work during magic and some don't?" he asked.

"For instance?"

"For instance, phones. Sometimes they work during magic and sometimes they don't."

He wanted to talk. Probably looking for some common ground. I'd be an asshole if I didn't oblige. "There are a couple of theories on that. One says that the intensity of the magic wave determines to what extent technology will fail."

"And the other one?"

I grimaced. "Magic is a fluid thing. It's not a strict system set in stone. Every one of us filters it through ourselves, and our thoughts and perceptions shape and change it. You've heard how powerful Pope is?"

"Yes."

"He derives his power solely from the faith of his congregation. Thousands and thousands of people believe he can heal the sick and so he can. Now let's take a car. How does it work?"

Derek frowned. "I'm not sure. There is an engine, which burns gasoline and turns it into gas. Gas expands and pushes something, a valve of some sort, which makes the wheels turn. Something like that."

I nodded. "Okay, now how does the phone work?"

He looked at me. "Ummm, your voice makes the wires vibrate?"

"Yes, but how does dialing a number translate into reaching the right person? And what if a bird sits on a wire? Does it still vibrate?"

Derek shrugged. "I have no idea."

"I don't either. And most other people don't. They never had to stop and think about how the phone works. It just does. Cars are a different matter. They require more maintenance and break down more often than a phone, and the repairs are a good deal more expensive, so any car owner will educate himself about his car's inner workings at least to some degree."

"To keep from being ripped off," Derek said.

"Yes. The theory is that since so many people are ignorant of the basic mechanical principles involved in making the phone work, to them it might just as well be magic. They believe blindly that it will work and it does. On the other hand, cars are viewed as the sum of mechanical parts which are prone to failure, therefore when magic hits, they fail."

"That's a cool theory," he said.

"Unfortunately, it makes my job that much harder."

The magic fluctuation crashed into us. The electric lamps went out and absolute darkness drenched the city. Just when my eyes adjusted to the lack of light, we turned the corner and were greeted by a row of feylanterns. One more turn and we'd reach Casino.

"Do you know where we're going?" I asked.

"To the People's shithole."

I shook my head, waving good-bye to any hopes of preserving my neutrality with him at my side. "I want this to be very clear. No matter what happens, I don't want you to change form unless you have no choice. They can't smell you, since you've showered. Unless you go furry, they have no way of knowing that you belong to the Pack, and I'd like to keep it that way."

"Why?"

"One, I want to keep my cooperation with the Pack out of the spotlight. It creates an appearance of impropriety."

"The People wouldn't be thrilled to know you have a wolfman with you."

"Yeah." Ted wouldn't be thrilled either. "And two, once you turn and fight, you'll have to be fed and given a peaceful spot to sleep it off. I don't always have a peaceful spot handy."

"Got it."

"Good."

The city, caught in the light and shadow web of the triumphant moon, lay empty and silent. Maybe the boy wonder would manage to keep his human skin on in the Casino. I certainly hoped so.

THE MAGIC HAD A SELECTIVE APPETITE. WHEN IT CAME to buildings, it gnawed on the sky scrapers first, from the top down, and then it pounced on anything large, complex, and new. The Bank of America Plaza went down first, followed by the SunTrust skyscraper. One Atlantic Center, the Peachtree Plaza, even the new Coca-Cola building took a dive. The Georgia Dome crashed before the proverbial dust cleared, and the rest of the monuments to the engineering might of man raced to commit seppuku in the face of the magic onslaught. So when one day the Georgia World Congress Center rumbled, quaked like a milk tooth about to come out, and collapsed in a huge dust cloud, the locals didn't even bat an eye.

Few expected the People to purchase the lot. Nobody expected them to clear it and raise their own private Taj Mahal in the ruin's place within five years. And when the ornate doors of the magic palace opened and the public saw gleaming rows of slot machines within, well, the city that had seen everything had to stop and stare. The shock lasted only until the first fool realized he had a few bucks in his pocket. Now the Casino was just one of the seven wonders of Atlanta, sucking in the crowds eager to pay the stupid tax. Fortunately for Derek and I, it was late even by the standards of degenerate gamblers and we didn't have to fight the human currents as we closed in on Nataraja's little nest.

I'd seen the Casino many times, and yet again, it caught me by surprise. Like an ethereal castle born from a mirage among the shifting desert sands, the People's HQ towered above the city. Alabaster-white in daytime, at night its walls glowed with gold and indigo, illuminated by powerful electric lamps or feylanterns.

The People had made some modifications. A total of eight slim minarets, instead of the original four, flanked the central domed building. High walls enclosed the complex, punctuated by blocky guard towers, equipped with howitzers and sorcerous ballistae. Solemn guards and occasional vampires patrolled the textured parapets. The place oozed necromantic magic.

We made our way between the brass statues of strange gods, poised above the waters of long, rectangular fountains. I recognized a few, but Hindu mythology was never my strong suit.

The largest of the statues stood in a circular fountain of its own just before the entrance. A strange figure, caught in the whirlwind of a fiery dance, balanced on one foot atop an ugly demon. Two pairs of arms protruded from its shoulders. One hand held a flame, the second beat a drum, the third pointed to the raised foot, and the fourth offered a blessing. A cosmic dancer, trampling the ignorance of the world, his body on fire, his face serene. Shiva as Nataraja, the Lord of the Dance.

Derek studied the statue, as I slowed before it, and scowled at the castle. "So he named himself after a god?"

"Yeah."

In this age it took a particular kind of nerve to take the name of a deity for yourself. Nerve was something the owner of the Casino had in abundance, but if Shiva was what he aspired to, he had a long way to go.

Nataraja served as the local lord of the People. The People styled themselves to be a new breed of human or a really old one, depending on whom you talked to. Like the Order, they had domains throughout the country, but unlike the Order, they appeared concerned with accumulating wealth to fund their research into the "mysteries of life and death," as their brochures put it. They had proficiency in a variety of both technological and magical fields; most showed a slant toward necromancy and necronavigation—the raising, studying, and caring for the dead.

The People had power in abundance. Dangerous as hell, they had raised necromancy to the level of art, demonstrating a high degree of professionalism in everything they did, which I admired. It didn't keep me from despising them.

The entrance to the Casino was open to the public. We tied our horses to the rails outside and walked in past the twin sentries wearing black cloaks over chainmail and brandishing scimitars. The scimitars had a worn look about them, the kind that originates from repeated sharpening after being dulled on something hard.

We entered the main floor. I hated casinos. The lure of easy money brought out the worst in people. The air smelled of greed, disappointment, and desperation.

Derek and I marched past the slot machines reconditioned to be run manually. Lost to the world in their concentration to feed more money into the machines, the slot players looked undead, going through the motions with the monotony of automatons. A woman won, jumping frantically as a waterfall of coins spilled, filling the receptacle of her machine. Her face, illuminated by delight, looked berserk, almost mad.

We passed the card tables, turned to a small service entrance, strode through it, and found ourselves in a small room opening into a staircase. A pair of lean guards, dressed in the same garb as the sentries outside, flanked the stairs. Almost immediately, as if on cue, a woman stepped into our view.

She stood a couple of inches above five feet, about half a foot shorter than me. Her emerald green dress left no aspect of her figure to the imagination. She was neither slender nor willowy. When writers of sappy romances ranted about "glorious curves tapering to a small waist" and "soft flesh that begged to be explored," they had her in mind. All in all, her body was a far cry from my own. I wasn't jealous. My body served me fine; it was strong, resilient, and equipped with quick reflexes, which let me kill things before they killed me.

I did envy her hair. Fiery red, it fell in curls and ringlets shining with red gold all the way to her hips. Derek's face split into a first-class leer. Rowena smiled as if he had just read her a poem.

"Kate! How pleasant to see you again." Her smile could launch a spaceship into orbit. Coupled with a contralto, tinted with a soft Polish accent, that smile made men lose the last remnants of their self-respect.

I glanced at Derek. The boy wonder didn't melt into a pile of goo, although his gaze was glued to Rowena's chest. Avoiding eye contact. Good strategy.

"Sorry we're late."

"Not a problem. Please follow me."

We did, climbing the staircase up the long hallway.

"You've been here before?" Derek asked, his gaze firmly fixed on Rowena's ass shifting under the shimmering green silk a few steps above us.

"Wiggles," I told him.

He blinked, then realized I wasn't referring to Rowena's backside. "Wiggles?"

"She's about fourteen feet long, triangular head, gray and blue scales . . ."

He was clearly drawing a blank. "Nataraja's pet snake," I explained. "It bolted a few weeks ago. I found it for him at the request of the Guild." Mentioning that I spent four solid days camped out in a swamp, covered in peat and muck, without a change of clothes, would have completely cramped my style.

An icy feeling came over me. The tiny hairs on the back of my neck rose. We rounded the bend and saw a vampire. It scuttled along the ceiling, heading in the opposite direction, ropy muscles working under the tightly stretched skin, probably dark during life, but now bluish purple. Rowena glanced at it and waved the way people in more technological times must've waved at the security cameras. I felt a particular magic flow from her in a sluggish wave. My stomach lurched and I swallowed, trying not to retch.

The undead sat unnaturally still. The urge to kill it almost overwhelmed me. My hand itched to touch Slayer, resting in its leather sheath on my back. I looked into the empty dead eyes and wondered what it would be like to slide my blade into one, scrambling the brain behind it. I would have liked to kill the man that piloted it even more.

The vampire shifted, springing into motion all at once, and moved on. "This way please," Rowena said, favoring us with another dazzling smile. And we had no choice but to follow while the vampire disappeared behind the turn of the corridor.

The hallway terminated in a huge arched door. It opened at our approach, splitting down the middle. Beyond, Nataraja's pentagonal throne room stretched like a hashish dream stolen from the mind of an ancient teller of *The Arabian Nights.* Graceful statues stood bathed in the glow of magic lamps that mixed with the gentle reflected radiance of Nataraja's gold throne. Velvet pillows dotted the Italian tile floor and priceless pieces of art struggled to add a touch of refinement to the shocking opulence. Nataraja himself reclined on his throne, like a sultan of legend.

The asshole wore white as he always did and his outfit looked to be worth my six months' salary. It's good to be the sultan.

His throne looked gold. It probably was gold, but my mind couldn't accept that such a concentration of wealth could be wasted on supporting someone's backside. Shaped like an egg set on its wide end and cut in half lengthwise, the throne reached the height of six feet. Stylized exotic animals, at one time considered mythical and now only extremely dangerous, covered the entire surface of the egg, both inside and out, and the precious gems that served as their eyes sparkled in the light of numerous lamps.

Nataraja rested on the throne, half-sitting, half-reclining on his elbow on a plush white cushion. His age was hard to determine. Judging by his features alone, he could not have been much older than forty but visual impressions didn't mean anything anymore. He *felt* old, much older than me. Two hundred years, maybe three, maybe more. A few years ago I would have said such longevity wasn't possible, since even a hundred years ago technology flowed full force, but my years as a merc had taught me to be very careful with words like "never" and "impossible."

Nataraja looked at me, slightly amused by my presence on his home turf. Olive-skinned and slight in build, he radiated power the way some men radiate strength. His hair, coal black and straight, framed an angular face, with a wide, high forehead, prominent cheekbones, and a weak chin, hidden by a carefully cut, ultra-short beard. His eyes, very dark and piercing, had a magnetic effect. When he stared, he appeared to look deep inside you, discovering the hidden thoughts and secreted ideas and taking them for his own. His gaze made it nearly impossible to lie to him. I still managed.

Wiggles hissed as I crossed the floor toward the throne. She fixed me with her empty hateful eyes and smelled the air, her long tongue shivering through the slit of the lipless mouth. Nice to see you too, sweetheart. Remember my cattle prod?

Rowena strode to the snake, her hand settling on the huge triangular head. Weighing nearly two hundred pounds, Wiggles could not be picked up and carried away, and snakes cannot be trained, since most of the time they assume that humans are warm walking trees. Wiggles, however, was a freak born of magic and genetic manipulation. She was still dumb by mammalian standards, but she knew that a hand on her head meant pain if she moved, so she settled into long languid coils at Rowena's feet.

Nataraja's voice came like a whisper of scales on rough stone. "Kate."

"Nate."

He grimaced. "I'm not in the mood to be disrespected."

"No wonder. It's quite late for a man of your age. Ever thought about retirement?" *You know you will do it and I know you will do it. Let's get it over with. Test me, you sonovabitch, so I can fight you off once again and then we'll talk.*

His power slammed into me, pressing, pushing me to the floor. His eyes grew into bottomless pits, commanding, all-powerful, sucking me into their awful depth, promising slavery and pain.

I clenched my teeth and held him, trying to shield Derek.

Nataraja pushed harder, his power welling like an avalanche, distorting the world, overwhelming it until nothing was left but his will and mine, locked against each other. A painful shudder pulsed through me. His face twisted and he bit his lip.

"Temper, temper," I said through my teeth.

"Aren't mood swings a sign of early senility?" Derek's strained voice said from beyond.

The awesome pressure ebbed for an instant and I gathered my magic, summoning every reserve I had. Strike against the kid, Nate. Strike so I can kill you.

The pressure fell abruptly and I was hurled back from a long black tunnel into the real world. Nataraja backed off, sensing the danger. Damn it.

I glanced at Derek. His face looked bloodless. His hands clenched into fists.

Nataraja was once again playing an amused host. "I see you brought a pet," he said. "He talks like you." *One day,* his face promised. *One day we'll settle this.*

"My bad habits rubbing off." *Any time.*

A whisper announced a new arrival. Ghastek came through the arched doors, carrying a briefcase and wearing khaki pants and a black V-neck sweater. He looked so absurd against the backdrop of Nataraja's vulgar throne room that I almost laughed.

Ghastek nodded to me and came to stand by his master's

throne. Both men were of slight build, but where Nate was slender, Ghastek was thin. A diet of steaks and hours in the weight room could make him lean and sinewy, but I doubted he ever looked at a dumbbell, let alone handled one. He was beginning to bald and the receding hairline added height to his forehead. His face was plain, saved from being unremarkable only by dark eyes betraying his intellect and that slight touch of distance particular to people who spend their time immersed in thought.

"Ahh, Ghastek," Nataraja said as if greeting a favorite pet. "I was just pondering Kate's new amusement. He would be her . . ."

I indulged him. "Apprentice."

"Apprentice." Nataraja rolled the word in his mouth, tasting it. "How modest. Considering his age, it's actually appropriate, although out of character."

"I hate to disappoint you, but our relationship is strictly professional."

Nataraja's laugh polluted the air. "Of course," he said, as if humoring a small child. "How insensitive of me."

I smiled at him. "Indeed. Now that we've established that you have appallingly poor taste, would you like a chance to chat with me as a representative of the Order or shall I make my exit?"

"Suddenly you're all business. Very well." Nataraja leaned back. "I'm dissatisfied with the direction your investigation has taken you."

I bared my teeth at him. "I find that amusing. I don't answer to you."

He didn't say anything, so I elaborated. "I work for the Order, and the last time I checked, the Order didn't report to Roland."

It was amusing to see the effect of the name. Both men jerked, as if shocked with a live wire.

"As you can see, gentlemen, I have access to the Order's database." Which was a blatant lie but they had no way of knowing it. Roland's name short-circuited their logic. If they realized how I knew the name of their leader, they both would suffer an instant apoplexy.

"Here is what I know, and please, correct me if I'm wrong. Ghastek's shadow vampire was tailing Greg Feldman. It was killed suddenly and you haven't been able to extract an image of the killer from the mind of the journeyman who had been piloting it. You've made no effort to disclose this information to the Order, which is understandable since you'd have to explain why your vampire was following the knight-diviner. What I don't understand is why you have been making so much noise over a single vamp."

A long pause stretched and then Nataraja jerked his wrist in a kind of "tell her" gesture and looked aside, seemingly losing all interest in our conversation. Rowena remained tranquil, her hand on the snake's head. I wondered what went through her mind.

"We've lost more than one vampire," Ghastek said.

"You have proof?"

Ghastek opened the briefcase and extracted a stack of photographs. Déjà vu. He walked forward to give the stack to me. Derek stepped between us, wordlessly took the pictures from his hand, and delivered them to mine.

I looked at a black-and-white image of a deceased vampire. The bloodsucker lay in a crumpled heap, its wiry body pitifully broken. Thick dark blood stained its pallid hide. The vamp was coated in it, as if someone had dipped his hand into the blood and smeared it all over its taut skin the way one would rub oil over the skin of a chicken to prepare it for roasting. The bloodsucker's bald cranium had been neatly cracked and wet emptiness glared at me where the brain had been.

The second photograph. The same vampire, this time placed

on its back to better display a long gash that split its torso from the genitals to midchest. Yellowish ribs protruded from the blackness of bloody tissue. Someone had used a very sharp knife to cleave the cartilage of several ribs on the left side, separating them from the sternum, not sawing but slicing in a single motion with awful force. The vamp must have been turned on its side to allow the stringy clot of its nearly atrophied intestines to fall out. There was no fat attached to the intestines, so the killer didn't have to bother with cutting it. Same with the bladder and colon; both organs had atrophied within weeks of undeath, so he didn't have to deal with the mess.

The diaphragm was neatly slit, both to remove the remaining intestines and to gain access to the esophagus. He must have peeled back the diaphragm and worked his hand up the chest cavity until he could grab the esophagus and cut it. Then he simply had to pull the esophagus out through the hole, and the blood-soaked, useless lungs and bulging heart would come out with it. I'd seen this before. That was how you gutted a deer.

"He took the brain, the heart, the lungs, what was left of the liver and kidneys, but discarded the intestines," Ghastek said.

I raised an eyebrow, since I didn't see the intestines, and he murmured, "The next photograph."

I looked and saw the ugly wet clump of innards in a puddle of blood. Unused, they had shrunk until they resembled tough twine.

"Admirable skill," Ghastek said dryly. "The cuts were made with almost surgical precision. He has an excellent knowledge of the vampiric physiology."

"Any chance of it being an inside job?"

Ghastek looked at me as if I had accused him of devouring small children.

"We are not stupid," he said, meaning *I'm not stupid*. "All of our people with that degree of skill are accounted for."

"Besides this one and the shadow, how many did you lose?" I asked.

"Four."

"Four? Four vampires?"

Ghastek shifted uncomfortably, looking as if he had tasted something slimy and sour. "We aren't happy about the situation."

"Where are the other photos?"

"We have none. The others were taken. We were not able to recover the bodies."

"What do you mean, taken?"

"Something killed them instantly, severing the link between their minds and the navigators who piloted them. Then their bodies were removed before our field team was able to recover them." He produced a piece of paper covered with neat typescript. "Here's the list of the locations, dates, and times."

Derek took the list from him and gave it to me. I glanced at it and put it in my pocket. Six vampires and seven shapechangers. Someone was trying to start a war between the Pack and the People, and was doing a damn good job of it. Who would benefit from it?

"You're out six vampires and you can account for only two of the bodies. Are you positive that the other four aren't active?" The idea of four unpiloted vamps running around the city made me hurt with dread.

"They are *deceased*, Kate!" Nataraja snapped out of his reverie. "Why don't you ask Curran and his pet lympago what was done to our property?"

A lympago was an inaccurate term to use for Corwin, but Nate seemed so happy to have found it that I let him wallow in his own ignorance.

"I spoke to the Pack," I said. "I've been able to clear Corwin to my satisfaction."

"That's not good enough for me," Nataraja said.

"It'll have to do." All of this verbal fencing strained my patience. "His m-scan didn't match."

"I saw the m-scan of the crime scene," Ghastek said, coming to life like a shark sensing blood in the water. "There was no power print except for our vampire and the diviner."

Shit. Me and my big mouth. I should carry a banner with a big sign, "Confidential Information Given Away Free!" At least it would let people know upfront who they were dealing with.

"You must not have been looking at the right m-scan. The one I saw had a clear power record of the murderer."

I could almost feel that formidable brain working behind Ghastek's eyes. "Would you be willing to provide us with a copy of this other m-scan?"

"Would you be willing to tell me why the hell your shadow vampire was tailing Feldman?"

"Perhaps we merely wanted to keep an eye on the diviner," Nataraja said.

I pretended to consider it. "No. I don't buy it. Keeping a vamp in the field is too expensive for casual surveillance."

"We have nothing further to discuss," Nataraja said.

"A pleasure seeing you, too," I said.

"Ghastek, escort the Order representative out of our territory." Nataraja grimaced. "We wouldn't want anything to happen to her. I simply couldn't bear it."

Ghastek gave me an odd look and walked out with us, leaving Rowena and Nataraja behind.

As soon as we were out of Nate's earshot, I stopped. "You don't really have to escort me."

"But I do."

"In that case I have a question."

Ghastek looked at me.

"If I were to taint a living animal with necromantic magic, how would I do it?"

"By taint you mean . . . ?"

There was no way out of this question without giving myself away. I was too stupid for this job.

"A sufficient amount of necromantic magic to produce a blended power print."

"What color?"

I strained to keep from gritting my teeth. "Pale orange."

He thought about it. "Well, the most obvious answer would be to feed an animal on necro-infused flesh. If a rat gorged itself on the flesh of a vampire, the necromantic magic would show up in its stomach contents. Some of it would make its way into the blood stream. But, since it's obvious, it's also wrong. I've scanned animals that fed on undead flesh before and the power print showed a pure necromantic arch."

"The magic of the undead flesh overwhelmed the magic of the animal?"

Ghastek nodded. "Yes. To produce a blended power print, the influence of the necromantic magic would have to be very subtle. In theory—and this is only in theory—it would have to involve reproduction."

"I don't understand."

"If you ask me nicely, I might explain," Ghastek said.

"Could you please explain this to me? It's important and I would very much appreciate it."

Ghastek allowed himself a smile. It touched his lips and vanished in a flicker, as if it was no more than a muscle twitch. I showed him my teeth.

"You're much more pleasant when you talk like a human being," Ghastek said. My smile failed to disturb him. "The bravado is amusing, but it becomes tiresome."

I sighed. "I'm a merc. I walk like a merc, I talk like a merc, I act like a merc."

"So you admit to being a walking stereotype?"

"It's safer that way," I said honestly.

For a moment I thought that he somehow understood the deeper meaning of my words. Then he said, "We were talking rats?"

"Yes. And I did ask nicely."

"In theory, if I take a female rat and feed it undead flesh, while allowing her to mate and carry offspring to term, then repeat the process with the offspring, somewhere down the line the descendants of the original rat may display permanent influence of necromantic magic, which will produce a blended power print. Something along light orange on the m-scan."

"Thank you."

"Thank *you*." He smiled.

THE WATER OF SHIVA'S FOUNTAIN WAS REFRESHING. I splashed it on my face, fighting an urge to lay down on the lovely cold concrete. Nataraja's little test had sapped my reserves, but I had once again prevented the show of power he was trying to provoke. I sat on the rim of the fountain. "I'm tired. I feel soiled and in need of a shower. How are you?"

Derek gripped the rim with his hands and dipped his head into the water. He shook, flinging droplets from his wet hair and washed his nostrils the way shapechangers did when they wanted to clear a strong smell from their noses.

"That place reeks of death," he said.

"Yeah. You know, it's not wise to mouth off to Nataraja."

"Look who's talking."

"He expects me to mouth off. Still, it was pretty funny. What did you think of Rowena?"

"You don't want to know," he said.

"You're right. I probably don't. She bothers me," I admitted.

"Why? Because she's prettier?"

I winced. "Derek, never, ever tell a woman that someone is prettier than her. You'll make an enemy for life."

"You're funnier than she is. And you hit harder."

"Oh, thank you. Please, continue to reinforce the fact that she's more attractive. If you say that I have a better personality, you'll find out how hard I can hit."

He grinned. We walked to our horses.

"Be careful on the way back," I said.

He gave me a puzzled look. "I'm the one protecting you. You be careful."

I shook my head. I finally got my knight in shining armor. Too bad he was a teenage werewolf.

"You think the People are gonna try something?"

"Not the People." I slowed down. "The Pack and the People lost roughly equal numbers and the murders took place right on the border between them. This string of killings feels carefully managed."

"By Nataraja?"

"By someone who would benefit from a war between the Pack and the People."

"Like Nataraja?"

"Would you let go of Nataraja already?" I frowned at him. "Nate above all is a businessman. Yes, he would like to diminish the Pack. In an outright conflict the People might even win, but it would leave them so weakened, a baby burp would knock them down. The war isn't cost-effective for the People right now, that's why we got invited into the Casino. For all of their posturing, the People are worried. Not only are they out six vampires, which are expensive to replace, but they also sense a deeper threat. Why do you think Ghastek is walking us home?"

"What threat?" Derek shrugged.

I had forgotten how good it felt to talk a theory out. "Have you ever heard people say 'pulled a Gilbert'? You know where the saying comes from?"

"No."

"About nine years ago a rogue Master of the Dead named Gilbert Caillard tried to take over the People by framing Nataraja in a sex-slave ring. Which is richly ironic—I doubt that snake ever had sex, let alone brokered it. Anyhow Gilbert's reasoning was that if the People were shamed and Nataraja got arrested, he could waltz in and take over the operation. He had power in abundance and almost pulled it off."

"You think he's back?"

"No, Gilbert's dead. Nataraja killed him and had his heart burned. He still carries the ashes in a little satchel on his neck. But this feels very much like a Gilbert. The plan has a certain brilliance to it: get the Pack and the People to battle it out and then come in and wrestle control from Nate's weak and hopefully dying fingers."

"Dying is good," Derek said.

"One, we have Pack people being torn apart by animals with necro taint, probably fed on undead flesh. Two, we have vampires being taken out by someone with advanced knowledge of vampiric anatomy. And three, Nate is scared. Look at the battlements.

He doubled their patrols. See, the People prize power most of all. They don't exactly encourage violent coups like this, but if the victor offers his obeisance to Roland and makes the appropriate noises, he'll most likely get away with it. I think we have a rogue Master of the Dead on our hands." That had to be it. It made perfect sense.

"Who's Roland?" Derek asked suddenly, intruding on my thoughts.

"Roland? He's the legendary leader of the People. It's rumored that he's been alive since magic last left the world, which was about four thousand years ago. He's supposed to have incredible power, almost godlike. Some say he's Merlin, some say he's Gilgamesh. He has some sort of agenda and uses the People to achieve it, although the majority of them have never seen him. There's no proof of his existence and lay people like you and I aren't suppose to know about him."

"Does he exist?"

"Oh yeah. He's real."

"How do you know about him?"

"It's my job to know." *And trust me, boy wonder, I know entirely too much. I know his habits. I know what food he likes to eat, what women he likes to take to his bed, what books he prefers to read. I know everything my father had known about Roland. I even know his real name.*

The flow of people to the white arch of the gates had ebbed. It was late or early, depending on the way you looked at it.

Skeletal claws of fear iced my spine. The small hairs on the back of my neck and arms stood on their ends. A vampire. Close.

Derek's gelding neighed, but Frau remained stoic. I loved this horse.

I turned slowly and watched the bloodsucker descend down

the snow-white wall of the Casino. It crawled headfirst like a mutated gecko, long yellow talons digging into the mortar. The pallid body, taut with dry, stringy muscle, dripped necro magic.

The vamp crept down until its head was level with mine and raised its face. It used to be female during life. Undeath had sharpened already delicate features, making it look like a concentration camp victim. The bloodsucker stared at me with haunted eyes. It raised a thin hand clutching a small object. Slowly it opened its maw. Its face twitched, trying to twist into a different set of features.

"I believe this is yours." Ghastek's voice said from the vamp's throat. The vamp's fingers opened and the object fell. I caught it: my throwing dagger. How considerate. He had even cleaned the bloodsucker blood off of it.

"Tell me, Kate," Ghastek said. "Why do you paint your daggers black?"

"So they don't shine when I throw them."

"Ahh. Obvious, come to think of it." The vamp's throat stank of death.

"Shall we depart?"

"Please."

"What's our destination?"

He knew perfectly well where Greg's apartment was. They probably kept the bloody place under surveillance.

"Just take me to the edge of your territory. Corner of White and Maple will do." Too late I remembered that Greg had died at that intersection. "This isn't necessary, you know."

"It is. If you died after a visit to the Casino, we would have to answer many unpleasant questions."

I petted Frau's neck, untied the reins, and mounted.

"A horse," Ghastek said with disgust. "I might have known."

"You have something against horses?"

"I'm allergic. Not that it matters under the circumstances."

He stabled the undead but good old horses made him sneeze.

"Go on ahead," I said. The vamp took off, running upright in a clumsy, labored manner. Bloodsuckers aren't built for running on the ground. It requires coordination and breathing, and the process no longer comes naturally to one who doesn't have to breathe.

I gave Frau's sides a gentle squeeze and she took off, breaking into an easy trot, Derek on his gelding close behind. I had a feeling that if the bloodsucker got within striking distance, Frau would try to find out if it was good to walk on.

Ghastek pushed the vamp for about a block and took it to higher ground. It scrambled up the side of the building and leaped across to its neighbor, defying gravity. Its gaunt form sailed along the third row of windows, talons clutching the wall long enough to push away, soundless, undetectable, a new horror.

We took the backstreets, staying away from the main road. A horseman passed us, riding a snow-white gelding, graceful and mean-eyed, a one-in-a-hundred kind of a horse. The rider wore an expensive leather jacket, edged with wolf fur. He gave me and Derek an appraising look and hurried on his way, adjusting the crossbow that rested on his back. I looked after White's retreating backside, searching for a sign that proclaimed *I'm wealthy, please rob me.* I didn't see one. I guess he figured his horse made enough of a statement.

Ahead, several kids crowded around a fire burning bright in a metal drum. The orange flames licked the drum's edges, throwing yellow highlights on their grimy, determined young faces. A scrawny boy in a dirty sweatshirt and with a tangle of feathers in his lanky hair chanted something dramatically and threw what looked like a dead rat into the fire. Everyone was a sorcerer these days.

The kids watched me as I passed them. One of them cursed with gusto, trying to get a reaction. I laughed softly and rode on.

If we did have a rogue Master of the Dead on our hands, then I had absolutely no idea how to ferret him out. Maybe if I had a big box leaning on a stake, and tied one of Ghastek's vampires under it . . .

We arrived at Rufus and turned north, heading toward the White Street. It was named for the snowfall of '14, when three inches of fine powder covered the street's ugly asphalt. Three inches of snow was not terribly unusual for Atlanta except that it had come in May and refused to melt in the following months despite the hundred-degree heat. Three and a half years later it finally gave in and thawed during an Indian summer.

I reached the corner and halted. The twisted form of Ghastek's vampire perched on top of a lamppost, wound about it like a snake around a tree limb. It looked at me, its eyes glowing with dim red, betraying an influx of magic. Ghastek was concentrating hard to hold it in place.

"Problems?" I asked softly.

"Interference." Ghastek's voice sounded like it came through clenched teeth. Someone was trying to wrestle away his control over the vamp.

I freed Slayer and laid it across Frau's back. The metal smoked. A thin sheen of moisture glistened on its surface. It could be reacting to Ghastek's vamp or to something else.

Behind me Derek's gelding neighed gently.

"Don't get off your horse," I said.

As long as Derek stayed in the saddle, he would remember to act human.

I dismounted and tied the horse to an iron fence. Ghastek's vamp uncoiled from the lamppost and slid soundlessly to the ground. It took a few unsure staggering steps into the intersection.

"Ghastek, where are you going?"

A cart drawn by a couple of horses thundered down the street at breakneck speed. The horses spied the vamp and shied, jerking the cart to the side, but not far enough. The cart's right wheel smashed into the vampire with a loud meaty thump, flinging it aside. The driver spat a curse and snapped the reins, forcing the horses into a frenzied gallop, rumbling down the street and vanishing in the space of a breath.

The vamp lay still in a pitiful crumpled heap.

How convenient.

Slayer in hand, I stepped into the street. "Ghastek?" I called softly.

I circled it, sword in hand. An ugly grimace froze the vampire's face. Its left foot twitched.

"Ghastek?"

A faint hiss tugged on my attention. I turned. Nothing. A small drop of liquid luminescence slid off my blade and fell onto the asphalt.

A blast of icy terror hit me like a sledgehammer. I whirled, lashing out on instinct, and felt the saber graze flesh as a grotesque shape plummeted at me from above. The creature twisted away from the sword in midair and landed softly to the side.

Derek's horse screamed and galloped into the night, carrying him off.

I backed away toward Ghastek's fallen vamp. The thing followed me on all fours. It was a vampire, but one so ancient that no trace of it having walked upright remained. The bones of its spine and hips had permanently shifted to adapt to quadruped locomotion.

The creature advanced, lean and wiry like a greyhound. An inch-high bone crest shielded its spine, formed by outgrowth of the vertebrae through the leather-thick skin. It paused, hugged the ground for a moment, and rose again, ruby-red eyes fixed on me.

Its face no longer bore any resemblance to a human. The skull jutted back in a bony hornlike curve to balance the horribly massive protruding jaws. The creature had no nose, not even a hint of the nose bridge. It opened its mouth, splitting its head in half. Rows of fangs gleamed against the blackness. It wouldn't just puncture and rip; it would shred me.

The creature's eyes focused on me. The owl-like pupils gleamed with red.

It leaped with inhuman speed. I aimed for the throat and missed, my blade sinking to the hilt into its shoulder. The thing swept me off my feet. I hit the ground hard. My head bounced off the pavement, and the world swam. Pressure ground into my chest, forcing the air from my lungs. I strained and sent a jolt of my power through Slayer's blade.

The saber's hilt was jerked from my hand and the pressure vanished. I sucked in a lungful of air and scrambled to my feet, the throwing knife in my hand.

The creature shivered a dozen feet away, dazed and uncertain. The thin blade of my saber protruded from its back. Two inches lower and to the left, and I would've hit its heart. The shoulder jerked, twisted by a powerful spasm as Slayer ground deep into the muscle seeking the heart. The flesh around the blade softened like melted wax.

The creature's head snapped, and it whipped around to face me. Two more inches. It would take Slayer at least three minutes to burrow that deep into the flesh. I had to survive for three minutes.

No problem.

I hurled my dagger. The tip of the blade bounced off the bony ridge just above the left orbit. Spectacular.

The creature leaped, sailing easily across the twelve feet separating us, and a furry shape smashed into it in midflight. They rolled, the vampire and the werewolf, one snarling, the other hissing. I chased them. For a moment Derek pinned the bloodsucker, his claws fastened into the vampire's gut, and then the vampire raked at the werewolf and shrugged him off.

I lunged. It didn't expect me to attack, and I delivered a clean kick to its shoulder. It was like kicking a marble column. I heard the bone crunch and hammered two quick thrusts to its neck. The creature swept at me, tearing at my clothes, in a whirlwind of teeth and claws. I parried the best I could. No sound issued from the monster's mouth. A claw raked at me. A hot whip of pain stung my ribs and my stomach. The fangs snapped an inch from my face. I jerked back, expecting the horrid maw to engulf me, but the vamp let go and took a step backward.

A set of new vampire arms was growing from its back. It spun, flailing, and I saw Ghastek's vampire clinging to its neck.

The bloodsucker rode the monster's back, clawing at the massive neck. The creature tore at the arms and reared. Derek clutched its hind legs. The vamp kicked, but Derek clung to him. I took a running start and hammered a kick into the vampire's ruined chest. Bone crunched. The vampire's flesh tore like an overfilled water sack, releasing a torrent of foul-smelling liquid.

The creature shrieked for the first time, an enraged, grating sound. The veins under its pallid hide bulged and its eyes smoldered deep blood-red, illuminating its face. It had sustained too much damage and was about to succumb to bloodlust, breaking from its master's control. It flung Ghastek's vampire away like a terrier flings a rat. Derek kept clawing at it, oblivious.

"Get away from it!" I kicked the werewolf. He snarled, furious, and I kicked him again. He let go and came at me, growling. I shoved him aside.

The creature screamed again and again, its body twisting, warping, as muscles knotted and snapped. Bony spikes pierced its shoulders, curving from its frame like horns. It reared and pawed at the ground, leaving cuts in the asphalt. I could see Slayer's blade through the hole in its chest.

The vampire charged me. It came with astonishing speed, impossible to stop. It smashed into me, and I grabbed Slayer's hilt and thrust with everything I had. We hit the asphalt and skidded until we crashed into a wall.

Good thing it was in our way. We might have kept going.

I lay very still. The creature's blood surged from its ruptured heart, drenching me. Colored circles blocked my view. Gradually I became aware of two eyes glowing gentle yellow above the vampire's shoulder. I blinked, bringing the furry nightmare of a face into focus.

"You okay?" My voice sounded hoarse.

With a short growling noise, Derek swiped the corpse off me and pulled me to my feet. "Thank you," I said.

Derek was bleeding. A long gash marred his right leg and jagged claw marks seared his shoulder. He saw me looking and snarled, swinging away, so I couldn't see his hip. I was bleeding, too. Fire bathed my waist, and it hurt to bend forward.

I put my foot onto the vamp and pulled out Slayer. It came away easily, the flesh enclosing the blade liquefied by its magic. Positioning myself, I swung the saber and sliced through the creature's neck. The deformed head rolled. I picked it up. The fire had gone out of its eyes. They looked empty. Dead.

Drenched in foul-smelling blood and hurting, I looked for Frau. Through all that, the mare stayed put. I couldn't believe it. I started toward her, stumbling a little. Walking, for some odd reason, proved to be troublesome. Halfway to Frau I changed my course and aimed for Ghastek's vamp instead.

The vamp lay on its stomach, its face toward me. I put the head down in front of it and tapped it with my finger.

"I guess that settles it. How old is it, Ghastek? Three hundred years? More?"

The vamp struggled to say something.

I shook my head. "Don't bother. I'll find out. Thanks for your help. You can tell Nataraja he can take his security and shove it."

The vamp moved its hand, clamping onto my foot. Gently I took the hand off my bloodstained shoe, stepped over it, and headed to the horse.

Derek stared at the bloodsucker with malice.

"Let him be. We need to get out, before the People's cleanup crew gets here."

I patted Frau and jammed the head into the saddlebag. The mare snorted, offended by the awful smell. "I'm sorry, sweetheart."

I took down a large army-issue waterproof bag. "Gasoline," I told Derek as if he couldn't smell it.

I splashed it over the spill, threw the bag aside, and reached for my matches. My fingers shook. I struck one match, then another, on the fourth the gasoline flared. Ghastek's vamp screeched as his evidence and my blood went up in smoke.

I walked Frau into the night and my loyal wolf followed me, limping.

WHEN WE REACHED THE DEAD-RAT-WIELDING KIDS, Derek collapsed. He fell forward, snout first into the asphalt. The kids stared, startled, but didn't bolt.

A soft shudder went through the werewolf, releasing a mist,

and leaving the naked human body curled on the ground. The kids looked on.

The gash on his thigh was deeper than I had thought. The creature's claws had severed the thick muscle shield of the quadriceps and cut deep into the calf. I peered into the wound and saw the shredded femoral artery. The injured flesh quivered. Torn blood vessels crawled toward each other amidst the muscle starting to knit together. The Lyc-V had shut his consciousness down to save energy for repairs.

Pain lanced my waist, tearing up into my chest. Gritting my teeth, I turned Derek on his stomach, worked one arm under his hips and threaded the other across his chest under his arms. He was heavier than he looked, weighing in at one fifty, maybe one fifty-five. No matter.

"Hey, lady!" said the kid with feathers in his hair.

The children stood huddled together. We must have made quite a spectacle, Derek, nude and no longer furry, and I, drenched in blood, with my sword still smoking in its sheath.

"You need some help?" the kid said.

"Yeah," I said, my voice hoarse.

He came forward, picked up Derek's feet, and looked back at his pack. "Mike."

Mike spat to the side and tried to look mean.

The kid with the feathers glared at him. "Mike!"

Mike spat again, for show—there wasn't much spit left—came over, and awkwardly clutched Derek's shoulders.

"Hold him under the armpits," I said.

He glanced at me, fear dancing in his eyes, set his jaw, and shifted his grip.

"On three," I muttered. "Three."

We heaved. The world swayed in the whirlwind of pain and then Derek was draped across Frau's back. He would be fine.

Lyc-V would repair him and tomorrow morning he'd be like new. I, on the other hand . . . A wet bloodstain was spreading from under my jacket at an alarming rate. If the blood started dripping, I'd be in a world of trouble. At least I still hurt.

"Thanks," I muttered to the children.

"My name's Red," the kid with feathers said.

I stuck my hand into the pocket of my pants. My fingers found a card. I handed it to him, careful to wipe the bloody smudge marring it on my sleeve. Not my blood. Derek's.

"If you ever need help," I said.

He took it solemnly and nodded.

THE STAIRS WERE DARK AS HELL.

I climbed, the steady pressure of Derek's body distributed over my back. If I bent over just right, the pain was bearable, and so I dragged Derek and the bag up the stairs one step at a time, trying to keep my angle steady and being careful where I put my feet. I wasn't certain if a werewolf could survive a broken neck. I knew I couldn't.

I paused on the landing to catch a breath and glanced up at my apartment's door.

A man sat on the stairs, his head leaning against the wall.

Gently I lowered Derek to the floor and went for my sword. The man's chest rose and fell in a smooth, even rhythm. I padded up the stairs, breathing through clenched teeth, until I could see his face. Crest. He didn't wake.

I tapped his head with the flat of Slayer's blade. When I awoke, I did so instantly and silently, my hand looking for my sword before my eyelids snapped open. Crest awoke like a man unused to danger, with luxurious slowness. He blinked and stifled a yawn, squinting at me.

I gave him a moment to recognize me.

"Kate?"

"What are you doing here?"

"I came to pick you up for dinner. We had a date."

Shit. I had completely forgotten about the date.

"I got held up until ten," he went on. "I called you but you didn't answer. It was too late by then, but I figured I'd drop by with a peace offering." He held up a paper bag full of white cartons, decorated with a stylized Chinese symbol in red ink. "You weren't here. I thought I'd wait a couple of minutes, sat down here on the stairs . . ." His brain finally registered my bloodied clothes, the sword, and the smudges of dried blood marring my face. His eyes widened.

"Are you okay?"

"I'll live."

I unlocked the door to the apartment, opening the ward.

"There is a naked man on the landing," I said hoping to forestall any upcoming questions. "I'm going to carry him into this apartment."

Crest threw the Chinese food into the apartment hallway and went down the stairs to get Derek without saying a word. Together we brought him inside and put him on the hallway carpet. I shut the door in the world's face and let out a breath.

I kicked off my shoes and turned the lantern switch. My shoes were bloody again. Oh well, nothing a lot of bleach wouldn't fix.

The tiny flames of feylanterns surged up, bathing the apartment in a comforting soft glow. Crest knelt to examine Derek's leg.

"He needs emergency care," he said. His voice had the brisk, professional, slightly distant tone good physicians adopted under stress.

"No, he doesn't."

He glanced at me. "Kate, the cut's deep and dirty and the artery's probably severed. He'll bleed to death."

Dizziness came, and I swayed a little. I wanted to sit down, but couches and chairs were harder to bleach than shoes. "He isn't bleeding."

Crest opened his mouth and looked back at the wound. "Shit."

"The Lycos Virus in action," I told him and went to the kitchen. There was no ready ice and scraping the freezer walls wasn't in me right that minute, so I put the bag into the sink and pulled off my shredded jacket in a flash of pain. The top underneath was soaked with blood. I tried removing it but it was stuck. I rummaged through the everything drawer for scissors, found some, and tried to cut off the vest.

The scissors got caught in the soggy fabric. I cursed and then Crest was beside me, his hand over the scissors. "I remembered you didn't have the Lyc-V," he said and the vest fell to the floor in a sodden, heavy mass.

He knelt to examine the jagged claw marks on my stomach.

"How bad?" I asked.

"Mostly shallow. Two deep lacerations, here and here." His finger grazed the skin lightly and still I winced.

"Hurts."

"I'd imagine. Would you like me to take *you* to the emergency room?"

"No. There is an r-kit on the table in the living room," I said. With magic this high, a regeneration-kit was almost as good as the spell doc. It cost an arm and a leg, but it was worth it. And its magic healed with very little scarring.

He looked at me. "Are you sure? We'd get it stitched in no time."

"I'm sure."

He went to get it. The trouble with regeneration-kits was that sometimes, like all things magic, they backfired and ate into the wound instead of healing it.

I shrugged off my pants, my panties, and my bra on the way to the bathroom and stepped into the shower. The water ran bloody. My stomach hurt. When blood no longer swirled around my feet, I shut off the shower and yelled for Crest to come in. He did, carrying the roll of brown paper.

"Do you know how to use one of those?" I asked.

"I *am* an M.D."

"Some M.D.s want nothing to do with the r-kits."

"You're not giving me a choice about it," he said. "Raise your arms."

I put my arms to my head and chanted the incantation. Crest untied the cord securing the paper and unrolled it. It contained a bandage and a long wide strip, smeared with brown ointment and covered with waxed paper. Crest peeled the paper off and held the strip by its edges. I chanted. The ointment on the strip obeyed, liquefying. A strong smell of nutmeg spread through the room.

Crest pressed the strip against my stomach. It adhered and a soothing coolness spread through my injured muscles, slowly transforming into warmth that suffused my stomach, drowning out pain.

"Better," I murmured. Crest bandaged my waist. After putting in a long day at work this seemingly normal guy would come all this way just to see me. Why? What would it be like to crawl home after a hard day and instead of licking my wounds in solitude in a dark and empty house, find him? On the couch, maybe. Reading a book. Maybe he would put it down and say, "I'm glad you've made it. Would you like some coffee?"

His hand grazed the tattoo on my shoulder. "Why a raven?"

"To honor my father."

The fingers continued to gently slide across my skin. "The writing under it, is that Cyrillic?"

"Yes."

"What does it say?"

"*Dar Vorona.* Gift of the Raven. I'm my father's gift."

"To whom?"

"That, my dear doctor, is a story for another time."

"The raven is holding a bloody sword," Crest said thoughtfully.

"I never said it was a nice gift."

He finished the bandage and was examining it critically. "You know those things are unreliable." His voice held just a touch of reproach.

"Eleven out of twelve work fine. I'd say that's better chances than getting an orgasm with a blind date, and women still try."

He blinked and laughed softly. "I never know what you'll say next."

"I don't either."

He rose and put his arms around me. So warm. I resisted the impulse to lean back against him. "Are you hungry?"

"Ravenous," I murmured.

"The food's probably cold by now."

"I don't care."

He kissed my neck. The kiss sent tingling warmth down into my fingertips. I turned and he kissed me again, on the mouth. I was so tired . . . I wanted to melt against him and let him hold me. "You're trying to take advantage of an injured naked woman."

"I know," he whispered in my ear, drawing me closer. "How awful."

Please don't let go. What am I thinking? Am I this desperate? I took a deep breath and pushed away from him gently. "I have to finish my work. I don't think you want to watch me."

"Do it after," he whispered and kissed me again. Somehow instead of breaking free, I pressed against him. I wanted nothing more than to stay wrapped up in him like this, smelling his scent, feeling his lips on mine . . . And then the vampire's head would lose the last of its magic and Derek and I would've bled for nothing. Poor Derek. "No," I said, my face a grimace. "By then it'll be too late."

"Work first. I see."

"Tonight. Not always."

"I'll watch," he said.

"You don't want to, trust me."

"It's part of what you do. I want to know."

Why? I shrugged and went to the bedroom to find some clothes. He didn't follow me.

IN THE KITCHEN I SET A LARGE SILVER TRAY IN THE MIDdle of the table. Supported by four legs, it rose above the surface of the table about three inches. Greg had kept an excellent supply of herbs in his apartment. Having combined them in the right proportions, I spread the aromatic mixture on the platter so it covered the metal completely. Crest sat on the chair in a corner and watched me.

I pulled the strings of the bag, took the head out, and placed the monstrosity onto the powder, balancing it on the stump of the neck.

"What the hell is that?"

"A vampire," I said.

"I've seen pictures. They don't look like that."

"It's very old. My guess is, at least a couple of centuries. Undeath brings certain anatomical changes. Some are immediate and some are slow. The older the undead, the more apparent those changes become. A vamp's never finished. It's an abomination in progress." The fact that vampires weren't suppose to have existed two hundred years ago when the tech was in full swing bothered me a great deal. My experience and education offered no explanation for this monster's existence, and so I put it aside, filing it for future reference.

I brought out a shallow glass pan, the kind used for baking lasagna, put it in front of the platter and slightly under, and dumped two quarts of glycerin into it. The clear viscous liquid filled the pan and settled.

I took one of my throwing daggers from my sheath. Crest grinned at the black blade.

"Fancy."

"Yeah."

This wasn't going to be pleasant and it wasn't the kind of magic I did often. Something in me rebelled at it, something born of my father's instruction and my own view of the world and where I stood in it.

The head rested on the herbs. In half an hour it would be useless.

I pricked my finger with the point of the dagger. A drop of bright blood swelled on the skin. Power pulsed in it and I touched the blood to the herbs. The bloodmagic inundated them, acting like a catalyst, fusing, shaping, molding the natural force of the dried plants. It surged upward, through the stump of the neck, spreading through the capillaries in the face, engulfing the brain, saturating the dead flesh. I guided it, helped it along, until the entire head sat suffused with magic. My finger touched the thick skin of the vamp's forehead, leaving a bloody smudge and sending a shock of power through the undead flesh.

"Wake!"

The dead eyes snapped open. The horrid mouth opened and closed soundlessly, contorting with impossible elasticity.

Crest fell off his chair.

The vamp's eyes stared wide at me, unblinking.

"Where is your master? Show me your master."

Dark magic boiled from the head, drowning the room. It swelled, vicious and furious, like an enraged animal ready to strike. In the corner Crest drew a sharp, loud breath.

A tremor rippled through the head. The eyeballs bulged from their sockets. The black tongue, long and flat, hung from between the reptilian lips and the sickle teeth bit into it, drawing no blood. Impaled on the teeth, the tongue jerked obscenely. I pushed harder, bringing the weight of my power upon the resilient necromagic.

"Show me your master!"

Red drowned the whites of the vampire's eyes. Two thick streaks of dark blood poured from what had once been tear ducts. The streams carved their paths down the face and into the herbs, mixing with a torrent of blood from the stump of the neck. The foul flood swept the dried herbs, falling into the glycerin and spreading in an uneven angry stain upon its surface. The blood darkened until it was almost black, and in it I saw a distorted but unmistakable image of a gutted skyscraper with a round Coca-Cola logo half-buried in rubble.

Unicorn Lane. Always Unicorn Lane.

The head jerked. The bones of the skull cracked like a broken nutshell. The flesh peeled off the vamp's face, curving in long slabs to the herbs. The exposed jellied mass of the brain glared through the fractured skull. The stench of putrescence filled the kitchen. I threw a plastic trash bag over the head and inverted the tray, sending the head and the herbs into the bag. I tied the bag and set it into the corner. The blood in the glycerin had clotted into an ugly rotting mass. I dumped it down the drain.

Crest rubbed his face.

"I did warn you."

He nodded.

I washed my hands and my arms up to the elbow with fresh-smelling soap and went into the living room, pausing on the way to check on Derek. He was sleeping like a baby. I sat on the couch, leaned back, and closed my eyes. This was the point when most men ran for cover.

I sat and rested. The desire for intimacy had passed and my longing now appeared unreal, ethereal like a half-forgotten dream.

I heard Crest walk into the room. He sat next to me.

"So that's what you do?" he said.

"Yeah."

We sat silent for a few breaths.

"I can live with it," he said.

I opened my eyes and looked at him. He shrugged. "I'm not going to watch again, but I can live with it." He leaned forward, resting his elbows on his knees. "Have you ever met someone and felt . . . I don't know how to describe it, felt a chance at having something that eluded you? I don't know . . . Forget I said anything."

I knew what he meant. He was describing that moment when you realize that you are lonely. For a time you can be alone and doing fine and never give a thought to living any other way and then you meet someone and suddenly you become lonely. It stabs at you, almost like a physical pain, and you feel both deprived and angry, deprived because you wish to be with that person, and angry because their absence brings you misery. It's a strange feeling, akin to desperation, a feeling that makes you wait by the phone even though you know that the call is an hour away. I was not going to lose my balance. Not yet.

I moved closer to him and leaned against his shoulder. We both knew that sex was out of the question.

"Do you mind if I stay anyway?" he asked.

"No."

I fell asleep leaning on him.

CHAPTER 6

I AWOKE BECAUSE SOMEONE WAS WATCHING ME.

"Don't you know it's not polite to stare, boy wonder?"

Derek gave Crest a derisive glance. The boy wonder was wearing sweats I didn't recognize. They didn't come from Greg's wardrobe. He must've gone out. Where exactly did he go?

During the night we had moved into a somewhat reclining position and I was lying on Crest's chest. I sat straight. "You disapprove?"

He shook his head. "It isn't my place."

"You don't like him all the same, though."

"He and you . . ." he made a put-together motion with his hands, fingers spread coming together but not quite touching. "You don't look right together."

"Why not?"

"You're harder than he is."

"What's wrong with that?"

"The man's supposed to be harder. So he can protect."

"Do you think I'm in need of protection?" The threatening overtone crept into my voice without intention.

"He will never tell you no," Derek said.

I stared at him until he lowered his gaze.

"Very few people tell me no," I said.

"Yeah."

"How's your leg?"

"Fine."

"Did you go out while I slept?"

"Yeah. Just a short jog."

"Maybe you should go for another one."

He left without saying a word. I woke Crest. "Time to go."

He rubbed his face with his palms. "Did I oversleep?"

"It's six thirty."

"Time enough to get home and change clothes. When will I see you again?"

I thought of the Coca-Cola logo half-buried in rubble and a two-hundred-year-old vampire. *Maybe never.*

"How about on Friday? Gives us a couple of days to cool off."

"It's Friday then."

He left. He didn't kiss me again.

I PRIED OPEN THE PAPER CONTAINER OF GENERAL TSO'S chicken and touched a piece with my finger. It was room temperature. The thought of dumping it into a pan and warming it to an edible temperature crossed my mind, but heating it on the stove would make the vegetables mushy and I hated overcooked vegetables. My father, a great believer in the nutritional properties of boiled vegetables and meat broth, had cooked hearty, hot soups. The memory of him watching in distress as I gagged on soft cabbage and half-dissolved onion flashed before my eyes. I smiled at the carton and extracted a fork from the kitchen drawer. Hot food was overrated anyway.

I speared a piece of chicken with my fork, carefully avoiding the lump of green pepper. Suddenly I was ravenous.

Someone knocked.

I paused, the chicken halfway to my mouth, and glared at the door. The knocking persisted. It wasn't Derek. His knock would be careful, almost apologetic. This bastard knocked like he was doing me a favor.

I looked at the chicken, glanced to the door, stuffed a whole piece into my mouth, and went to see who dared to make demands on my time.

The door swung open, revealing Curran. He wore old jeans and a green sweatshirt, and carried a brown paper sack. He raised his face and sucked air in through his nostrils in the manner of shapechangers. "Tso's, seafood delight, and fried rice," he said. "You're going to share?"

I leaned against the wall. The door was open but the ward still blocked his entrance, affording me a bit of leisure. "Oh, it's you." I dug in the container with my fork. "I thought it was somebody important."

Curran stepped forward, brushing against the ward. A flash of carmine rippled through the magic barrier and the lord of shapechangers withdrew.

"A ward," he said.

"A good one."

He put his palm against the ward and pushed. Red pulsed from his fingers, spreading through the ward like waves from a pebble tossed into a quiet pond.

"I can break it," Curran said.

I raised an eyebrow at him. "Be my guest."

Shapechangers had a natural resistance to wards, so his promise had some substance. Still, I had reinforced all of Greg's wards. If Curran did break it, the resonance from the collapse would give me one hell of a migraine, but I doubted he could. It was a good ward.

He considered it. I could see it in his eyes, and for a moment I thought he would try it. Then he shrugged. "I could break it, or we can be civil and you can let me in."

Getting tired of power demonstrations, are we, Your Majesty? I unlocked the ward. A wave of silver rolled from the top of the doorframe to dissipate on the floor. "Come on in."

He strode toward the kitchen and stopped halfway, his face a snarl. "What the hell do you have in your pantry, a dead vampire?"

"No. Only the head of one." I had double-bagged the head, sealing it in plastic, and still he smelled it.

I perched on the edge of the table and nodded toward the gathering of white cartons. "Help yourself. There's fried rice in there somewhere."

He put his paper bag on the floor, picked a carton indistinguishable from any other, took the spoon I offered him, and popped the carton open. "Peas," he said with disgust. "Why the hell do they always put peas in it?"

"So what brought you here so bright and early?"

He used his spoon to pick out the peas with great care, depositing them into the trash. "Heard that you got something."

"Boy wonder snitched on me?"

"Yeah."

"When? This morning?"

Curran nodded. "It's the blood oath. For example, if he were to get his leg ripped to shreds, it's his duty to warn us that he can no longer guard you to the best of his ability. Someone had to come and assess the situation."

"Since when is 'someone' you? Don't you have plenty of flunkies to run your errands?"

He shrugged. "Just checking on the kid."

"Last night his leg looked like it went through a shredder. He won't let me look at it, but I think the bone is intact." A shapechanger's body healed the flesh wounds within a couple of days. Mending bones took much longer.

Curran swallowed a mouthful of rice. "Figures. He's young. It's important to be stoic when you're a young guy. You didn't fuss over him, did you?"

"No. He should be limping in pretty soon."

"You're going to show me what screwed up his leg?"

"After I'm done eating."

"Weak stomach?"

"No. It's a pain in the ass to wrap it back up."

A careful, measured knock interrupted us. I went to open the door and let Derek inside. He saw Curran and stopped. He wasn't exactly at attention, but he came close.

Curran waved him in, and Derek took a chair out of the way. I looked at Curran. "Any more rice in there?"

He chose another container and gave it to me. I opened it and pushed it toward Derek. "Eat."

He waited.

He had to be ravenous. The amount of calories his body burned to repair itself ensured that the mere hint of food filled his mouth with drool.

"Derek, eat," I said.

He smiled and sat still.

Something was wrong here. I glanced at Curran and put two and two together.

"This is *my* house."

They both looked at me with the patient expression Japanese traditionalists adopt when silly *gajin* ask them why they go through all that trouble just to drink a cup of tea.

"He doesn't eat until I tell him or until I'm done," Curran said. "Doesn't matter whose house it is."

I set my chicken on the table and crossed my arms. I could argue the point with them until I turned purple in the face and neither would relent. The low-ranking wolves didn't feed before their Pack King. It was the way of the Code. They lived by its rules or they lost their humanity.

Curran put another spoonful into his mouth. Time stretched as he chewed the food. Derek sat still. The urge to slap Curran was almost too much for me.

The Beast Lord scraped the bottom of his container, licked the spoon, reached over the table and took away Derek's rice, replacing it with the brown paper sack he had brought. Derek glanced into the sack and retrieved a bundle of waxed paper tied with a cord. He snapped the cord and unwrapped the bundle. A five-pound shoulder roast looked back at him.

Curran jerked his head toward the hallway. "Don't make a spectacle of yourself."

Derek rose, gathering the roast, and disappeared into the depths of the apartment. I glared at Curran.

"I like fried rice," he said with a shrug. He slid the spoon under the paper flaps of the other small paper box, forced them open, and proceeded to pick out the peas.

The low rumble of a predator feeding came from within the apartment.

"Keep it down," Curran said without raising his voice.

The snarling died.

"So what do you have?"

I sketched it out for him, concluding with the vamp's head. The undead flesh had liquefied over night, turning into putrid black goo. The stench of rot was so strong that by the time I opened the second trash bag both the Beast Lord and I were gagging in a most undignified manner. Curran took one look at the distorted skull and tied the bag shut.

"Should've done it before we ate," he observed when we managed to secure the head.

"Yeah." I opened the window, letting a gust of cold wind into the kitchen.

"So you're planning on taking this on by yourself? No backup?"

"No."

"Going to notify the cops?"

I grimaced. It had nagged at me since I awoke. To go to the cops would mean bringing in the Paranormal Activity Division, and as soon as the Division gave the MSDU their mandatory notification, the military would try to step in and eat the whole pie by themselves. The Division would cry jurisdiction and the whole thing could stretch for several days. By then my friendly nemesis could be gone or worse, he could have gained leadership of the People. The fact that I had a lot of assumptions and a strange skull wouldn't exactly make the authorities abandon the departmental rivalry and hurry on my account.

The Guild would offer no assistance. There was no money involved, and if I as much as squeaked to the Order that some asshole tried to start a war between the Pack and the People, and herded two-hundred-year-old vampires to do it, Ted would take me off the case faster than I could exhale. On the other hand, trying to confront a rogue Master of the Dead by myself was suicide. I was homicidal but not stupid.

I became aware that Curran was watching me. "I don't know," I said.

"I can solve that problem for you," he said. He was offering the Pack's resources. I would be crazy not to take him up on that offer.

I bent an eyebrow at him. "Why?"

"Because I have sixty-three rats who buried their alpha three days ago. They've been howling for blood, while I've been sitting around with my thumb up my ass."

"That's a big risk to take just for the sake of appearances."

He shrugged. "Power is all about appearances. Besides, who knows? It did snow in May once, so even you could be right."

I let the barb go. "And if I'm not?"

"Then at least I've tried."

It made sense in an odd way. "Who'll come?"

"A few people."

"Jim?"

"No."

"Why?"

"Because someone from the Council has to stay behind to hold the Pack together if I die. The alpha-wolf has hurt himself, and Mahon stayed behind the last time. The new alpha-rat doesn't have enough experience."

"What happened to the alpha-wolf?"

"LEGOs."

"Legos?" It sounded Greek but I couldn't recall anything mythological with that name. Wasn't it an island?

"He was carrying a load of laundry into the basement and tripped on the old set of LEGOs his kids left on the stairs. Broke two ribs and an ankle. He'll be out of commission for two weeks."

Curran shook his head. "He picked a hell of a time. If I didn't need him, I'd kill him."

I ARRIVED AT THE COCA-COLA BUILDING UNMOLESTED and hid in the shadowy alcove of an abandoned phone booth, half a block from the ruined skyscraper. The logo lay partially buried in the remains of what must have been a magnificent building in its time—even now its skeleton covered the entire block. It had been only ten years old when the flair, a freakishly strong magic fluctuation, took it down.

The shapechangers were nowhere in sight. Across the street a ravaged building careened amidst waist-tall heaps of dusty broken glass. Good place to hide. It took me a minute to find a gap in the crumbling wall. I squeezed through and found fiery eyes glaring at me.

They were battle ready. Pink and black tongues licked mismatched jaws and huge teeth, and long claws made faint scraping noises on the concrete floor. Eight pairs of eyes sought prey, fueled by hunger. The primitive savage of my subconscious howled and yelped in terror.

"Oh, it's you," Curran's voice said quietly. "I thought it was an elephant."

"Don't mind him," murmured a lean shape to the left. "He was born rude." A lupine female in a midform. That bordered on cheeky. She was either his main squeeze or the female alpha of the wolves.

An enormous shaggy Kodiak bear towered to the left, a dark mountain of fur and muscle, his muzzle light with old scars. Mahon had changed all the way. Next to him rose something huge, almost eight feet tall. Vaguely humanoid in shape, it stood on two columnar furry legs. Hard muscle corded its frame, and a shaggy, grayish mane crowned the head and the back of the massive neck. Long stripes crisscrossed its chest, faint like the smoke marks on the pelt of a panther.

I glanced at its face, and the power in its gold eyes rooted me to the floor. Goose flesh marked my limbs. I couldn't move. It could have pounced on me and I couldn't have done anything to stop it. The mammoth muscles of its neck bulged as it rolled its head one way, then another, stretching. The twin pads of its upper lip split, revealing three-inch-long canines. The monster licked his lips, long lines of whiskers twitching, and spoke in a deep growl. "Pretty, aren't I?"

Curran. In midform. I broke from his gaze. "Adorable."

The nightmare made a barely perceptible nod, and a ratman scuttled forward with superhuman agility and leaped, finding purchase on sheer wall. Up he went to the gap twelve feet above the floor and dove through it. The scout was off.

Curran turned and walked to the wall, where a long crack split the side of the decrepit building. A furry, taloned hand hit the crumbling barrier, and the wall exploded outward, pelting the street with concrete and rock dust. The King of the Beasts ducked through the opening he had made and we followed, single file.

CURRAN HALTED. TO HIS LEFT THE BEAR RUMBLED TO A stop. To the right, Jennifer, the female alpha-wolf, carefully put her clawed foot down into the grime and stood still. We froze in silence, a scattering of bizarre statues in the Gorgon's backyard, waiting for something I couldn't see or hear.

The stench of death was overwhelming.

We stood in a wide foyer, its once polished tiled floor now a dusty mess of dirt and rubble. Massive cracks creased the filthy walls, growing into dark uneven holes. To the left a wide fissure slashed through the floor. Ahead rock dust and garbage choked the once splendid staircase. The new Coca-Cola building was on its last breath.

The faint sound of claws scuttling on stone came from the left. A pair of red-coal eyes blazed from the darkness of a crack in the concrete wall, and the sleek furry shape of the ratman filled the gap and dropped to the floor. While the werewolves were nightmarish, the ratman leaned toward repulsive. Thin and shaggy, he was covered with dark fur, except for the face, forearms, and wood-hard calves, where the exposed skin was light pink and looked soft, almost human. He had huge feet and hands, the size resulting from the long, large-knuckled digits tipped with sharp claws. The beginnings of a misshapen rodent muzzle guarded the mouth, filled with uneven yellowish teeth. Jerky, quick twitches troubled the ratman as he moved, and his human eyes darted to glare in random directions.

The ratman closed the distance to Curran in short, rapid leaps, his paws raising small clouds of dust from the foyer floor.

"Dourrnstahrs," he said, his horrid jaws crippling the word. "Big roum."

He offered something white to Curran. The Beast Lord took the object into his massive hand, glanced at it, and tossed the thing to me. I caught it. A human femur. Someone with sharp teeth and a lot of persistence had stripped away the cartilage that once sheathed its ends, leaving narrow scratches on the shaft. I turned it, trying to make the most of the dim moonlight filtering through the fissures in the walls and the crooked arch of the entrance. Stripes of smoother, glossy connective tissue crossed the bone in two places—the mark of the Lyc-V knitting the shaft together after it had been broken. I held the femur of a shapechanger.

The ratman scuttled across the foyer to the gap in the floor, and we followed. The fissure ran some ten feet in length and about three feet wide at the widest place. I leaned over the edge and peered into it. There was a clear drop to the floor, sixteen feet below.

Behind me the Bear made a rumbling noise. Curran nodded and the enormous Kodiak turned away. He would never fit.

One by one the shapechangers dove into the gap, until I alone stood by the edge. I sat on the filthy floor, swinging my legs into the hole, lowered myself, shortening the distance as much as I could, and dropped down. The hard shock of landing on the stone floor resonated into my feet and died.

Nobody waited for me. The shapechangers had departed. How nice.

Ahead, a long tunnel, narrow and dark, offered a faint glow. Behind me the remains of an underground garage stretched into the distance. I turned to the tunnel and trotted down, careful to leap over the concrete boulders littering the floor.

The tunnel ended, opening into a large room, of which I could see very little since a gathering of furry, muscled backs blocked my view. The warm glow came from the torches, thrust into rungs in the walls. They burned with smokeless white fire that had to be magic. The ceiling rose impossibly high, decorated with plaster molded into ornamental design. The floor may have been parquet at one point.

Some sort of banquet hall.

A woman spoke, her voice harsh and laced with metal. "Welcome to the end of your journey, half-breed. Here you will die like the rest of your kind."

A half-breed? What an odd thing to call a shapechanger. I moved to Jennifer's side and saw the Master of the Dead. Or rather, the Mistress. She stood in the center of the room, straight and rigid as a mast, wearing a flowing dress that started off white around her shoulders, transmuting into blue around her waist, darkening to a deeper purple and finally blazing blood-red at the hem. Her hair, long and glossy black, was knotted into a complex plait and tied with long stringy twine. A cascade of small plastic beads hung from the twine. I looked closely. On second look, they probably weren't plastic. Few people made plastic beads in the shape of human finger bones.

I felt no power emanating from her. No shadow, no hint, nothing, except her age. She felt older than Nataraja.

"I am Olathe," she said with the same gravity Greek gods must have used to introduce themselves to their mortal children. "The Mistress of the Dead. The favored concubine of Roland, the Father of the People."

Alrighty then.

"Care to repeat that?" Curran said. His voice was a deep snarl, but his diction was perfect. "I missed the part where I was supposed to be impressed."

Olathe looked down on him. Not easy to do considering he was nearly two feet taller than her. She may have been Roland's concubine but it had cost her: once probably beautiful, she looked worn-out, like an old manikin whose grimy paint had begun to peel. He had drained all of her vivacity, her spark, her humor. Only the eyes remained alive on the soulless face: huge, prideful, and driven.

Something shifted behind her in the shadows of the far wall. A twisted silhouette, then another, and another. I reached toward it with my magic, felt the cold wall of her defenses, and withdrew. No need to provoke her before Curran was ready.

"I'm curious, how long did he fuck you?" Curran strode forward, one enormous foot padding after another. The shapechangers followed him. "How long did you last? A year? Six months?"

"Thirteen years," she said.

Curran kept moving forward. The longer he kept talking, the closer to her we would get. He was going out of his way to be offensive, although for him it didn't take much effort. "Thirteen years. Finally grew bored with you, didn't he? Found somebody younger, prettier, fresher. And now you're here, hiding in some shit hole, forgotten and discarded, like a used rubber. Nothing to show for all those years."

She reeled back. "I've held his body in mine. I've tasted his flesh and he passed a blessing of power onto me."

Technically that would be true. If they had shared body liquids, she would have gained some of his power.

"A blessing of power," Curran laughed, the echoes of his snarls scattering to the walls. "How about a child?"

She did not answer.

"Oh, wait." Curran paused. "I forgot. The Father of the People is too afraid to make a child of his blood. Or maybe he found you lacking in power?"

She laughed. The loud hollow sound ricocheted from the walls, seemingly coming from everywhere. "Oh, no, half-breed. Power is something I *do not* lack."

Her defenses dropped. I felt the shadows behind her, the enraged, ravenous vampires, younger than the one I had beheaded, but formidable all the same. Evil magic clung to them, like a rotting mantle, fueling their frenzy.

She spoke a single harsh word, and the phantoms behind her burst from the shadows, reeking of undeath and hungry for blood.

The shapechangers broke away into a loose fighting formation, leaving me in the middle of the floor. Curran's talking had gained us about twenty feet, and the vampires' charge came with astonishing speed. I hit the ground. The first vamp sailed over me.

I rolled onto my back. Another vamp leaped over me. My blade slid into the flesh of its withdrawn gut. A black gush of its blood drenched the floor an inch away from my head. The vamp aimed for Curran, oblivious to the wound. The Beast Lord roared. *Happy hunting.*

I leaped to my feet and launched myself toward Olathe. She spun, a small sickle knife in her hand. My curved blade slit her forearm. The power of her blood slammed into me, and I rocked back, dizzy. She whirled, her hair flying, her eyes wild and bulging. The blood from the cut sprayed around her, falling to the ground in a wide circle. The red drops ignited, and a wall of carmine flames rushed upward, enclosing her in a protective circle of magic. A blood ward. The only way to penetrate it was with the blood of a relative or with overpowering magic. *Shit.*

A vampire hit me from the side. It clung to me, jaws snapping as we skidded across the floor. Pain shot through my stomach. *Not again!* The magic inside me boiled. I grabbed Slayer's blade with my hand, oblivious to the icy burn, and jammed it into the pale dead eye. Slayer hissed, triumphant. The vamp crashed to the floor and thrashed, dying. I kicked myself free.

Another monster rushed at me. I sidestepped, lunged, and grazed its neck with Slayer's tip. The vamp spun around and buried its claws in my thigh. I rammed my saber into its throat, severing the arteries and slicing through the bones of the neck. The vamp's mouth hung open, spewing blood. My kick hammered into its leg. The bone snapped with a crunch. The vamp dropped on its gut, flailing. I jerked my sword free and went looking for Olathe. Behind me the last spark of the vamp's magic dissipated into thin air.

A third bloodsucker leaped, horrid mouth gaping open.

My blade cut into its chest, sliding smoothly between its ribs into the bulging sack of its heart and out again before the twisted body hit the ground. I kept walking.

The hall was drenched in blood. The shapechangers fought in pairs, their movements coordinated with military precision. In a corner two furry bodies were down, with Curran standing over them, beset by three bloodsuckers at once.

I saw Jennifer and someone spotted like a leopard battling back to back, pressed by four vampires. She dropped and kicked the first one, her claws ripping into its side, wrenching free the bloody shard of a rib. Her partner fell onto the bloodsucker, tearing into its neck. More vamps swarmed on top of them.

Nobody paid me any mind. In the battle of monsters, I was just a human. I kept moving.

The east wall shuddered. Dusty plaster exploded, scattering across the floor and something huge charged through the gaping hole, roaring like a tornado. It hit the clump of the vampires with awesome force. An undead body flew through the air, slamming against the wall. The vampire twisted on reptilian feet and leaped back. A colossal paw swept it from midflight, snapping the spine like a dry twig. The Bear of Atlanta had arrived.

Olathe's blood wall shimmered before me. She stood within the barrier, watching the slaughter. The blood from her forearm slid onto her fingers, dripping to stain her dress. She looked at me and smiled. What the fuck was she so happy about?

She kept grinning, her face bright with sick glee.

"You like blood?" I snarled. "I'll show you blood."

Slayer's blade slit my arm and across the hall the bloodsuckers paused for a single beating of my heart. They knew the blood, knew whose power flowed through my veins. They stood still, mesmerized, paying homage to the magic, and then slashed back into their victims.

I thrust my bloody arm into the red fire. It seared me and solidified, cracking like a fractured windshield. The smile bled from Olathe's face. The carmine fire shattered. A myriad of tiny flames fell at my feet. I leaped into the circle and thrust.

Olathe made no move to counter my sword. It sliced into her stomach with a wet sucking noise. I dragged it upward, cutting through the intestines, cleaving the liver. She sagged forward on the blade, and in her eyes I saw the satisfaction of recognition. She knew my blood, too.

I jerked the blade free and let her fall. She sagged to the filthy floor and lay on her back, drawing hoarse short breaths. A dark stain blossomed on her dress above her navel and spread through the fabric. She possessed an unnatural vitality, but soon the magic that sustained her would dissipate. She expelled it from her body with every labored breath.

I watched the blood stain grow. My anger died. I was tired. My thigh hurt and my stomach felt like someone had taken a red-hot rake to it.

The bloodfire had surged anew after I had passed through it. It would burn until the last of Olathe's blood dried or decomposed, and the banquet hall shimmered red past the translucent wall of ruby flames. It was almost over.

I rolled my head back, cracking my neck, and saw why Olathe had been grinning.

The ceiling teemed with vampires.

Dozens of them, nude, twisted, wriggling obscenely against each other, packed tighter than sardines in a can. They covered the plaster completely, like a medieval painting of hell that had somehow sprung to life, and more were coming, squirming one by one through a dark hole in a corner.

How many? Forty? Fifty? A hundred? How many of them

were pre-Shift, pre-magic? I tried to feel and was swamped in the wave of icy hate. At least twenty.

The undead blanket writhed. A sweet surprise Olathe probably planned to spring on us when we thought we had won. Except that in a moment she would die, releasing all of them from her control, leaving them to blood frenzy.

A horde of ravenous undead left to their own bloodlust. We would all die here. Curran, Mahon, Jennifer. Me. And death would spread, when the undead monstrosities burst into the streets after they finished us off.

Across the room Curran tore a vampire in half, throwing the mangled pieces to the floor.

Dozens of now peacefully sleeping people would perish. They would see their children torn to pieces while they screamed.

I dropped to my knees and cleaved Olathe's chest. The flesh and cartilage parted before the blade and I pulled her rib cage open like a bear trap. She hissed at me. I reached into her chest and grasped her heart, forging a link between us. Through her blood I felt the multitude of vampire minds, drowning in their own madness.

That's the wrong way, my father's voice said from my memory. *Don't give in to this.*

There is no right way.

I cut my arm deeper, letting my blood mingle with Olathe's, slowly gaining control. She shuddered, her heels kicking the floor. If I let her die, turning the vampire horde loose, they would scatter before my mind could fasten on them. I lacked the proper training in piloting the undead, and my only option was to merge our power through the bloodlink, controlling the moment of her death, so when she passed on, fading from the undead's minds, they would find me already there.

She knew what I was doing. Her teeth bared in a feral grimace, but she didn't have the power to resist the bloodlink. The magic of my blood overwhelmed hers. My power spread, flooding the vampiric minds. Clenching my teeth, I squeezed, crushing her heart and her life with it. Power exploded in my fist, forcing me to my feet.

Olathe jerked. Her eyes rolled back into her skull and the full weight of the horde settled upon me.

The room shuddered. Too many. There were too many.

A fiery band enclosed my chest, engulfed my throat, my head, and compressed, crushing me. I stumbled. My knees quivered. My mouth hung open. I couldn't breathe. There wasn't enough air.

I knew I hadn't gotten them all, despite the bloodlink. Through the hammer of their minds I could feel individual stragglers, drowning in bloodlust. I sent the horde against them. The ceiling churned with bodies tearing into each other. A chunk of plaster broke off and plummeted to the floor, breaking into dust two feet away from me. The bloodflames blocked the sound from the rest of the room.

My arms held wide, trying to balance, I looked through the eyes of the vampires and saw a long crack in the plaster. *Thank you, God.*

The ceiling quivered as dozens of talons ripped into it.

Dimly I saw Jennifer through the shimmering wall of the flames. My lips shaped a word.

"Go."

She stared at me, unable to hear through the bloodwall.

"Go."

Suddenly Curran was beside her. He said something, but I couldn't hear.

"Go. Now. Go."

He thrust his hand into the fire and leaped back, his fur melted, his skin red with future blisters.

Another chunk of plaster crashed to the ground outside the circle. To me it made no sound, but they heard the dull thud, jumped, and looked at the ceiling. Jennifer cringed like a whipped dog.

Curran stared at me.

"Go now. Go. Go."

He understood. His clawed hand grasped Jennifer's shoulder and pushed her back. The she-wolf hesitated for a moment and ran.

My sight faded completely. The beating of my heart filled my ears like the tolling of a great bell. I couldn't feel my body, as if it no longer existed. Blind and deaf, I remained in the middle of nothing, swaying, while above me the undead brought the ceiling down. They dug through the plaster and cement to the framework of steel support beams, holding the five stories of concrete above us. Thin arms grasped the beams and pulled with supernatural strength.

God. I haven't been very good.

The metal whined in protest.

I could have tried harder. I could've been a better person. I stand before you now as I am. I make no excuses.

The beams gave, bending.

Please, have mercy on me, Lord.

In my mind's eye I saw the enormous beams breaking. I saw tons of plaster, cement, and steel falling down, onto vampires, onto me, burying us beneath the rubble, sealing a tomb from which not even a vampire could get out.

I felt their hate-filled hungry minds vanishing one by one. Finally I could let go. I released the awful burden and the awareness left me.

CHAPTER 7

SLAYER LAY IN ITS SHEATH ACROSS A NIGHT TABLE, next to a man reading an ancient paperback. On the cover of the book a man in a brown suit and fedora held an unconscious blonde in a white dress. I tried to focus on the title but the white letters blurred.

The man reading the book wore blue scrubs. He had cut the pantlegs midway down his thighs, and faded blue jeans showed below the blue fabric. I crooked my neck so I could see his feet. Big heavy work boots caught the jeans.

I leaned back onto the pillow. My father had been right: there was Heaven and it was in the South.

The man lowered the book and glanced at me. Of average height and stocky, he had dark skin, glossy with an ebony sheen, and graying black hair, cut military style. The eyes peering at me through the thin-framed glasses were at once intelligent and brimming with humor as if someone had just told him an off-color joke and he was trying his best not to laugh.

"Lovely morning, isn't it?" he said, the unmistakable harmonies of coastal Georgia vibrating in his voice.

"Shouldn't it be 'ain't it'?" I said. My voice sounded weak.

"Only if you are an uneducated fool," the man said. "Or if you wish to appear country. And I'm too old to appear anything that I'm not."

He moved by my side and took my wrist in his hands. His lips stirred, counting the heartbeats, then his fingers lightly touched my stomach. Pain lanced through me. I flinched and drew a sharp breath.

"On a scale from one to ten, how much does it hurt?" he asked, his fingers probing my shoulder.

I grimaced. "About five."

He rolled his eyes. "Lord, help me. I have another hard case on my hands."

He jotted something on a yellow legal pad. We were in a small room, with cream-colored walls and a paneled ceiling. Two large windows spilled sunlight onto the floor, and light blue sheets covered my legs.

The man put down his pen. "Now, whoever told you, little lady, that you can slap on an r-kit and charge right down the mountain into the battle needs a good wallop. Anything magic hits it and the damn thing will go screwy on you every time."

"Screwy," I said. "Is that a medical term?"

"Of course. Follow the finger with your eyes, please. No turning the head now."

He moved his left index finger around and I followed it with my eyes.

"Very good," he said. "Count backward from twenty five."

I did and he nodded, satisfied.

"It appears, mind you, only appears, that you've avoided a concussion."

"Who are you?"

"You may call me Dr. Doolittle," he said. "I've sailed through the night and day, in and out of weeks, to where the wild things are and now I'm their private physician."

"That was Max." The pain twisted my hip and I groaned. "Not Dr. Doolittle."

"Ah," he said, "what a pleasure to meet an educated mind."

I stared at him for a moment, but he just laughed at me with his eyes.

"Where are we?"

"In the Pack keep."

"How did I get here?"

"You were carried."

I felt an urge to rub my forehead and found an IV dangling from my arm.

"Who carried me here?"

"That's an easy one. His Majesty carried you out of the building, then you were slung over Mahon's back and brought to my doorway."

"How did Curran get a hold of me in the first place?"

"From what I understand, he leaped through some sort of a fire, grabbed you, and leaped back out. Which accounts for his third degree burns. Curiously, there are no burns on you. A mangled hip, some severe injuries to the stomach, massive blood loss, but no burns. Now why is that?"

"I'm special," I told him.

Curran had gone through the bloodward fire. Twice. To get me. *Idiot.*

"You won't tell me."

"No."

"That's gratitude for you," he sighed with mock sadness. "After you were brought here, I spent roughly four hours repairing your body, most of which"—he glared—"were spent on fixing your stomach."

"Third degree burns," I said.

"Yes. You haven't heard a word I said."

"I heard everything: four hours, stomach, hip, blood loss. You didn't do a blood transfusion, did you?" There was no telling what the magic in my blood would do to foreign plasma.

"Heaven forbid. I do believe you think me to be an amateur." He ended "amateur" with a "tuar."

"What about bandages?"

He shook his head. "I've sworn a medmage oath, my lady, and I have yet to breach it. Your bloody bandages, clothes, and all such were incinerated personally by me."

"Thank you."

"You're welcome."

"A third degree burn means that all the layers of skin are burned," I said.

"That's right." Dr. Doolittle nodded. "It looks bad but it feels much worse."

"On a scale of one to ten?"

"About eleven."

I closed my eyes.

"Our lord developed a lovely golden crust," Doolittle's soft voice said. "I do believe he could have gotten a part in an old-fashioned horror picture. He's quite comfortable now, floating, I imagine."

"Floating?"

"I prescribed the tank. It's an oversized aquarium, filled with a certain solution yours truly developed in his youth. If His Majesty were an ordinary person, the only way to restore his epithelium would be through grafting. Since he's not an ordinary person, he will float in the tank for a few days and then come out with new skin. His shoulder will take longer. Which reminds me." He rose, walked to the door, and stuck his head out. "Tell the Bear our guest is awake."

He returned and rummaged through the vials on the table.

"Shoulder?" I asked.

"I gather a small piece of a ceiling had the misfortune to land on him. Crushed his left shoulder blade."

He turned, a syringe in his hand.

"No," I said firmly.

"The tech hit twenty minutes after I was done with you," he said. "You're in pain and I'm goin' to give you an old-fashioned pain killer."

"No, you won't."

"This is Demerol. It's quite mild."

"No. I don't like Demerol. It makes me light-headed." It's not enough I was weak and in the middle of the Pack compound, now he wanted to mess with my head, too.

"Nonsense. Be a good girl and take your medicine." He stepped forward.

"You come near me with that needle," I said, putting as much malice into my voice as I could muster, "and I'll shove it up your ass."

He laughed. "Precisely the thing Jennifer said when I tried to put stitches on the cut across her buttock. Luckily for me, I don't have to stick you with this needle."

He showed me the empty syringe. I blinked and felt a rush of soothing cool. He must have squirted the bloody Demerol into my IV. *Asshole.*

I closed my eyes. I felt light-headed and tired. And I still hurt.

Heavy footsteps echoed through the room. I had a visitor and there was only one shapechanger that didn't bother to move like an assassin.

I opened my eyes and saw Mahon nod to the good doctor and say in his deep, quiet voice, "Well done."

Mahon approached, pulled up a chair, and sat next to me, his massive forearms leaning on his legs. His huge back stretched the black fabric of an oversized T-shirt, but despite barely fitting him in the shoulders, the shirt was a foot too long. The shapechangers had a fondness for sweats, and Mahon was wearing gray sweatpants and no socks. His hairy feet rested on the sun-warmed floor.

His brown eyes met my gaze. "The Pack appreciates your sacrifice."

"There was no sacrifice. I'm alive." And Curran is burned to charcoaly crispness.

He shook his head. "The sacrifice was intended and we're grateful. You have earned the trust and friendship of the Pack. You may visit us when you wish. You may ask us for help in a time of need, and we'll do our best to aid you. It's no small thing, Kate."

I probably should have said something formal and flowery, but Demerol kept tangling my thoughts. I patted his big hand and mumbled, "Thanks."

Mahon's eyes were warm. "You're welcome."

IT WAS FRIDAY AND I WAS WALKING. DRESSED IN matching gray sweats and sneakers that were too wide, both courtesy of the Pack, I conquered the hallway at a slow but persistent pace. I was dizzy and had to fight off the urge to spin right, which would have rammed my head into the wall.

Doolittle's wizardry had doused the pain in my stomach, muting it to a dull ache that gnawed on me when I bent the wrong way. He promised minimal scarring on the abdomen and I believed him. My thigh wasn't so lucky. The vamp had bitten off a chunk of flesh, and despite Doolittle's efforts, I'd carry a reminder for the rest of my days. I didn't care. I was grateful I had any days left.

The hallway opened into a wide room the size of a large gym. Assorted devices filled it, positioned with care on the stone floor, some born of technology, others of magic, and a few convoluted hybrids of both.

A wiry, medium-sized woman about my age sat on a padded square cot by the door. The cot resembled an oversized dog bed. The woman munched on saltine crackers. Probably a wererat. They ate constantly.

The woman glanced at me through a cascade of tiny dark braids. A wooden bead secured each braid.

"Yeah?" she said.

Friendly.

"I have an appointment," I told her.

"So?" she said.

I shrugged and walked past her. She didn't stop me.

The tank sat near the left wall, half-hidden by a large slab of stone on which someone had written cabalistic symbols in chalk. The symbols looked to be bullshit: a misshapen *veve* that should have been drawn in red; two Egyptian symbols, one for Nile and the other for Canopus; and something vaguely resembling the Japanese symbol for dragon.

I skirted this waste of space and approached the tank. Eight feet tall, it was cubical in shape. Its glass walls contained an opaque greenish liquid and I could make out dim contours of a human shape hanging motionless in the green water.

I knocked on the glass. The body moved and Curran surfaced with a splash. He took the oxygen mask from his mouth and held on to the edge of the tank for support, which resulted in the rest of him pressing against the glass. Just what I needed. Pasty Beast Lord in all his nude glory against the backdrop of swamp water.

His new skin was very pale. The thick blond hair of his scalp and eyebrows was now barely longer than morning stubble.

"Thank you," I said, keeping my gaze fixed on his face.

"You're welcome."

Feeling awkward, I fought an urge to shift from foot to foot. "I'm leaving."

"When?"

"After I talk to you."

"Doolittle's released you?"

The memory of the aging doctor glaring at me in outrage popped into my head. "He didn't have much choice."

"You can stay if you need to." Curran wiped the moisture dripping from his chin.

"No thanks. I appreciate it and all, but it's time to go."

"Places to go, people to meet?"

"Something like that."

"Sure you don't want to join me in the tank? The water is fine."

I blinked, at a loss for words. Curran laughed, clearly enjoying every second.

"Ahh, no," I managed.

"You don't know what you're missing."

Was he coming on to me or just messing with me? Probably the latter. Well, then, two could play that game. I looked pointedly at his midsection. "No thanks," I said. "I know exactly what I'm missing."

He grinned.

I said, "I've come to talk about Derek."

Curran managed to shrug while still holding on to the wall. "I've released him from his blood oath."

"I know. He insists on tagging along and I don't want him to.

I tried to explain that I do dangerous work for little money and that being in my vicinity is bad for his health."

"What did he say?"

"He said, 'Yeah, but will I get chicks? In truckloads?'"

Curran laughed, submerging like a dolphin, and surfaced again. "I'll talk to him."

"Could you do it sooner rather than later? He thinks he's going to drive me home."

"Alright. Tell Mila at the door to send him to me."

"Thanks."

I turned.

"How did you get through the fire?" he asked.

Oh crap. "It wasn't fully up," I said. "Dumb luck. Couldn't get out of it though. I guess she was hell-bent on bringing that ceiling down on my head."

"I see," Curran said. I couldn't tell if he believed me or not.

I turned around and made a little mocking bow that made my stomach hurt. "Would there be anything else, Your Majesty?"

He waved me off with a flick of his wrist. "Dismissed."

Curran was too dangerous to know. Too powerful, too unpredictable, and worst of all, possessing an innate ability to infuriate me, throwing me off balance.

Hopefully our paths would not cross again.

A young wolf whose name I didn't know drove me to Greg's apartment. I thanked him and walked up the stairs to find a white stain of a note pinned to my door. It said, "Kate, I tried to call but you didn't answer. I hope we're still on for tonight. I've made a reservation at Fernando's for six o'clock. Crest." I tore the note off the door, crumpling it, and tossed it aside. The wards shimmered shut. The sturdy door separated me from the rest of the world, and I breathed a sigh of relief. Kicking off the Pack's sneakers, I crawled into the bed and fell asleep.

WHEN I AWOKE, LATE AFTERNOON WAS SLOWLY BURNing down to evening. I felt drained and uneasy, unsettled, as if I'd missed an important deadline. Searching my brain for the causes of my rotten mood produced no results and I felt worse.

I lay in bed and looked at the ceiling, considering calling Crest and telling him to forget it. That would be the sensible thing to do. Unfortunately, sensibility was not among my virtues. To miss the date was somehow equivalent to giving up without trying.

I shambled to the bathroom and washed my face with cold water. It didn't help.

There was only one dress I could wear to Fernando's, both because it was the only formal dress I owned and because it was the only dress hanging in Greg's guest closet. I had worn it to a formal function he had dragged me to in November, where I had spent two hours listening to people who loved hearing themselves orate.

I took the dress from the closet and dropped it onto the bed, then went to the kitchen and poured myself a glass of water. I had lost a lot of blood. I forced one glass down, refilled it, and came back, sipping the water. The dress lay on the sheets, bathed in the last rays of the tired sun. Of a simple cut, it had an unusual color, a nameless shade somewhere on the crossroads between peach, khaki, and brass. Anna had picked it out for me. I remembered her going through the dresses hanging on wire hangers, briskly sliding them out of the way one by one, while an impossibly thin saleswoman watched in distress. "You don't need thinning," Anna had explained, "or padding. What you need is softening, which is a touch more complicated but can be done with the right dress. Lucky for us, you have the right complexion for the color. It will make you look darker, which in itself isn't a bad thing."

I looked at the dress and recalled the unsettling feeling of not recognizing myself when I put it on. I was proportionate, even lean, but not slender. Most women don't bulk easily, but if I flexed my arm, I could see definition. No matter how hard I tried to lose weight or become thinner, all I managed to do was to wind more muscle on my frame, so I'd quit trying to match the willowy standard of beauty when I was fourteen years old. Survival took precedence over fashion. Sure, I didn't weigh a hundred and ten pounds, but my narrow waist let me bend and I could break a man's neck with my kick.

This dress camouflaged the muscle, tricking the eye into seeing soft flesh where there was none. The trouble was, I wasn't sure I wanted to wear it today for Crest.

I touched the soft fabric and wished Anna would call.

The phone rang.

I picked it up and heard Anna's voice say, "Hello."

"How do you do that?"

"What? Calling when you want to talk to me?" She sounded amused.

"Yes."

"Most clairvoyants are slightly empathetic, Kate. The empathy with the person serves as a bridge for the things we do. I've known you for a very long time—I remember when you were learning to walk—and I've formed a permanent bond. Think of it as being tuned to a certain radio station that's off-line most of the time."

I sipped my water. I knew she wouldn't mention the vision, unless I asked her about it, and I didn't feel like asking.

"How's the investigation?"

"I've found Greg's killer."

"Aha. What did you do to him?"

"Her. I disemboweled her and then crushed her heart."

"Lovely. What did she do to you?"

"I'll have a scar on my upper thigh and my stomach is still healing. But at least I had a professional medic this time."

Anna sighed. "I suppose it's not too bad for one of your outings. Are you satisfied?"

I opened my mouth to tell her yes and stopped. The cause for my unease became clear.

"Kate?"

"No, I'm not satisfied." I told her about Olathe and her pre-Shift vampires. "Too many loose ends," I said. "One, I'm still not sure who killed Greg. I'd thought it could be one of her vamps, but that doesn't explain the animal power prints on the m-scanner and I saw no animals during the fight."

"There is no way to check now?"

"No. The building is kaput. Two, where are the missing women and why were they kidnapped?"

"As food for the vampires?" Anna ventured.

"Four women wouldn't have sustained her stable for more than a day. Why didn't she grab more?"

"I don't know."

I sipped my water. "Neither do I. And the enemy in your vision was male. There is more, but I can't remember right now. I have this awful feeling that I've overlooked something. Something ridiculously obvious."

I fell silent. Anna waited on the line.

"Anyhow," I said finally. "I'll have to wait until my brain sorts this out."

"Ah," Anna said. "Is there something more pressing?"

"A handsome plastic surgeon expects me at Fernando's at six."

"Aha. Did you happen to mention that you abhor Fernando's?"

"No," I said. "But I expected him to figure it out. Formal dining isn't me, Anna."

"Understatement of the year," Anna murmured. "Is he fun?"

"Who?"

"The plastic surgeon. Is he fun? Does he make you laugh?"

"He tries," I said.

"Doesn't sound like he's successful."

"I think I may have tried to force this thing too hard," I said.

"Which part? Intimacy or sex?"

"I suppose both." For me casual sex was an oxymoron. Sex placed me in a position of vulnerability and there was nothing casual about that. I never slept with a man I didn't trust and admire. I didn't know enough about Crest to either admire or trust him, yet I had wanted to get him into the sack. I had paraded naked in front of him, for God's sake. "It bothers me. I think it has something to do with Greg's death."

There was silence on the line. Finally Anna's voice murmured, "Lo and behold, a chip in your armor."

"I intend to repair it tonight."

"You're a maximalist, Kate. All or nothing. Perhaps he deserves a chance."

"I didn't mean that I would break it off. I'll just reassess the situation. I'll try to see if he is fun."

Anna sighed. "Will you wear the dress we bought that time?"

"Yes."

"A word of advice," she said. "Let your hair down."

I WALKED INTO FERNANDO'S WITH MY HAIR DOWN. IT fell to below my waist, framing my face and softening the edges. With makeup on my face, a dress and matching heels, at least I looked like the kind of woman that would be eating at Fernando's. The heels made my hip hurt.

I gave my name to an impeccably dressed host and he led me

deeper into the restaurant. My shoes made faint clicking noises on the marble floor as we walked past the round tables draped with crisp white tablecloths. Men in expensive suits and well-groomed women wearing gowns worth more than I made in a month conversed at the tables, eating at their leisure. Several vines heavy with pungent white flowers grew from ceramic urns. Someone had taken a lot of care in arranging their stems on the walls with artful precision.

I hated this place.

Crest sat at a corner table, studying the menu. He looked glum. He glanced up, saw me, and froze. It was shallow but the dumb look on his face made me feel better. Beautiful I would never be. Striking, that I could manage.

Moving with the grace of a dancer, the host held the chair for me. I thanked him—which was probably against the rules—and sat. Crest stared at me.

"Have we met?" I asked.

"I think so," he said. "You look different."

It was time to break the illusion. "Different? Amazing, radiant, gorgeous, any of those might get you laid, but I don't know about different."

It worked. He stopped staring. "I didn't think you were coming."

"Work," I said. "Besides, since I've tortured you with Las Colimas, the least I could do is let you return the favor."

"You don't like it here?"

No. The atmosphere is stuffy, the food is bad, and the only thing I can afford is a bowl of grits. Do they even serve grits here? I shrugged. "It's not too bad. Do you come here often?"

"Every three weeks or so."

Oh boy.

The waiter showed up and engaged Crest in conversation that I didn't understand and didn't listen to. I watched the patrons until the waiter murmured the code words, "And the lady?"

"What salads do you serve?"

I ordered a twenty-two-dollar salad and the waiter departed.

"No main course?" Crest asked.

"Not today."

A silence reined. Crest seemed content to gaze at me while I had no idea what to do with myself.

"You look stunning," he said finally. "So different."

"It's an illusion," I told him. "I'm still me."

"I know."

He smiled. By the way he looked at me, I knew he was wondering what I would be like in bed. Why wasn't I wondering the same thing about him? He did cut a nice figure in the dark suit. A few women overtly glanced at him.

I caught a man looking at me from a table nearby. I suppose I should've been flattered.

"So how's work?" I finally said to say something.

"I'm thinking of leaving the practice," he said.

"Oh?"

"I'd like to spend more time studying Lyc-V," he said. "I think it's fascinating, particularly how the very structure of bones changes under the influence of magic. To develop that ability further would mean incredible advances for reconstructive surgery. No invasive procedures, no implants, no recovery, just the elimination of imperfections through will."

I smiled at him. Perhaps one day I'd introduce him to Saiman.

The waiter arrived with the wine menu. Crest ordered and then rattled on about the fascinating nature of Lyc-V, going into more technical detail than my limited comprehension could handle. I dutifully watched him, wondering why Olathe kidnapped the women. Something about it just didn't add up.

Crest fell silent and I blinked, turning off the autopilot.

"You're not listening, are you?"

No. "No, please go ahead."

"Do I bore you?"

"A little."

"I'm sorry," he said.

I shrugged. "Please don't be. You're being yourself and I'm being myself. For you shapechangers are a new and interesting frontier. For me, they are a part of my work. They are violent, often cruel, paranoid, and extremely territorial. When I see one, I see a possible adversary. You get excited because they can change their bone structure, while I get pissed off because their jaws don't fit together well in midform and they drip spit on the floor. And they smell awful when they're wet."

Crest looked at me.

"Besides, I lack the medical expertise to understand most of what you've said during the last five minutes. I hate feeling like a layman. It's too much for my fragile ego."

He reached over and touched my hand. His skin was warm and dry, and for some unknown reason his touch comforted me.

"I'm shutting up," he promised solemnly.

"You don't have to," I said. "Let's talk about something else, though. Books, music, something not related to work."

"Yours or mine?"

"Both."

The world skipped a beat as the magic crashed. The conversation at the tables died for a moment and resumed as if nothing happened. Our dinner arrived. My salad consisted of leaves of lettuce, tastefully arranged to frame the thin slivers of orange, and a scattering of other greenery. I poked at the lettuce with a fork. For some reason I wasn't hungry.

"How's your salad?" he asked.

I speared a slice of orange with my fork and ate it. "Good."

He smiled, pleasure evident on his face, and I recalled the advice given to me by someone a long time ago. If a man takes you to a restaurant of his choosing, don't compliment him. Rave about the quality of the food and he'll be thrilled, because he took you there. It wasn't in me to rave.

We spoke for a few minutes about nothing at all, but the conversation kept dying. Whatever we had at Las Colimas had fled and we couldn't recapture it. I poked at my salad, looked up, and saw Crest glancing past my shoulder. "Is there a problem?"

"That guy keeps staring at you," Crest said. "It's going beyond polite. I think I might go over and ask what his problem is."

I turned and saw a familiar figure two tables down. Leaning against the chair, half-turned so he could have a better view of our table, sat Curran.

Why me?

A stunning Asian woman wearing a tiny black dress occupied the other chair at his table. The woman appeared nervous, her slender fingers twisting the corner of the napkin. She gave me a startled glance, like a gazelle at a waterhole, and turned away quickly. Curran appeared unconcerned.

Our gazes met and Curran grinned.

"I don't think talking to him is a good idea," I said.

"An old boyfriend?" Crest said.

"Lord, no. We've met professionally."

I motioned to the waiter and he glided over. "Yes, ma'am?"

I nodded toward Curran. "See that man over there with very short hair? Next to a beautiful woman?"

"Yes, ma'am."

"Would you please deliver a saucer of milk to him with my compliments?"

The waiter didn't even blink, a testament to Fernando's excellent service. "Yes, ma'am."

Crest looked at me, obviously itching to ask for an explanation.

The waiter delivered the milk, murmuring to Curran. Curran's smile turned predatory. He took the saucer and raised it in a kind of salute. His eyes flashed gold. The gleam flared and vanished so quickly that if I hadn't been looking straight at him, I would've missed it. He brought the saucer to his mouth and drank from the edge.

"He looks out of place in jeans," Crest said.

"Trust me, he doesn't care. And nobody working at Fernando's is insane enough to bring it up." Actually, Fernando's didn't seem like Curran's kind of restaurant. I had pegged him for a steak-and-shrimp or Chinese place kind of guy.

"I see." Crest was trying to give Curran an intimidating stare. If he kept it up, Curran might collapse laughing. Suddenly I was angry.

Crest's gaze lingered on Curran's date. Something new reflected in his eyes, interest, admiration? Attraction, maybe? Curran winked at him.

Crest folded his napkin and put it on the table. At least half of his chicken breast remained on his plate. "I think we should go," he said.

I pushed away my mostly intact salad. "Good idea."

A waiter materialized by our table. Crest paid cash and we walked out into the night. Outside Crest turned to the left.

"My car is that way," I said, nodding to the right.

He shook his head. "I've got a surprise planned. Since we cut our dinner short, we might be early. Do you mind walking?"

"Yes, actually." Not in these heels and not with a red-hot needle in my hip. "Would you mind driving me?"

"It would be my privilege."

As we walked to his car, I felt someone watching me. I paused to adjust the strap on my shoe and made him across the street, leaning against the building. The leather jacket and spiky hair was unmistakable. Bono. Ghastek was keeping an eye on me, but this time instead of a vampire he sent his journeyman. Nice choice. Bono still had a grudge against me for our little chat at Andriano's. Had Ghastek found out that I'd squeezed the journeyman who had clued me in on Ghastek's unmarked vampires? Or maybe I was thinking about it all wrong.

Bono shifted slightly to keep me in his view. Why keep surveillance now, when Olathe was dead? Unless Bono had served Olathe. It made sense. If she had wished to take over Nataraja's operation, she would've tried to recruit young journeymen, and with her looks and power, luring them to her side wouldn't have been that hard. Was Bono here for revenge? Or was there another player to this drama and now Bono took orders from him?

It wasn't over. My instincts told me that it was too easy, too convenient, and now I had the confirmation from Bono. What did he know that I didn't? I thought about crossing the street and beating it out of Bono, pummeling him into pulp until he told me every last detail he knew. I could ram his head against the bricks and take him deeper into the dark of the alley. Or even better, smash him against the wall and take him to the car. In this neighborhood nobody would pay attention to a woman in an evening dress and her handsome companion that had a touch too much to drink and had to be supported by her. I could stuff him into the car and drive him someplace secluded.

"Kate?"

Crest's pleasant face came into view. Bloody hell.

"Which one is your car?"

"That one."

I smiled at him, or at least I tried. Casting one last look after Bono, I let Crest open the door of his vehicle for me and forced myself to sit down. Later, Bono. I can always find you.

CREST'S RIDE WAS EXPENSIVE, METALLIC GRAY, AND bullet shaped. He held the door open for me and I arranged myself on the leather passenger seat. He got in and we took off. The inside of the car was spotless. No used tissues wadded and stuffed into the cup holder. No old bills or worn receipts littering the floor. No grime on the panels. It looked immaculate, almost sterile.

"Tell me, do you own a single pair of worn jeans?" I asked. "Just one pair so old that it has permanent dirt in it?"

"No," he said. "Does it make me a bad person?"

"No," I said. "You do realize that most of my jeans have dirt embedded in them?"

"Yes," he said, his eyes laughing. "But then I'm not interested in your jeans, only what's in them."

Not tonight. "Okay, just as long as we're clear."

The city scrolled by us, its streets channeling an occasional gasoline-burning car feeding on the death throes of technology. I counted as many horsemen as I did cars. Fifteen years ago the cars had dominated the streets.

"So who was that man?" Crest said.

"That was the Beast Lord."

Crest glanced at me. "*The* Beast Lord?"

"Yes. The top dog." Or cat.

"And that woman was one of his lovers?"

"Probably."

A snow-white Buick cut us off, squeezing into the lane and

screeching to a halt before the traffic light. Crest rolled his eyes. The traffic light flickered, flaring with blinding intensity and dying to a weak glow.

"Residual magic?" Crest wondered.

"Or faulty wiring." The good doctor was picking up the magic jargon. I wondered where he'd learned about the residual magic effects.

"It makes sense." Crest parked next to a large building. "We're here."

A valet opened my door. I stepped out onto the pavement. Crest's car was in distinguished company. All around us Volvos, Cadillacs, and Lincolns spewed well-dressed people onto the sidewalk: women smiling so wide their lips threatened to snap and men inflated with their own importance. The couples proceeded to make their way up to the tall building before us.

The valet got into the car and drove off, leaving us standing in full view. People looked at me. They looked at Crest, too.

"Do you remember the Fox Theater?" Crest said, offering me his elbow. Opening doors was one thing. Hanging on his elbow was another. I ignored it, walking to the door with my hands loosely at my sides.

"Yes. It was demolished."

"They took the stones from it and built this place. Great, isn't it?"

"So instead of building a new, fresh, sterile building, they dragged all of the agony, heartbreak, and suffering that permeated the stones of the old place into the new one. Brilliant."

He gave me an incredulous look. "What are you talking about?"

"Artists emanate a great deal. They agonize over their looks, over their age, over the competition. A very minute detail can become a matter of great gravity. The building in which they perform soaks in their failures, their jealousies, their disappointments like a sponge and holds all that misery in. That's why empaths don't go to anything above the level of spring fair performances. The atmosphere overwhelms them. It was incredibly stupid to transfer the weight of so many years to the new place."

"Sometimes I don't understand you," he said. "How can you be so damn pragmatic?"

I wondered what nerve I struck. Mister Smooth had suddenly turned confrontational.

"After all, there are other emotions." His tone was irate. "Triumph, exultation at the magnificent performance, joy."

"That's true."

We stepped into the dim lobby, lit with torches despite the presence of electric bulbs. People around us moved in a steady stream toward the double doors at the far wall. We went with the flow, passing through the doors and into the large concert hall, filled with rows of red seats.

People looked at us. Crest looked pleased. We were the center of attention, tall, dapper Crest and his exotic date in a distinctive dress with a scar snaking its way down her shoulder. He didn't see how much the crowds bothered me; he didn't notice that I was beginning to limp. If I told him, it would only make matters worse. I kept walking and smiling, and concentrated on not falling.

We sat smack in the middle and I let out a tiny breath of relief. Sitting was a lot easier than standing.

"So who are we waiting for?" I asked.

"Aivisha," Crest said with gravity.

I had no idea who Aivisha was.

"It's the last performance of the season," he continued. "It's getting too warm. I didn't think she would perform this late, but the management assured me that she will have no difficulties. She can use the residual magic."

I leaned back in my seat and waited quietly. Around us people settled into their seats. An old woman, dressed in an impeccably white gown and escorted by a distinguished older gentleman, stopped by us. Crest jumped to his feet. Oh dear God, I would have to get up. I rose and smiled and waited politely until we completed the introductions. The woman and Crest chattered for a few minutes while the escort and I quietly shared each other's misery. Finally she moved on.

"Madam Emerson," Crest told me and patted my hand. "Probably the last true Southern socialite. You did very well. I think she likes you."

I opened my mouth and clamped it shut. I hadn't done anything but stand still and smile. Like a well-behaved child or a disciplined dog. Had he expected me to hump her leg?

A bell rang, commanding quiet from the crowd. A hush claimed the concert hall and slowly the velvet curtain parted to reveal a short woman. She was dark-skinned and heavy, with glossy coils of raven black hair styled high on top of her head. A long gown of silvery fabric cascaded in folds and plaits off her shoulders, shimmering, as if it was woven of sun-lit water.

Aivisha looked at the audience, her dark eyes bottomless, and took a tiny step forward, the cascade of silver moving all around her. She opened her mouth and let her voice pour forth.

Her voice was incredible. Startling in its clarity and beauty, it rose, gaining strength, building on itself, and power streamed from her, permeating the concert hall and the astonished crowd. I forgot about Crest, about Olathe, about my work, and listened, lost in the harmony of the enchanting voice.

Aivisha raised her hands. Thin slivers of ice grew from her fingers, spiraling, twisting, in perfect accord with her song. Like impossibly complex crystal lace, the ice stretched across the stage to climb up the side columns, blossoming into bundles of needle-thin feathers. It hugged the folds of Aivisha's gown, a dutiful pet, happy to please, and I couldn't tell where the silver of the fabric began and the crystal purity of ice ended.

Aivisha sang and sang, and ice danced for her, obeying her every whim. She commanded us, and mesmerized, we held our breath until her voice climbed to an overpowering crescendo. A burst of blue light pulsed from her, saturating the ice in an instant. The crystal lace burst, evaporating into the air. The curtain fell, hiding Aivisha from the audience. For a moment we sat stunned. And then the concert hall erupted in applause.

Crest squeezed my hand and I squeezed back.

Forty-five minutes later we pulled into the parking lot before my apartment building.

"Can I walk you to the door?" Crest asked.

"Not tonight," I murmured. "I'm sorry. I just wouldn't be good company."

"Are you sure?" Crest asked, hope dying in his eyes. I felt bad, but I couldn't do it. Something told me I should just stop this right here.

"Yes," I said. "Thank you for the dinner and company."

"I was hoping the evening wouldn't end this soon," he said.

I touched his hand with my fingertips. "I'm sorry. Perhaps some other time."

"Oh, well," he said. "There is always tomorrow night."

I opened the door and let myself out of his car. He lingered for a moment and then sped off. Too late I realized that he had expected a good night kiss.

MY HIP HURT MORE AND MORE, AND BY THE TIME I crossed the parking lot, the ache had graduated to a full pain, spiced with sharp spasms.

"Just great." I slipped off my shoes. Barefoot, with heels in hand, I headed toward the door.

My foot found an imperfection in the pavement. I slid and almost landed on my ass. Pain bit my leg. I bent forward, waiting for it to pass and growling wordless curses under my breath.

"Do you need me to carry you?" a voice whispered into my ear. "Again?"

I spun and hammered an uppercut into the speaker's midsection. My fist met a wall of solid muscle.

"Good punch," Curran said. "For a human."

Yeah, yeah. I heard you exhale when I hit you. You felt it. "What do you want?"

"Where is your pretty date?"

"Where is yours?"

I started toward the building again. The only way to get away from him was to climb up the stairs and shut the ward in his face.

"Home," he said. "Waiting for me."

"Well, do me a fucking favor and go see her."

I reached the stairs and sat down. My leg demanded a break.

"Hurts?"

"No, I like sitting on filthy steps in an expensive evening dress."

"You're a bit surly tonight," he observed. "Not getting laid will do that."

I looked at the night sky, at the tiny dots of stars. "I'm tired, my leg hurts, and there's shit that needs answers and I can't find any."

"Like what?"

I sighed. "One, I don't know who killed Greg and why. Two, we found no evidence of the necro-tainted animals that killed your people. Three, Greg's file mentioned women. Why did Olathe take them and what did she do with them?"

He bent low toward me. "It's over," he said. "And you've got a bad case of spotlight deprivation."

"A bad case of what?"

"You're a no-name merc and all of a sudden everyone wants to talk to you. The power brokers of the city know your phone number. Makes you feel important. And now the dance is done. I sympathize." His voice dripped derision. "But it's over."

"You're wrong."

Curran walked away.

"She called you a half-breed," I told his back. "Why?"

He ignored me.

I forced myself to my feet and went upstairs. I got into the apartment, changed clothes, threw together a bag of stuff I didn't want to be without, took Slayer, and went downstairs again. I started Karmelion, biting off the words of the chant like a snapping dog, and pulled out of the parking lot. I'd had it with this whole bloody city. I was going home. To my real home.

CHAPTER 8

DAYLIGHT STREAMED THROUGH THE WINDOW, TICKling my face. I yawned and snuggled under the covers. I didn't want to wake up. Not yet. In retrospect driving out of the city close to midnight, and with an aching hip, wasn't the brightest idea, especially considering that the tech hit around four, leaving my truck marooned a mile away from the house, but I had gotten in just before the sunrise and now none of it mattered. I was home.

I stuck my face into the pillow, but daylight persisted and I stretched, sighing. My bare feet hit the sun-warmed floor and I happily padded to the kitchen to make coffee.

Outside the late morning was in full swing. The clear sky was luminescent with blue. No wind troubled the leaves on the myrtles. The kitchen window begged to be opened. I unlocked it and pushed the bottom half up to let the coastal, sea-spiced air into my house. Home. Finally.

In the yard, positioned so it could be noticed from either kitchen or porch, rose a stick. On the stick was a human head.

Long hair hung in blood-caked strands. Pale eyes bulged from their sockets. The mouth gaped open and green flies were breeding among the torn lips.

It was so out of place in my sunlit world that for a moment it didn't seem real. It couldn't be real.

An unmistakable stench of rot crept into my kitchen

I sprinted to the bedroom, wincing at the pain, grabbed Slayer, and went to the front door. My wards were up. Cautiously I opened the front ward and stepped onto the porch.

Nothing.

No sound. No power.

Nothing except a rotting head in my front yard.

I approached the head and circled it slowly. It belonged to a young woman. She had died recently—the expression of horror was still frozen on her face.

A large nail pinned a folded piece of paper to the back of her head. I raised the paper with the tip of Slayer's blade. Uneven letters glared back at me.

Do you like my present? I made it special for you. When you see your half-breed friend, tell him I won't waste his head like this. I'll strip every shred of meat off his bones. I'll gorge myself on his carcass until I can't walk and let my children finish the rest, while I sleep it off with half-breed women. Half-breed meat tastes like shit but it has good texture. Olathe never did appreciate it. It's a shame about her dress. I was partial to it.

I walked inside and dialed Jim's number.

THE DEAD HEAD LOOKED AT JIM. JIM LOOKED AT THE head.

"You know some fucked up people," Jim said.

"Her name's probably Jennifer Ying," I said. "The hair has Mongoloid texture. She's one of the missing women whose names I found in Feldman's file. The head wasn't here when I came in, which was around four thirty this morning."

Jim sniffed at the head. "Fresh kill. A day, maybe a day and a half at most," he said. "You need to call Curran."

"He won't listen to me. He thinks I'm a glory hound."

Jim shrugged. We'd worked together long enough to know that neither of us was interested in fame.

"You aggravate the hell out of him."

"There is more." I led him to the porch. A gathering of human bones lay arranged on canvas, spanning the entire porch.

"You rob a graveyard?"

"I wondered how he came so close to the house without setting my wards off, so I went looking and found these. He arranged them in a circle around the property in the tree line. It's a form of a ward. Very old."

"How old?"

"Neolithic. Primitive hunters would lay out the bones of their prey around their settlements. The idea is to form a chain of Rock, Bone, and Wood. You use Rock and Wood to obtain the Bone, binding all three, so if you return the Bone to the Rock and Wood after you're done with it, it will afford you protection. He created himself a safe passage so he could wander around my yard whenever he wanted. It's an easy spell to break. All you have to do is to remove the bones, and that's why nobody uses it anymore. Unfortunately, you can't detect it unless you stumble over it."

I picked up a skull and handed it to him. Jim took it and recoiled, hissing. His eyes flooded with green.

Folklore correctly stated that in death a shapechanger's body would revert to the form it had at birth, be it human or animal, but Lyc-V did some permanent things to bone structure, which remained in life or in death. Several long, glossy strips of Lyc-V-created bone marked the skull in telltale places above the jaw and along the cheekbones.

"A wererat," Jim said, handing me the skull as if it was hot. "Guess how many I found?"

"Seven."

"And at least three vampires. The skeletons are not complete. Some bones are missing, but there are eight pelvises and nine skulls, three of which have bloodsucker fangs."

Jim glared at the bones. "You have to put the vamps separate."

"What?"

"Put the bloodsucker bones separate," he repeated. He was agitated and low snarls crept into his voice.

"Why don't you get off your ass and help me?"

"I'm not touching *them*."

I sighed. "Jim, I'm not a criminalist. Without a bloody loup and an m-scanner, I don't know which bones are vamp. You, on the other hand, can tell by the scent."

He glared at me, his eyes a little wild. "You look through it, and if you have trouble, you let me know."

He marched into the yard. I sighed and went about sorting the bones.

I SAT ON THE PORCH BETWEEN TWO PILES OF BONES, watching the werejaguar in my yard make small circles around the stick supporting the rotting head of a young woman. I had failed her. *I* had looked at the evidence. *I* had drawn the wrong conclusions. But I was still here, sitting on my porch, while she had paid for my stupidity. And my arrogance.

Jim kept walking, placing each foot softly in front of the other, stalking an invisible prey around a circle. Yellow flooded his eyes, and his upper lip quivered once in a while, showing his fangs. Unless the cat was yawning in your face, you wouldn't see his fangs until he was ready to sink them into you. Jim was ready to sink them into *someone*. He would have to wait in line.

"Stop it. You're wearing a hole in my yard."

Jim stopped pacing to glare at me.

A dark van pulled into the driveway. It was magic and water powered like Karmelion and it made enough noise to match my horror of a truck. Four stone-faced shapechangers stepped out and approached me, carrying several canvas bags. I got up and stood aside, giving them access to the bones. They began packing the fractured skeletons of their dead into the bags, sorting as they went along, handling the bones with the same care a china dealer employs when touching his best merchandize.

Doolittle stepped out of the van, wearing denim overalls and carrying a portable m-scanner. He paused to murmur a few words to Jim and proceeded to the head.

Jim approached the porch. "Curran wants you in the city."

I shook my head. "I can't go. After you're done, I'll have to call the cops. You got your bones back. The Ying family deserves to receive their daughter's."

"What the fuck do I tell Curran?"

Doolittle plucked the note from the nail, flipped it over. "Looks like he wrote on the back of some sort of magazine page."

I took the note from his fingers. The page was from *Volshebstva e Kolduni*, the "Spells and Warlocks" rag-sheet whose credibility Saiman had so easily dismissed.

"Kate?" Jim asked.

I wanted to cry. How could I have been so stupid? I brought the Almanac out to them and handed the upir article Bono had given me to Doolittle. He read a few words. "It says here this creature feeds on dead human flesh. It will mate with animals and produce half-breed sons, neither animal nor human. Where did you get this?"

"One of Ghastek's journeymen gave it to me."

"Ghastek knew," Jim snarled. "He knew the whole time. I'll rip his heart out!"

"'Driven by the need to produce an heir, the upir will mate with women of power, for only a woman of power can carry a true upir to term . . .'" Doolittle looked at me. "You cannot stay here, Kate. You must come to the keep."

I opened my mouth but he silenced me with a wave of his hand. "There are seven of us and one of you. We'll carry you if we have to."

THE PACK COUNCIL SAT IN PADDED CHAIRS AROUND A table. In the middle of the table sat the head of Jennifer Ying, brought in as evidence by Doolittle and placed under a glass hood laced with preserving spells. She bore silent witness to all that was said. Next to her a speaker phone relayed Saiman's cool voice.

"All upiri are male. The history of their breed is quite old: it's likely they were an integral part of the fertility cults in early agrarian societies of the Bronze Age. During the rites young women, embodying the Goddess, were brought to the upir so he could play out his role of her son-consort by copulating with them. Of course, often the copulation resulted in the woman's death, in which case, the upir would complete the rite full circle, devouring her body.

"The arrival of the Iron Age with its patriarchal gods-heroes signaled the end of the Goddess cult, and the upiri gradually migrated to the remote regions, finding the vast Russian forests particularly suitable. Although they are driven by the urge to procreate, the upiri are interested only in producing a powerful male, another upir. All female children are born dead. Once a son is produced, the upir feeds the mother to the child and casts him out, driving him out of his territory. It must be noted that only a woman of significant magic power is able to sustain enough magic to produce a baby upir."

"What about the animal children?" Curran demanded.

"The upir will mate with any animal he can anatomically penetrate. The resulting offspring, although viable, is usually sterile. A single upir may have scores of these servant-creatures. Also, since an agrarian cult of fertility centers on regeneration, the upir is likely to have vast recuperative powers. My source lists him as immune to metal, wood, tooth, and claw. He is virtually impossible to kill."

Curran nodded at Mahon. The Bear spoke, "The Pack thanks you for your information."

"I appreciate the gratitude of the Pack. You will receive my bill within three days."

Mahon turned off the phone.

"What if it's Max?" I murmured.

"Could it be Maximillian Crest?" Curran asked Jim.

Startled, I asked, "How do you know his name?"

"I know more about you than you do. Do you really think I would deal with you without following your every step?"

"You had Derek spy on me. You promised me he would do no such thing."

"Actually I put a scout in the apartment above you," Jim said. "Greg's place isn't soundproof."

I shut up, stunned by the betrayal. I should've known better—the Pack always came first. They were professionally paranoid.

"How did you and Crest meet?" the alpha-wolf asked.

I didn't answer.

Jim reached over and touched my hand. "Kate, this is one of those times when silence isn't golden."

There was nothing left to do. No way out. If Crest was an upir, I couldn't take him on my own. "I went to the morgue to examine a deceased vamp found at the knight-diviner murder scene. I was looking for the brand and he walked in on me. He stated that he was a cosmetic surgeon performing what he called 'charity duty' at the morgue. He wore scrubs and the stripes of a unit supervisor. He asked me to join him for lunch. I refused."

"How did he react?" said a heavyset woman. She was middle-aged and plump. Her graying hair perched in a bun atop her head. The others called her Aunt B, for what reason I didn't know. She looked like every child's favorite grandmother. She was also the alpha female of the twelve hyenas the Pack counted among its members.

"He appeared surprised."

A light murmur rippled through the Council.

"He has access to the morgue," Jennifer said. "A lot of corpses."

"And being a plastic surgeon, he would meet many pretty women," added the alpha-rat through a mouth full of potato chips. The rotting head did nothing to dull his appetite.

"Why didn't he mate with Olathe?" Jennifer wondered. "It's obvious they were working together. He would help her take over the People, and in return, he'd get all the vampire flesh he wanted. Plus fresh corpses."

"She was barren," Jim said. "Roland probably had her fixed before he fucked her."

"Did you go to lunch?" Aunt B wanted to know.

"Yes. It was a normal lunch. The next time I saw him was after Derek and I encountered that vampire. Crest was asleep on the stairs when I brought Derek home."

"Did you sleep with him, dear?" asked Aunt B. "We need to be clear."

I tried to keep from gritting my teeth. "No."

"Then you haven't seen him in an uncontrolled environment." Aunt B shook her head. "He could've been cloaking the entire time."

"His cloak would have to be exceptional," I said. "I felt no magic. Nothing at all."

Curran, who had been leaning against the wall, crossed his arms over his chest. "To sum up, he's never appeared at the same time as the upir. He seems to pop up in her life whenever she makes any headway. She's never seen his place or met any of his friends."

"He's familiar with tech." I finally thought of something smart to say. "He owns a car."

"Anything else?" Mahon asked.

"He's fascinated with Lyc-V."

"I like him for it," Jim said. "And the kid thinks he's an asshole."

Thank you, Derek.

Curran pushed himself from the wall. "Either he's the upir or he's not. How would we find out?"

Doolittle stirred. "The only way to know for sure, m'lord, is to scan a blood sample. Blood can't hide the magic when separated from the body. Time is of the essence in this matter. The less time the blood has to degrade, the better. I suggest we take a portable scanner."

"If he is what we think he is," the alpha-wolf said softly, "we'll have to go in force."

"And I doubt he would volunteer the sample." Mahon said.

"We can't compel him," the alpha-wolf said.

To compel a person to give a blood sample with the purpose of scanning it was illegal. It was a violation of privacy and the courts had been adamantly enforcing it. If Crest proved to be human, he could make enough of a stink to keep the Pack in hot water for years.

"Not to mention that he'll know who all of you are," I said.

They mulled it over.

"It doesn't matter," Curran said. "We solve this now."

"DOESN'T FEEL SO GOOD, DOES IT?" JENNIFER SAID TO ME as we left the black van that ferried us to Crest's apartment.

"No."

"It'll be okay," she said and we both knew she lied.

The tight pack of shapechangers cleared the stairs to the lobby. A clerk was on duty, a thin, red-headed man, who started to rise at our approach. Curran nodded to him as if they had known each other for years, and the man sank back into his seat.

The six of us took the stairs at a run, Curran in the lead, followed by Jim, Jennifer, Doolittle, and me. Aunt B's oldest son brought up the rear. He chose to carry a shotgun.

We reached the door to Crest's apartment. Behind me Aunt B's son blocked the stairs. I wondered if the shotgun was for me, in case I developed second thoughts.

My stomach tightened. It felt wrong. I should've come alone. I shouldn't have let them pull me along. *I will not put myself into this situation again.*

Curran knocked on the door. Crest's voice said, "Hello?"

Curran looked at me.

"This is Kate," I said. "I'm not alone and I need to talk to you."

A silence issued as he digested it and the door swung open.

Crest looked slightly disheveled. He gazed at the stone-faced gathering outside his doorstep and stepped back. "Come in."

We did. The shapechangers spread through the house, and Crest found himself enclosed in a ring. They maintained their distance, a few feet between them and the human in the middle. Just enough room to gain momentum for a leap without getting in each other's way.

"Mind telling me what this is about?" Crest said. His gaze flickered to Curran.

"These people are shapechangers," I said. "Several of their pack mates are dead. I'm involved in the investigation and the murderer has developed an unhealthy fascination with me. He left a rotting head in my yard with a love note."

Crest's face lost its expression. "I see," he said. "You think that I'm the guy."

Doolittle stepped forward. "If you'd be so good as to volunteer a blood sample, the matter can be cleared up within minutes."

Crest was looking at the kid with the shotgun. Wrong. Excluding himself, the kid was the least dangerous of those present. "And if I don't volunteer?"

"You should," Curran said flatly.

Crest looked at me. "Kate? You believe that I'm the killer?"

"No. But I have to know for sure."

A mix of emotions twisted his face. He thought that I had betrayed him. So did I.

"You said you wanted to be part of what I do," I said softly. "Now you are. Please give us the blood, Dr. Crest." *I don't want to see you hurt.*

Crest clenched his teeth. Around me the shapechangers tensed. His gaze fastened on my face, Crest rolled up the sleeve of his shirt and held out his arm. "Might just as well get it over with."

Doolittle tied his biceps with a strip of rubber. A long needle pierced the skin and the dark blood squirted into the clear tube.

"So tell me," Crest said. "What exactly am I supposed to be? I assume since Kate's involved, I'm not an ordinary human. What am I guilty of?"

"She thinks you feed on the dead," Jim said.

"Really?"

"Yeah. You hunt them. In the night. Human, vampire, Pack, doesn't matter. You hunt them, you kill them, and then you eat the corpses."

"Lovely." Crest's gaze didn't waver. Doolittle carried the sample to the scanner.

"Oh, it gets better, Doc." Jim was on a roll. Sonovabitch. "You also kidnap young women. You fuck them, then eat them. You mate with animals and make kids. Hordes of little misshapen Crests that roam the city in search of human meat."

"How nice."

The scanner chattered, printing out the signature. Jim shut up and leaned forward, his eyes fixed on his prey. The shapechangers hovered on the verge of shedding their humanity, ready to rip into the warm meat. They breathed deep, their muscles taut with concealed motion, their eyes hungry and unblinking. And their prey, the human in the middle of the room, stood surrounded and alone, looking at me like a lost child. I slid Slayer from its sheath and held it ready.

"Human," Doolittle said. "He's clean."

"You sure?" Curran said.

"Not a scintilla of doubt."

A shiver passed through the group as if someone turned off an invisible switch. I put away Slayer. Curran looked at me. His face was calm, that particular calm that contained a storm. "Do me a favor," he said. "Next time you get a hunch, don't tell me."

He turned to Crest. "On behalf of the Pack, I offer you a formal apology and our friendship. A suitable compensation will be rendered for the offense to your person. You would honor us by accepting it."

Crest made a dismissive gesture with his hand. "Don't worry about it."

Curran strode past me, and the shapechangers filed out of the room one by one, until only Crest and I were left.

"You really thought I was a monster." Crest's voice held quiet wonder. "Tell me, how long did you suspect me? Did you go to dinner with me thinking that I rape and kill women so I can feed on their corpses?"

"No."

"No? Why should I believe you?"

"If I suspected you then, I would've tried to kill you then."

"As opposed to being ready to kill me now?" He paced, suddenly breaking into motion as if standing still had become too great of an effort. "I saw your eyes. If that printout had said anything but what it said, you would've run me through with that sword. And it wouldn't have bothered you!"

"It would've bothered me a great deal."

He spun about. "You know, I really thought we had something there. Something nice. But I was wrong."

No reply would have been a good answer to that, so I kept my mouth shut. Crest's face had gone pale with bitterness, his mouth a narrow straight slash. "Worst of all, I think you would've preferred it to be the other way. You wanted me to be that thing."

I shook my head.

"No, you did. What was it, Kate? Did you just have to be right or was I too much of a departure from your world? Do I have to be a monster for you to fuck me?"

Coming from him the expletive gained an edge, like a knife. "I'm sorry."

He shook his hands in front of him, trying to grasp the air. "Sorry doesn't begin to cover it!" He glared at me and exhaled forcefully. "I'm through with this conversation and I'm through with you. Go. Just go away."

I left. He closed the door behind me. I wished he would've slammed it, but he closed it very carefully.

Nobody waited for me on the stairs. I got down to the lobby and walked up to the clerk. "Is there a back door out of here?"

He pointed down the hall. I took it, walked out of the building, and kept walking. The shapechangers could find me by scent. If they really wanted to track me down, there wasn't a thing I could do to stop them. But I had a feeling Curran was too disgusted with me to care one way or the other. I hailed a horse buggy and paid the driver fifty bucks to take me to the ley point.

CHAPTER 9

I SAT ON MY PORCH, ALTERNATING BETWEEN A BOTTLE of hard lemonade and Boone's Farm Sangria, and watched the night breathe. It was very quiet. The night breezes had died and nothing troubled the dark leaves on poplar branches. Not a blade of grass stirred on the lawn below.

I took a big swig of sangria and another of lemonade. Not drinking so much, but getting drunk. Making my body feel as bad as my mind. I wished I had some beer to chase down the wine. It would make me sick faster.

I'd accomplished quite a bit. It was hard to sit here and not be proud of myself. I'd failed to find Greg's killer. He would murder again, he would kill young women, he would kill shapechangers, and I didn't even know where to look for him. I'd pissed away whatever meager credibility I'd had with the Pack. And with the Order, for that matter. I had a thing going with a nice guy. It wasn't perfect, but he *liked* me. He had tried pretty hard. A normal, decent guy. And I had broken our little relationship beyond all repair. He wasn't a part of my world so I brought him into it. On my terms.

I turned one of the bottles upside down, guzzling the liquid without tasting it, until I almost choked, and raised it in a salute to the distant line of trees. "Nice going."

The trees said nothing. I shook my head and reached for the other bottle.

And saw a monster in my yard.

It sat on its hunches, sniffing at the wind. A large bastard, at least a hundred and sixty pounds. Long grayish fur grew in patches on its lean carcass. Bare skin, pale and wrinkled, showed between the irregularly shaped spots of fur, especially on the stomach, where long, ragged scars crisscrossed the flesh. A small hump protruded from the beast's back, and the fur covering it was longer and coarser, forming a matted mane that flared just behind the large head crowned with round human ears.

The thing's hind legs were heavy and muscled and shaped somewhat like those of a canine, but with longer digits. Its front paws, smaller and disturbingly human in shape, clutched something dark. I squinted at the wet fuzzy clump. A squirrel. The creature sniffed at its prize with a long, wrinkled muzzle, opened massive jaws, and tore into the squirrel. A sickening crunching of broken bones disturbed the night's silence.

It chewed with gusto, squeezing the bloody stump in its hands, and looked at me. The small bloodshot eyes that glared from the beast's face were undeniably human. When you looked into the eyes of a shapechanger, you saw a beast clawing to get out. When I looked into this thing's eyes, they burned with understanding, dim yet significant intelligence, betraying sadness and a capacity for suffering.

The thing raised its horrid maw to the sky and made an eerie lingering noise, as if a dozen voices murmured the same phrase in a dozen languages at once. Then it turned to the squirrel and bit off another morsel.

A faint scraping of claws reached my ears. I glanced about me. Grotesque shapes hid in the shadowy corners, some small, some large. They perched on the rails, they slunk below, around the porch stairs, and darted under the truck in the driveway, shifting and moving all around me.

The rim of the bottle touched my lips and I drank, as the beasts drew closer.

"Poor Crest," a velvet voice murmured. "I've been alive for three hundred years and I can't remember the last time I laughed so hard."

I set the bottle down with marked slowness and looked toward the voice. "It's you," I said. "Shit. I would've never thought."

Bono smiled at me, showing even teeth, white and inhumanly sharp. There were too many of them, too. Funny how I never noticed it before.

The black, spiky, gel-saturated hair was gone, and long, sleek strands fell to his shoulders. They were gray, the odd dark gray of dirty duct tape. His skin was pale and smooth, and I was seeing too much of it, since Bono chose to appear nude, except for something resembling a kilt or a skirt that hung from his hips, doing a piss-poor job of covering whatever it was supposed to cover.

The world went fuzzy. I rubbed my forehead. The wine was kicking in.

Bono slid from the rail on which he had been perching. He moved with liquid slickness across the porch, seamlessly coming to all fours and lowering himself to the floorboards to sit beside me.

There was something so alien in the way he moved, in how he sat, how he smelled, how he looked at me with eyes brimming with hate, something so inhuman that my brain stopped, smashing against that inhumanity like a brick wall. He made me want to scream.

I forced myself to sit still. The effort burned some alcohol and the view didn't seem as blurry.

In the yard several smaller creatures waited impatiently as the large one finished his squirrel.

"It's hard for you, isn't it?" the upir said softly. "It's hard to sit next to me like this. You want to scream and run, run as fast as you can across the grass, never looking back, knowing that you can't escape but running still because it's better to die with your back to me. Do you know why that is? Because your body knows that you are food, to be used, eaten, and discarded."

I brought the bottle to my lips and took a small sip. "How many cheesy novels did you have to read to come up with that one?"

He leaned, lowering himself until he lay on his side, his head supported by the arm bent at his elbow. "Laugh, Kate. It's the last opportunity you'll have."

I shrugged. In the yard the squirrel hunter took a swipe at a smaller, hideous thing that darted to nip at the tuft of fur in his hand. The smaller creature yelped, readied for another pass, and froze, its short, nearly translucent tail quivering, gripped by an invisible hand. It stood stiff, thick legs far apart. The quivering spread up its spine, until its neck trembled. The phantom hand squeezed hard one last time and released it. The creature jerked and collapsed. Shaking, it gained its feet and stumbled away, whining softly, its tail between its legs.

"Children misbehave sometimes," Bono said. "They need to be punished. If you're wondering, I can do it to my women, too."

He stared at the big creature and it walked toward us. "Let's get the introductions out of the way," the upir said. "This is my eldest son at the moment. I call him Arag. Arag, this is a future dinner. Future dinner, this is Arag."

Arag's human eyes, sunken deep into his deformed skull, teared up.

"What the hell did you . . ."

"Baboon." The upir shook his head. "Strong, cruel, aggressive. Unfortunately, he got a little more from me than from his mother. He can speak. Say something for Kate, Arag."

The monster looked down at his hands. He shifted from foot to foot, unsure, and emitted a long distorted screech, like nails scraping against chalkboard. "Bloood," he shrieked.

"Sad, isn't it?" Bono smiled. "He walks the Earth, a pitiful, wretched creature, uttering words at random, longing for something—he himself doesn't know what—and hating everyone and everything. I tried ripping out his vocal cords, but the damn things just grow back."

"Blooood." Arag sighed.

The upir waved him away. "Go on."

Arag returned to his post in the yard. The upir sighed. "I'm thinking of killing him when we're done here. You think I should?"

I swallowed more wine.

"It won't help," Bono said.

I shrugged and drank some more. "Why make an alliance with Olathe?"

"Why not? It was a good plan. Sooner or later the half-breeds and the necromancers would've warred, and Olathe would take over the vampire stables. I'd have enough vampire meat to gorge myself sick. Vampire flesh is the best, Kate. It's aged and flavorful, like a fine wine."

"You ate shapechangers, too."

"Their magic strengthens me." Bono grimaced. "But they taste like shit."

His fingers touched my hair. He picked up a strand and raised it to his nostrils.

"I bet the original plan was to put a bun in Olathe's oven."

He bared his teeth. "The bitch was barren—can you believe that?" He twisted my hair around his fingers and looked through it at the moon. I pulled away and he let the strands slip from his hand with a chuckle. "But then I stumbled onto you. And you're not barren, Kate."

"Why me?"

He leaned close, his breath hot on my cheek. "I know what you are. I've climbed the hill and sniffed the grave of that rotting sack of bones you called Father. I smelled his stink and I know his blood isn't in your veins. And I know whose is. All of that power crammed into a tight, sweet little package. Did you know your real father hunted my kind thousands of years ago? Your puny little mind can't comprehend the extent of my hate for him. You will give me a son, Kate. And all of the magic of your bloodline will belong to me."

He laughed softly and I had to swallow a scream. "Why did you kill Greg?"

"He was getting too close to me. Olathe's little subterfuge failed to fool him. I knew I would have to kill him sooner or later. The trick was to do it so you'd leave your precious warded house and come after the killer."

"You wanted me to confront Olathe. You wanted to know if my blood was stronger than hers."

"Yes. It took you so long to figure it out. I practically drew a map for you. I hand-fed you every crumb. All you had to do was to follow the trail but you meandered and backtracked. An ape could've gotten it faster. But then, you and an ape are only a small step apart."

He licked my cheek. "The magic is thick tonight and I grow hungry. There is a fresh corpse waiting for me at my place. And more will be coming. There are many necromancers among the People who would rather serve me than that fool on his gilded throne. Let's end this, what do you say?"

I said nothing.

"No clever remark? Are you scared, Kate?" His voice dropped to a whisper, but the words he said thundered with power. *"Estene aleera hesaad de viren aneda." And now, you are forever mine.*

Oh Dear God. For him power words were a language. The strength of the ancient magic gripped me, crushing my mind with its enormity. The whirlwind of light swirled about me, carrying me away into unknown depths. I bit my tongue and tasted my blood. Something furious and defiant rose inside me and screamed. Blinded by the light, I heard myself speak a single word.

"Dair."

Release.

The light dimmed and I saw Bono's eyes staring into mine. Unfamiliar words came, surfacing from someplace long forgotten, their meaning somehow clear. *"Ar ner tervan estene." I'll kill you first.*

I smashed the bottle against the stairs. The glass shattered, spilling across concrete. I rammed the razor-sharp edge into his throat. Blood sprayed over me.

"Ud." Die.

The ground shook with the power I sank into the word. The upir fell, blood gushing from his throat. I lunged to the door and dove through. The ward flowed closed behind me.

An odd gurgling noise came from the upir. It struggled from

his ruined throat, bubbling forth with the gushes of dark blood. Bono reached for the bottle. His fingers closed about the blood-slicked glass, slid, fastened around the edge, the glass slicing into the flesh of his fingers. He pulled and ripped the bottle from his neck, dropping it gently onto the boards.

The gurgling noise strengthened, expelling blood with each tortured cough. Glass shards slid from the wound, carried down by the crimson flow. A hideous creature crept onto the porch to sniff the bloody bottle. Bono grabbed it with one hand and flung the forty-pound thing over the rails like a kitten.

His fingers grazed the awful cut, wiping away the blood. The wound was closing. As it sealed shut, the gurgling noise mutated, growing louder, and I realized that Bono was laughing.

"Nice try," he said, displaying his unscarred neck. "My turn."

He leaped at the open door. An explosion of crimson rolled through the doorway and he howled, thrown back. He flipped and spun about, his eyes blazing. Silver from his eyes leaked onto his cheeks, staining the skin. There was nothing at all human about him now.

He lunged again and saw the sharp, angular vampire bones guarding the doorway from the inside.

"Bitch!"

"Rock, wood, and bone, Bono," I said dully. "Your ward is reinforcing mine."

He screamed. The windows vibrated. I threw my hands against my ears. Bono pounded his fists against the porch floor and the boards exploded.

"Won't work," I told him. "You can demolish the whole house. The ward will still stand."

He stared at me, silvery streaks wetting his face as if he cried metal instead of tears. His offspring shivered and hugged the ground. "This isn't over," he howled. "I will murder all that give you protection. I'll kill the cat and I'll devour his flesh. His magic will be mine and then I'll come back. No ward will guard you then!"

He leaped from the porch, racing into the night, and his brood followed him.

I leaned my head against the wall. The booze made it hard to think. He didn't die. I hadn't expected him to. One who can weave the power words into sentences wouldn't die from a single word.

The cat? He said he'd kill the cat. Was he talking about Jim? No, Curran, it had to be Curran. Jim wasn't strong enough to threaten my ward. Curran was. All shapechangers had a natural resistance to warding spells. It had to do with the animal part of their nature. Curran's resistance was the strongest. I could call Jim and warn him.

Who would believe me?

"'And men my prophet wail deride!'" I mumbled and dragged myself to my feet.

I called Jim anyway. He didn't answer the call and the answering machine did not pick up.

THE JOLT OF A WARD BREAKING RIPPED THROUGH MY skull. My headache exploded and sleep fled.

Someone was in my house.

I slipped my hand under the pillow, found the handle of a throwing dagger, and pulled the blade free.

I lay awake, breathing quietly. Silence and dark filled the rooms. There was no need to go hunting. Whoever it was would come to me.

A man-sized shadow loomed in the hallway, a deeper darkness against the wall. It hesitated for a breath and approached. I closed my eyes, watching it through my eyelashes.

Six yards. Breathe in and breathe out.

Five.

Four. Close enough.

I hurled the dagger. The black blade spun through the air and bit into the shadow's shoulder. Crap. Missed.

The shadow lunged for me. I went for Slayer, but the bastard was too fast. I kicked, both feet hard. The shadow swatted my kick aside and grabbed my right wrist. Steel fingers squeezed, and my hand went numb. I hit the shadow in the throat with my left hand. It growled and I found myself staring into yellow eyes.

"Let go of my hand, asshole!"

Curran let go, and I rubbed my wrist. "Damn it, don't you know how to talk?"

He stared at me, uncomprehending. I reached for the lamp, remembered that the magic was up, and took a candle from the night table instead. I struck a match. The narrow blade of a candle flame flared into existence. Curran stood before me, his eyes wide, unblinking. Tiny red marks covered his face and hands, blending into a uniform coat of crimson. I reached out and touched his palm. Magic stung my fingertips. Blood. Curran was covered with blood, miniscule drops of it swelling from every pore. He had broken through my ward and it had exerted a price.

"Curran?"

He gave no indication of hearing me. He must be dazed from shattering the spell.

The headache pounded at my skull like a hammer. Gaining my feet, I took Curran by the hand, led him to the bathroom, and nudged him into the shower. I turned on the cold water and let the icy cascade splash on his face.

Lowering the toilet cover, I sat down and rested my head on my hands. The water poured. I would've killed for an aspirin.

Curran drew a sharp, ragged breath and exhaled. Awareness

crept into his eyes. "Cold," he said. Shuddering, he shut off the water and shook himself. The drops extinguished the candle and darkness swallowed us.

I reached blindly and threw a towel at him. Finding the door, I started toward the kitchen. Halfway through the short hallway something fell onto my head. I leaped to the side and grabbed at it. My fingers held a twig.

What the hell?

I looked up and saw the night sky. A large, irregular-shaped hole gaped in my roof. Curran had picked the highest point of the building, where the ward would be the weakest, and punched through the ward and the roof with it.

I ground my teeth, went into the kitchen, and found a fey-lantern. With a little coaxing, it ignited, its gentle blue flame spreading soft light. Curran appeared in the doorway.

"You broke my roof," I told him.

"It was easier than the door," he said. "I knocked. You didn't answer."

I rubbed my temples. From now on, no more wine.

Something clanked. I looked up. Curran put my dagger on the table.

"How's your shoulder?"

"Sore," he said.

Telling him that I had been aiming for his throat wasn't in my best interest.

"You were right," he said. "It's not over."

"I know," I said softly.

"There is an upir."

"I know."

"He has Derek."

I stared at him.

"I sent Derek and Corwin to the Wood," Curran said. "He attacked them at the pickup point and took Derek. The last Corwin remembers, the kid had a broken leg but was alive."

"What about Corwin?"

"He's hurt," Curran said.

"How bad?"

"He's dying."

"THIRD TREE FROM THE LEFT," CURRAN SAID.

We stood on the porch, shoulder to shoulder, the night stretching before us.

"I see him." A reptilian-looking thing crouched in the branches of the poplar, its long scaly tail wrapped around a tree limb. The watcher Bono had left to keep an eye on me.

"We can't kill it. Bono thinks I'll sit in the house and hide behind my wards. If we kill it, he's going to know. He has some sort of telepathic bond with them."

Curran strode to the tree. The thing watched him with huge round eyes. Curran jumped, caught a low branch, and pulled himself onto it. The reptilian monster hissed. I went to the shed and brought back a coil of cable wire. Curran grabbed the thing by the neck. It squealed and let go of the branch. He hurled it down and I stepped on it and tied the wire around its neck. Its skin was translucent and colored pale olive, glistening with transparent scales. Curran jumped down and we tied the other end around the tree.

We headed toward the ley line.

WE SAT ON A NARROW WOODEN PLATFORM, HASTILY thrown together from bits of discarded lumber. They were called ley taxis, cheap wooden constructs that lay in stacks near every ley point. Nothing living could ride the ley line without having some sort of support under its feet. If you were foolish enough to try, the magic current would sever your legs just above the knee.

The ley line dragged us north toward Atlanta at nearly ninety miles an hour. Magic held the taxi completely immobile, so much so that it appeared the rough wooden platform hung still, while the planet merrily rotated past it.

"Explain the bone ward to me again," Curran said quietly.

"He killed the vampires and fed on them. The flesh he consumed created the bond between their bones and him. By bringing the bones inside and binding them to the stone foundation and the walls, I forced him to fight against himself. It's nearly impossible to break this kind of ward. I had also dropped the ward-markers all around the yard so he would have a clear passage to my porch. He was too happy to see me to notice."

"You baited him?"

"Yes."

"So the bone ward can be reversed, but blood wards can be overcome by a person of similar blood?"

"Apples and oranges," I said dully. I felt tired and restless at the same time. "The blood ward draws its power directly from the blood, while the Rock-Wood-Bone ward is an environmental ward. It draws power from the magic itself. The presence of bones just defines it, similar to a lens that allows only light of a certain color to pass. He can't enter my house when magic is up. And since he is magic, he must be too weak to try during tech."

I watched the planet rotate by, the darkness-drowned valleys and hills rolling on both sides of us. Poor Derek. I clenched my teeth.

"Don't," Curran said.

"I should've found somebody to listen." We didn't look at each other, choosing instead to stare into the night's face.

"Wouldn't have mattered," Curran said. "I would've still sent them to the Wood. It was the safest place for them."

"In retrospect, it all fits." My voice was bitter. "He was Ghastek's journeyman, right in the middle of the People's recon crew. He knew when vamps went out and where they headed. He knew which route your people took coming back into the city from Keep. And he spent all his free time picking up women at the bar." I leaned back. I'd had the benefit of Anna's vision and I still missed it. "So stupid."

Curran didn't say anything.

The stars shone bright, mocking us from above, laughing at two humans on a piece of junk. I closed my eyes, but sleep refused to come.

"I put a broken bottle into his throat," I said.

"I saw the bloody glass."

"He laughed. The bottle was in his neck. He was bleeding all over and laughing at me."

"He won't be laughing when I find him." He said it without bravado, flat, the same way most people promise to pick up a loaf of bread on the way home.

The Almanac said that the upir was immune to metal, wood, stone, tooth, and claw. How the hell were we going to kill him?

Curran reached over. His warm hand rested on my forearm for a moment and moved on. For some reason that made me feel better. There was no reason why it should have, but it did. I closed my eyes, put my head on the damp-smelling boards, and fell asleep.

A LIGHT TOUCH ON MY SHOULDER WOKE ME. "LEY point," Curran said.

I sat up and saw the break in the ley line up ahead, where the view of the normal world grew distorted. Several tall figures waited for us.

"Friend or foe?"

"Friend," Curran said.

The platform buckled, trying to contract on itself. The old boards creaked, taut under the strain, and grew slick as the damp wood expelled the moisture. The line quaked with a spasmodic jolt and spit us into the deformed arms of a dozen shapechangers. Clawed hands reached to help me off the platform. I got up to my feet on my own.

"How many are left?" Curran asked the head female.

She snarled, mismatched jaws snapping, and a shapechanger in a human form stepped forward. "Two groups, m'lord," he said. "A small family from Waynesville and nine people from Asheville. There was a freak mudslide and they have to dig through the sludge to get to the point."

Curran nodded and strode up the dirt road, flanked by dense brush. Far ahead I could hear the horrible growl of a reconditioned vehicle.

"A horse would be quieter," I said.

"I don't like horses," he said.

All around us the brush was alive with lithe shapes. Glowing eyes watched us, drinking in every movement. The Pack was mobilizing, pulling into Keep. No shapechanger would remain outside its walls, and until the last of them crossed the threshold of their fortress, the roads leading to it would remain heavily fortified.

"Nobody can remain on full alert forever," Curran said, as if answering my thoughts. "After we killed Olathe, I'd let them go."

Except that it wasn't over.

The roar of the water-powered car grew too loud to talk. We rounded the bend in the road and I saw the reconditioned Jeep guarded by three wolves. We climbed in and Curran drove to Keep.

CORWIN'S LABORED BREATHING ECHOED ACROSS THE Pack's infirmary like the toll of a mourning bell.

His misshapen face looked haggard, gray skin sagging from the bone. His feverish eyes fastened on me.

"The Wood is calling," he whispered. I touched his hand, and wicked claws shot out, tearing my skin. "A good hunt," the lynx-were said.

"He doesn't know who you are," Doolittle said over my shoulder.

Gently I freed my hand and patted the furry throat.

"It won't be long now," Doolittle said.

"I hurt," Corwin rasped.

I looked to Doolittle, but he shook his head. "There is nothing I can give him to stop that kind of pain."

"He was impaled on a broken lamppost when we found him," Curran said softly.

Corwin jerked upward. Massive hands gripped my shoulders and green eyes blazed, suddenly lucid. "I'm dying," he rasped.

"Yes," I said, while Doolittle said "No" at the same time.

The cat clung to me. "You never came to the Wood," he said.

"No." I held him gently. His chest shuddered, raked by pain. "I never did."

"Too bad . . ." the cat whispered.

He sagged in my arms and I lowered him to the pillow. He trembled. A bloody waterfall drenched the sheets, leaving a lynx among the tangle of bandages. His fur was matted and bloody.

"Shit!" Doolittle spat, shoving me aside.

I backed away from the bed, as he feverishly grabbed for a

syringe. Curran took me by the shoulders and turned me toward the bed at the opposite wall.

"There is someone I need you to ID for me," he said.

I looked at the bed and saw a man lying on his back covered to his chin with a blanket. There was something unnatural about his rigid pose. Curran pulled the blanket aside and I saw that the man was strapped to the bed. I took in the filthy brown hair and the hard face. There was something familiar about him. I'd seen him before. The man's eyelids snapped open and I took a step back, instantly recognizing the promise in the pale eyes. The bum from Ted's office. The pieces clicked. How stupid of me.

"We found him next to Corwin, knocked out cold," Curran said. "Apparently he jumped into the fight for Derek, but he won't tell me why."

"Untie him," I said.

Curran looked at me. "He has trouble controlling himself."

"Untie him," I repeated. "You shouldn't keep a Crusader of the Order tied up in your infirmary, Curran."

A tortured noise came from Corwin's bed, the hoarse painful yowling of an animal in agony. For a moment Curran looked like he would pound his fist into the wall, but the slip lasted a mere breath and the calm expression reasserted itself on his face.

"Get him to behave," Curran said, "and I'll untie him."

I sat down on the edge of the bed. The Crusader's gaze had a touch of insanity to it. All crusaders were crazy. It was in their job description. If at this moment, he broke free of his restraints, he would try to kill everyone in the room.

"I know who the upir is," I told the Crusader. "I know what he wants." The Crusader's eyes fixed on me. Once he looked at you, *really* looked you in the eyes, you started to sweat, your muscles tensed, and you knew you had only two options: fight or flight. He wasn't giving me his hard stare now. He was listening. "The upir can't stay away," I said. "Soon he'll come here and then I'll fight him." I pointed to Curran. "So will he. While Curran and I are fighting and bleeding, a man will be lying here, tied to the bed because he was too stubborn to compromise."

The Crusader spoke. "They took my weapons."

Curran nodded. "He can have them back if he promises not to assault my people. And to stay in Keep. I can't have him running around, fucking shit up right now. He cooperates or he stays tied to the bed."

I looked to the Crusader. The madness flared in his eyes and died. "Agreed," he said.

I took a knife from my belt and sawed through the restraints securing his arms. The Crusader sat up, rubbing his wrists. I offered him the knife and he cut the bonds on his ankles.

"What's your name?" I asked.

"Nick," he said. He wore the Pack's trademark sweats and smelled clean.

I looked to Curran. "Did you force him to bathe?"

"We dipped him," Curran said. "He had lice."

"My weapons," Nick said.

Curran motioned us to follow and we did. He led us out of the room to the hallway, down the corridor, and to a small room. "I have to go," he told me, his hand on the door handle. He turned to Nick and the two men locked stares, sizing each other up. "Stay put," Curran said.

"He will," I told him. The crusaders were insane, but they were still Knights of the Order. Their word was binding.

Curran opened the door for us and walked away, while we entered the room.

A lone bed flanked the wall next to a small dresser and a desk cluttered with metal. The place didn't look lived in—no personal items on the furniture, no loose clothes. A heavy punching bag hung from the ceiling and I wondered if that was standard equipment for Keep's rooms. Nick went to the desk, while I sat on the bed.

He had been loaded for bear when the shapechangers took him. A dozen shark teeth gleamed on the table, next to a 9mm Sig Sauer, a .22, a shotgun, several clips, and boxes of assorted ammo. A long chain lay coiled by the shotgun. Silver, judging by the color of its metal. A short gladius-shaped sword lay on the side, flanked by several sharp dirks and a crescent-shape serrated blade designed to slice the throat. A tangle of cord and wooden parts occupied the corner of the desk—a garrote. There was a utility belt, two leather bracers, designed to hold the shark teeth, a back sheath, an r-kit, and bandages.

Nick stripped to the waist, displaying a hard scarred torso. His left shoulder was bandaged. He pulled the bandages off, exposing a raw, jagged wound, and slapped the r-kit onto it. Taking a fresh roll of gauze from the table, he began to dress the shoulder. I got up, stood behind him, and passed the bandage over his back.

We worked in silence until the wound was dressed. He put the shirt back on and strapped the utility belt over his waist.

"How long have you been tracking him?" I asked.

He didn't look at me, his attention captured by the metal on the table. "Four years." He slid the shark teeth one by one into their places on the bracers. "First Quebec, then Seattle. Tulsa."

I touched the desk. "Nothing here will kill him."

He thrust the gladius into his belt. It didn't matter that he had nothing. He would still try.

"How did you know the upir would attack the kid?"

"The kid's been bound to you. A natural target."

"I'm a better target."

"No. He wants you alive. To breed." He stepped toward me

and touched my arm. Pale luminescence shimmered on his fingertips and vanished. "Power," he said. "Draws him like a moth to a flame."

He didn't need demonstrations of power. He could tell by touch. I tried to remember if he had touched me back in Ted's office. We'd brushed against each other.

"You took responsibility for the kid," he said. "You let him be taken."

He was right. "Coming from a man who let himself be captured by the Pack and strapped to a bed, that doesn't carry much weight. Tell you what, come back to me with the upir's head and then you can judge me."

He stared at me for a moment, his face blank, and then said in his grating voice, "Fair enough."

We moved at the same time and I stared into the barrel of his Sig Sauer while Slayer's tip pressed against his jugular. I wasn't sure how I knew he'd move.

The door opened slowly. Someone stepped into the room and halted. Neither of us was willing to look away. A long moment passed, and the newcomer exited. The door clicked, closing. A loud knock broke the quiet.

I grimaced at Nick. "You going to do something, do it, so I can slit your throat and move on."

The gun barrel pointed upward and vanished back into the holster with a safety's click. "Not now," he said. I slid Slayer back into its sheath.

The knocking persisted. "Come in," I said.

The door opened, revealing a female shapechanger. She turned to me. "Curran wants you," she said.

The woman led me to the Council room in the back of the auditorium and held the door, motioning us to enter. I stepped inside and saw a dead girl on the floor. She lay on her side, her legs spread obscenely, her arms stretched forward. Moisture stained her torn T-shirt. A tiny heart on a long gold chain, the kind a teenage girl might buy for herself, spilled through shredded fabric to rest on the ground. Long scratches scarred the wooden floor, where her claws had scraped the boards. She must have changed shape before she died.

Her head stuck out at an unnatural angle, blind blue eyes staring at the ceiling. She looked young, frighteningly young, fourteen at the most. Someone had broken her neck, quickly, cleanly, in a single devastating jerk.

Curran was looking at her corpse from the gloom. Mahon sat at the wall, rubbing his forehead. There was a white piece of paper in his hand.

"The upir sent a phone number," Curran said.

Mahon put his hand over his face. A scene played itself before my eyes: the girl lunging forward, blue eyes insane with the upir's thoughts, changing into a snarling beast in midleap; Mahon stepping forward, huge arms grabbing her, snapping fragile bones on instinct, before the brain reacted; the girl changing back and falling to the floor . . . I didn't ask where on her body they found the note.

"Are you going to call him?" I asked.

"Yes," Curran said. "Suggestions?"

"He loses his temper when things slip from his control," I said. "And he thinks with his dick." It wasn't much.

Curran picked up the speakerphone and dialed the number. The long tone sounded through the room once, twice. A click announced that the phone was picked up and Bono's voice said, "I see you've got my message."

"I got it," Curran said.

"Did you kill the little girl, cat? Is she lying on the floor someplace? Are you looking at her now, wondering if she would've been good to fuck? I can help you with that. She was sweet, clumsy and dumb, but sweet. A bit dry too, but she bled a lot, so that evened things out."

Curran's face was relaxed, almost tranquil.

"Is your girlfriend there with you?" Bono asked. He was babbling, excited, as if high on something. "The tall, dark-haired one with sharp eyes? I looked for her, but she was gone, so I took the human blonde you had before her. I'm going to have her for lunch tomorrow. The trick with fresh meat is to soften it someplace warm. But then you eat your meat raw, so educating you on the subtleties of cooking is a waste of time. My children are getting your girl ready to fillet. Would you like to hear her scream?"

There was a sound of a door swinging open and a woman's voice cut through. "Please no," she begged in sheer panic. "Please, please, please . . ." Me. It should've been me. There was nothing I could do but listen.

Curran's face was still calm. He picked up a chair and bent its metal legs into twisted curves.

Suddenly the woman choked, reaching a new intensity of terror, and broke into sobs, loud, heart-wrenching cries. Her desperation filled the room. She had no hope. She knew she was dying and she knew that there would be no escape. She screamed sharply once, twice, and fell silent.

Bono's voice snarled, "Idiot!" and Arag's unforgettable, inhuman whimper emanated from the phone.

"He punctured an artery," Bono's voice returned. "It's so simple—cut the stomach and pull out the intestines, but no, he manages to get his claws into an artery. Now I'll need to wash the innards. I'll have to kill him after all."

The whimpering receded, moving farther from the phone. "So

tell me," Bono said, "did she sound like that when you fucked her? She wouldn't scream for me, she only sobbed. A real disappointment, that one. Are you there, half-breed?"

"I'm here. And I too have something for you to hear. Say hello, Kate."

"Hello," I said.

There was silence on the phone. "It's not her," Bono said. "She's still in her house."

"How's the neck?" I asked. "Still spitting up glass?"

"She *is* here," Curran said. "*With me.* Tonight, while you're waiting for your corpse to get soft, think of me and her. Think of her begging me for it."

"I'll get her in the end." Bono's voice was taut with strain.

Curran made a loud sigh. "What is it about you and my sloppy seconds?"

Bono slammed the phone. I turned and left the room.

I WANDERED THE HALLWAYS UNTIL I FOUND THE ROOM where the Crusader and I almost had our little showdown. Nick was gone. I hoped he had enough sense to stay in the compound. Pissing Curran off right now was pure suicide.

I closed the door and went to the window. It was raining. The gray sky spewed gray water onto the dull grass far below. The grayness from the outside seeped into the room, leeching the color from the sparse furnishing. The rain would end eventually, leaving the grass and the trees brilliant green, vivid with fresh color. Strange how something so colorless and drab could rejuvenate the world.

There was a pair of gray sweats and nothing else in the small dresser by the bed. I placed Slayer and its sheath onto a Spartan blue blanket, stripped, and put on the sweats. I started slow, stretching, jumping an invisible rope, until warmth spread through my muscles. I cracked my neck and attacked the punching bag.

I wasn't sure how much time had passed. Sweat drenched my sweatshirt and the T-shirt under it, and the fabric stuck to my back. Sometime after my legs began to hurt, I heard a knock. My brain brushed the sound aside. I launched another kick, connected with a solid thump, launched another before my mind put on the brakes. "Come in."

Curran stepped into the room and closed the door. I wiped the sweat from my forehead and stretched. He sat down on a chair, hands resting on his knees, looking at the floor, and waited for me to finish.

"He called back," he said when I was done.

"What did he say?"

"He raved for a while. Promised to kill me. He won't attack Keep."

"You expected him to?"

"No. I hoped."

I sat on the bed. It wouldn't play out the way we hoped it would. Bono refused to be provoked into something rash, where numbers would be on the Pack's side. In this new age, combat between individuals decided the fate of many.

Bono would challenge Curran. It was inevitable. Curran had threatened his masculinity; he had made it personal, and when the challenge came, Curran would have to accept it. He was the Pack leader, the alpha male who didn't have the luxury of backing down. He would not hide in the safety of Keep, while the upir raged, murdering everyone whose death he thought likely to bring us pain.

I looked at Curran. "Your . . ." I paused searching for the right word. Girlfriend seemed inadequate, woman too impersonal. "Your lady," I finally said. "Is she safe?"

"Yes," he said. "She's here."

I nodded, screams of another woman echoing in my ears. Curran looked up at me, his eyes haunted. He looked older and tired.

"It's not that I don't care," he said. The screaming didn't stop for him either.

"I know."

"I can't let him intimidate me."

"I know," I repeated quietly.

"I'm sorry," he said and I wasn't sure exactly what for.

He left.

I sat on the bed and thought. Everyone had a weakness. It was the law of nature that for each being there was a predator or a disease or a vulnerability built into their very core. The upir had to have a weakness. It wouldn't be in any book. If that was the case, the Crusader would have found it by now.

I thought about everything that had happened since Greg's death, carefully going over events, trying to recall every detail. I thought about Bono, the places he visited, the people he might have met, the things he did.

The rain pounded harder. The sweat-drenched clothes grew cold on my back.

My room had no phone. I got up and went down the hall, trying different rooms, until I found one that did. I closed the door and dialed the number.

"Hello," said a male voice with the smoothness of someone for whom courtesy was a part of the job description. "You have reached the People's inner office. How may I help you?"

"I need to speak to Ghastek."

"Mr. Ghastek is busy at the moment . . ."

"Put him on. Now."

He didn't like what he heard in my voice. The phone clicked and Ghastek came on the line against the background noises.

"Hello?"

I heard quiet voices discussing something. He wasn't alone.

"You had to know," I said. "He was your journeyman for two years."

"I fail to understand . . ."

"Don't," I snarled.

There was so much fury in my voice that he fell silent.

"Tell me, Ghastek. Tell me what you know."

"No," he said.

I closed my eyes and tried to think clearly. I could go down there and slaughter everything in my way. I had a lot of frustration to vent. By the time they pulled me down, the People's stable would be awash in blood. I could do that. I wanted to do it very much, but then it wouldn't solve my bigger problem.

"He will come back for you," I told him. "He loathes you. He's committed now, and after he kills everyone he hates, he'll find you and you'll be raising vampires for him and his brood. You'll be his short-order cook."

"Do you think I haven't thought of that?" Ghastek whispered fiercely.

"Then tell me what you know. Tell me!"

Silence answered me. A moment passed, then another.

"I have nothing to tell you," Ghastek said and the line went dead. I fought the urge to hurl the phone against the wall.

"Asking the People for information is both futile and stupid," said Nick behind me. "They wouldn't sell you a spare umbrella in a shit storm."

I turned. Nick's hair, pulled back from his face into a ponytail, looked two shades lighter. The stubble had vanished, leaving a hard but pleasant, open face. He crossed the room, moving like a mature martial artist, fully confident in his skill and no longer competing to prove himself, but still too young and too fit to grow a sensei paunch. I could tell he was both quick and trained, armed with a muscle memory that would allow him to counter a kick or a punch without pause or thought.

He stopped a respectable distance away, and I realized he smelled like Irish Spring soap. For a moment I wasn't sure if I was looking at the same man and then our gazes met. The familiar urge to step back flooded me.

"Why, you're adorable," I said, trying not to break into a nervous laugh. "All that you need is one of those little earrings in one ear."

He gave me his hard stare.

"I'm just curious," I said. "When you do that to people, do they usually start to shake and fall to the ground quivering with fear?"

"They usually just die surprised," he said.

"Must not have worked on the upir then."

He swung a large knapsack over his shoulder.

"Going somewhere?" I wondered, sitting down on the bed. My reaction time was probably close to his, and there was enough distance between us. If he tried anything, I had time to evade.

"Yes."

"And how are you planning on getting past the Pack sentries?"

"I'm planning on you getting me out," he said. "They took away my wolfsbane, but I know you have some."

I rubbed my face with my hands. I did have wolfsbane—I would have been an idiot to venture within the Pack's territory and not bring any. And I was probably better at using it, too. "Why would I help you escape? Do you have any idea how pissed Curran will be? I might as well slit my wrists now."

"Considering how the upir plans to use you, it might not be a bad idea."

Nick stepped to me, reached out slowly, and brushed my hand with his fingers. A sharp tingle of magic nipped at my skin and his fingers glowed with white radiance, as if he had dipped his hand in fluorescent paint.

I pulled away. "Would you stop doing that?"

His gaze probed me. "Who are you? Where do you come from?"

"I'm pretty sure I came from my mom and dad," I said. "See, when a man puts his penis inside a woman's vagina . . ."

"I know how to kill him," he interrupted.

I shut up.

Nick crouched next to me. "Back in Washington, I tracked him down to the Shrine of the Gorgon. He'd helped himself to the priestesses and slaughtered the priests, but before Archiereus of the shrine died, he told me how to kill him. But I need my tools. Help me make it out of here, and I'll come back with a weapon to fight him."

"Why not just tell Curran?"

He shook his head. "The Beast Lord won't listen. He's got tunnel vision: keep the Pack safe. He won't let me out."

"Tell me," I said.

"Will you help me?"

"Tell me first and I'll do what I can."

Nick leaned toward me. "Bone of prey," he whispered. "You kill him with bone."

"I'll help," I said. "But while you're out, I need you to do me a favor. Bring me a present, Nick."

CURRAN LOOKED AT ME. HE WASN'T GIVING ME A HARD stare. He was just looking at me with no expression at all.

"Where's the Crusader?" he asked. His voice was level.

"He needed some 'me' time," I said. "I might be wrong, but I don't think he's a team player."

There were seven of us in the room: Curran, Jim in his jaguar shape, Mahon, two lupine sentries, the stable master, and me. The sentries and the stable master looked decidedly uncomfortable. Their eyes still watered from the wolfsbane and the left sentry had a full-blown allergic reaction, complete with red rash and a running nose he probably desperately wanted to wipe. If it wasn't for Curran, he might have made a mad dash for the handkerchief, but the Beast Lord's presence kept him rooted at attention, and so he just stood there, both faucets dripping.

Curran nodded calmly, feigning understanding. He was too composed for my liking. In his place I would've exploded. I flexed my wrist lightly, feeling the edge of the leather bracer full of silver needles rub against my skin. Mahon had politely requested to hold Slayer for me while Curran and I had our little talk. Just as well. It's not like I could kill Curran now. *Should.* It's not like I *should* kill Curran now. I could always try. Later.

The Beast Lord crossed his arms on his chest. His face looked placid. Calm before the storm . . .

The jaguar at my feet tensed and tried to look smaller. Nick needed a bit of a distraction while he rode like a bat out of hell on the horse commandeered from the Pack stables. I'd provided that distraction by leading Jim and his posse of pissy shapechangers on a merry chase through the countryside.

"Just so we're clear," Curran said. "You *did* understand that I didn't wish you or the Crusader to leave Keep?"

"Yes."

"That's what I thought," Curran said.

He grabbed me by the throat and slammed me against the wall. My feet felt no floor. His fingers crushed my neck.

I clasped the hand that held me and jammed a long silver needle into his palmar nerve between the index finger and thumb. Curran's fingers trembled. His hand opened, releasing me. I slid to the floor, dropped, and swiped at his legs. He fell. I rolled away and came to my feet. On the opposite side of the room Curran rose to a half crouch, his eyes burning gold.

The whole thing took maybe two seconds. The stunned audience never got a chance to react.

Curran reached for the needle, pulled it out, and dropped it to the floor, never taking his eyes off me.

"It's okay," I told him. "I have more."

He lunged from a half crouch into a spectacular pounce. I dashed forward, aiming to come under him and flick the needle into his stomach. And we both crashed into Mahon.

"No!" the Bear growled.

I bounced off his leg and sat onto the floor, stupidly blinking. Mahon grabbed Curran by his shoulders and struggled to keep him still. Huge muscles bulged on his shoulders and arms, splitting the seams of his sleeves.

"Not now," Mahon grunted. His reasonable voice had no effect. Curran locked his hands on Mahon's arms. I could see the beginnings of a judo style hold there, but Curran did not follow through. Instead it degenerated into a brute contest of strength. Mahon's face went purple with effort. His feet slid.

I got up. Mahon's arms trembled, but Curran's face had gone pale from the strain. The Bear against the Lion. The room was so thick with testosterone, you could cut it with a knife. I looked at the sentries.

"You and Jim might want to leave," I told them.

The younger lycanthrope stirred. "We don't take orders from . . ."

The older male cut him off. "Come."

They filed out the door, taking the jaguar with them.

I went to the locked men and very gently took Curran's right wrist and tugged on it. "Let go, Curran. Please, let go. Come on. You are mad at me, not at him. Let go."

Slowly the tension drained from his face. The gold fire ebbed. His fingers relaxed and the two men broke off.

Mahon puffed like an exhausted plow horse. "You are bad for my blood pressure," he said to me.

I shrugged and jerked my head in Curran's direction. "I'm even worse for his."

"You left," Curran said. "You knew how fucking important it was and you still left."

"Nick knows how to kill him. He needs a weapon and you wouldn't let him out," I said.

"And if the upir had caught you," Mahon said softly. "What would you have done then?"

I took a sphere Nick had given me from my pocket and showed them. The size of a walnut, it was metallic and small enough to perfectly fit into the palm of my hand. I squeezed the sides gently and three spikes popped from the sphere, moist with liquid.

"Cyanide," I explained.

"You can't kill him with that." Curran grimaced.

"It's not for him. It's for me."

They stared at me.

"People were dying," I said. "He was laughing, and all I could do was to sit tight and be safe."

Curran growled. "You think it's easy for me?"

"No. But you're used to it. You have experience with responsibility for people's lives. I don't. I don't want anybody else to die for me. I'm up to my knees in blood as is."

"I had to send three patrols out," Curran said. "Because of you. None of them died, but they could have. All because you couldn't stand to not be the center of attention for a few minutes."

"You're an asshole."

"Fuck you."

I started sniffing. "What the hell is that stink? Oh, wait a minute, it's you. You reek. Did you dine on skunk or is that your natural odor?"

"That's enough," Mahon roared, startling both of us into silence. "You're acting like children. Curran, you've missed your meditation, and you need one. Kate, there is a punching bag in your room. Make use of it."

"Why do I have to punch the bag while he meditates?" I mumbled on the way out.

"Because he breaks the bags when he punches them," Mahon said.

I was almost to the room when it occurred to me that I had obeyed Mahon without question or even doubt. He had that eternal father-thing about him that managed to throw me off track every time. There was no defense against it or at least I didn't know of one. He didn't use it when he fought with Curran. I tried to figure out why while I dutifully punched the bag. My punches were rather pathetic. Then exhaustion settled in. A mere twenty minutes later I gave up, took a shower, and fell onto my bed without finding an answer.

CHAPTER 10

SOMEONE STOOD OVER ME. MY EYES SNAPPED OPEN AND Curran's face slammed into focus. He leaned against the wall next to the bed looking at me.

"What?"

"He called," Curran said.

I sat up in bed. "He decided he wants a fight?"

"Yeah. He put Derek on the line. He broke the kid's legs and is keeping him in the leg irons so the bones can't heal."

Better and better. "Bono give you any terms?"

"Me, the Crusader, and you. Tonight."

How nice. A party for the top three on the upir's most wanted list. "Where?"

"Southeastern ley point. He says he'll let us know from there."

"Are you bringing backup?"

"No," he said. He didn't mention any reasons but I knew them all: his word, his pride, his duty, the fact that the upir would kill Derek. Any one of those would do.

I rubbed the sleep from my face. "What time is it?"

"Noon."

The patrols caught me at seven in the morning and I had gone to bed around eight, which gave me a grand total of four hours of sleep. "When do we have to leave?"

"Seven thirty."

I lay back down, pulled the blanket up, and yawned. "Fine, wake me up at seven then."

"So you're coming?"

"Did you expect me to hide here?"

"He referred to you as his little snack."

"He's a sweetie."

"He's also all about screwing you."

I raised my head enough to look at him. "Look, Curran, what do you want from me?"

"Why does he want to mate with you?"

"I'm a good lay. Go away, please."

Curran brushed my quip aside. "I want to know why he's got a hard-on for getting you knocked up."

There was a pun in that sentence somewhere but he didn't look like he was in the mood to notice. "How should I know?" I said. "Maybe the idea of torturing my child gets him hot. I've had four hours of sleep. I need at least four more, Curran. Go away."

"I will find out." He made it sound like a threat.

"You read too much into it."

He peeled himself from the wall. "How will I find the Crusader?"

"He'll be here in a couple of hours. He thought he'd get an invitation. Please don't take his weapons away this time. He comes of his own will."

Curran walked out. I took a deep breath and forced my mind to go blank.

NICK WALKED THROUGH THE DOOR AT TWENTY MINutes till four. I was awake and putting on my boots.

He closed the door and leaned against it. His face had gained stubble and his hair looked greasy again.

"What do you do to your hair?"

"Dust, hair gel, and a little gun oil."

"Ever thought of patenting the recipe?"

"No."

I stood up. He locked the door and took a leather roll from the inside of his trenchcoat. He put it on the table, untied the string securing it, and unrolled it with a snap. Inside lay two yellowish blades, one almost a foot long and the other about the size of my hand. I picked up the larger one. It was filed from a human femur split in half, and a long groove ran along the center of the blade where the bone marrow had been.

"Too heavy," I murmured.

"And brittle," he said softly. "I broke four."

"Why didn't you have one when you and Bono fought over Derek?"

His eyes flashed. "I did," he said. "It shattered in my coat when he kicked me."

I ran my finger along the blades. Considering how little time he had, they were amazingly well made.

"I won't get anywhere near him with this one." I put the large blade down and picked up the smaller one. With this one I'd have to get close to the upir. Very close.

"You get one shot," Nick said.

I nodded and tucked it into my knife sheath.

"You still have the sphere?" he asked.

I nodded.

"Still planning to use it?"

My hand twitched to check the comforting weight of the metal in my pocket. Somewhere deep down I knew I wouldn't use it. I would fight to the end, fight until he would be forced to cut me to pieces. I would make him kill me if I had to. After all I was only human. It wouldn't take much.

I glanced at Nick and realized he knew exactly what I was thinking. "Only if I have no choice," I said.

I RODE ONE OF THE PACK'S HORSES, A SOLID, THICK-muscled creature of an undeterminable shade somewhere half-way between mud and soot. He pounded the ground with his hooves as if suspecting that the thin layer of soil masked a nest of wriggling snakes and he could get at them if he just stomped hard enough.

"Wind," the surly werewolf had told me after presenting me with the reins. Given that I had smothered his face with wolfs-bane less than twenty-four hours ago, I wasn't high on his list of favorite people. "His name's Wind."

I had thought of asking him what possessed someone to give this illegitimate offspring of a knight's war stallion and an over-sized plow horse a star-of-the-racetrack name but had decided against it. Now Wind was merrily pounding his way through the darkened city at the velocity of a tired speed walker. Curran's howling Jeep wasn't even getting a workout and Nick I couldn't see. His red gelding had taken off at the first snarl of the magic-powered engine and insisted on maintaining the distance.

I patted the charger's neck. "At least you're not skittish."

Might just as well have screamed into a tornado. The bloody Jeep drowned any sound in its tortured battle for sonic supremacy.

The magic was thick and growing thicker, flooding the sleepy city with untapped power. It mixed with the light of the old moon, swirling in the alleys, churning among the ruined carcasses of gutted buildings, feeding on concrete and plastic. As we rode through the derelict industrial district, heading toward Conyers and the ley point, we watched the crumbling wrecks of once proud structures disintegrate slowly into nothing while all things magic triumphed. It was impossible not to find significance in the situation. A superstitious person would've viewed it as an omen, a gloomy forecast of things to come. I scowled at the cemetery for human ambition and kept riding. Tonight I would have given ten years of my life to have the tech reassert itself for a few hours. As it was, I probably didn't have ten years to give.

The ley point shimmered ahead, a short, controlled jerk of reality pricked by a magic needle. We reached it at the same time, the snarls of Curran's Jeep sending Nick's gelding into near panic.

"Would you shut that thing off!" I screamed over the noise.

"No! Takes too long to warm up!" Curran roared back.

"Why won't you ride a horse!"

"What?"

"A horse! Horse!"

Curran's gesture plainly told me what I could do with the horse in question.

An animal scuttled forward and paused before us, poised until it was sure we noticed it. It resembled a bobcat but only vaguely. It was too large, close to sixty pounds, its spine and legs too long and disproportionately narrow, like those of an adolescent cat. The top part of its face was unmistakably feline, while the bottom half boasted an almost perfect human jaw with a small, pink-lipped mouth. The effect was too disturbing for me.

At least now I had a good idea who had left those hairs at Greg's murder scene.

Convinced that we'd seen it, the nightmarish bobcat took off down the highway with unexpected speed. Nick chased it and so did Curran in his Jeep. After a few moments of prompting, Wind realized that I wanted him to move and happily obliged.

We followed the bobcat out of the city and along the highway for the better part of an hour. The horses began to tire, but the beast showed no signs of slowing down. Finally it darted off onto a side road, under a canopy of tall pines. The pavement had crumbled, splitting under the pressure of the roots. It would slow the horses down and stop the car flat.

Nick pursued the cat, while I lingered long enough to see Curran park his Jeep on the side of the highway and shut it off. He pulled himself out of the cab, showing every intention of running after us. I squeezed Wind's sides with my knees—he didn't seem to understand subtle clues—and my faithful mount pounded after Nick.

I caught up with the Crusader at the end of the road, where the trees parted, bordering a large clearing. A massive, forbidding structure of red brick and concrete stood before us. An eight-foot-tall concrete wall secured the building, and only the three upper stories were visible. I looked around. Overgrown and unkempt, the clearing showed signs of past landscaping, and a straight streak of pavement, half-choked by weeds, led to the gap in the wall, where heavy metal gates stood partially ajar, offering a glimpse of the inner yard. The bobcat thing bounded up the walkway and dove between the gates.

There was something familiar about the building. It was simple, almost crude in construction, just a blocky box of about four stories with narrow windows blocked by metal grates, yet the sight of it filled me with dread.

Curran came around the bend in the road, running at an easy pace. No sweat marked his face.

"Red Point," he said grimly, stopping beside me. "It had to be Red Point."

Nick looked at me.

"A local prison," I told him. "The left wing inmates kept complaining that ghosts were trying to kill them. Nobody paid attention until the walls came to life during a strong magic fluctuation and swallowed the prisoners. They found partially entombed bodies."

"Prisoners half-buried in brick," Curran said darkly. "Most were still alive and screaming."

I shifted in the saddle. What I took to be a pile of debris to the left of the main building now took on a definite shape of a decrepit guard tower. How the hell did the trees grow so fast? They looked decades old.

"I thought MSDU leveled this place years ago," I muttered.

"No." Curran shook his head. "They just condemned it when the walls wouldn't stop bleeding. They don't kill it unless they know they can't use it."

I reached out, feeling for the power, and recoiled. Thick dire magic clothed the prison. It permeated the walls, drowning the building, flowing from it like an invisible octopus spreading its tentacles out in search of its prey. I quested again and found a tangle of necro-tainted threads within the thickness of the magic. Something fed on the power of the prison, digesting it to fuel itself. Something undead and enormously powerful.

"A zombie?" I whispered.

"Smells like one." Curran grimaced, upper lip quivering lightly to reveal his teeth.

The metal gates stood partially ajar, inviting us in. I didn't want to go. A crazy thought popped into my head—I could just ride away. I could turn my horse around and ride away, far away, and never look back.

I don't have to enter.

I dismounted and tied Wind to a tree. It wasn't fair to take him into that place. Reaching for Slayer, I freed it from the back sheath.

"Ever twist your elbow doing that?" Curran asked.

"No. I've had a lot of practice."

Nick dismounted and tied his gelding to a tree next to Wind.

Not waiting for him, I started toward the gate.

"You're going to take him on by yourself?" Curran's voice asked at my side. He sounded amused.

"If I wait any longer, I won't go in," I said. My knees trembled. My teeth chattered in my mouth.

He grabbed me and kissed me. The kiss sent a wave of heat from my lips all the way to my toes. Curran's eyes laughed. "For luck," he whispered, his breath a hot cloud on my ear.

I broke free and wiped my mouth on the back of my hand. "When we're done with the upir," I growled, "I'll give you that fight you've been wanting."

"Much better," Curran said.

"If you lovebirds are done," Nick said. "Get out of my way."

Curran changed in an explosion of ripping clothes. I wasn't sure what was more frightening, whatever awaited us beyond the gate or the awful meld of human and prehistoric lion next to me, but at the moment I didn't care. The weight of the cyanide sphere tugged on my pocket.

Together we stalked toward the gates. Curran hit them once and they flew open, revealing the yard beyond, illuminated by three bonfires. I took a step inside and stopped, stunned.

The upir stood in the middle of the yard, bathed in the light of the flames. He wore a kilt. A belt of wide silver disks enclosed his waist, and charms of fur and bone hung from the links on leather cords. Ornate spaulders of silvery metal guarded his shoulders, joined by a chain of metal disks across his bare chest. Matching vambraces shielded his arms from the wrist to the elbow, leaving his hands exposed. His shins were bound in cloth but no boots protected his feet and he stood lightly poised, ready to leap. He held a spear, tipped by a foot-long blade, curved like a scimitar. The blade shimmered with borrowed firelight, matching the gleam in his eyes. He looked so odd, standing there in the middle of the yard, against the backdrop of a crude modern building, a being ancient but alive, a contradiction in terms, as if time itself had torn and spit him from its depths complete with the kilt and wild gray hair.

"Damn," Curran growled. "I didn't know this was a costume party."

His voice jarred the illusion. I snapped my fingers. "Oh, hell. I should've brought my French maid outfit."

The upir laughed, sharp teeth gleaming. "Look at the windows, Kate. Look at your sisters."

I glanced up and saw them, positioned in the windows like pale statues. Women. At least two dozen, standing rigid and still in torn, bloody clothes on the windowsills. Some of them looked dead, others were—several corpses hung from a large chain stretched from the roof. They all looked the same, robbed of their souls by identical expressions of fear twisting their faces. They hadn't been there when I had surveyed the place from beyond the wall.

Slayer smoked, feeding off my fury, and thick opaque liquid slid shimmered from the tip of its blade, evaporating before it hit the ground.

Something moved within a giant pile of rubble at the far wall. The hill of garbage and refuse shuddered, breathed, and surged upward, impossibly high. A nauseating stench hit me. I gagged. Garbage fell, revealing yellow bones and shreds of rotting flesh oozing putrid juices. Flies swarmed, thick like a black cloud. An enormous skull fixed me with deep-sunken, dead eyes. Gargantuan jaws gaped open and clanged together, forcing teeth as long as my arm to scrape against each other. The horrid corpse shifted. A taloned paw rose and touched the ground, sending tremors through the yard. The bonedragon advanced.

"A dragon for a knight," the upir called. "Aren't you happy, Crusader? I gave you an excuse not to fight me."

Nick charged past me, the silver chain whipping from his sleeve. He swung at the upir and Bono danced away. An enormous putrid foot slammed before Nick, separating him from the upir. The bonedragon snapped at the Crusader.

A horde of the upir's offspring burst from the doors and swarmed upon me. I sliced, nearly splitting a furry carcass in two just before I saw Curran leap onto the dragon's shoulder. He lingered for a mere moment and pounced down, behind the creature, where Bono stood grinning.

The beasts surged about me. Slayer cut and hissed. Sharp claws dug into my foot and withdrew.

Something was wrong.

I cut at a piggish snout and saw the light die in the creature's human eyes. The shaggy body crumpled to the ground. Its siblings closed the ranks above it. I raised my hand for a new blow.

The beasts didn't attack. They snarled and pawed the ground, but no fangs ripped into me. I lowered the blade.

They were there to contain me. Fodder for my saber to keep me busy and away from the fight. I advanced. The creatures stood their ground and snarled. A wide-jawed spotted thing snapped, missing my arm by a hair. So they wouldn't let me move.

I could just kill all of them. I should just kill all of them.

Something in me rebelled at the idea of slaughtering these

pitiful half-animals while they looked at me with human eyes. I swung about, looking for a leader and found Arag, half-crouched, swaying softly. His horrid face had a slack, muted expression.

"Arag," I said.

The monster gave no indication he heard me. His jaws hung open, exposing yellow fangs and a thick tongue.

"Arag!"

The creature stared at me stupidly. I moved to skirt him to the left and he snarled, coming to life. I kept going. He charged me. His huge head hammered my side with awesome force. I fell and saw his fangs above me. Drool dripped on my face, stretching from his teeth. He hovered above me, black lips quivering, legs rigid. The slack expression reasserted itself and he moved back, returning to his place in the ring of furry beasts.

I gained my feet. Not trusting his offspring, Bono was keeping them on a short telepathic leash.

Beyond the line of furry backs, the bonedragon bit at Nick. The Crusader ducked and hurled something into the gaping mouth of the zombie. I waited for the loud boom, but none came. Nick's grenades wouldn't work. The magic here was too thick.

Far to the left, Curran and the upir battled. Bono moved fast, matching the shapechanger in both speed and agility. His wild hair flying, he leaped and spun like a dervish. His weapon was a blur in his hands, forming a wall Curran had trouble penetrating. A long laceration marred Curran's back, swelling with blood. It wasn't healing—the spearhead had silver in it.

Bono fought Curran and held his children in check. A man of many talents.

Time to jam a stick into his wheel.

I surveyed the horde before me and picked a thick, bald beast. It stood on disproportionately thin legs, staring at me with dull eyes. Its fat gut hung low, almost reaching the ground.

I flicked my wrist. The heavy round head rolled to the dirt in a gush of blood. The beast's heart pumped a few times, not knowing that the creature was dead, and more blood bubbled from the stump of the neck, saturating the air with a sharp metallic scent.

The horde trembled. The beheaded carcass crumpled to the ground and the ring of beasts around me nodded in tandem, mesmerized by its fall. I slashed the beast's gut and a clump of tangled bloody intestines spilled into the dirt.

I cut a piece of steaming entrails, speared it with Slayer, and dipped it in a puddle of blood. The horde's eyes fixated on the flesh. I raised it on the tip of my blade and held it before Arag's nose.

"Blood," I told him.

Arag's baboon nostrils flared. He sucked in the scent. A thick tongue rolled from his mouth, greedily licking the air. The quivering piece of intestine beckoned, dripping blood to the ground. I moved back a step and Arag moved with me, his gaze glued to the slimy morsel.

I took another step. Arag followed and jerked, checked in midmotion. The bloody, tender piece of flesh hung before his nose, so close that he had only to lean forward to touch it. And he wanted it. He wanted it very badly. Yet Arag did not move.

Bono's hold on them was too strong. There was nothing I could do to break it. Every moment I delayed was costing Curran and Nick in blood.

The twisted monstrous horde looked at me, seeming so pitiful.

I flicked the piece of flesh from Slayer's blade, sending it arching high into the night air. Arag died before it hit the ground.

Bono had never seen me kill before. I cut them down one by one, quickly, methodically, working with mechanical precision. Some fought when threatened, others just stared stupidly as the smoking blade sliced into them, cleaving muscle and tendon. In three minutes' time it was over and I ran across the yard to Curran and Bono.

The bonedragon charged to intercept. Its skeletal tail swept at me, and I rolled to the side as the dragon pounded its enormous paw into the ground, blocking my way. The zombie snapped at me, jaws clanking inches away. I leaped to my feet and slashed at the rotting paw. Slayer sliced through decaying tissue in a spray of putrid sluice. The dragon's tail smashed into me. Pain exploded in my side as if I had been hit by a truck. I flew through the air and fell into the carnage I had wrought.

I leaped to my feet and slid on the blood of Bono's children, sprawling headfirst onto their corpses. Where the hell was Nick?

The dragon closed in for the kill. Huge teeth reached for me, and I pushed away from a corpse, sliding on my back across the bloody mess. The skeletal jaws dug into the spot where I had been a moment earlier.

The dead orbs of eyes swiveled, focusing on my new position, and the dragon attacked. I squirmed to the side. Great teeth scraped the ground next to me and I jammed Slayer into the undead beast's cheek, sending a jolt of magic through the point where its jaws met. The dragon jerked its head up, taking me with it. I hung twenty feet above the ground as the zombie's jaws opened and closed, trying to crush my sword. The stench of decay choked me. Through the gaps in the dragon's teeth, I saw a ribbon-thin, half-rotten tongue flailing against the cage of fangs.

Slayer ate through the undead flesh, liquefying gristle and muscle. The dragon shook its head like a dog gripping a dead rat in its mouth. Something within its skull popped with a light crack. The enormous mandible broke free and crashed to the ground, taking me with it. I flipped in the air, trying to land on my feet and fell onto the jagged teeth. A sharp bone shard jabbed through my ribs. I cried out and pushed myself off the bones. Above me a clawed foot replaced the sky. I dove to the side and the dragon's paw crushed its broken jaw.

It didn't matter. I could hack it to pieces and it would still keep coming at me limb by limb.

I clenched my teeth, fighting the fire in my side and saw Nick above me pulling himself onto the roof of the building. He was aiming for the far end, where several silhouettes crouched by a vent. The navigators.

The dragon bounded after me. I backed away, almost stepping into a fire.

Nick sprinted across the roof to the clump of figures. It would take several navigators to pilot the dragon. If Nick knocked one of them out of the lineup, the zombie might collapse. Or break free.

I grabbed a branch from the fire and hurled it at the dragon. It arched across the sky and splashed across the undead chest. The rotting tissues failed to ignite. The dragon kept coming, undaunted. I ran around the blaze, keeping the flames between me and the dragon.

The beast snapped at me but stayed away from the fire. Above me, Nick smashed into the beings on the roof and a shaggy body tumbled to the ground, screaming out its life on the way down.

The dragon skirted the bonfire, forcing me to move. I dug my fingers under my T-shirt as I ran. They touched broken bone, sending a shock of blinding pain through me, and came away slick. Not good.

The dragon hesitated and twisted away from me, huge head rising on an impossibly long neck to reach the roof.

A distraction. Lord, please, let the dragon's pilot be a coward. A couple of minutes, that's all I need.

I began to chant low, under my breath. The magic surged to me, coalescing about me, stalking my tracks like an opportunistic cat smelling tuna. I plunged Slayer into the ground and put my other hand against my ribs. Warm blood coated my palm and I thrust my hands into the fire. Flames licked my skin and blood hissed, evaporating. I kept chanting.

On the roof Nick struggled with something tall and clawed as the dragon snapped, trying to skewer them both with its fangs.

Magic grew, flowing into me and through my blood and flesh, bonding with the fire. My hands blistered as I paid the fire for its service.

"Hesaad," I whispered to the flame. *Mine.* Suffused with my blood, the fire flinched like a living thing, no longer a simple reaction of oxidation, but a force alive with the power it borrowed from magic. *"Amehe." Obey. "Amehe, amehe, amehe . . ."*

The flames detached from the refuse that served as its fuel. An enormous fireball hovered before me. With a wave of my hand, I released it. It streaked across the yard, roaring with fury, and smashed into the dragon's jagged spine. The impact broke the dragon in two. The back half fell, burning, while the front, lacking support, sagged to the ground, the huge head stretching helplessly, still trying to reach the combatants on the roof.

The flames consumed the undead flesh. It was so tempting to sink to the ground and watch them, but if I did that, I would not get up again.

I gripped Slayer's hilt and the skin on my right hand split. I cried out and let go. The pain was too much. My charred fingers found a vial of anesthetic in my belt. Numb. I had to make my hands numb. The belt wouldn't release the vial and my ruined fingers were so clumsy. Tears wetted my cheeks. Finally the vial came free and I gripped the cork with my teeth, pulling it out. I spat the cork to the ground and shook the vial, throwing a cloud of dust into the air. I walked into the dust, my hands before me. The world swayed, growing distorted, and numbness came.

I watched myself reach for the sword and grip the handle I couldn't feel and pull the sword free. Turning I walked across the yard to where Curran still fought with the upir.

A piercing howl cut through the roar of the fire, a scream of pure towering fury, so potent it could only be human. Two bodies plummeted to the ground from the roof. One of them wore a trenchcoat.

"Good-bye, Nick," I whispered, as the bodies smashed into refuse. The Crusader's scream died with him. The dragon shuddered and melted, decomposing before my eyes into a pile of bone and ooze. The abomination's pilot was dead.

I dragged myself across the yard. I could see the bloodstain on my T-shirt now. Not that much time left.

I saw Curran, exhausted and bleeding from a dozen places. Bono's body looked misshapen, as if he was missing pieces of himself. It looked like whole sections of muscle had been torn from his body and his skin had simply closed over them.

The upir spun the spear off his neck, catching it with ease, and rammed its point into Curran's thigh. Curran snarled and ripped into the upir, tearing great chunks of meat from Bono's chest. The upir cried out and danced away. His skin knitted itself over the wound.

My legs failed me and I fell. The poison sphere rolled out of my pocket beyond my reach. *Nice going, Kate. Nice going.*

I bent my neck and watched the battle upside down, unable to flinch when their blood splashed me.

They were tired. Both of them. There were no taunts, no showy roars. Just fighting, grisly, bloody, and painful.

Once again Bono danced away, light on his feet. Curran snarled low and saw me. His gaze locked on me for a moment and I knew that this was it.

Bono lunged. Curran knocked away the spear, ripping at the

upir's leg and missing, deliberately too slow. The spear came back in a shiny arch. Bono thrust. The razor-sharp point slid into Curran's stomach and out his back, pinning him to the ground. But Bono had leaned forward, putting all his strength into the thrust. Curran's massive hands gripped him by the shoulders. Enormous muscles strained. A horrible snarl ripped from Curran's mouth. Bones broke, muscle snapped, and I saw light through Bono's chest, as Curran tore his torso in two. For a moment the two halves of the chest were upright, the head and neck on the left half sticking out at a strange angle, and then the upir lost his balance and tumbled into the dirt.

Curran sagged against the spear. Blood poured from his mouth and his face went slack. "No," I heard myself whisper. "Please, no."

The upir's body jerked. His mangled chest shuddered and slowly he rose to his knees. He remained upright for a moment, fell again, and pushed himself forward across the soot-stained ground toward me.

I watched him crawl, his body straining to mend the damage. His head came level with mine. I could see the red sack of his heart pulsing through the gap in his chest half-hidden by ruined spongy lungs.

"Nice fight," he said through the bloodstained lips. His right eye wouldn't stop blinking. "Something to remember on our honeymoon."

I jammed the bone blade into his heart.

Bono screamed. His unearthly howl shook the prison and the windows exploded. His hands flailed, trying to reach the dagger, but failed to find the small blade. He clawed at my neck, but I couldn't feel it. It didn't matter. That final thrust had taken everything I had.

There was nothing left to do but to lie here. I'd see him die before I did. That would be enough for me.

Bono lay on his back. "I don't want to die," he whispered between short, hoarse breaths. "I don't want to die . . ."

His body began to smoke. First a thin sheen of indigo fog coated his skin and then it grew, curling into long tendrils and escaping into the night sky.

"My power . . . leaving me," Bono rasped. The smoke thickened and the upir began to whisper in the language of power. His words made no sense to me. He chanted feverishly, trying to hold onto life or simply praying, I wasn't sure which.

A shudder troubled his ruined body. His speech faltered. His heels dug into the ground. The blue smoke vanished, like the light of a candle snuffed out by someone's breath. The upir's unblinking eyes stared into the night. It was over.

I wished I could push myself farther and reach Curran. Maybe I'd have someone to fight with in the afterlife if we went together.

It was a hell of a kiss . . .

Darkness claimed me.

EPILOGUE

HELL LOOKED A LOT LIKE MY HOUSE.

I lay under what appeared to be one of my blankets on what appeared to be my bed. A dull gnawing pain chewed on my ribs. Do people still feel pain in the afterlife?

There was a glass of water sitting on the night table next to the bed. Suddenly I was very thirsty. I reached for the glass and discovered that both my hands were heavily bandaged. I stared stupidly at the bandages then at the glass.

A hand wearing a cutoff glove picked up the glass and offered it to me.

"For a second I thought I might actually be alive," I said, looking at Nick's unshaven face. "Now I know—I've gone to Hell and you're my nursemaid."

"You're not as funny as you think," he said. "Drink the water."

I did. It hurt going down.

He took the glass away from me and got up, trenchcoat brushing the edge of my blanket.

"Careful with the germs there," I said.

"My germs are the least of your problems," he said. He reached over, swiped his fingers across my arm, and studied the glow. "Doesn't usually shine this bright. Or last this long." He turned slowly, surveying my place: the old, beat-up couch, the scratched night table, the ancient rug, the basket full of clean laundry, all threadbare jeans and faded T-shirts, and waved his shimmering fingers. "See? Still going."

I raised my bandaged hand and put it on his fingers, smothering the glow. So many people died because of me. Every time I thought about it, my chest ached, and I wanted to grab onto someone and make them tell me it would be alright, the way I wanted to hear it at my father's funeral. But there was nobody left. And if someone did reassure me, they would be lying.

I always went out looking for other people's trouble. Strangers hired me to solve their problems. I'd spent years making sure problems did not ram my door and tear my life apart. And it didn't work. So much time wasted. And what did I have to show for it, except the body count?

"Responsibility is a bitch," Nick said.

"Yeah."

He took my hand off of his. A faint white radiance still danced on his skin. He shook his head, as if in wonder. "If I were on my own, packing some power, and for some reason not wanting to be found, I might lay low for a while. But I'd know that sooner or later I'd have to come out and play, because whoever's looking for me would eventually find me. I'd start building some connections. The thing about a lone wolf? Once you corner it, it has no one to turn to."

He put a small rectangle of paper on the blanket and walked away. I swiped the card. A phone number without any name or address. I stuck it under my pillow.

"Curran?" I called after him.

"He made it," Nick said.

Later Doolittle came to visit me. He replaced my bandages, helped me to the bathroom, and told me how Mahon had sent a scouting party looking for us despite Curran's orders and how the scouts missed us because of the enchantment placed on Red Point. We might have died where we lay if Nick hadn't stumbled out of the gates.

They had found sixteen women in Red Point, battered and abused to the point of near death. For seven others we had come too late. Their corpses escaped the horror of the Red Point in body bags. They found Derek too, locked in one of the small rooms.

Someone finally called the cops, and the Paranormal Activity Division had descended onto the old prison like a pack of dogs onto a lost kitten. They unearthed a graveyard of human bones in one of the cellars, enough skeletons to keep the morgue busy for the next year.

Doolittle forbade me to mess with my bandages for another forty-eight hours and left, promising to send a nurse in his stead. While he was gone, the magic hit and I spent two hours muttering the chants to repair my hands and the wards about my house. By the time the nurse arrived, the defenses were up and she couldn't get in. I listened to her yell for about twenty minutes and then she left.

I didn't want anyone with me. Solitude felt good for now.

I lay in bed, once in a while making a heroic journey to the bathroom, and thought a lot. There wasn't much else to do but think.

Later, I received a visit from the Paranormal Activity Division, whom the ward, unfortunately, didn't deter. Two plainclothes detectives alternatively tried to charm and bully me into giving them a statement without a Guild representative present. I lost my patience forty-five minutes into our conversation and pretended to fall asleep, forcing them to leave.

The next morning I was walking, not very well, but walking. Considering my rapid progress, I pulled the bandages off my hands. I had no nails, but other than that, my hands looked normal. Very pale, but normal. If it wasn't for magic, they would've taken months to heal. But then if it wasn't for magic, I wouldn't have ended up in this mess.

Anna called. We spoke and after a few minutes our conversation grew increasingly strained until she said, "You've changed."

"In what way?"

"You sound like you've aged five years."

"A lot happened," I said simply.

"Will you tell me about it?"

"Not right now. Later sometime."

"I see. Do you need help?"

I did, but I didn't want her there and I wasn't sure why. "No, I'm fine."

She didn't insist and I was grateful.

The next evening brought another visit from Doolittle, who fussed until I let him in. He released my ribs from the bandages, revealing a long jagged scar snaking its way across my ribcage. He thought it might dissolve in time. I didn't think so. Even if it did, the damage to my person was already done and no amount of magic would wipe it away.

A week passed without any news. As soon as I was able to manipulate a pen to my satisfaction, I wrote a long report detailing the investigation, tied a pretty blue ribbon around it, addressed it to the Order, including a request to forward a copy to the Guild, and left it for the mailman.

My nails started to grow, for which I was grateful. My fingers had looked odd without them. The pile of unopened mail grew too, slowly building in the basket by my door. I ignored it. There were bound to be some bank notices in there, threatening to do horrible things to me unless I fixed my overdraft. I didn't want to deal with them.

I thought a lot while sitting in the sun drinking iced tea during the day and coffee in the evenings, and read. Anna called again, but sensing that I didn't want to talk, she kept the conversation embarrassingly short.

During one of those sunshine-filled days, I raided the cabinet where I kept my wine and dumped it into the sink, leaving myself a single bottle of Boone's Farm Sangria. For a special occasion.

The next Sunday I awoke early, disturbed by a loud banging. It echoed through the house, ricocheting from the walls. I listened to it for a few moments, making sure it wasn't a figment of my imagination, then grudgingly hauled myself out of the bed and went to investigate.

A quick reconnaissance identified the sound's point of origin, namely my roof, and I went into the yard to get a good look at it. The sun was already up and beginning to grill the ground. I looked at the top of the house and saw the Beast Lord in a torn T-shirt and paint-stained jeans. He held a hammer in a very businesslike manner and was applying it to my roof. Derek sat next to him, dutifully passing him shingles.

The world had gone insane.

"Can I ask you a question?" I called.

Curran stopped hammering and looked at me. "Sure."

"What are you doing on my roof?"

"I'm teaching the kid a valuable skill," Curran said.

Derek coughed. I chewed on that for a moment and opened my mouth, but before I could say anything, the phone rang.

"Get off my roof," I said and went to pick it up.

"Ms. Daniels?" said an unfamiliar male voice into the receiver.

"Kate."

The hole above my hallway was almost gone. Curran showed no signs of stopping.

"Kate, this is Detective Gray with PAD."

"You would be which of the two bulldo . . . law enforcement professionals that came to my house?"

"Neither."

The hammering gained new intensity as if Curran was trying to pound the house into the ground. I guessed he was trying to get the nails all the way in with one hit.

"I'm here with Knight-protector Monahan. He informed me of your involvement with the Red Point Stalker murders."

Red Point Stalker. Ugh. Sounded like some half-baked made-for-TV mystery.

The hammering had reached deafening levels.

"We're impressed. If you don't mind me asking, what is that banging?"

"Just a minute." I put the receiver on the table and yelled, "Curran!"

"What?"

"Could you hold a minute? I'm on the phone with PAD."

He growled something, but the hammering ceased.

"I'm sorry. You were saying . . . ?" I asked the phone.

"I was saying that we're very impressed with your work. We contacted the Pack, and the Beast Lord had very good things to say about you."

"He did?"

"Yes."

"Just a minute." I lowered the receiver. "Curran?"

"What?"

"Did you get a call from PAD about me?"

"I may have."

"What did you tell them?"

"I don't recall. I think I mentioned your discipline and ability to follow orders. I may have said something about you being a team player."

Derek emitted a strangled cough.

"Why?" I demanded.

"It seemed like a good idea at the time." Curran resumed hammering.

"I'm sorry," I said into the phone, sticking my finger into my other ear so I could hear. "His Majesty tends to exaggerate things. I'm not a team player. I'm undisciplined and I have a problem with authority. Also, the Beast Lord can't hammer for shit."

On the roof Derek was laughing his head off.

"I wasn't looking for a team player," Gray said.

"Oh."

"What do you know about Marduk?"

"An ancient deity. Prefers human sacrifice. He's particular about how it's prepared. Why?"

"I'm looking for an Order representative to assist my team with one of our cases. Your name came up."

"I'm flattered but I have no authority to represent the Order."

"Knight-protector says that you do."

"Oh." "Oh" was a nice word. Short and neutral.

"I spoke to the Guild; they are on board. They recognize a need for a liaison between themselves and the Order, and it seems everyone would be happy if you took the job."

Liaison between the Guild and the Order. A salary. An actual salary—probably embarrassingly small—but still, a salary. Unfortunately, in my current financial state "small" would prove to be a problem. "I'm sorry," I said. "I would love to help you but I can't. I'm broke. As a matter of fact, at the moment I'm less than penniless, and I'll have to take a regular Guild gig before I can commit to anything else."

There was a muffled sound of distant conversation and Gray said, "The knight-protector's asking if you've checked your mail lately."

I poked the pile of correspondence with my foot and it spilled onto the floor.

"Is there something in particular I should be looking for?"

"A blue envelope."

I fished the blue envelope out of the pile and opened it, cradling the receiver between my shoulder and my ear. A beautiful statement looked back at me, boasting of six thousand dollars being deposited into my account. The caption stated, "For services rendered as stated in accordance with Article M1." M1 covered crusaders. Unlike most knights, they didn't draw a salary but were paid per job.

"Please tell him thank you for me." I'd never become a crusader, Ted and I both knew it. But I was grateful for the rescue.

"I will," Gray said. "So will you take the job?"

Thank you, Ted. "Yes," I said. "I will."

"Great. When can you start?"

I looked outside where a beautiful day was just beginning and thought of the two shapechangers on my roof.

"Tomorrow," I said. "I can start tomorrow."

Magic Bites

Bonus Material

KATE DANIELS SERIES FREQUENTLY ASKED QUESTIONS

The world has suffered a magic apocalypse. We pushed the technological progress too far, and now magic has returned with a vengeance. It comes in waves, without warning, and vanishes as suddenly as it appears. When magic is up, planes drop out of the sky, cars stall, electricity dies. When magic is down, guns work and spells fail.

It's a volatile, screwed-up world. Magic feeds on technology, gnawing on skyscrapers until most of them topple and fall, leaving only skeletal husks behind. Monsters prowl the ruined streets; werebears and werehyenas stalk their prey; and the Masters of the Dead, necromancers driven by their thirst for knowledge and wealth, pilot blood-crazed vampires with their minds.

In this world lives Kate Daniels. Kate likes her sword a little too much and has a hard time controlling her mouth. The magic in her blood makes her a target, and she has spent most of her life hiding in plain sight. But sometimes even trained killers make friends and fall in love, and when the universe tries to kick them in the face, they kick back.

FAQ

Is the entire world like this or is Atlanta the only place that's messed up?

The entire world has been affected by magic.

What caused the magic to start flooding the world?

I'll let Kate explain since we already wrote it once, and I'm lazy:

> *Theory said that magic and tech used to coexist in a balance. Like the pendulum of a grandfather clock that barely moved, if at all. But then came the Age of Man, and men are made of progress. They overdeveloped magic, pushing the pendulum farther and farther to one side until it came crashing down and started swinging back and forth, bringing with it tech waves. And then in turn, technology oversaturated the world, helped once again by pesky Man, and the pendulum swung again, to the side of magic this time. The previous Shift from magic to tech took place somewhere around the start of the Iron Age. The current Shift officially dawned almost thirty years ago. It began with a flare, and with each subsequent flare, more of our world succumbed to magic.*

Are Kate and Curran going to be a couple?

You have to read more books to find out. ☺

What is Saiman?

See the answer to the previous question.

What is Kate?

See the answer to the previous question.

What is Curran's beast?

That we can answer. Curran transforms into *Panthera leo atrox*, a species of prehistoric American lion. One of the largest predatory cats that ever existed, the American lion roamed the Americas, hunting prehistoric bison, deer, North American camels, and mammoths. It ruled the food chain until roughly eleven thousand years ago, when climate changes forced it into extinction. The American lion was a muscular animal, with long legs and a lightly striped pelt, with some specimens weighing close to nine hundred and fifty pounds. It had a very large brain, and scientists theorize that it was capable of complex social relationships. The American lion lived in mated pairs rather than prides. We took some liberties in the portrayal of Curran's beast in the name of artistic license. For example, the American lion had no mane, but Curran has one because it's a little difficult to imagine a male lion without a mane.

What kind of badger is Dr. Doolittle?

Dr. Doolittle is a honey badger.

Can you explain the m-scanner colors?

Pure white or silver—the color of Divine: a deity or possibly a demigod. Appearance of a true god is extremely rare.

Pale blue, blue-gray, or silver-blue—the color of Human Divine: someone who derives his power from faith. Monks, priests, diviners, prophets.

Blue—the color of Human Magic: someone using purely human magic. Elemental mages, psychics, telekinetics, empaths, etc.

Green—the color of Wereanimals: shapeshifters who derive their ability to change forms from Lyc-V. Werewolves, werejaguars, bouda, etc.

Olive green—the color of Animal-weres: animals who derive their ability to change forms from Lyc-V. Occasionally shamans and druids will also register this color.

Pale peach or very pale yellow—the color of Animals. The m-scanner registers their magic as very faint, and often it does not show up at all.

Red—the color of Undeath. It's rare to find pure red without the addition of some other color into it. Usually only undead animals register as pure red and only because animal magic is too weak to significantly impact the color.

Purple—the color of Human Undead. Vampires, reanimated corpses, ghasts, etc. The older the undead, the weaker the human influence and the darker and redder its color or appearance is on the m-scan.

What's it like to write together?

You know, people ask this all the time and some of them hope for a really dramatic answer. They usually want to know if we get in fights over characters and if one of us has to sleep on the couch because we disagreed over a particular character. Writing together is a lot like being married: we compromise and try to compensate for each other's weaknesses. It's very rarely confrontational. We don't throw dishes or punch walls. We might squabble occasionally, but nothing makes it into the finished manuscript unless we agree on it.

How did you come up with the idea for this world?

It came together from a variety of influences. We both really liked eighties cartoons, like *Thundarr the Barbarian* or *He-Man*, which featured a mix of magic and technology. When Gordon was younger, he read a book (sorry, don't recall the name now) where there was a god Tech. He was a very small god, who started out when the first bow was made. Other gods made fun of him. But the more humans developed, the stronger he grew until he finally became incredibly powerful. It seemed like a really neat idea.

There are so many stories where the magic is going out of the world. Tolkien's work, for example, explores that theme. And it always makes you so sad to read about magic dying. We yearn for magic. Look at the film industry—we use cutting-edge technology to create magic on-screen. It's an integral part of being human: to want a touch of something mystical and unexplained. It seemed natural to bring about a "reverse" apocalypse: magic is back with a vengeance. We hope you'll like it.

CHARACTERS

KATE DANIELS

APPEARANCE

Age: 24

Gender: female

Height: 5′7″

Build: lean, muscular

Hair: dark brown, long

Eyes: dark brown, almond shaped, slightly elongated

Skin: tan

Distinguishing marks: a tattoo on her left shoulder of a raven holding a bloody sword with the words *Dar Vorona* (Raven's Gift)

AFFILIATION

Guild, later the Order of Knights of Merciful Aid

SPECIALTY

Killing things, with much bloodshed. Talking trash, infuriating authority. Driving the Beast Lord crazy.

FUN FACTS

Kate is short for Ekaterina, but Kate never thinks of herself as that. Daniels is not her real surname; it was randomly chosen by her adoptive father, Voron.

CURRAN LENNART

APPEARANCE

Age: 31

Gender: male

Height: 5′11″

Build: muscular, defined, gives off a sense of coiled strength about to explode

Hair: blond, typically cut short except during the flare, when it grows into a mane within a few days

Eyes: gray, luminescent with gold when excited or angry. Curran's gaze is extremely difficult to hold.

Skin: naturally pale, but he tends to bake himself in the sun every chance he gets

Distinguishing marks: a broken nose that didn't quite heal right, very unusual for a shapeshifter

Beast form: an enormous gray lion, striped with darker gray, like smoke blown against gray velvet

AFFILIATION

Pack. Curran is the Beast Lord. Tremble.

FAVORITE MODE OF FIGHTING

Grows teeth the size of dinner forks and bites people's heads off. Roars afterward.

SPECIALTY

While Curran's physical power is overwhelming, he rarely has to use it. He's observant and shrewd, and tends to employ diplomacy and intimidation, breaking into violence only as a last resort. He moves extremely quietly and enjoys sneaking up on Kate.

JIM SHRAPSHIRE

APPEARANCE

Age: 33

Gender: male

Height: 6′2″

Build: lean, muscular, sinewy and very defined but not bulky like a bodybuilder

Hair: dark brown, short

Eyes: dark brown

Skin: dark

Face: Jim cultivates a thuggish appearance because he likes when people underestimate him. He is not a handsome man, but he is masculine and confident.

Voice: Jim has a melodious voice. He clearly can sing, but nobody has ever heard him do it.

Beast form: American jaguar, *Panthera onca veraecrucis*

AFFILIATION

Pack, alpha of Clan Cat, chief of security; Mercenary Guild member.

SPECIALTY

Suspecting plots, hiding things in odd places, obsessing to the point of paranoia, berating Dali for driving too fast, berating Kate for doing stupid things, berating Curran for not following security protocol.

Jim is the Pack's chief of security. His attention to detail is meticulous. He notices everything and forgets nothing. He is fiercely independent and a powerful opponent. He is Curran's best friend. He accepts Curran's authority as Beast Lord; however, Jim enjoys a greater degree of autonomy than other Pack alphas, because Curran is aware that Jim is smarter than he, and he generally leaves Jim to do his job as he sees fit. Jim has many aliases, including Jim Black, as he's known in the Mercenary Guild.

MAHON

APPEARANCE

Age: 62

Gender: male

Height: 6′

Build: broad shouldered, heavily muscled, looks like you could hit him with a truck and the truck would fold about him like a crushed Coke can

Hair: very dark and curly, typically worn shoulder length; a thick beard that Mahon keeps neatly trimmed

Eyes: brown

Skin: ruddy. Mahon looks like he spends a lot of time outdoors.

Distinguishing marks: a long scar reaching from over his left eye to the temple, only visible if you look very closely

Beast form: a huge Kodiak bear, *Ursus arctos middendorffi*. Mahon has never been weighed in beast form, but rumors say he tops fifteen hundred pounds.

AFFILIATION

Pack. Mahon is the Pack's executioner.

FAVORITE MODE OF FIGHTING

Mahon prefers to charge, using his weight as a weapon. Like Curran, he can crack a shapeshifter's skull with a single blow of his paw.

SPECIALTY

Kingmaker. Mahon is a strong believer that the Pack requires a powerful leader to survive. He groomed Curran to take that position, supported him in his rise to power, and now he assists him unconditionally, even though they don't always see eye to eye.

TED MOYNOHAN

APPEARANCE

Age: 51

Gender: male

Height: 5'10"

Build: Once very fit, Ted now runs to hard fat: he won't be running any races for fun, but if you slammed a door in his face, he'd punch through it. He looks like a middle-aged heavyweight boxer who developed love of Twinkies and Western clothes.

Hair: salt-and-pepper, short, hides his bald spot under his hat; sometimes grows a short beard, sometimes prefers to be clean-shaven

Eyes: brown

Skin: pale. Despite cowboy clothes, Ted hasn't seen a ranch for years and years.

AFFILIATION

Atlanta chapter of the Order of Knights of Merciful Aid, knight-protector. As the knight-protector, Ted oversees the activity of the Atlanta Order office.

FAVORITE MODE OF FIGHTING

Ted prefers a large heavy mace but is also fond of modified guns, especially revolvers.

SPECIALTY

Seems to always know more than people expect he does. Demands exceptional results in unreasonable time, and when his subordinates deliver, he takes it as a given. Dislikes any deviation from the human norm. Ted is very stubborn and has been known to dig in his heels when it suits him.

FACTIONS

MERCENARY GUILD

The Atlanta Mercenary Guild is a loosely structured organization of independent contractors, which takes care of magic "hazmat" too minor to attract the attention of the Order of Knights of Merciful Aid or the Paranormal Activity Division of the Atlanta Police Department.

The Guild has two divisions: administrative, which is located in a former Sheraton Hotel on the edge of Buckhead, and merc, which consists of all of the mercenaries who actually do the work in the field. The individual mercenaries, called mercs, are employee-owners of the Guild: as long as they are within the Guild, they own a tiny share in it. The admins may or may not be employee-owners, as some of them are employed on a temporary basis.

Each merc is assigned a "zone," a small geographical area that is his or her territory. Mercs are grouped into "chains," according to their ability and location. A typical chain has eight to ten links.

The day-to-day Guild business takes place as follows:

The admin division receives a trouble call, which may come by phone, in person, or by some other means.

The admins evaluate the call, making sure that the Guild is authorized to take the job and that no other agency or individual has been simultaneously employed to handle the same problem. Mercs are a violent lot, and the primary function of the admin division is to keep the detached-body-part count to a minimum. If the Guild is clear to proceed, the trouble call is logged in as a "gig."

The admins determine into which zone the gig falls and alert the mercenary assigned to that zone. If the merc declines the gig, the job is passed on to the next person in their chain. Occasionally, the job is too difficult for a single merc, and the "owner" of the gig may choose to team up with another merc. It is up to the individual mercs to determine how they want to split the bounty.

The merc performs the job and delivers proof to the admins. In cases where the job was done remotely, the person who has made the trouble call or the local police agency usually has to confirm that the problem has been resolved. The merc then collects the bounty, 30 percent of which goes to the Guild to pay for medical and dental insurance for the mercs, admin maintenance and salaries, lawyer fees, and other various expenses. Most mercs also contribute up to 10 percent of their bounty to their pension fund. No one has yet gotten rich enough to live in style on their pension, but it has kept a few retirees off the streets.

Well-Known Mercs:

Solomon Red: the Guild's reclusive founder who lives in administrative headquarters

Mark: Solomon's right hand and the Guild's chief admin, responsible for day-to-day operations

THE PEOPLE

The People defy categorization. Part cult, part corporation, part scientific institution, the People concern themselves with necromancy: study, raising, and care of the undead. Like the Order, the People have a national presence, with bases in most major cities.

The People are obscenely wealthy and seemingly interested solely in increasing their wealth. They control the largest vampire stable on the continent and are not shy about wielding their influence.

VAMPIRES

Vampires are mindless creatures. They have no ego, no consciousness, and no ability to formulate thoughts. Left to their own devices, they would slaughter every living thing until nothing was left; and then they would turn on one another. Because their brains do not atrophy like most of their internal organs, vampires provide an ideal anchor for a person gifted in necromantic magic. Such people are called navigators. The navigators "ride" or "pilot" the mind of the vampires, experiencing the world both through their own eyes and ears, and through the eyes and ears of the vampires. Vampires hunt by sight and hearing. Their sense of smell is underdeveloped and doesn't translate to the navigator.

Vampire creation is a strictly controlled process, overseen by the government. A person may legally choose to become a vampire after death provided he or she is of sound mind when the contract is made. To replenish and expand their stable, the People offer a sizeable amount of money to the prospective "vamps-to-be," and they are never short on applicants. The prospect of money usually attracts terminal patients. Once the contract is signed, the applicant may terminate the contract at will at any point. The applicant is closely monitored. In the moment of clinical death, he is injected with Immortuus pathogen. His body is then secured for the duration of the incubation, which usually takes ten to twelve days. Upon undeath, the vampire becomes the property of the People.

JOURNEYMEN AND MASTERS

To become a member of the People, one has to pass rigorous ability tests. If the applicant demonstrates necromantic ability, he is hired as a journeyman. Journeymen are assigned to a Master of the Dead, an experienced necromancer, who is able to raise and navigate the undead. The journeymen do the grunt work of the vampire care and receive instruction in navigation. Most do not possess enough talent to ever reach Master of the Dead status. While impeccably dressed during business hours, in their time off journeymen often adopt Goth attire and show a strong preference for bright blood-red accessories.

Masters of the Dead wield a great deal of power. They have the authority to select their own candidates for the vampires out of the pool of potential applicants. Because the People pursue wealth with single-minded dedication and often own casinos, funeral homes, and security firms, most Masters of the Dead are wealthy. However, the People's agenda runs deeper than their surface addiction to material comforts. The People are ruled by Roland, a shadowy figure unknown to laymen. Roland is rumored to possess almost godlike powers. The People are his creation, and he uses them to further his own ends. What those ends are, nobody knows.

Currently the Atlanta chapter of the People has seven Masters of the Dead.

THE ORDER OF KNIGHTS OF MERCIFUL AID

The Order of Knights of Merciful Aid offers exactly what it promises: merciful aid on the edge of the sword or by the burn of a bullet. Powerful and disciplined, the Order is a nationwide organization, which consists of elite warriors and scholars. Each major city has its own Order chapter.

Members of the Order are called knights. The Order's mission, rules, and regulations are outlined in the Order's Codex, a book that many of the knights strive to memorize. When asked, the knights state their mission as simply "Protection of mankind." The knights are lethal, honorable, and, unfortunately, convinced that they are always right. Like the Mercenary Guild, the Order protects humanity against the dangers of magic, but unlike the Guild, the Order charges according to income, meaning that if an indigent person petitions the Order for help, the knights will assist him pro bono. The Order has a strange, semiofficial status and is considered to be a part of the Law and Order triumvirate, which also includes the Military Supernatural Defense Unit (special forces of the U.S. Army) and the Paranormal Activity Division (police).

KNIGHTS

To become a knight, one usually has to pass the Order Academy's legendary entrance exams. Upon acceptance, the prospective knight is given the rank of squire. Squires live and study within the Academy's walls for four years. They are not permitted to leave the grounds for longer than twenty-four hours even on holidays.

The course of study is strenuous and includes weapons and magic training and extensive mental conditioning. The Order isn't simply interested in producing effective knights. These knights must also be true believers in the Order's cause.

Only one in eight squires lasts long enough to graduate and be knighted as a knight-defender. Of those, one in twelve will die within the first year, and of the remaining, only one in three will make it to retirement.

The knights are ranked according to their ability and experience:

Knight-Defender: The rank and file of the Order. Knight-defenders usually have two to ten years of experience. If in that time they fail to distinguish themselves in a way that would permit the Order to assign them a new classification, they assume the rank of master-defender.

Knight-Questor: Once called knight-inquisitors, the questors specialize in investigations. They often enter the ranks of the Order after having served in the military or in law enforcement.

Knight-Diviner: Knight-diviners derive their power from faith. Buddhist monks, Taoists, Christians, pagans, and scholars of the Torah have all been known to serve as knight-diviners. Like all magic users, knight-diviners project their own magic field. This field is the reason why strong knight-diviners are particularly effective against vampires. When confronted with the human divine magic, the vampiric pathogen, which fuels vampires' insatiable thirst, fails to recognize the source of the magic as human. In other words, vampires view knight-diviners as moving pieces of scenery rather than targets. The knight-diviners act as counselors and psychiatrists. The Order recognizes their special status, and the Codex bestows protection onto petitioners who come to see knight-diviners: they do not need to identify themselves, nor do they have to disclose the reason for their visit to any other knight.

Master-at-Arms: Masters-at-arms are knights distinguished by their supreme knowledge and ability with weapons. Masters-at-arms have a specialized designation according to their chosen weapon: "master-at-arms, blade," "master-at-arms, blunt," "master-at-arms, firearm," etc.

Master-at-Craft: Masters-at-craft are knights who possess exceptional magical knowledge and ability. Like masters-at-arms, they are distinguished by their specialization: "master-at-craft, medicine," "master-at-craft, conjuration," "master-at-craft, battle," etc.

Knight-Crusader: Crusaders have a special rank. Unlike most knights, they are not tied to a certain chapter, but are free to travel as they see fit. Crusaders are the Order's equivalent of a lancet. Got a nasty boil ready to rupture? Throw a crusader at it. He will take care of the problem and move on. Deadly fighters, the crusaders are extremely dangerous and unpredictable. They are the most shadowy of the knights and tend to be loners who value their privacy.

Knight-Protector: Knight-protectors spearhead the individual Order chapters. They are skilled leaders and proven fighters.

THE PACK

The Pack is the largest shapeshifter society in the South, possibly in the nation, rivaled only by the werebuffalo herd in the Southwest and the Ice Fury Pack in Alaska. By the latest official count, the Pack includes twelve hundred shapeshifters and is constantly growing. Organized with military discipline, the members of the Pack value loyalty, obedience, restraint, and duty above all else.

SHAPESHIFTERS

To understand the Pack one has to understand the shapeshifters. In every shapeshifter, a monumental struggle is taking place, a battle between man and beast. When a beast wins, the shapeshifter becomes a loup, a homicidal maniac. Loups feed on human meat. They revel in cruelty and commit atrocities. They are irrational and incapable of leading a life within human society. They die young and don't leave pretty corpses. If a loup is sighted and apprehended, it is killed. There is no rehabilitation and no going back.

When a human wins, he does so through adhering to the Code, a collection of writings, which the shapeshfiters treasure. The Code outlines principles of shapeshifter behavior and teaches control and discipline through mental exercise. The shapeshifters who follow the Code view themselves as free of the burden of the beast and refer to themselves as Free People of the Code.

The individuals who emerge from that crucible practice restraint in all things. They exist in a strictly regimented Pack structure. The Pack is segregated into clans according to the species of the beast. Within each clan there is an alpha male and an alpha female and a beta male and a beta female. The alphas rule the clan with absolute authority. They also bear the ultimate responsibility for the welfare of their clan. Should the clan be threatened, the alphas will be the first to fight and the first to die.

The betas assume the position of second in command. Alphas create policies, but betas are often responsible for implementing them. Should one of the alphas die or become unable to perform his or her duty, the beta will step in and assume the alpha status and responsibilities.

More often than not, the alphas are married to each other, but not always. The most notable exceptions are Clan Bouda and Clan Rat. Clan Bouda's alpha, Aunt B, is a widow and her son serves as the Clan's alpha male. Clan Rat's alpha male, Robert Lonesco, is homosexual and his spouse, Thomas, is considered to be a beta male, while Margaret Killian serves as the clan's alpha female.

The alphas make up the Pack Council, the function of which is to assist the Pack alpha in governing the shapeshifters. The Atlanta Pack alpha is known as the Beast Lord, due to the unusually large size of the Pack and the manner in which the current Beast Lord, Curran Lennart, came to power. While the Council has the ability to influence Curran, they can't challenge his authority or override him.

The life of the shapeshifter is difficult. If they survive the hormonal surge of puberty without going loup, they become members of the Pack. Young shapeshifters quickly find out that not all humans welcome them, and most come in contact with prejudice sooner or later. While the Pack rules of conduct may seem draconian, this lifestyle works for most because within the Pack they find warmth and understanding and safety. The alphas care about their people and will, and do, lay down their lives to keep them secure.

While each clan has its own base, they come together at Keep, a huge fortress built specifically for the Pack over the course of two decades. No modern machinery was used during the construction, and Keep is magic-proof. Besides Keep, the Pack owns several large tracts of land, including a huge forested region in Virginia they call the Wood. The Pack also keeps several offices within Atlanta. Because the Pack's influence is increasing, the People view them as rivals, and the animosity between the two factions grows with every day.

CLANS

Clan Wolf: The largest of the clans and the most disciplined. Wolves are warriors. They work well in groups and prefer a team approach to most problems. Wolves also have the largest percentage of pups who turn loup at puberty: almost one in four. The pups who turn loup have to be killed. Wolves are maniacal in their loyalty to Curran.

Clan Rat: The second largest of the clans, the rats are scouts, spies, and deadly assassins. Due to an unusually high metabolism, they eat continuously. The rats are prone to shakes, crippling fits that result from severe depletion of nutrients. Like wolves, they work well in a group or on their own.

Clan Hyena: Counting only two dozen members, hyenas, or boudas as they like to be called, still wield a fair amount of influence. Boudas are extremely violent fighters. They are prone to berserk rages, and other clansmen learn the hard way to steer clear. Boudas are also notoriously adventurous in their sexual explorations. Just like in nature, women dominate this clan, with men taking the secondary role. Boudas don't play fair. Common Pack wisdom says that if you make an enemy of the boudas, you will never be forgiven. They will smile in your face and break your neck the second you look away.

Clan Cat: Clan Cat consists of large and small felines. By nature, cats are loners. They bind into a clan only out of necessity, so they can have a representative on the Council. Of all the clans, cats are the most lethal and the most independent. They occasionally balk at orders simply because they can. They are also prone to cruelty. Currently Clan Cat has forty members.

Clan Jackal: Clan Jackal is a quiet clan. The jackals are known not for their superior fighting abilities, but for their cunning. They are family-oriented and peaceful. However, occasionally the long-standing rivalry between Clan Jackal and Clan Wolf rears its head. Like hyenas, jackals are susceptible to frenzy.

Clan Heavy: Clan Heavy includes all of the shapeshifters with large beast forms who do not fit into any other clan: bears, boars, moose, badgers, etc.

Clan Nimble: Clan Nimble includes all of the shapeshifters with small beast forms who do not fit into any other clan: mink, stoat, wolverine, fox, etc.

THE NEO CULTS

The Neo Cults worship pagan gods, some ancient and some new. Some are benevolent, like the druids, and some are malevolent, like the Children of Mephisto. The cults have no central authority. They are not actually a faction, but just a convenient way to classify practitioners of religious magic.

Greek, Celtic, and Scandinavian pantheons command the largest number of followers among the neocultists, with Native American and Hindu gods being a close second.

Cults exclude the following major religions and denominations: Buddhism, Hinduism, Judaism, Christianity, Islam, and Taoism.

Cults can be loosely classified by their beliefs:

Classical: Greek and Roman pagans, worshipping one or more deity or creature from the classical mythology

Traditionalist: Scandinavian (Viking) pagans, druids, volhv (Russian druids), Japanese pagans, Chinese pagans, etc.

Sect: odd offshoots of major religions, rejecting the doctrine of the majority, such as Satanists and the Order of the Broken Cross

Modern: cults based on an entirely new belief system, such as the presence of extraterrestrial beings

FACTION QUIZ

FIND YOUR PLACE IN KATE'S ATLANTA

Answer the questions honestly and write down the letter of your answer to each one.

1) ***Laws must be obeyed***

   a) As long as they don't conflict with the higher purpose

   b) As long as they don't endanger your people

   c) As long as they don't interfere with profits

   d) As long as they don't conflict with the natural course of things

   e) Always

   f) As long as they don't get you into hot water with the cops

2) ***You see a man breaking into your favorite mom-and-pop store in your neighborhood. You***

a) Pull out your sword, go over, and ask him what he is doing

b) Sneak up behind him and punch him in the face

c) Get your flunky to go over and stab him

d) Watch him do his dirty deed, find out where he lives, and poison him a week later

e) Pull out your gun and yell at him to get down on the ground before you blow his brains out

f) Walk away. It doesn't concern you one way or another.

3) ***You see your best friend's spouse making out with another person. You***

a) Confront the spouse after and explain that what she is doing is morally wrong

b) Tell your best friend what you saw and be ready to guard his back because there is going to be a brawl

c) Observe the couple, trying to deduce reasons behind the affair

d) Let them be. Each person is free to choose their own path.

e) Confront them on the spot

f) Wait until the date is over and try to blackmail the cheaters for money or sex

4) *The most important factor in deciding whether to take a job is*

a) Will it benefit the majority of people?

b) Will it benefit your family?

c) Does it hold scientific value and is it intellectually stimulating?

d) What are its consequences?

e) Is it legal?

f) Does it pay well?

5) *You're throwing a party. You provide*

a) Good food, good liquor, nothing fancy, moderation is encouraged

b) A feast: lots of food, lots of beer and wine, no hard liquor

c) Expensive food, expensive wine, only the best will do

d) A chance to drink and celebrate being yourself

e) Hard liquor and BBQ

f) A room. This party is strictly BOB—bring your own booze.

6) *The perfect pet is*

a) A mastiff: loyal and devoted

b) A mutt, a cat, a rat: as long as it has fur, it's all good

c) A snake: clean, sleek, calculating, and deadly

d) A bird: free, independent, with a clear view of the whole picture from above

e) A German shepherd: it obeys orders, it tracks people, and it protects you

f) A horse: you have to have one to get around, so at least the damn creature is useful

7) ***Your favorite computer-game genre is***

a) Role-playing: being savior of the world is always a good thing

b) Fighting and adventure: nothing better than fast reflexes, agile characters, and triple-kicking your opponent's head off his shoulders

c) Building sims: taking fifteen minutes to figure out just the right way to position the building is worth it if the city is perfect in the end

d) Puzzles: there is a pattern in all things. You just have to trust in your intuition to find it.

e) First-Person Shooter: blow heads off enemies with a high-powered rifle. If your buddy can play with you, it's even better.

f) MMO RPG: life is about grinding and getting better gear. Kill X amount of enemies; get X amount of money. Simple and profitable.

8) The most useful subject in school is

a) History: learn from your yesterday's mistakes to ensure survival tomorrow

b) Civics: without politics, civilization, and social interaction, people are just animals

c) Chemistry, genetics, and anatomy: a human body is a fascinating thing

d) Philosophy, biology, and ecology: we only have one planet. Might as well find our place in it.

e) PE and team sports: the world is a tough place. Might as well learn how to act together according to the rules of the game.

f) Basic math: you have got to know how much change you ought to get back when you give somebody twenty dollars to buy ammo

9) A parent must

a) Teach a child that sometimes life requires personal sacrifice

b) Keep a close eye on a little tyke so he doesn't go crazy

c) Provide a lot of interesting toys to help a child develop early

d) Get a pet, something small and cuddly to teach a child responsibility and compassion for those around him

e) Teach a kid that there is right and there is wrong, and you've got to pick a side

f) Pay for chores—if you work, you get paid; that's a good lesson to learn

10) Your car is

a) Four wheels and a motor—as long as it gets you from point A to point B on time, does it really matter what it looks like?

b) A Jeep or a Land Rover—functional, you can load a bunch of people in it, and it goes anywhere

c) A black SUV—not gaudy, but powerful and stylish

d) My two legs—I prefer to walk

e) A Ford Mustang—a good solid muscle car, goes fast

f) A Hummer, armored—it tells people two things: one, the owner is a badass, and two, if you're going to shoot at it, there is a whole lot of steel between you and the driver, so you better start running

HOW TO SCORE YOUR RESULTS

Count the letters you wrote down.

If You Answered Mostly A:
You are a knight of the Order of Knights of Merciful Aid. You're disciplined, competent, and organized. You serve a higher purpose and you tend to take a rational approach to most problems. Your mission is simply to protect mankind, even if it means protecting it from itself. You are lethal, honorable, and, unfortunately, convinced that you are always right.

If You Answered Mostly B:

You are a shapeshifter of the Pack. Family is the most important thing to you. You don't trust outsiders, and while you're fanatically loyal to your friends, you're courageous and aggressive and emotions occasionally tend to get the better of you. You value loyalty, restraint, and courage above all.

If You Answered Mostly C:

You're a member of the People. You pilot undead for a living and believe that most problems can be resolved through application of reason, money, or a vampire. You believe in the pursuit of academic excellence, as long as it doesn't conflict with your financial well-being, you like the finer things in life, and you feel that those who work hard should be able to show off the fruits of their labors.

If You Answered Mostly D:

You are a witch of the Covens. You believe in balance: for every action, there must be an equal and opposite reaction. He who disrupts the harmony of the world will get his comeuppance one way or another. You're independent and comfortable in your own skin, you live and let live, and you look to nature for guidance in resolving your problems.

If You Answered Mostly E:

You are a cop of the Paranormal Activity Division. You have a strong sense of right and wrong, and tend to see the world in black-and-white. The laws are there for a reason and you make sure that they stay in place. You live hard and party hard because you never know when you might have to put yourself between a crazed maniac armed with a fireball and a random citizen who just happened to be in the wrong place at the wrong time.

If You Answered Mostly F:

You are a mercenary of the Guild. Life is hard, but you're harder. You tend to look out for number one. You risk your hide to provide for you and yours, you work hard, and you don't let anyone get the better of you. When you take a job, you get it done, but you always keep your eyes on the prize, and if it gets too nasty, you aren't above walking away from the whole thing.

CURRAN POINTS OF VIEW

We've received numerous requests from our readers asking us what this or that character thought about certain scenes from the books. However, nobody has garnered as many requests as Curran. Finally, in the summer of 2009, Gordon decided to write a scene from the Beast Lord's point of view, and since then Curran POVs, as these scenes came to be called, have become a favorite with the fans. Some people even resort to bribing Gordon.

You can read many of these at www.ilona-andrews.com, our blog, but this is the first time they officially appear in print, and we're very grateful to Ace for giving us an opportunity to bring them to you.

UNICORN LANE

I was in Unicorn Lane at night. A bad time to be in a bad place. Anything can happen there, but it's never something good.

No one was in charge of Unicorn Lane. None of Atlanta's many supernatural factions could claim dominion over it. It was populated by those once human and those who had never been, and they hid in the dark ruins, feeding on each other and making visitors unwelcome. Thus Unicorn Lane was recognized by all as neutral territory, a no-man's-land you entered at your own risk. The scared hovered at the edge, the stupid died not far from it. I was here to meet someone, and if she made it far enough to find me, I would know she was neither.

I leaned back, feeling the cold stone of the abandoned building with my back. Moonlight seeped through the holes in the roof, illuminating a gap in the wall. She would come through there. The night shadows hid me, so I'd have plenty of time to look her over.

The Unicorn lay quiet. The night is never truly silent, but right now the monsters minded their manners. None of them knew why I was here, but all of them recognized they didn't want to be the reason for my visit.

What I did know of the merc came from Jim, my chief of security. He'd worked with her in the Mercenary Guild. That gave me pause. Jim was a cat and preferred the solitary hunt. It was rare for him to let anyone outside the Pack watch his back. He said she was fast, for a human, and good with a blade. He also said she had a big mouth and fought when she should run. None of this endeared her to me. Mercs were bottom-feeders. No honor, no integrity, no loyalty. They didn't stand for anything. I wasn't in the habit of personally meeting lowlife thugs who wanted to be tough guys. I had people for that.

However, I was willing to take a chance this time since Jim had vouched for her. Jim had seen her come out of situations that should have ended her, and he didn't believe all of her cards were on the table. She was likely hiding strong magic, which meant she came with baggage. That was fine if it made her useful. Something was hunting my people, the Free People of Atlanta.

We were shapeshfiters and we had the best trackers in the city, but we had yet to catch it.

Normally, we solved our own problems. We kept it in the family. Humans saw us as freaks, and I saw no need to give them more ammunition. But the murders had been too numerous, and some of the vampires had been destroyed as well. No big loss. The Order of Knights of Merciful Aid got involved. The only human I trusted in that organization of fanatics, a knight-diviner of the Order, had been investigating the case and was killed for it, presumably by the same creature. I have little love and less use for humans, but Greg Feldman had died helping us, and that counted for something. Incredibly, this merc was his estranged ward and had inherited the case along with a temporary position with the Order.

I would find this thing that murdered my people. I would stand over it and taste its blood as the light faded from its eyes. Nothing would change that. But with the Order's help, I would find it faster. If Greg's ward was looking for revenge, all the better. It would mean she was willing to take risks that could help me get my teeth on this creature's throat.

The night wind brought a mixture of scents to my tongue. Leather—old boots. A touch of sweat, clean and unmistakably feminine. A mix of rosemary, chamomile, lavender—shampoo, an herbal fragrance foreign to this dank and moldy place, nice. A very faint trace of cloves and steel—oil for the sword. She was near and moving closer.

She was quiet, nearly soundless for a human. Interesting. What was she?

Finally, the faint sound of a step. *Come closer, little mouse, you're almost there.*

The night shadows swallowed me. She would come in right across from me—it was the only way—and I would see her before she saw me, should I choose to let myself be seen. Perhaps if she looked as good as she smelled, I would give her that privilege.

A slight scratch of a foot sliding on stone. I leaned forward to get a better look.

Moonlight from gaps in the ceiling illuminated the scene as she put first a foot through the gap. She came in sideways, slowly and carefully, carrying a sword. An odd-looking blade, pale. She held it like she knew what she was doing, but her faith in its ability to protect her was misplaced. The tips of my claws itched the inside of my skin, wanting to come out. She had one sword, but I had ten claws.

She scanned the area, stopped to listen, then moved forward stealthily, like a dancer, hiding in the nearest shadow before I caught a glimpse of her face. The draft brought another whiff of her scent. She paused, and I knew she was peering into the gloom, trying to find me. I liked the way she moved, balanced and light, neither tiptoeing nor stiff. Nice body. *Come to me, mouse, don't be scared.*

She took a step forward and I saw her in profile. Exotic, strong features, not pretty, but I liked what I saw.

I drew my fingers through the dirt, scraping the floor a little.

She pivoted on one foot, turning her sword. Fast. Her head snapped toward me. Dark eyes stared straight at me. I detected no fear. Instead it was a look of challenge. So not a mouse after all but something more. This could be interesting. I'd let her dance in the dirt a bit more. She was fun to watch.

She crouched with her hand out. What the hell was she doing . . . ?

"Here, kitty, kitty, kitty."

Oh my God, she was retarded, and I was going to kill Jim.

She blinked and stared at me. She'd seen my eyes glow.

I let go, shifting in the dark into my true form. If you want a kitty, little girl, I'll give you one you'll never forget.

I stepped into the moonlight. She froze.

That's right. No sudden moves. I padded toward her slowly and circled her, allowing her take it all in. Do you like the kitty now? I could smell her surprise and fear. Our gazes met. Her eyes went wide and she fell on her ass.

Heh. A bow would have been sufficient.

I retreated into the shadows of the corner. I was not sure what effect a laughing lion would have on her, and I did not want her to faint. I reverted to human form and changed into sweats and a tee. Any other time, I might have walked out to her as is, but this was a business meeting. Best to keep it that way.

I gave her a few seconds to recover. She was dusting off her jeans.

"Kitty, kitty?"

She jumped a bit. Smart girl. Most shapeshifters can't switch back and forth like that. I'm not most shapeshifters. I am the Beast Lord.

"Yeah," she managed weakly. "You caught me unprepared. Next time I'll bring cream and catnip toys."

Toys wouldn't be necessary. "There may not be a next time."

I stepped out, and she turned toward me. She seemed almost relieved that I wasn't naked. Most women had the opposite reaction. Her loss.

I hit her with my hard stare. She met my gaze and did not look away or cringe. Points for her. She was tall for a woman, maybe two or three inches shorter than I. Young, maybe early or mid-twenties. She looked strong and lithe, like an athlete or martial artist.

"What kind of woman greets the Beast Lord with 'here, kitty kitty'?"

"One of a kind."

She continued to hold my stare. She might not have been as

funny as she thought she was, but she wasn't a coward. Good. I could work with brave.

I took a step toward her. "I am the Lord of the Free People."

FERNANDO'S

I sat at a table at Fernando's. It wasn't my favorite place—too posh, too public—but Myong liked it. The service was good, the food was okay, but people didn't really come to Fernando's to eat. They came to be seen. Most of them were self-important people indulging themselves. It wasn't my crowd, and I didn't care to be seen by them.

Myong glanced up from her menu. She, on other hand, fit into Fernando's quite well. She was beautiful, and she had that cultured elegance that went along with wealth and privilege. Any of the men here would've loved to have her on their arm. It was almost as if she were one of the rewards of power—a gorgeous woman suitable for a successful man, and she did nothing to break that impression. And now I was that guy with her. I was in a restaurant I didn't like, among people I couldn't stand, and I was bored.

I surveyed the patrons—men and women, sitting around identical tables, murmuring in quiet voices, drinking their wine. A woman walked between the tables, led by a waiter. She wore a champagne-colored gown, and something about the way she moved, perfectly balanced, caught my eye. Most people would be focusing on the waitress, but she seemed aware of her surroundings, not anxious but ready, cataloging the possible dangers and summing people up.

The waiter turned. The woman turned after her, and I saw her face.

Kate.

Kate Daniels. Here, in Fernando's. I put down my menu.

Where in that really revealing dress was she hiding her sword? Did she have it strapped to her thigh?

Kate kept gliding in her heels. She looked stunning. Her hair was down, framing her face and falling past her shoulders and down her back. The dress fit her well, almost as if it had been tailor-made to flatter her lean, strong frame, displaying all of the things jeans and those ugly sweatshirts usually concealed. She looked, well, feminine. Long legs. Supple. Bare shoulders. The dress softened her, but she had definition on her arms. Don't see that often in a human woman.

In the short time I had known her, she had struck me as many things, brave, competent, smart-ass, but tonight she looked beautiful. It made me regret that she had declined my earlier offer of joining me in the tank.

The waiter led her to the table, where a man sat alone. She was on a date. And the poor fool wasn't even armed. He didn't stand a chance.

Kate circled the table, giving me a lovely view of her backside. Mm. She stood by a chair that would let her see the door. Ha. I wondered for a moment if she would flip it over and sit cowboy style, with the back of the chair protecting her stomach.

"Is something funny?" Myong asked.

"No."

Her date, a handsome man in an expensive dark suit, stared at her, his mouth hanging slightly open. *You and me both, brother.*

The waiter held the chair for her. Her date didn't even rise. *Come on, fancy lad, stand up, say something charming, hold her chair for her. Did they not teach etiquette at Little Lords Academy?*

Kate sat. The fancy lad kept staring.

Gods, man, act like you've been out with a lady before.

He finally recovered and said something. She said something back. He smiled. They managed to engage in some small talk.

I glanced across the table at my own date. Myong looked lovely as always, in her perfect little black dress. She caught me looking, and as usual, she looked down demurely. *Yes, yes, I get it, you're not offering me a challenge.* I didn't need a show of submission every time I looked at her. This beauty and the beast routine was getting stale.

Where Kate radiated strength and a capacity for violence, Myong's beauty was far more fragile, like an exquisite crystal bird. The contrast was striking. I glanced at Kate again. If I walked over to their table and started trouble, Myong would, despite being a shapeshifter, seek safety rather than risk injury, possibly under the table, clutching a fork as a weapon. She once confided that she found violence—how had she put it—"distasteful." I was very frequently distasteful.

Still, she was intelligent and cultured, and I wanted her take on them.

"Glance causally at the couple two tables down and give me your impression of them both, please."

Myong looked surprised but did as asked. She studied them carefully, and after a moment, she spoke softly. "His haircut is in fashion and expensive. The suit is custom-made, and the tailoring is impeccable. His shoes are Italian leather. His hands are elegant and well taken care of. I don't think he's a fighter. He has no calluses or scars, and his nails are manicured. He seems at ease here, an important man. The waiter seems to know him, so he must be a regular. She is not. The dress is suitable but seldom worn. The heels are the appropriate height and coordinate well with the dress, but she doesn't like wearing them. If she has to run or fight, she will take them off." Myong paused and allowed herself a small, slightly superior smile. "If something untoward occurs, she might use them as weapons."

A waiter came by our table to refill Myong's water. He took care to stand as far away from me as possible and look down. Once again, somebody recognized me, and the appropriate instructions had been issued to the staff. Don't provoke the psychopath in charge of the shapeshifters, or he might slaughter us all. The violent animal can't control himself. Ugh.

"Who's that man over two tables down?" I asked.

"Dr. Maximillian Crest," the waiter said.

"Medical doctor?"

"I believe he's a plastic surgeon."

The waiter fled, no doubt grateful to escape unharmed.

Crest, that was his name, was meanwhile droning on, while Kate seemed to be only half listening. I could not hear him clearly, but I could guess at the gist of it.

"Blah blah blah, I am handsome, I make a lot of money, this suit is expensive, and my shoes are made of the finest Corinthian leather handstitched by virgins under the moonlight. Of course, I could have gone into pediatrics, but for one of my amazing skill, really, plastic surgery was the only option. Beauty is so important, don't you think? Oh, Kate, you are nearly as attractive as I. Why then should we not be beautiful together?"

The way he looked at her bugged me. As if he studied her face searching for tiny flaws that he could correct. Kate could do better.

I pressed Myong further. "What is your impression of them as a couple?"

Without a moment of hesitation, she said, "He could do better."

"Really?" I allowed a slight edge to creep into my voice.

She seemed to shrink into herself, and I could tell she regretted the remark. "My lord," she began.

Every time I gave my chain a little slack, she cringed. This just was not working out.

"It's fine. Don't worry about it."

It was not Myong's fault that she found him appealing. He was handsome, and he was probably a decent human being. I had no reason to dislike him this much except that he was at the table. I offered her a dip in my tank. And she declined, so she could go and dress up like that for him.

Crest was wearing a custom-made suit and expensive shoes, while I, one the other hand, was dressed in faded jeans and a comfortable tee. The interesting thing was that Kate looked as uncomfortable as I did, despite her fancy dress and shoes. Hmm. I wondered what would happen if I walked over there and asked her to blow this joint and grab a burger with me. She'd probably laugh. But then again, she seemed to like the spotlight. Maybe she was enjoying being the center of attention at Fernando's. There were enough men looking at her. Her clothes were crap, and from what Jim said, money was tight for her. This must've been her rare opportunity to shine, and she pounced on it.

Crest finally caught me staring and said something to her. Kate turned. Her eyes widened. *Surprised to see me?*

Her gaze lingered over Myong and slid back to me. I grinned. *Yeah, my date is almost as pretty as yours, baby.*

Kate motioned to the waiter, while pretty boy looked at me. He was actually trying to stare me down. I hid a smile. *Dear Doctor, you don't want any of this. Trust me.*

He kept looking. I returned the stare. I was kind of curious if he would have the nerve to come over and do something about it.

Then again, who knows, maybe he just was wondering if he could fix my nose. *Believe me, Doc, you don't wanna see my other face.* I thought about giving him just a quick peek. Just a hint of a fang.

A waiter approached our table, carrying a silver tray with a bowl on it. Now what?

The waiter deposited the bowl in front of me. Milk. Ha!

"Compliments of the lady at that table, sir."

Oh this was too good. I locked eyes with Kate and picked up the bowl. She was looking. I raised the dish and drained it. *Salute! Your move, baby.*

She smiled.

Crest was glaring now. He tossed his napkin on the table. Oh-oh. I wondered if I was supposed to faint or flee.

He shifted his gaze and let it linger over Myong. It was meant to provoke me, but instead he just looked at her, caught off guard, as if he just realized for the first time that she was there and she was gorgeous. He was wondering what she would look like out of her tight black dress. Your guess is as good as mine, pal. Every time I tried to touch her, she made this face, as if she was going to bravely endure. She didn't have to worry. I would never put my "big rough hands" all over her unless I thought she wanted it. She would consent, but she didn't want me, and that killed it for me.

I realized that another male was openly staring at my date, and I didn't really give a damn. What did that say about me and Myong, exactly? Nothing that would ever go anywhere.

Kate had that look in her eyes that said she was contemplating punching me in the face. *Settle down, buttercup. I'm not going to embarrass Dr. Dreamboat in front of you and ruin your chances of entering the upper echelons of society.*

I gave Crest a little wink, just to screw with him.

He startled. He said something to Kate. She glanced at me, almost with regret, or maybe I was reading too much into it. They rose. He didn't hold the chair for her again. Seriously?

They walked out. And just when we were starting to get along.

Where the hell were they going? He was probably going to try to impress her with the opera or something. I looked back at Myong. She smiled. Very dutiful.

Kate was leaving with Crest. Possibly she'd spend the night with him. And I was going home alone. I'd drop Myong off and try to salvage what was left of my evening.

A Questionable Client

A Prequel Story to *Magic Bites*

THE PROBLEM WITH LEUCROCOTTA BLOOD IS THAT IT stinks to high heaven. It's also impossible to get off your boots, particularly if the leucrocotta condescended to void its anal glands on you right before you chopped its head off.

I sat on the bench in the Mercenary Guild locker room and pondered my noxious footwear. The boots were less than a year old. And I didn't have money to buy a new pair.

"Tomato juice, Kate," one of the mercs offered. "Will take it right out."

Now he'd done it. I braced myself.

A woman in the corner shook her head. "That's for skunks. Try baking soda."

"You have to go scientific about it. Two parts hydrogen peroxide to four parts water."

"A quart of water and a tablespoon of ammonia."

"What you need to do is piss on it . . ."

Every person in the locker room knew my boots were shot.

Unfortunately, stain-removal methods was one of those troublesome subjects somewhere between relationship issues and mysterious car noises. Everybody was an expert, everybody had a cure, and they all fell over themselves to offer their advice.

The electric bulbs blinked and faded. Magic flooded the world in a silent rush, smothering technology. Twisted tubes of fey-lanterns ignited with pale blue on the walls as the charged air inside them interacted with magic. A nauseating stench, reminiscent of a couple of pounds of shrimp left in the sun for a week, erupted from my boots. There were collective grunts of "Ugh" and "Oh God," and everybody decided to give me lots of personal space.

We lived in a post-Shift world. One moment magic dominated, fueling spells and giving power to monsters, and the next it vanished as abruptly as it appeared. Cars started, electricity flowed, and mages became easy prey to a punk with a gun. Nobody could predict when magic waves would come or how long they would last. That's why I carried a sword. It always worked.

Mark appeared in the doorway. Mark was the Guild's equivalent of middle management, and he looked the part—his suit was perfectly clean and cost more than I made in three months, his dark hair was professionally trimmed, and his hands showed no calluses. In the crowd of working-class thugs, he stood out like a sore thumb and was proud of it, which earned him the rank and file's undying hatred.

Mark's expressionless stare fastened on me. "Daniels, the clerk has a gig ticket for you."

Usually the words "gig ticket" made my eyes light up. I needed money. I always needed money. The Guild zoned the jobs, meaning that each merc had his own territory. If a job fell in your territory, it was legitimately yours. My territory was near Savannah, basically in the sparsely populated middle of nowhere, and good gigs didn't come my way too often. The only reason I ended up in Atlanta this time was that my part-time partner in crime, Jim, needed help clearing a pack of grave-digging leucrocottas from Westview Cemetery. He'd cut me in on his gig.

Under normal circumstances, I would've jumped at the chance to earn extra cash, but I had spent most of the last twenty-four hours awake and chasing hyena-sized creatures armed with badgerlike jaws full of extremely sharp teeth. And Jim bailed on me midway through it. Some sort of Pack business.

That's what I get for pairing with a werejaguar.

I was tired, dirty, and hungry, and my boots stank.

"I just finished a job."

"It's a blue gig."

Blue gig meant double rate.

Mac, a huge hulk of a man, shook his head, presenting me with a view of his mangled left ear. "Hell, if she doesn't want it, I'll take it."

"No, you won't. She's licensed for bodyguard detail, and you aren't."

I bloody hated bodyguard detail. On regular jobs, I had to depend only on myself. But bodyguard detail was a couple's kind of dance. You had to work with the body you guarded, and in my experience, bodies proved uncooperative.

"Why me?"

Mark shrugged. "Because I have no choice. I have Rodriguez and Castor there now, but they just canceled on me. If you don't take the gig, I'll have to track down someone who will. My pain, your gain."

Canceled wasn't good. Rodriguez was a decent mage, and Castor was tough in a fight. They wouldn't bail from a well-paying job unless it went sour.

"I need someone there right now. Go there, babysit the client through the night, and in the morning I'll have a replacement lined up. In or out, Daniels? It's a high-profile client, and I don't like to keep him waiting."

The gig smelled almost as bad as I did. "How much?"

"Three grand."

Someone whistled. Three grand for a night of work. I'd be insane to pass on it. "In."

"Good."

I started to throw my stink-bomb boots into the locker but stopped myself. I had paid a lot for them and they should have lasted for another year at least, but if I put them into my locker, it would smell forever. Sadly, the boots were ruined. I tossed them into the trash, pulled on my old spare pair, grabbed my sword, and headed out of the locker room to get the gig ticket from the clerk.

WHEN I RODE INTO ATLANTA, THE MAGIC WAS DOWN, so I had taken Betsi, my old, dented Subaru. With a magic wave in full swing, my gasoline-guzzling car was about as mobile as a car-sized rock, but since I was technically doing the Guild a favor, the clerk provided me with a spare mount. Her name was Peggy, and judging by the wear on her incisors, she'd started her third decade some years ago. Her muzzle had gone gray, her tail and mane had thinned to stringy tendrils, and she moved with ponderous slowness. I'd ridden her for the first fifteen minutes, listening to her sigh, then guilt got the better of me, and I decided to walk the rest of the way. I didn't have to go far. According to the directions, Champion Heights was only a couple miles away. An extra ten minutes wouldn't make that much difference.

Around me, a broken city struggled to shrug off winter, fighting the assault of another cold February night. Husks of once-mighty skyscrapers stabbed through the melting snowdrifts encrusted with dark ice. Magic loved to feed on anything technologically complex, but tall office towers proved particularly susceptible to magic-induced erosion. Within a couple of years of the first magic wave they shuddered, crumbled, and fell one by one, like giants on sand legs, spilling mountains of broken glass and twisted guts of metal framework onto the streets.

The city grew around the high-tech corpses. Stalls and small shops took the place of swanky coffee joints and boutiques. Wood-and-brick houses, built by hand and no taller than four floors high, replaced the high-rises. Busy streets, once filled with cars and buses, now channeled a flood of horses, mules, and camels. During rush hour, the stench alone put hair on your chest. But now, with the last of the sunset dying slowly above the horizon, the city lay empty. Anyone with a crumb of sense hurried home. The night belonged to monsters, and monsters were always hungry.

The wind picked up, driving dark clouds across the sky and turning my bones into icicles. It would storm soon. Here's hoping Champion Heights, my client's humble abode, had someplace I could hide Peggy from the sleet.

We picked our way through Buckhead, Peggy's hooves making loud clopping noises in the twilight silence of the deserted streets. The night worried me little. I looked too poor and too mean to provide easy pickings, and nobody in their right mind would try to steal Peggy. Unless a gang of soap-making bandits lurked about, we were safe enough. I checked the address again. Smack in the middle of Buckhead. The clerk said I couldn't miss it. Pretty much a guarantee I'd get lost.

I turned the corner and stopped.

A high-rise towered over the ruins. It shouldn't have existed, but there it was, a brick-and-concrete tower silhouetted against the purple sky. At least fifteen floors, maybe more. Pale tendrils of haze clung to it. It was so tall that the top floor of it still reflected the sunset, while the rest of the city lay steeped in shadow.

"Pinch me, Peggy."

Peggy sighed, mourning the fact that she was paired with me.

I petted her gray muzzle. "Ten to one, that's Champion Heights. Why isn't it lying in shambles?"

Peggy snorted.

"You're right. We need a closer look."

We wound through the labyrinth of streets, closing in on the tower. My paper said the client's name was Saiman. No indication if it was his last or first name. Perhaps he was like Batman, one of a kind. Of course, Batman wouldn't have to hire bodyguards.

"You have to ask yourself, Peggy, who would pay three grand for a night of work and why. I bet living in that tower isn't cheap, so Saiman has money. Contrary to popular opinion, people who have money refuse to part with it unless they absolutely have to do it. Three grand means he's in big trouble, and we're walking into something nasty."

Finally, we landed in a vast parking lot, empty, save for a row of cars near the front. Gray Volvo, black Cadillac, even a sleek gunmetal Lamborghini. Most vehicles sported a bloated hood—built to accommodate a charged-water engine. The water-engine cars functioned during magic waves by using magic-infused water instead of gasoline. Unfortunately, they took a good fifteen minutes of hard chanting to start, and when they did spring into action, they attained a maximum speed of forty-five miles per hour while growling, snarling, and thundering loud enough to force a deaf man to file a noise complaint.

A large white sign waited past the cars. A black arrow pointed to the right. Above the arrow in black letters was written "Please stable your mounts." I looked to the right and saw a large stable and a small guardhouse next to it.

It took me a full five minutes to convince the guards I wasn't a serial killer in disguise, but, finally, Peggy relaxed in a comfortable stall, and I climbed the stone stairs to Champion Heights. As I looked, the brick wall of the high-rise swam out of focus, shimmered, and turned into a granite crag.

Whoa.

I squinted at the wall and saw the faint outline of bricks within the granite. Interesting.

The stairs brought me to the glass-and-steel front of the building. The same haze that cloaked the building clouded the glass, but not enough to obscure a thick metal grate barring the vestibule. Beyond the grate, a guard sat behind a round counter, between an Uzi and a crossbow. The Uzi looked well maintained. The crossbow bore the Hawkeye logo on its stock—a round bird-of-prey eye with a golden iris—which meant its prong was steel and not cheap aluminum. Probably upward of two hundred pounds of draw weight. At this distance, it would take out a rhino, let alone me.

The guard gave me an evil eye. I leaned to the narrow metal grille and tried to broadcast "trustworthy."

"I'm here for one fifty-eight." I pulled out my merc card and held it to the glass.

"Code, please."

Code? What code? "Nobody said anything about a code."

The guard leveled a crossbow at me.

"Very scary," I told him. "One small problem. You shoot me, and the tenant in one fifty-eight won't live through the night. I'm not a threat to you. I'm a bodyguard on the job from the Mercenary Guild. If you call to one fifty-eight and check, they'll tell you they're expecting me."

The guard rose and disappeared into a hallway to the right. A long minute passed. Finally, he emerged, looking sour, and pushed a button. The metal grate slid aside.

I walked in. The floor and walls were polished red granite. The air smelled of expensive perfume.

"Fifteenth floor," the guard said, nodding at the elevator in the back of the room.

"The magic is up." The elevator was likely dead.

"Fifteenth floor."

Oy. I walked up to the elevator and pushed the up button. The metal doors slid open. I got in and selected the fifteenth floor, the elevator closed, and a moment later faint purring announced the cabin rising. It's good to be rich.

The elevator spat me out into a hallway lined with a luxurious green carpet. I plodded through it past the door marked 158 to the end of the hallway to the door under the exit sign and opened it. Stairs. Unfortunately in good repair. The door opened from the inside of the hallway, but it didn't lock. No way to jam it.

The hallway was T-shaped, with only one exit, which meant that potential attackers could come either through the elevator shaft or up the stairs.

I went up to 158 and knocked.

The door shot open. Gina Castor's dark eyes glared at me. An AK-47 hung off her shoulder. She held a black duffel in one hand and her sword in the other. "What took you so long?"

"Hello to you, too."

She pushed past me, the thin, slightly stooped Rodriguez following her. "He's all yours."

I caught the door before it clicked shut. "Where is the client?"

"Chained to the bed." They headed to the elevator.

"Why?"

Castor flashed her teeth at me. "You'll figure it out."

The elevator's door slid open, they ducked in, and a moment later I was alone in the hallway, holding the door open like an idiot. Peachy.

I STEPPED INSIDE AND SHUT THE DOOR. A FAINT SPARK of magic shot through the metal box of the card-reader lock. I touched it. The lock was a sham. The door was protected by a ward. I pushed harder. My magic crashed against the invisible wall of the spell and ground to a halt. An expensive ward, too. Good. Made my job a hair easier.

I slid the dead bolt shut and turned. I stood in a huge living room, big enough to contain most of my house. A marble counter ran along the wall on my left, sheltering a bar with glass shelves offering everything from Bombay Sapphire to French wines. A large steel fridge sat behind the bar. White, criminally plush carpet, black walls, steel-and-glass furniture, and beyond it all an enormous floor-to-ceiling window, presenting the vista of the ruined city, a deep darkness, lit here and there by the pale blue of feylanterns.

I stayed away from the window and trailed the wall, punctuated by three doors. The first opened into a laboratory: flame-retardant table and counters supporting row upon row of equipment. I recognized a magic scanner, a computer, and a spectrograph, but the rest was beyond me. No client.

I tried the second door and found a large room. Gloom pooled in the corners. A huge platform bed occupied most of the hardwood floor. Something lay on the bed, hidden under black sheets.

"Saiman?"

No answer.

Why me?

The wall to the left of the bed was all glass, and beyond the glass, very far below, stretched a very hard parking lot, bathed in the glow of feylanterns.

God, fifteen floors was high.

I pulled my saber from the back sheath and padded across the floor to the bed.

The body under the sheets didn't move.

Step.

Another step.

In my head, the creature hiding under the sheets lunged at me, knocking me through the window in an explosion of glass shards to plunge far below . . . Fatigue was messing with my head.

Another step.

I nudged the sheet with my sword, peeling it back gently.

A man rested on the black pillow. He was bald. His head was lightly tanned, his face neither handsome nor ugly, his features well shaped and pleasant. Perfectly average. His shoulders were nude—he was probably down to his underwear or naked under the sheet.

"Saiman?" I asked softly.

The man's eyelids trembled. Dark eyes stared at me, luminescent with harsh predatory intelligence. A warning siren went off in my head. I took a small step back and saw the outline of several chains under the sheet. You've got to be kidding me. They didn't just chain him to the bed; they'd wrapped him up like a Christmas present. He couldn't even twitch.

"Good evening," the man said, his voice quiet and cultured.

"Good evening."

"You're my new bodyguard, I presume."

I nodded. "Call me Kate."

"Kate. What a lovely name. Please forgive me. Normally I would rise to greet a beautiful woman, but I'm afraid I'm indisposed at the moment."

I pulled back a little more of the sheet revealing an industrial-sized steel chain. "I can see that."

"Perhaps I could impose on you to do me the great favor of removing my bonds?"

"Why did Rodriguez and Castor chain you?" And where the hell did they find a chain of this size?

A slight smile touched his lips. "I'd prefer not to answer that question."

"Then we're in trouble. Clients get restrained when they interfere with the bodyguards' ability to keep them safe. Since you won't tell me why the previous team decided to chain you, I can't let you go."

The smile grew wider. "I see your point."

"Does this mean you're ready to enlighten me?"

"I'm afraid not."

I nodded. "I see. Well then, I'll clear the rest of the apartment, then I'll come back and we'll talk some more."

"Do you prefer brunettes or blondes?"

"What?"

The sheet shivered.

"Quickly, Kate. Brunettes or blondes? Pick one."

Odd bulges strained the sheet. I grabbed the covers and jerked them back.

Saiman lay naked, his body pinned to the bed by the chain. His stomach distended between two loops, huge and bloated. Flesh bulged and crawled under his skin, as if his body were full of writhing worms.

"Blonde, I'd say," Saiman said.

He groaned, his back digging into the sheets. The muscles under his skin boiled. Bones stretched. Ligaments twisted, contorting his limbs. Acid squirted into my throat. I gagged, trying not to vomit.

His body stretched, twisted, and snapped into a new shape: lean, with crisp definition. His jaw widened, his eyes grew larger, his nose gained a sharp cut. Corn-silk blond hair sprouted on his head and reached down to his shoulders. Indigo flooded his irises. A new man looked at me, younger by about five years, taller, leaner, with a face that was heartbreakingly perfect. Above his waist, he was Adonis. Below his ribs, his body degenerated into a bloated stomach. He looked pregnant.

"You wouldn't tell me what you preferred," he said mournfully, his pitch low and husky. "I had to improvise."

"WHAT ARE YOU?" I KEPT MY SWORD BETWEEN ME AND him.

"Does it really matter?"

"Yes, it does." When people said shapeshifter, they usually meant a person afflicted with Lyc-V, the virus that gave its victim the ability to shift into an animal. I'd never seen one who could freely change its human form.

Saiman made a valiant effort to shrug. Hard to shrug with several pounds of chains on your shoulders, but he managed to look nonchalant doing it.

"I am me."

Oh boy. "Stay here."

"Where would I go?"

I left the bedroom and checked the rest of the apartment. The only remaining room contained a large shower stall and a giant bathtub. No kitchen. Perhaps he had food delivered.

Fifteenth floor. At least one guard downstairs, bullet-resistant glass, metal grates. The place was a fortress. Yet he hired bodyguards at exorbitant prices. He expected his castle to be breached.

I headed to the bar and grabbed a glass from under the counter, filled it with water, and took it to Saiman. Changing shape took energy. If he was anything like other shapeshifters, he was dying of thirst and hunger right about now.

Saiman's gaze fastened on the glass. "Delightful."

I let him drink. He drained the glass in long, thirsty swallows.

"How many guards are on duty downstairs?"

"Three."

"Are they employed by the building owners directly?"

Saiman smiled. "Yes. They're experienced and well paid, and they won't hesitate to kill."

So far so good. "When you change shape, do you reproduce internal organs as well?"

"Only if I plan to have intercourse."

Oh goodie. "Are you pregnant?"

Saiman laughed softly.

"I need to know if you're going to go into labor." Because that would just be a cherry on the cake of this job.

"You're a most peculiar woman. No, I'm most definitely not pregnant. I'm male, and while I may construct a vaginal canal and a uterus on occasion, I've never had cause to re-create ovaries. And if I did, I suspect they would be sterile. Unlike the male of the species, women produce all of their gametes during gestation, meaning that when a female infant is born, she will have in her ovaries all of the partially developed eggs she will ever have. The ovaries cannot facilitate production of new eggs, only the maturation of existing ones. The magic is simply not deep enough for me to overcome this hurdle. Not yet."

Thank the universe for small favors. "Who am I protecting you from and why?"

"I'm afraid I have to keep that information to myself as well."

Why did I take this job again? Ah yes, a pile of money. "Withholding this information diminishes my ability to guard you."

He tilted his head, looking me over. "I'm willing to take that chance."

"I'm not. It also puts my life at a greater risk."

"You're well compensated for that risk."

I repressed the urge to brain him with something heavy. Too bad there was no kitchen—a cast-iron frying pan would do the job.

"I see why the first team bailed."

"Oh, it was the woman," Saiman said helpfully. "She had difficulty with my metamorphosis. I believe she referred to me as an 'abomination.'"

I rubbed the bridge of my nose. "Let's try simple questions. Do you expect us to be attacked tonight?"

"Yes."

I figured as much. "With magic or brute force?"

"Both."

"Is it a hit for hire?"

Saiman shook his head. "No."

Well, at least something went my way: amateurs were easier to deal with than contract killers.

"It's personal. I can tell you this much: the attackers are part of a religious sect. They will do everything in their power to kill me, including sacrificing their own lives."

And we just drove off a cliff in a runaway buggy. "Are they magically adept?"

"Very."

I leaned back. "So let me summarize: You're a target of magical kamikaze fanatics, you won't tell me who they are, why they're after you, or why you have been restrained?"

"Precisely. Could I trouble you for a sandwich? I'm famished."

Dear God, I had a crackpot for a client. "A sandwich?"

"Prosciutto and Gouda on sourdough bread, please. A tomato and red onion would be quite lovely as well."

"Sounds delicious."

"Feel free to have one."

"I tell you what, since you refuse to reveal anything that might make my job even a smidgen easier, how about I make a delicious prosciutto sandwich and taunt you with it until you tell me what I want to know?"

Saiman laughed.

An eerie sound came from the living room—a light click, as if something with long, sharp claws crawled across metal.

I PUT MY FINGER TO MY LIPS, FREED MY SABER, AND padded out into the living room.

The room lay empty. No intruders.

I stood very still, trying to fade into the black walls.

Moments dripped by.

A small noise came from the left. It was a hesitant, slow clicking, as if some creature slunk in the distance, slowly putting one foot before the other.

Click.

Definitely a claw.

Click.

I scrutinized the left side of the room. Nothing moved.

Click. Click, click.

Closer this time. Fear skittered down my spine. Fear was good. It would keep me sharp. I kept still. Where are you, you sonovabitch . . .

Click to the right, and almost immediately a quiet snort to the left. Now we had two invisible intruders. Because one wasn't hard enough.

An odd scent nipped at my nostrils, a thick, slightly bitter herbal odor. I'd smelled it once before, but I had no clue where or when.

Claws scraped to the right and to the left of me now. More than two. A quiet snort to the right. Another in the corner. Come out to play. Come on, beastie.

Claws raked metal directly in front of me. There was nothing there but that huge window and sloping ceiling above it. I looked up. Glowing green eyes peered at me through the grate of the air duct in the ceiling.

Shivers sparked down my back.

The eyes stared at me, heated with madness.

The screws in the air-duct cover turned to the left. Righty tighty, lefty loosey. Smart critter.

The grate fell onto the soft carpet. The creature leaned forward slowly, showing me a long conical head. The herbal scent grew stronger now, as if I'd taken a handful of absinthe wormwood and stuck it up my nose.

Long black claws clutched the edge of the air duct. The beast rocked, revealing its shoulders sheathed in shaggy, hunter green fur.

Bingo. An endar. Six legs, each armed with wicked black claws; preternaturally fast; equipped with an outstanding sense of smell and a big mouth, which hid a tongue lined with hundreds of serrated teeth. One lick, and it would scrape the flesh off my bones in a very literal way.

The endars were peaceful creatures. The green fur wasn't fur at all; it was moss that grew from their skin. They lived underneath old oaks, rooted to the big trees in a state of quiet hibernation, absorbing their nutrients and making rare excursions to the surface to lick the bark and feed on lichens. They stirred from their rest so rarely that pagan slavs thought they fed on air.

Someone had poured blood under this endar's oak. The creature had absorbed it, and the blood had driven it crazy. It had burrowed to the surface, where it swarmed with its fellows. Then the same someone, armed with a hell of a lot of magic, had herded this endar and its buddies to this high-rise and released them into the ventilation system so they would find Saiman and rip him apart. They couldn't be frightened off. They couldn't be stopped. They would kill anything with a pulse to get to their target, and when the target was dead, they would have to be eliminated. There was no coming back from endar madness.

Only a handful of people knew how to control endars.

Saiman had managed to piss off the Russians. It's never good to piss off the Russians. That was just basic common sense. My father was Russian, but I doubted they would cut me any slack just because I could understand their curses.

The endar gaped at me with its glowing eyes. Yep, mad as a hatter. I'd have to kill every last one of them.

"Well, come on. Bring it."

The endar's mouth gaped. It let out a piercing screech, like a circular saw biting into the wood, and charged.

I swung Slayer. The saber's blade sliced into flesh, and the beast crashed to the floor. Thick green blood stained Saiman's white carpet.

The three other duct covers fell one by one. A stream of green bodies charged toward me. I swung my sword, cleaving the first body in two. It was going to be a long night.

THE LAST OF THE ENDARS WAS ON THE SMALLER SIDE. Little bigger than a cat. I grabbed it by the scruff of the neck and took it back into the bedroom.

Saiman smiled at my approach. "I take it everything went well?"

"I redecorated."

He arched his eyebrow again. Definitely mimicking me. "Oh?"

"Your new carpet is a lovely emerald color."

"I can assure you that the carpet is the least of my worries."

"You're right." I brought the endar closer. The creature saw Saiman and jerked spasmodically. Six legs whipped the air, claws out, ready to rend and tear. The beast's mouth gaped, releasing a wide tongue studded with rows and rows of conical teeth.

"You provoked the volhvs." It was that or the Russian witches. I bet on the volhvs. The witches would've cursed us by now.

"Indeed."

"The volhvs are bad news for a number of reasons. They serve pagan Slavic gods, and they have thousands of years of magic tradition to draw on. They're at least as powerful as druids, but unlike druids, who are afraid to sneeze the wrong way or someone might accuse them of bringing back human sacrifices, the volhvs don't give a damn. They won't stop either. They don't like using the endars, because the endars nourish the forest with their magic. Whatever you did really pissed them off."

Saiman pondered me as if I were some curious bug. "I wasn't aware that the Guild employed anyone with an education."

"I'll hear it. All of it."

"No." He shook his head. "I do admire your diligence and expertise. I don't want you to think it's gone unnoticed."

I dropped the endar onto his stomach. The beast clawed at the sheet. Saiman screamed. I grabbed the creature and jerked it up. The beast dragged the sheet with it, tearing it to shreds. Small red scratches marked Saiman's blob of a stomach.

"I'll ask again. What did you do to infuriate the Russians? Consider your answer carefully, because the next time I drop this guy, I'll be slower picking him back up."

Saiman's face quivered with rage. "You're my bodyguard."

"You can file a complaint, if you survive. You're putting both of us in danger by withholding information. See, if I walk, I just miss out on some money; you lose your life. I have no problem with leaving you here, and the Guild can stick its thumb up its ass and twirl for all I care. The only thing that keeps me protecting you is professional pride. I hate bodyguard detail, but I'm good at it, and I don't like to lose a body. It's in your best interests to help me do my job. Now, I'll count to three. On three, I drop Fluffy here and let it go to town on your gut. He really wants whatever you're hiding in there."

Saiman stared at me.

"One. Two. Th—"

"Very well."

I reached into my backpack and pulled out a piece of wire. Normally I used it for trip traps, but it would make a decent leash. Two minutes later, the endar was secured to the dresser, and I perched on the corner of Saiman's bed.

"Are you familiar with the legend of Booyan Island?"

I nodded. "It's a mythical island far in the Ocean, behind the Hvalynskii Sea. It's a place of deep magic where a number of legendary creatures and items are located: Alatyr, the father of all stones; the fiery pillar; the Drevo-Doob, the World Oak; the cave where the legendary sword Kladenets is hidden; the Raven prophet; and so on. It's the discount warehouse of Russian legends. Anytime the folkloric heroes needed a magic object, they made a trip to it."

"Let's concentrate on the tree," Saiman said.

I knew Slavic mythology well enough, but I hadn't had to use it for a while and I was a bit rusty. "It's a symbol of nature. Creatures of the earth at its roots, the serpent, the frog, and so on. There is a raven with a prophetic gift in the branches. Some myths say that there are iron chains wrapped around the tree's trunk. A black cat walks the chain, telling stories and fables . . ."

Saiman nodded.

Oh crap. "It's that damn cat, isn't it?"

"The oak produces an acorn once every seven years. Seven months, seven days, and seven hours after the acorn falls from the tree, it will crack and grow into the World Oak. In effect, the tree manifests at the location of the acorn for the period of seven minutes."

I frowned. "Let me guess, you stole the acorn from the Russians and swallowed it."

Saiman nodded.

"Why? Are you eager to hear a bedtime story?"

"The cat possesses infinite knowledge. Seven minutes is time enough to ask and hear an answer to one question. Only the owner of the acorn can ask the question."

I shook my head. "Saiman, nothing is free. You have to pay for everything, knowledge included. What will it cost you to ask a question?"

"The price is irrelevant if I get an answer." Saiman smiled.

I sighed. "Answer my question: Why do smart people tend to be stupid?"

"Because we think we know better. We think that our intellect affords us special privileges and lets us beat the odds. That's why talented mathematicians try to defraud casinos and young brilliant mages make bargains with forces beyond their control."

Well, he answered the question.

"When is the acorn due for its big kaboom?"

"In four hours and forty-seven minutes."

"The volhvs will tear this high-rise apart stone by stone to get it back, and I'm your last line of defense?"

"That's an accurate assessment. I did ask for the best person available."

I sighed. "Still want that sandwich?"

"Very much."

I headed to the door.

"Kate?"

"Yes?"

"The endar?"

I turned to him. "Why were you chained?"

Saiman grimaced. "The acorn makes it difficult to control my magic. It forces me to continuously change shape. Most of the time I'm able to keep the changes subtle, but once in a while the acorn causes contortions. Gina Castor walked in on me during such a moment. I'm afraid I was convulsing, so my recollection may be somewhat murky, but I do believe I had at least one partially formed breast and three arms. She overreacted. Odd, considering her profile."

"Her profile?"

"I studied my bodyguards very carefully," Saiman said. "I handpicked three teams. The first refused to take the job, the second was out due to injuries. Castor and Rodriguez were my third choice."

I went back to the bed and ducked under it. They'd chained him with a small padlock. Picking locks wasn't my strong suit. I looked around and saw the small key on the dresser. It took me a good five minutes to unwrap him.

"Thank you." He rose, rubbing his chest, marked by red pressure lines. "May I ask why?"

"Nobody should die chained to the bed."

Saiman stretched. His body swelled, twisted, growing larger, gaining breadth and muscle. I made a valiant effort not to vomit.

Saiman's body snapped. A large, perfectly sculpted male looked at me. Soft brown hair framed a masculine face. He would make any bodybuilder gym proud. Except for the bloated gut.

"Is he preferable to the previous attempt?" Saiman asked.

"There is more of you to guard now. Other than that, it makes no difference to me."

I headed into the living room. He followed me, swiping a luxurious robe off a chair.

We stepped into the living room. Saiman stopped.

The corpses of endars had melted into puddles of green. Thin stalks of emerald green moss sprouted from the puddles, next to curly green shoots of ferns and tiny young herbs.

"The endars nourish the forest," I told him.

He indicated the completely green carpet with his hand. "How many were there?"

"A few. I lost count."

Saiman's sharp eyes regarded my face. "You're lying. You know the exact number."

"Thirty-seven."

I zeroed in on the fridge. No telling when the next attack would come, and I was starving. You can do without sleep or without food, but not without both, and sleep wasn't an option.

Saiman trailed me, taking the seat on the outer side of the counter. "Do you prefer women?"

"No."

He frowned, belting the robe. "It's the stomach, isn't it?"

I raided the fridge. He had enough deli meat to feed an army. I spread it out on the bar's counter. "What do you do for a living, Saimain?"

"I collect information and use it to further my interests."

"It seems to pay well." I nodded to indicate the apartment.

"It does. I also possess an exhaustive knowledge of various magic phenomena. I consult for various parties. My fee varies between thirty-six and thirty-nine hundred dollars, depending on the job and the client."

"Thirty-six hundred per job?" I bit into my sandwich. Mmm, salami.

"Per hour."

I choked on my food. He looked at me with obvious amusement.

"The term 'highway robbery' comes to mind," I managed finally.

"Oh, but I'm exceptionally good at what I do. Besides, the victims of highway robbery have no choice in the matter. I assure you, I don't coerce my clients, Kate."

"I'm sure. How did we even get to this point? The stratospheric fee ruined my train of thought."

"You stated that you prefer men to women."

I nodded. "Suppose you get a particularly sensitive piece of information. Let's say a business tip. If you act on the tip, you could make some money. If you sell it, you could make more money. If both you and your buyer act on the tip, you both would make money, but the return for each of you would be significantly diminished. Your move?"

"Either sell the information or act on it. Not both."

"Why?"

Saiman shrugged. "The value of the information increases with its exclusivity. A client buying such knowledge has an expectation of such exclusivity. It would be unethical to undermine it."

"It would be unethical for me to respond to your sexual overtures. For the duration of the job, you're a collection of arms and legs that I have to keep safe. I'm most effective if I'm not emotionally involved with you on any level. To be blunt, I'm doing my best to regard you as a precious piece of porcelain I have to keep out of harm's way."

"But you do find this shape sexually attractive?"

"I'm not going to answer that question. If you pester me, I will chain you back to the bed."

Saiman raised his arm, flexing a spectacular biceps. "This shape has a lot of muscle mass."

I nodded. "In a bench-pressing contest, you would probably win. But we're not bench-pressing. You might be stronger, but I'm well trained. If you do want to try me, you're welcome to it. Just as long as we agree that once your battered body is chained safely in your bed, I get to say, 'I told you so.'"

Saiman arched his eyebrows. "Try it?"

"And stop that."

"Stop what?"

"Stop mimicking my gestures."

He laughed. "You're a most peculiar person, Kate. I find myself oddly fascinated. You have obvious skill." He indicated the budding forest in his living room. "And knowledge to back it up. Why aren't you among the Guild's top performers?"

Because being in top anything means greater risk of discovery. I was hiding in plain sight and doing a fairly good job of it. But he didn't need to know that. "I don't spend much time in Atlanta. My territory is in the Low Country. Nothing much happens there, except for an occasional sea serpent eating shrimp out of the fishing nets."

Saiman's sharp eyes narrowed. "So why not move up to the city? Better jobs, better money, more recognition?"

"I like my house where it is."

Something bumped behind the front door. I swiped Slayer off the counter. "Bedroom. Now."

"Can I watch?"

I pointed with the sword to the bedroom.

Saiman gave an exaggerated sigh. "Very well."

He went to the bedroom. I padded to the door and leaned against it, listening.

Quiet.

I waited, sword raised. Something waited out there in the hallway. I couldn't hear it, but I sensed it. It was there.

A quiet whimper filtered through the steel of the door. A sad, lost, feminine whimper, like an old woman crying quietly in mourning.

I held very still. The apartment felt stifling and crowded in. I would've given anything for a gulp of fresh air right about then.

Something scratched at the door. A low mutter floated through, whispered words unintelligible.

God, what was it with the air in this place? The place was stale and musty, like a tomb.

A feeling of dread flooded me. Something bad was in the apartment. It hid in the shadows under the furniture, in the cabinets, in the fridge. Fear squirmed through me. I pressed my back against the door, holding Slayer in front of me.

The creature behind the door scratched again, claws against the steel.

The walls closed in. I had to get away from this air. Somewhere out in the open. Somewhere where the wind blew under an open sky. Someplace with nothing to crowd me in.

I had to get out.

If I left, I risked Saiman's life. Outside the volhvs were waiting. I'd be walking right into their arms.

The shadows under the furniture grew longer, stretching toward me.

Get out. Get out now!

I bit my lip. A quick drop of blood burned on my tongue, the magic in it nipping at me. Clarity returned for a second and light dawned in my head. Badzula. Of course. The endars failed to rip us apart, so the volhvs went for plan B. If Muhammad won't go to the mountain, the mountain must come to Muhammad.

Saiman walked out of the bedroom. His eyes were glazed over.

"Saiman!"

"I must go," he said. "Must get out."

"No, you really must not." I sprinted to him.

"I must."

He headed to the giant window.

I kicked the back of his right knee. He folded. I caught him on the way down and spun him so he landed on his stomach. He sprawled among the ankle-tall ferns. I locked his left wrist and leaned on him, grinding all of my weight into his left shoulder.

"Badzula," I told him. "Belorussian creature. Looks like a middle-aged woman with droopy breasts, swaddled in a filthy blanket."

"I must get out." He tried to roll over, but I had him pinned.

"Focus, Saiman. Badzula—what's her power?"

"She incites people to vagrancy."

"That's right. And we can't be vagrants because if we walk out of this building, both of us will be killed. We have to stay put."

"I don't think I can do it."

"Yes, you can. I'm not planning on getting up."

"I believe you're right." A small measure of rational thought crept into his voice. "I suppose the furniture isn't really trying to devour us."

"If it is, I'll chop it with my sword when it gets close."

"You can let me up now," he said.

"I don't think so."

We sat still. The air grew viscous like glue. I had to bite it to get any into my lungs.

Muscles crawled under me. Saiman couldn't get out of my hold, so he decided to shift himself out.

"Do you stock herbs?"

"Yes," he said.

"Do you have water lily?"

"Yes."

"Where?"

"Laboratory, third cabinet."

"Good." I rolled off him. I'd have only a second to do this, and I had to do it precisely.

Saiman got up to his knees. As he rose, I threw a fast right hook. He never saw it coming and didn't brace himself. My fist landed on his jaw. His head snapped back. His eyes rolled over, and he sagged down.

Lucky. I ran to the lab.

It took a hell of a lot of practice to knock someone out. You needed both speed and power to jolt the head enough to rattle the brain inside the skull but not cause permanent damage. Under normal circumstances, I wouldn't even try it, but these weren't normal circumstances. Walls were curving in to eat me.

If I did cause too much damage, he would fix it. Considering what he had done to his body so far, his regeneration would make normal shapeshifters jealous.

Third cabinet. I threw it open and scanned the glass jars. Dread mugged me like a sodden blanket. *Ligularia dentata, Ligularia przewalski* . . . Latin names, why me? *Lilium pardalinum, Lobelia siphilitica.* Come on, come on . . . *Nymphaea odorata,* pond lily. Also known to Russians as odolen-trava, the mermaid flower, an all-purpose pesticide against all things unclean. That would do.

I dashed to the door, twisting the lid off the jar. A gray powder filled it—ground lily petals, the most potent part of the flower. I slid open the lock. The ward drained down, and I jerked the door ajar.

Empty hallway greeted me. I hurled the jar and the powder into the hall. A woman wailed, smoke rose from thin air, and Badzula materialized in the middle of the carpet. Skinny, flabby, filthy, with breasts dangling to her waist like two empty bags, she tossed back grimy tangled hair and hissed at me, baring stumps of rotten teeth.

"That's nice. Fuck you, too."

I swung. It was textbook saber slash, diagonal, from left to right. I drew the entirety of the blade through the wound. Badzula's body toppled one way, her head rolled the other.

The weight dropped off my shoulders. Suddenly, I could breathe, and the building no longer seemed in imminent danger of collapsing and burying me alive.

I grabbed the head, tossed it into the elevator, dragged the body in there, sent the whole thing to the ground floor, sprinted back inside, and locked the door, reactivating the ward. The whole thing took five seconds.

On the floor, Saiman lay unmoving. I checked his pulse. Breathing. Good. I went back to the island. I deserved some coffee after this, and I bet Saiman stocked the good stuff.

I SAT BY THE COUNTER, SIPPING THE BEST COFFEE I'D ever tasted, when the big-screen TV on the wall lit up with a fuzzy glow. Which was more than a smidgen odd, considering that the magic was still up, and the TV shouldn't have worked.

I took my coffee and my saber and went to sit on the couch, facing the TV. Saiman still sprawled unconscious on the floor.

The glow flared brighter, faded, flared brighter . . . In ancient times people used mirrors, but really any somewhat reflective surface would do. The dark TV screen was glossy enough.

The glow blazed and materialized into a blurry male. In his early twenties, dark hair, dark eyes.

The man looked at me. "You're the bodyguard." His voice carried a trace of Russian accent.

I nodded and slipped into Russian. *"Yes."*

"I don't know you. What you do makes no difference to me. We have this place surrounded. We go in in an hour." He made a short chopping motion with his hand. *"You're done."*

"I'm shaking with fear. In fact, I may have to take a minute to get my shivers under control." I drank my coffee.

The man shook his head. *"You tell that* paskuda, *if he lets Yulya go, I'll make sure you both walk out alive. You hear that? I don't know what he's got over my wife, but you tell him that. If he wants to live, he has to let her go. I'll be back in thirty minutes. You tell him."*

The screen faded.

And the plot thickens. I sighed and nudged Saiman with my boot. It took a couple of nudges, but finally he groaned and sat up.

"What happened?"

"You fell."

"Really? What did I fall into?"

"My fist."

"That explains the headache." Saiman looked at me. "This will never happen again. I want to be absolutely clear. Attempt this again, and you're fired."

I wondered what would happen if I knocked him out again right there, just for kicks.

"Is that my arabica coffee?" he asked.

I nodded. "I will even let you have a cup if you answer my question."

Saiman arched an eyebrow. "Let? It's my coffee."

I saluted him with the mug. "Possession is nine-tenths of the law."

He stared at me incredulously. "Ask."

"Are you holding a woman called Yulya hostage?"

Saiman blinked.

"Her husband is very upset and is offering to let us both go if we can produce Yulya for him. Unfortunately, he's lying, and most likely we both would be killed once said Yulya is found. But if you're holding a woman hostage, you must tell me now."

"And if I was?" Saiman rubbed his jaw and sat in the chair opposite me.

"Then you'd have to release her immediately, or I would walk. I don't protect kidnappers, and I take a very dim view of violence toward civilians, men or women."

"You're a bewildering woman."

"Saiman, focus. Yulya?"

Saiman leaned back. "I can't produce Yulya. I am Yulya."

I suppose I should've seen that coming. "The man was under the impression he's married to her. What happened to the real Yulya?"

"There was never a real Yulya. I will tell you the whole story, but I must have coffee. And nutrients."

I poured him a cup of coffee. Saiman reached into the fridge and came up with a gallon of milk, a solid block of chocolate, and several bananas.

Chocolate was expensive as hell. I couldn't remember the last time I'd had some. If I survived this job, I'd buy a couple of truffles.

I watched Saiman load bananas and milk into a manual blender and crank the handle, cutting the whole thing into a coarse mess. Not the chocolate, not the chocolate . . . Yep, threw it in there, too. What a waste.

He poured the concoction into a two-quart jug and began chugging it. Shapeshifters did burn a ton of calories. I sighed, mourning the loss of the chocolate, and sipped my coffee. "Give."

"The man in question is the son of Pavel Semyonov. He's the premier volhv in the Russian community here. The boy's name is Evgenii, and he's completely right, I did marry him, as Yulya, of course. The acorn was very well guarded and I needed a way in."

"Unbelievable."

Saiman smiled. Apparently he thought I'd paid him a compliment. "Are you familiar with the ritual of firing the arrow?"

"It's an archaic folkloric ritual. The shooter is blindfolded and spun around, so he blindly fires. The flight of the arrow foretells the correct direction of the object the person seeks. If a woman picks up the arrow, she and the shooter are fated to be together."

Saiman wiped his mouth. "I picked up the arrow. It took me five months from the arrow to the acorn."

"How long did it take you to con that poor guy into marriage?"

"Three months. The combination of open lust but withholding of actual sex really works wonders."

I shook my head. "Evgenii is in love with you. He thinks his wife is in danger. He's trying to rescue her."

Saiman shrugged. "I had to obtain the acorn. I could say that he's young and resilient, but really, his state of mind is the least of my concerns."

"You're a terrible human being."

"I beg to differ. All people are driven by their primary selfishness. I'm simply more honest than most. Furthermore, he had the use of a beautiful woman, created to his precise specifications, for two months. I did my research into his sexual practices quite thoroughly, to the point of sleeping with him twice as a prostitute to make sure I knew his preferences."

"If we get out of this, I need to remember never to work for you again."

Saiman smiled. "But you will. If the price is right."

"No."

"Anyone will work for anyone and anyone will sleep with anyone if the price is right and the partnership is attractive enough. Suppose I invited you to spend a week here with me. Luxurious clothes. Beautiful shoes." He looked at my old boots, which were in danger of falling apart. "Magnificent meals. All the chocolate you could ever want."

So he'd caught me.

"All that for the price of having sex with me. I would even sweeten the deal by assuming a shape preferable to you. Anyone you want. Any shape, any size, any color, any gender. All in total confidentiality. Nobody ever has to know you were here. The offer is on the table." He placed his hand on the counter, palm down. "Right now. I promise you a week of total bliss—assuming we survive. You'll never get another chance to be this pampered. All I need from you is one word."

"No."

He blinked. "Don't you want to think about it?"

"No."

He clamped his mouth shut. Muscles played along his jaw. "Why?"

The TV screen ignited. Evgenii appeared in the glow. Saiman strode to the screen with a scowl on his face. "I'll make it short." His body boiled, twisted, stretched. I shut my eyes. It was that or lose my precious coffee. When I opened them, a petite red-haired woman stood in Saiman's place.

"Does this explain things enough?" Saiman asked. "Or do I need to spell it out, Evgenii?"

"You're her?"

"Yes."

"I don't believe it."

Saiman sighed. "Would you like me to list your preferred positions, in the order you typically enjoy them? Shall we speak of intimate things? I could recite most of our conversation word for word, I do have a very precise memory."

They stared at each other.

"It was all a lie," Evgenii said finally.

"I call it subterfuge, but yes, in essence, the marriage was a sham. You were set up from the beginning. I was Yulya. I was also Siren and Alyssa, so if you decide to visit that particular house of ill repute again, don't look for either."

Oh God.

The glow vanished. Saiman turned to me. "Back to our question. Why?"

"That man loved you enough to risk his own neck to negotiate your release. You just destroyed him, in passing, because you were in a hurry. And you want to know why. If you did that to him, there's no telling what you'd do to me. Sex is about physical attraction, yes, but it's also about trust. I don't trust you. You're completely self-absorbed and egoistic. You offer nothing I want."

"Sex is driven by physical attraction. Given the right stimulus, you will sleep with me. I simply have to present you with a shape you can't resist."

Saiman jerked, as if struck by a whip, and crashed to the floor. His feet drummed the carpet, breaking the herbs and fledgling ferns. Wild convulsions tore at his body. A blink and he was a mess of arms and legs and bodies. My stomach gave up, and I vomited into the sink.

Ordinarily, I'd be on top of him, jamming something in his mouth to keep him from biting himself, but given that he changed shapes like there was no tomorrow, finding his mouth was a bit problematic.

"Saiman? Talk to me."

"The acorn . . . It's coming. Must . . . Get . . . Roof."

Roof? No roof. We were in the apartment, shielded by a ward. On the roof, we'd be sitting ducks. "We can't do that."

"Oak . . . Large . . . Cave-in."

Oh hell. Would it have killed him to mention that earlier? "I need you to walk. You're too heavy, and I can't carry you while you convulse."

Little by little, the shudders died. Saiman staggered to his feet. He was back to the unremarkable man I'd first found in the bedroom. His stomach had grown to ridiculous proportions. If he were pregnant, he'd be twelve months along.

"We'll make a run for it," I told him.

A faint scratch made me spin. An old man hung outside the window, suspended on a rope. Gaunt, his white beard flapping in the wind, he peered through the glass straight at me. In the split second we looked at each other, twelve narrow stalks unfurled from his neck, spreading into a corona around his head, like a nimbus around the face of a Russian icon. A bulb tipped each stock. A hovala. Shit.

I grabbed Saiman and threw him at the door.

The bulbs opened.

Blinding light flooded the apartment, hiding the world in a white haze. The window behind me exploded. I could barely see. "Stay behind me."

Shapes dashed through the haze.

I slashed. Slayer connected, encountering resistance. Sharp ice stabbed my left side. I reversed the strike and slashed again. The shape before me crumpled. The second attacker struck. I dodged left, on instinct, and stabbed my blade at his side. Bone and muscle. Got him between the lower ribs. A hoarse scream lashed my ears. I twisted the blade, ripping the organs, and withdrew.

The hovala hissed at the window. I was still blind.

Behind me, the lock clicked. "No!"

I groped for Saiman and hit my forearm on the open door. He ran. Into the hallway, where he was an easy target. I lost my body. God damn it.

I sprinted into the hallway, trying to blink the haze from my eyes. The stairs were to the left. I ran, half-blind, grabbed the door, and dashed up the stairs.

The blinding flare finally cleared. I hit the door, burst onto the roof, and took a kick to the ribs. Bones crunched. I fell left and rolled to my feet. A woman stood by the door, arms held in a trademark tae kwon do cat stance.

To the right, an older man grappled with Saiman. Six others watched.

The woman sprang into a kick. It was a lovely kick, strong, with good liftoff. I sidestepped and struck. By the time she landed, I'd cut her twice. She fell in a crumpled heap.

I flicked the blood off my saber and headed for Saiman.

"You're Voron's kid," one of the men said. "We have no problem with you. Pavel's entitled. His son just threw himself off the roof."

Ten to a million, the son's name was Evgenii.

I kept coming. The two men ripped at each other, grappling and snarling like two wild animals. I was five feet away, when Pavel head-butted Saiman, jerking his right arm free. A knife flashed, I lunged, and saw Pavel slice across Saiman's distended gut. A bloody clump fell, and I caught it with my left hand, purely on instinct.

Magic punched my arm. A pale glow erupted from my fist.

Saiman twisted and stabbed something at Pavel's right eye.

The volhv stumbled back, a bloody pencil protruding from his eye socket. For a long moment he stood, huge mouth gaping, then toppled like a log. Saiman spun about. The muscles of his stomach collapsed, folding, knitting together, turning into a flat washboard wall.

The whole thing took less than three seconds.

I opened my fist. A small gold acorn lay on my palm.

The golden shell cracked. A sliver of green thrust its way up. The acorn rolled off my hand. The green shoot thickened, twisted, surging higher and higher. The air roared like a tornado. Saiman howled, a sound of pure rage. I grabbed him and dragged him with me to the stairs. On the other side, volhvs ran for the edge of the roof.

The shoot grew, turning dark, sprouting branches, leaves, and bark. Magic roiled.

"It was supposed to be mine," Saiman snarled. "Mine!"

Light flashed. The roaring ceased.

A colossal oak stood in the middle of the roof, as tall as the building itself, its roots spilling on both sides of the high-rise. Tiny lights fluttered between its branches—each wavy leaf as big as my head. Birds sang in the foliage. A huge metal chain bound the enormous trunk, its links so thick, I could've lain down on it. A feeling of complete peace came over me. All my troubles melted into distance. My pain dissolved. The air tasted sweet, and I drank it in.

At the other side of the roof, the volhvs knelt.

Metal clinked. A black creature came walking down the bottom loop. As big as a horse, its fur long and black, it walked softly, gripping the links with razor-sharp claws. Its head was that of lynx. Tall tufts of black fur decorated its ears, and a long black beard stretched from its chin. Its eyes glowed, lit from within.

The cat paused and looked at me. The big maw opened, showing me a forest of white teeth, long and sharp like knives.

"Ask."

I blinked.

"You were the last to hold the acorn," Saiman whispered. "You must ask the question, or it will kill all of us."

The cat showed me its teeth again.

For anything I asked, there would be a price.

"Ask," the cat said, its voice laced with an unearthly snarl.

"Ask, Kate," Saiman prompted.

"Ask!" one of the volhvs called out.

I took a deep breath.

The cat leaned forward in anticipation.

"Would you like some milk?"

The cat smiled wider. "Yes."

Saiman groaned.

"I'll be right back."

I dashed down the stairs. Three minutes later, the cat lapped milk from Saiman's crystal punch bowl.

"You could've asked anything," the creature said between laps.

"But you would've taken everything," I told it. "This way, all it cost me is a little bit of milk."

IN THE MORNING, PETERS CAME TO RELIEVE ME. NOT that he had a particularly difficult job. After the oak disappeared, the volhvs decided that since both Pavel and Evgenii were dead, all accounts were settled, and it was time to call it quits. As soon as we returned to the apartment, Saiman locked himself in the bedroom and refused to come out. The loss of the acorn hit him pretty hard. Just as well. I handed my fussy client off to Peters, retrieved Peggy, and headed back to the Guild.

All in all, I'd done spectacularly well, I decided. I lost the client for at least two minutes, let him get his stomach ripped open, watched him stab his attacker in the eye, which was definitely something he shouldn't have had to do, and cost him his special acorn and roughly five months of work. The fact that my client turned out to be a scumbag and a sexual deviant really had no bearing on the matter.

Some bodyguard I made. Yay. Whoopee.

I grabbed my crap and headed for the doors.

"Kate," the clerk called from the counter.

I turned. Nobody remembered the clerk's name. He was just "the clerk."

He waved an envelope at me. "Money."

I turned on my foot. "Money?"

"For the job. Client called. He says he'd like to work exclusively with you from now on. What did the two of you do all night?"

"We argued philosophy." I swiped the envelope and counted the bills. Three grand. *What do you know?*

I stepped out the doors into an overcast morning. I had been awake for over thirty-six hours. I just wanted to find a quiet spot, curl up, and shut the world out.

A tall, lean man strode to me, tossing waist-long black hair out of the way. He walked like a dancer, and his face would stop traffic. I looked into his blue eyes and saw a familiar smugness in their depths. "Hello, Saiman."

"How did you know?"

I shrugged and headed on my way.

"Perhaps we can work out a deal," he said, matching my steps. "I have no intentions of losing that bet. I will find a form you can't resist."

"Good luck."

"I'm guessing you'll try to avoid me, which would make my victory a bit difficult."

"Bingo."

"That's why I decided to give you an incentive you can't refuse. I'm giving you a sixty percent discount on my services. It's an unbelievable deal."

I laughed. If he thought I'd pay him twenty-six dollars a minute for his time, he was out of luck.

"Laugh now." Saiman smiled. "But sooner or later you'll require my expertise."

He stopped. I kept on walking, into the dreary sunrise. I had three thousand dollars and some chocolate to buy.

ABOUT THE AUTHORS

Ilona Andrews is the pseudonym for a husband-and-wife writing team. Together they are the coauthors of the #1 *New York Times* bestselling Kate Daniels urban-fantasy series and the romantic urban-fantasy novels of the Edge. They currently reside in Texas with their two children and numerous pets. For sample chapters, news, and more, visit ilona-andrews.com.